AN INTRIGUING INTERLUDE

"Why won't you let me go with you?" Victoria demanded. "You're the one who said we had to trust each other if I was going to work for you. Why is that so damned difficult for you to do?"

Hunter's hand suddenly came up, startling her. As if embarrassed that she had interpreted the action as hostile, he let it hover between them, unsure of how to continue.

"I'm sorry, Victoria," he said softly, his fingertips just inches from her jaw. "I have my reasons. Reasons that I just can't share with you—or with anyone—right now."

Victoria grabbed his hand. Even through her gloves, she could feel the electricity of his touch. To her surprise, Hunter's fingers tightened on hers instead of wrenching away.

"Thank you for being so concerned," he murmured, his face coming close to hers. For a moment, she wondered if he would kiss her, but he was still locked inside his own painful secrets. "And now I really do need you to go," he said. "Please."

Also by Christina Hamlett

The Magic Touch
Charade

Available from HarperPaperbacks

HUNTER'S HEART

◆ ◆ ◆

Christina Hamlett

HarperPaperbacks
A Division of HarperCollinsPublishers

HarperPaperbacks *A Division of* HarperCollins*Publishers*
10 East 53rd Street, New York, N.Y. 10022

Cover photograph by Herman Estevez

First printing: May 1994

Printed in the United States of America

HarperPaperbacks, HarperMonogram, and colophon are trademarks of HarperCollins*Publishers*

❖ 10 9 8 7 6 5 4 3 2 1

This book
is dedicated
with love and appreciation
to the Three Silver Knights,
whose humor has slain the best of dragons
in the worst of times
and to
Citi,
whose courage still protects me
from the darkness

When, in disgrace with fortune and men's eyes
I all alone beweep my outcast state
And trouble deaf heaven with my bootless cries,
And look upon myself, and curse my fate,
Wishing me like to one more rich in hope,
Featured like him, like him with friends possessed,
Desiring this man's art and that man's scope,
With what I most enjoy contented least;
Yet in these thoughts myself almost despising,
Haply I think on thee, and then my state,
Like to the lark at break of day arising
From sullen earth, sings hymns at heaven's gate;
For thy sweet love remembered such wealth brings
That then I scorn to change my state with kings.

—William Shakespeare
Sonnet XXIX

HUNTER'S
HEART
◆ ◆ ◆

Prologue

There were very few things in life that intimidated Elliott Bowman. Thirty-four years of seasoned practice in the Fairfax County courts had honed the southern attorney's ability to handle almost any situation or personality with unflappable calm. "Elliott could take on the devil and win," his spouse was fond of boasting, well versed in her husband's judicial achievements and always elated to recite them, even to total strangers at the Dixie Mart.

The impending task of delivering unpleasant news to his firm's most prestigious client, however, was a duty he would gladly have delegated at that moment to one of his two partners. Mr. O'Hare was not one to passively take no as an acceptable answer, nor did he have a reputation for compromise. All or nothing, he had told the law firm.

The crux, naturally, was that Hunter O'Hare wanted it all.

Elliott resignedly closed the leather portfolio in his lap and reached up to slide the wire-framed glasses off his hawkish nose, catching as he did so a glance at his watch. As if to supplement his own observation, the hollow chime just then of the hallway Biedermeier confirmed the hour, startling him with its coincidental intrusion on the silence.

Nearly fifteen minutes had passed since his host had excused himself from the room to take a telephone call. Fifteen minutes. Too short a time to be considered a reprieve, he thought, and yet an interminable delay in reporting what he must.

"It's Tokyo on the line, sir," the housekeeper had announced from the doorway before they even got started on their meeting, a nonchalant statement as if such calls for her employer on his unlisted phone were the norm and not the exception. Considering his client's reputation on the international business scene, of course, anything was possible.

"This will only take a minute," he had promised the attorney, flashing the charismatic smile that could seal alliances or topple entire empires. "Just make yourself comfortable."

I'd feel more comfortable on my own turf, Elliott had wanted to say, regretting that he hadn't insisted on meeting at the office in Alexandria. Surrounded by the kindly and familiar visages of Washington, Lincoln, and Roosevelt that graced his office walls, the senior partner would have found a quiet strength in numbers. Here at the estate he was on his own and maneuvering at the outset from a defensive position. It wasn't a role he enjoyed.

Elliott looked down at the portfolio again, half-wishing that—if he opened it just once more—a magical answer might materialize on the front page that would earn him Mr. O'Hare's undying gratitude and an increased retainer fee.

No such luck, his conscience chided him. He had scrutinized Sir Patrick O'Hare's will for the past month to the point of memorization.

Elliott laid the portfolio atop the desk, quietly damning it for making the last thirty days so exasperating.

"Find a loophole," was all that O'Hare had asked of him.

It was a request that should have been simple. Yet try as he might to discern a poorly executed clause within the document, the assignment had met with dismal failure.

Telling that to his client, of course, was roughly equivalent to a root canal without anesthesia, the latter being almost preferable to the embarrassment of admitting defeat to someone who expected perfection and had the resources to pay for it.

The minutes dragged onward.

With a sigh, Elliott redirected his attention to studying the room where he waited for his client's return.

It was an interior as rich and awe-inspiring as Hunter O'Hare himself and probably more magnificent than any room he'd ever see in his lifetime. The room was like an elegant showplace straight from the glossy pages of *Architectural Digest*.

As far as Elliott was concerned, the rest of the house need not even have existed. The library alone was proof of heaven.

Its most engaging feature, of course, was the triple set of French doors along the room's west side, affording a sunny and panoramic view of lush green lawns and a sprawling lattice of white fences to segregate the gentleman's collection of thoroughbred horses.

Elliott would kill for a view like that, content as he was with the Foggy Bottom brownstone he and his wife had lived in since the Carter Administration.

Not fifty yards from where the house stood, O'Hare had told him, Yankee and Confederate troops had met in bloody skirmish on what were previously open fields. It was hard to believe to look at the grounds now, for the fertile pastureland bore no visible scars of historical battle, only the signs of contemporary wealth.

The furnishings were an extension of O'Hare's success as an American industrialist. The repetition of dark mahogany, antique brass fixtures, and forest green fabric conveyed a timelessness and grace that would have been at home on either side of the Atlantic. Floor-to-ceiling bookcases of leather-bound volumes invited cozy browsing, though Elliott wondered when his client ever had the time for such casual pursuits.

What did the man do for fun? he wondered, marveling at just how little he really knew about his client.

Even Hunter's mention of family was sparse, though Elliott had gleaned a few more pieces of the puzzle on his own from the past month's work. Two cousins, a maiden aunt, an eccentric great-grandfather with a twisted sense of humor.

Perhaps I wouldn't make mention of family, either, Elliott thought, recalling some of the more peculiar things he had heard about O'Hare's Irish relations.

As he shrugged the memory away, Elliott's glance suddenly fell on something he hadn't noticed before. Nestled between a slender Egyptian statue and an onyx paperweight on the left side of O'Hare's desk was a five-by-seven picture frame.

Curiosity tugged at Elliott's brain, daring him to turn it around, to steal a peek at the mystery subject who had earned the privilege of gracing the Irishman's private sanctuary.

Elliott glanced over his shoulder toward the open door of the library, his spirits lifted twofold by the fact that the hallway was empty and that the floors were hardwood. Certainly any sound of approaching footsteps on their polished surface would be ample warning to return the frame to its proper place.

Without further hesitation, he reached for it.

A gasp escaped Elliott's lips at the sight of what the frame contained, for he found himself staring at the picture of the most beautiful young woman he'd ever seen.

Twenty? Twenty-five? Elliott had never been a good judge of female ages, owing to their tricks with makeup and hair. His first impression, though, was that she was quite a bit younger than O'Hare.

A *Nicole Kidman type*, he thought, her heart-shaped face almost overwhelmed by a curly mane of strawberry blond hair that fell past her shoulders and defied any semblance of taming. Wide blue eyes and an impish, lip-glossed grin could even place her age somewhere in the high teens, Elliott speculated, all of which made her relationship to O'Hare more puzzling.

Who *was* she? For that matter, *where* was she? Cursory exposure that he had had to the house, the presence of a young woman in it would have been noticeable by now.

Whoever she was, Elliott decided, her picture would inspire anyone to great things. No wonder O'Hare kept it so close at hand.

The sudden sound of a footfall nearly made him drop it. With a quick lunge, Elliott thrust the frame back on the desk just as O'Hare entered the room.

"Sorry to keep you," Hunter apologized, striding across the room with the hard grace of someone in total control and not averse to showing it. "It was a call that couldn't wait."

"No apology necessary," Elliott assured him, jarred back to the reality of having to tell the man who now sat opposite him that he wasn't going to get what he wanted.

"Well?" O'Hare said pleasantly. "Shall we get on with it?"

As Elliott reached for the portfolio, his glance was automatically drawn again toward the frame. Would O'Hare notice that it wasn't at exactly the same angle? Elliott hoped that he wouldn't notice until their business was concluded and he was behind the wheel of his car heading back for Alexandria.

"My partners and I have been over your great-grandfather's will a number of times," Elliott began. "As I mentioned on the telephone with you, we've also been in regular communication with Mr. Tapping in London."

His eyes met O'Hare's across the desk and he could already read in their steel gray depths that his client was impatient.

"Why do I have the feeling," O'Hare interrupted him a moment later, "that this isn't going to go the way I'd like?"

Elliott cleared his throat. "Never having met Sir Patrick, I can only say that the conditions of his will are a reflection of the pride he felt for his—and your—Irish heritage."

"The conditions," O'Hare retorted, "are the ravings of a hundred-year-old lunatic. A *stubborn* hundred-year-old lunatic."

At least one can see where you inherited it, Elliott would have pointed out if he had had the license to speak his mind.

"Whatever his mental state," Elliott continued, "I'm afraid that his attorney, Mr. Tapping, successfully covered all of the bases."

O'Hare leaned back in his chair, quietly contemplating the ceiling.

"Read it to me again," he said.

"Which part?" Elliott queried.

"The stupid part," O'Hare replied with an edge of snarl in his baritone voice. "The part about the castle."

In spite of the circumstances, Elliott nearly smiled at

the irony of a man as self-confident as Hunter O'Hare being defeated by a clause concocted in the land of leprechauns. Elliott wondered if Hunter had ever lost anything in his entire life.

In response to O'Hare's request, he thumbed through the pages to the one he wanted, the page that had kept him up nights and taxed his capacity to turn mistakes into assets. Elliott skipped over the jumble of heretofores, party of the first parts, and Latin phraseology to the single paragraph that had caused them both so much vexation.

"... and should my great-grandson choose not to reside in said property and make it his permanent home, all acquisitions, titles, and benefits described herein shall be divided equally between my late daughter's two surviving children, Mr. Sean Michael Gleavy and his sister, Miss—"

"There must be *something* you can do," O'Hare cut in.

Elliott regarded him over the tops of his wire-framed glasses, wondering why a seven-hundred-year-old castle that his client had never set foot in had become such a bone of contention. Nor did it make sense that a man as wealthy as Hunter O'Hare would even miss the forefeiture of his great-grandfather's financial holdings.

"As I said," Elliott reiterated, "his terms are quite explicit. If you're set on inheriting what Sir Patrick left you, I'm afraid the castle is a major obstacle you have to deal with."

"No such thing as obstacles," O'Hare muttered under his breath. "Just temporary inconveniences." As he turned to smile at Elliott, his gaze was diverted to something on the desk. Without saying a word, however, O'Hare reached over and adjusted the frame to his liking.

"We're going to have to get an answer back to Tapping by the thirtieth," Elliott reminded him.

O'Hare looked off toward the French doors and the

pastoral view beyond, resting his cleft chin on steepled fingers.

"Tell me again what it all means," he said. "In twenty-five words or less."

Elliott took a deep breath. "It means that, to claim your inheritance, you have to move to his castle in Ireland."

O'Hare cocked a brow. "Hmmm."

"Excuse me?"

"The will only says I have to *live* in the place," he repeated. "Is that right?"

"Yes," Elliott said, puzzled by the beginnings of a smile on his client's face.

"What it *doesn't* say," O'Hare remarked, "is that the castle has to stay where it is. . . ."

1

Five Years Later

It was not one of her better mornings. The first real
storm of the season had knocked the power off north-
west of New Hampshire Avenue sometime during the
night, and though it had been restored less than two
hours later, Victoria Cameron remained blissfully
unaware of it until well past her second cup of coffee and
half a poppyseed bagel. Assuming that she was ahead of
schedule, she had sat down for a leisurely breakfast
instead of eating it in stages throughout her apartment
as she usually did.

Because the sky was dark with clouds, the first clue
that she was running late was a commuter advisory on
the radio.

"It's a chilly eight-thirty in the nation's capital," the
announcer said, "and out there on the Rock Creek Parkway—"

"Damn!" Victoria muttered after checking the one clock
among many that wasn't electric and had, thus, eluded

◇ **9** ◇

Mother Nature's tempestuous mischief. Abruptly abandoning breakfast, she flew to her bedroom to resume the
now-hasty task of dressing and finishing her hair.

Some would argue that Victoria could step out in a
ponytail and knee-length grubby sweatshirt and look
more put-together than women who spent hours fussing
over their looks. From her actress mother, she had inherited high cheekbones, a creamy complexion, and titian
locks that she meticulously pinned each morning into a
chignon at the base of her neck. From her college track-
coach father came long-lashed eyes of jade green, a defiant chin, and a discipline for physical exercise that kept
her tall frame in shape despite long hours at a desk job.
A desk job that had more than enough paperwork on it
that Monday morning than she cared to think about.
Running late didn't help matters one bit.

Not that Elliot Bowman was any kind of tyrant who
parked himself at the front door with a pocket watch and
a stern expression. He and his two partners at the law
firm—Thatcher Williams and John Johnson—were
among the nicest men she had ever worked for.

Linked by the common denominators of silver hair,
stocky bodies, and grandfatherly ages, Victoria always
imagined them as three medieval knights who had been
called out of retirement to ensure justice in the Virginia
courts.

That they treated their staff so well rather than intimidating them was the reason Victoria gave a hundred and
ten percent to her work—the same reason she hated not
getting there on time.

In annoyance, she glared at her reflection in the bathroom mirror, dismayed that the same hair she had effortlessly been pinning into place for most of her adult
career life was now refusing to cooperate.

Nor was she entirely happy with the white sweater she had pulled on, its shoulder pads seemingly twice the size that she remembered from the last time she wore it. The wool sienna dress would have been better, she thought, though it was now too late to change. With a last scowl at her hair, Victoria swept a handful of bobby pins off the marble counter, resolving to repair her image to the conservative norm when she got to the ladies' room at the office.

Fate, however, clearly had no intention of letting her off so easily. Two chipped nails, a misplaced set of keys, and a mud puddle later, she finally found herself crossing Teddy Roosevelt Bridge and heading south to Virginia.

Maybe the rest of the world is running late, too, she thought, from the crawl of suburban traffic and timid drivers acting as if they had never experienced October rain before. At the rate she was going, it would be morning coffee break by the time she pulled into the garage.

In nice weather, she would simply have caught the Metro, a smooth train trip punctuated by a few blocks of healthy walking. Inclement conditions on the East Coast, though, were no picnic, a realization she had come to after almost three years in Washington, D.C. Still, she wouldn't trade it for anywhere else.

It was the excitement, for one thing. Lured by the glitter of politics and the intrigue of international relations, Victoria had acted on a friend's recommendation and landed her first job with a congressman from her home state, an administrative position that enabled her to deal on a daily basis with the kind of movers and shakers that most people only knew by their mention in the newspapers and on television.

Her appetite whetted by the knowledge that she was taking part in the government process, Victoria had

made up her mind after only one week with Congressman Hoffart that Washington was a place where she
could happily spend the rest of her life.

It was also as far as she could move from her mother
and still be a U.S. citizen.

It wasn't that she and Marcine were estranged. To the
contrary, America's beloved soap star of "Niagara's Tears"
had always overcompensated for her celebrity status by
striving to be her daughter's best friend. Not until her
intentions had spilled over into Victoria's career plans a
tad too much did the latter realize it was time for a break.

"But you're so pretty!" Marcine insisted. "Just give the
television thing a chance. Okay, sweetums? You'll like it."

Victoria, however, had been smart enough to recognize even back in high school that the Hollywood
lifestyle wasn't for her and never would be. While her
peers were literally falling all over themselves for
Marcine's attention—and a referral to her agent—Victoria
herself was studying political science. While girlfriends
were taking acting classes, she was taking typing and
shorthand to get a job.

The first proverbial cutting of apron strings had come
in college, though San Diego was still close enough to
LA for Marcine's long arm of influence. Even Victoria's
move to a law firm in Denver hadn't been distant enough
to sever the ties—or the hope on Marcine's part—that a
second Cameron woman would grace the afternoon tube
and plaintively murmur lines like, "Oh, Kenneth, if only I
had known you felt this way. . . ."

"Washington?" Marcine had gasped when Victoria told
her about the job with Lawrence Hoffart. "What on earth is
happening there that you can't find back here at home?"

Reality, Mother, she had wanted to reply but didn't.
Though they would always be mother and daughter and

love each other dearly, they would never see eye to eye.

She had yet to mention to Marcine, in fact, that she had been working for the firm of Bowman, Johnson, and Williams since the first of August. Nor had Marcine, in her isolated world of bright lights and double-spaced scripts, ever inquired what happened to their staff people when politicians lost their bid for reelection during the June primary. Hoffart's surprise defeat to Dill Deguchi had obviously made headlines in every paper except the one weekly tabloid Marcine read religiously.

For that matter, the only interest Victoria had ever known her mother to take in elections at all was when Reagan got elected.

"He almost did a walk-on with us," Marcine proclaimed, "but something came up with—oh, I don't know. . . . I think it was the Russians or somebody." That the soap opera shoot had never been rescheduled was a personal grudge the older redhead would carry to her grave . . . and hold all of the nation's capital accountable for.

"It would've been such a good episode, too," Marcine still maintained. "The plot line had him wounded by a gunman and brought to Bayside General." Marcine clearly marveled at how the scriptwriters kept coming up with such original ideas.

The remembrance of her mother's naïveté caught Victoria smiling as she took the first turnoff to Alexandria. Were it not for their astonishingly similar looks, it often occured to her that she could have been left at childbirth by gypsies on the doorstep of her parents' Sherman Oaks mansion, gypsies who forgot to write down the address so they could come back later to claim her.

As Victoria eased her car down the ramp of the garage and around the first corner, the last thing she wanted to see was another vehicle parked in her usual stall right next to the elevator. Yet there one was—a charcoal gray Mercedes sitting there—looming there, in fact—as if it owned the place.

I should've just called in sick today, Victoria thought to herself, wondering if all the setbacks thrown in her path weren't some profound clue the universe was trying to impart.

As she drove past it, she was tempted to park her own car directly behind it and block the driver's exit.

While spaces in the garage weren't officially assigned, there was an unspoken rule among coworkers that everyone took the same space every day, a right guaranteed even when they were running late.

Obviously the usurper was an outsider, she determined, for only ignorance or arrogance would have compelled someone to sail in out of the storm and commandeer whatever slot suited them.

HUNTER 1, the shiny license plate read.

Victoria smirked at the incongruity. A plate that boasted one's passion for killing ducks and Bambi's mother belonged on a rusty pickup truck with a gun rack and Confederate flag in the rear window.

What such a personage would be doing in the garage of one of Virginia's most prestigious law firms—much less driving an expensive sedan—was a mystery, of course, that she couldn't fathom. And only because HUNTER 1 presumably *did* have business with someone in the firm did she drop the temptation of complicating the sedan's departure.

Let there be a wicked pair of antlers out there somewhere with his name on them, she quietly wished instead.

It was bad enough to have been jostled in the elevator on the descending ride from the cafeteria and had coffee spilled down the front of her sweater. To emerge on her floor in such a sloppy state and simultaneously encounter the most sexy, breathtaking man she had ever seen was further testimony that the gods were out to get her. Their eyes met for only that initial second, his glance abruptly diverted downward to the tan drench of caffeine that had already taken on the shape of Illinois.

Usually quick-witted in awkward situations, Victoria found herself tongue-tied, concurrently dazzled by the tall Adonis and embarrassed that she looked like a wild-haired klutz.

This isn't like me, she thought to herself in a flushed flash of reflection. Appreciative as she was of attractive men, her prior exposure to some of Hollywood's most handsome faces had sufficiently immunized her against heady first-glance sensations like the one she was experiencing.

Feeling neither confident nor composed enough under the circumstances to say something bright and memorable, Victoria exchanged places with him without saying anything, conscious that he gave her a wide berth in stepping past.

The doors thudded closed behind her before she could turn for a second look at him, even if she had entertained so obvious a flirtation. All that remained was that fleeting moment of involuntary appraisal, that split-second image of dark blond hair, a rugged square jaw and smoldering eyes that penetrated her like a hawk.

To steal a favorite line from Marcine, he was central casting's answer to Indiana Jones in a suit.

Whoever the gorgeous hunk was, though, he was already gone. Unlike the paperwork that she knew was waiting on her desk.

"Oh, there she is!" the voice of John Johnson boomed out, breaking from his hallway confab with Williams to greet her before she could duck into the ladies' room for cosmetic first aid.

"Is that a new look or what?" Thatch ribbed her, indicating the coffee on her sweater.

"The hair's different, too," John observed. "Maybe it's not Tory after all. What do you think, Thatch?"

"Nope, it's her," Thatch affirmed, his blue eyes sparkling. "I'd know that wicked grimace anywhere."

"Oh, bite the wall," she retorted, accustomed to their teasing but nonetheless too much at odds with the entire day to enjoy their unrehearsed humor.

"'Bite the wall?'" Thatch echoed.

"It's a California expression."

"Ah, California!" he sighed. "Do they still put their wagons in a circle every night?"

John made a melodramatic show of checking his watch. "Keeping banker's hours now, Tory?"

"Some idiot with a macho plate was parked in my spot," she replied.

"So where'd you have to park?" Thatch inquired. "Baltimore?"

"What's a 'macho plate'?" John asked.

"Hunter 1," Victoria answered.

The two men exchanged a quick glance with one another, a starkly meaningful glance that did not escape the young woman's notice.

"Something going on that I don't know about, gentlemen?"

"What don't you know about gentlemen?" Thatcher asked. "Anything we can tell you? Not that we're the best resource. . . ."

Victoria smirked and looked to John for explanation.

"Elliott was looking for you," he said, his manner shifting from jovial to serious.

"Am I in trouble?" she asked.

John looked toward Thatcher again before answering. "Not yet," he said, "but be careful what you say about Hunter."

"Yes," Thatcher agreed. "You could be treading on dangerous ground."

2

It *wasn't like the two of them* to withhold secrets from her, and she immediately challenged them on it. "So what's the mystery about Hunter?" Victoria pressed, sliding her leather purse strap off of her shoulder.

John avoided the issue. "Elliott's call on this one," he said. "Nothing major. Just watch your step, kiddo." The wry but indulgent glint in his eyes perplexed her even more.

"So is this Hunter person a client or what?"

"What," Thatch predictably replied, much to her aggravation.

"You're hiding something," she accused him.

"From the looks of it," John interjected, facetiously pretending to steal a glance behind Thatcher's back, "he's hiding an entire Third World country."

Thatch took the jocular insult without batting an eyelash.

"Come on, guys," Victoria interrupted their banter. "Who's Number One Hunter, and why the advice to watch my step?"

There was no prying further detail from either man

about the cryptic remark, however. Both of them seemed peculiarly anxious to now change the subject or go back to what they were doing.

"Not going to help me out, huh?" she queried in reference to Elliott's summons of her. "Last chance to come clean."

"Your guess is as good as mine," Thatch said.

"Probably better," John added, inclining his head toward his cohort. "Worst guesser I ever met in my life. Half the time, he can't even figure out 'Murder, She Wrote.'"

"Seriously," Thatch said, "I've got no idea what E.B. wants. He just asked to see you as soon as you got here."

In his eyes, though, Victoria had already read what he tried to conceal by his calculated state of confusion. Something was definitely in the works. Something major.

Taking only the time to hang up her raincoat and throw her purse in her desk, she headed for Elliott's corner office, feeling guilty that she had already kept him waiting for her long enough.

"Come in," Elliott beckoned her when she poked her head around the opened door. Like his portly counterparts, his face immediately registered recognition that her appearance that morning was different. Further, that it was not a change for the better. "If I've caught you at a bad time—" he started to say.

Victoria dismissed his remark with a shake of her head. How like Elliott to be sensitive that she wasn't in top form for an impromptu meeting. I must *really* look like hell, she thought to herself. "Right now's fine," she assured him. "Sorry I was running a little late this morning."

"No apology necessary," he assured her.

"What's on your mind?"

"Have a seat," he offered, removing his glasses and laying them atop the yellow legal-size tablet on which he had been writing. "This may take a while to explain." The intrusive buzz of the intercom on his telephone preempted him. "All right, put him through," he instructed the receptionist, "but would you hold the rest of my calls until I get back to you, Linda? I'm in a meeting right now."

Cued by Elliott to stay where she was while he spoke to a client, Victoria settled back into her chair, using the time to study his office and the framed photographs that so richly personalized it. Many of them had been taken by Elliott himself.

That her mentor was an avid shutterbug was well known throughout the firm. If and when Elliott ever retired, Victoria thought to herself, the man would probably be content to roam the countryside with his camera and record the change of seasons for posterity. Thatch and John frequently teased him about running out of wall and credenza space to display his efforts.

He had already done his level best to record most of the highlights of Europe and the Far East. Extensive travels with Ruth and their three daughters had yielded the recognizable landmarks of Paris, London, and Rome. Even Diamond Head and Waikiki Beach at dusk had earned a spot in Elliott's Kodak montage.

Victoria's favorite, though, was still the castle.

Maybe because it *wasn't* a famous place—at least it wasn't as far as she knew—she had been drawn to it the very first time she saw it.

Precariously perched on the sea side of a rocky cliff, the most striking thing about the medieval structure was the odd gradation of color between the castle's gray base and its lighter cylindrical towers.

The more she looked at the photograph—as she was looking at it now—the more Victoria wished that she knew its history, for certainly a castle in such isolated, windswept surroundings had been built there for a purpose. I'll have to remember to ask Elliott where it is, she reminded herself, nudged back to the present by the sight of him hanging up the receiver.

"Sorry," he apologized for the interruption. "Where was I?"

"You were just getting started," Victoria said.

Elliott cleared his throat. "As you know," he began, "we're starting to get into the holidays around here. . . ."

A warning bell went off in Victoria's head. Uh-oh, she thought, he was going to ask her to coordinate the office Christmas party. In the course of her working experience, it was practically a given that new staff members were always targeted to plan the Christmas parties, spearhead the United Way campaigns, and muster enthusiasm among the staff to donate a record number of pints to the annual blood drive. *Don't let it be something like that*, she silently prayed.

" . . . I've been talking the whole thing over with Thatch and John," Elliott was saying, "and they concur that there won't be enough work to keep a full staff busy. . . ."

Victoria's initial impression that she was being recruited for an undesirable holiday task was now replaced by the plummeting suspicion that she was, instead, about to be laid off.

"Excuse me?" she murmured, embarrassed that her sudden preoccupation with impending unemployment had caused her to miss what Elliott had just said.

"I want you to know, Victoria, that I wouldn't even consider doing this if Mr. O'Hare weren't one of our more . . ." Elliott searched a moment for the right adjective . . . "important clients. I guess what I'm saying is that your professionalism puts you at the top of the list of people we feel confident enough to send."

"Send where?"

"To work for Mr. O'Hare," he replied. "If you want to, that is."

"He's another attorney?" Victoria inquired, puzzled by Elliott's prior use of the word "client."

A smile creased his face, the preface to a broad chuckle. "O'Hare? No, not at all. Even though he *does* have the smarts to make a first-rate prosecutor. I often wonder, in fact, why a man of his background never went into law."

"Maybe you should take this from the beginning," Victoria recommended.

"The beginning?" The avuncular lawyer leaned back in his chair. "I suppose the beginning for *our* purposes would be five years ago. . . ."

"So, are you going to do it?" Thatch asked poised over his second Scotch and soda.

In spite of the storm, he and John had decided to hail a cab and spirit their favorite administrative assistant off to lunch a few hours later at The Declaration, a waterfront pub at the end of King Street. Even before the menus were placed in front of them, both men had bombarded her with more questions than she'd been asked on the exam for her driver's license. Halfway through salad, she was still vacillating between answers.

"I don't know yet," she said, as flattered as she was perplexed to be singled out for so strange an assignment with a man Elliott respectfully referred to the entire time as "Mr. O'Hare." "The whole thing seems to be happening too fast."

"I understand he's going to pay double your salary," John said.

"Which means," Thatch cheerfully concluded, "you could buy *our* lunch."

"Why doesn't he save himself the difference and go through a clerical service?" Victoria asked, cognizant of the booming business that the District's proliferation of employment agencies enjoyed in hiring out temporary staffers. "Wouldn't that make more sense?"

"I don't think money's really an object," John murmured as he dolloped extra dressing on his greens.

Victoria smirked. "Obviously not, from the sounds of it. You'd just think he'd spend it more wisely."

"Still," Thatch interjected, "you've got to admit that the man has spunk."

"Spunk or an overdose of arrogance," Victoria said.

"Whatever it is, seems to work for him," John pointed out.

It was hard for Victoria to share their obvious admiration of the millionaire's accomplishments, her head still spinning from what she had learned that morning.

The background story Elliott related to her had struck only a vague chord of remembrance as she listened. Totally absorbed in her legislative work at the time with Congressman Hoffart, she had barely noticed the splashy newspaper account a few years back of some Virginia millionaire moving an entire castle across the Atlantic.

While the eight-figure price tag of relocation had captivated gossip-seekers around the globe, to Victoria Cameron, it had held about as much significance as another Elvis sighting.

If anything, the blatant eccentricity of someone financing such a frivolous endeavor as castle-moving when so many of the country's homeless lived on the edge of survival had left a sour taste in her mouth.

Nor was she sure that she even wanted to *meet* a man so pompous and egocentric, much less work for him through the end of December.

"So is Hunter his real name?" she inquired, "or does he like to shoot bag ladies for sport?"

Thatcher helped himself to another roll and passed the basket to John. "Do you get the feeling," he asked him, "that Elliott's Irishman made a bad first impression on her?"

"Nothing gets by you, does it, Thatch?"

"'Elliott's Irishman'?" she echoed.

"He's the only one O'Hare likes to deal with," John replied.

"Not that he wouldn't deal with us if he had to," Thatch said. "It's just that he and E.B. are on the same wavelength."

"I find *that* hard to believe," she said, unable to fathom a credible liaison between someone as kind and altruistic as Elliott Bowman and a rich manipulator like O'Hare.

"Definitely a bad first impression," Thatch repeated.

"I'll probably like the man even *less* in person," Victoria predicted.

John arched a silver brow. "You mean Elliott didn't introduce the two of you this morning?"

Victoria shook her head. "He'd already left when I got there," she informed them. That both of them had known O'Hare was on the premises, of course, now explained why they had tried to shush her from being too vocal about his car being in her slot.

"Oh," they jointly responded.

"Oh? That's all you're going to say?"

"That's all *I* was going to say," Thatch shrugged. "How 'bout you, John?"

"Ditto."

"Another glass of wine?" Thatch offered.

"I'd rather have the truth."

"Can *I* have her wine then?" John asked.

Victoria folded her arms. "Come on, guys. Enough games. You obviously knew about this whole thing. And," she emphasized, "you obviously also know more about this Hunter O'Hare person than you're telling me."

Thatcher pensively scratched his chin. "What exactly is it that you want to know?"

"For openers," she said, "what's he like? Besides an arrogant, conceited spendthrift who likes to move tons of rock?"

"Oh, I think that about sums it up," Thatch nodded. "What do *you* think, John?"

"Maybe she wants to know what he looks like," John speculated. "After all, she missed that chance this morning."

Victoria waited for their reply, wondering if the description would coincide with the one she had fashioned on her own—an ancient, Lon Chaney clone with a definitive hump who had a room in the bell tower.

"Well," Thatcher said, "he's short."

"Very short," John agreed. "And ugly."

"Definitely ugly."

"Ugly is probably being kind."

"Too kind."

"Although," John added, "you shouldn't judge a book by its cover."

"True," Thatch said, "but we're talking a truly ugly book here. I don't think you can get around that."

"Maybe we *shouldn't* let Victoria go work for him. . . ." The bearded attorney's thought trailed off, unfinished.

"And why is that?" Victoria asked.

"Because you're such a beauty, of course." Thatch toasted her with his drink.

"And O'Hare," John joined in, "is an absolute beast."

3

"*I'm sorry I can't go out* there with you this afternoon," Elliott apologized to her a few days later.

Not as sorry as I am, Victoria thought to herself. Acting on Elliott's advice that a courtesy interview was a good icebreaker, O'Hare had extended an invitation to both of them to join him on Thursday for tea.

"It'll be a nice, no-pressure way to get to know each other," the attorney had told her when it was first set up. "And if you two just don't click, well, no real harm done."

Or money lost, Victoria silently added, still perplexed as to how the millionaire had engaged her, sight unseen.

"I'm looking forward to it," she had lied, thankful at the time her boss wasn't sending her by herself, a proverbial lamb to the wolf.

A morning mix-up in courtrooms, however, had forced Elliott to drop out at the last minute.

"Maybe we should just reschedule it," she proposed. While Thatch and John's claims about the millionaire were obviously exaggerated, Victoria nonetheless felt reluctant to fly solo on her initial meeting with him. "Would tomorrow work?"

"Tomorrow's out . . . and most of next week," Elliott murmured, confirming it with a quick perusal of his desk calendar. "Besides, the sooner you two get squared away on preliminaries, the better."

"Trying to get rid of me?"

Elliott chuckled. "I'm sure I'd never hear the end of it from a certain quarter if I did."

His reference to the fondness his two partners had for her filled Victoria with a momentary rush of warmth.

"No," he continued, "since we couldn't all connect on Monday, I wanted to wrap this up before we get too far along." Elliott winked. "I know he's anxious to meet his new employee."

"*Temporary* employee," Victoria felt compelled to add.

"Oh, yes, that's a given," he said, though a hint of puzzlement underscored his words. "Something on your mind?"

"I guess I'm still adjusting to your volunteering me," she confessed. "Not that I'm not flattered by it."

"Well," Elliott explained, "we just like to go that extra mile for some of the clients who have been good to us over the years. I'm sure Mr. O'Hare will be as appreciative of your work as we are. I also know he's impatient for you—or whomever—to get started, his workload being what it is." The "whomever" had been thrown in too hastily to convince her that it was an option.

"All the same—" she started to say.

Elliott was shifting through the files on his desk, a cue that she had come to recognize as his nonverbal closure on chitchat. "You'll do fine, Victoria. Don't even give it a second thought."

"That's not what I was worried about."

"Something else, then?"

Victoria took a breath, wishing now that she had

spent more time rehearsing her argument. After all, she was conversing with a man who could easily give Perry Mason a run for his money.

"I'm afraid there's some real potential for a personality clash. I mean, in my dealing with someone as affluent as Mr. O'Hare." Affluent was the best euphemism she could come up with for the sentiments she was actually feeling.

"Conflict?" A perplexed scowl flickered across the attorney's age-worn face. "In what way?" he queried. "I'd think with your background of growing up in Los Angeles—"

"And with a celebrity mother?" Victoria filled in. She shook her head. "Washington's a long way from that lifestyle," she went on. "When I worked with Larry, I was putting my energy into work that was meaningful, that was going to help people *get* somewhere." The congressman's tireless crusade for better housing, outreach education, and senior health programs had made his defeat that summer all the more crushing to her, leaving her to wonder if his successor could ever be as empathic to the masses. "I just feel like maybe Mr. O'Hare and I are coming from opposite sides. . . ."

Elliott nodded as she talked, the lines of concentration deepening along his brows and under his eyes as he sought to understand her concerns.

"So you see your assisting Mr. O'Hare as running counterpoint to those objectives?" he finally spoke.

"Don't you?"

"We all have our reasons for doing things," he quietly replied. "I think you may be judging him prematurely."

"I just wanted you to know how I feel about it and that I was worried." Victoria stole a purposeful glance at her watch, still hoping that her boss might reconsider her discomfiture and make other arrangements before it was too late.

"At least you don't have to worry about getting lost today," Elliott assured her, sidestepping her appeal for a new judgment. "He's sending his driver to pick you up." Case closed.

Had the remark about getting lost come from anyone else, Victoria would have been prompted to point out that she hadn't been lost since age ten and that furthermore, she was perfectly capable of finding some silly castle in the Virginia countryside. After all, how many could there be?

Elliott, however, was from that generation of men who—in spite of working with women on a daily basis in the business environment—still harbored notions that members of the opposite sex could not survive ten minutes on their own, much less decipher something as complicated as a map.

Victoria let the comment slide, accepting it at face value as the older man's interest in her well-being.

"I could take a cab," she suggested. "No sense in his chauffeur coming all the way to town."

Elliott shrugged it off. "I'm sure he just wants to make you feel welcome."

Or *make me feel controlled*, Victoria thought. The Irishman clearly had a zeal for complete power over the people he considered his servants. Even Elliott seemed to be counted among them.

"I guess the bottom line is that I'm still a little confused," she replied instead. "It's hard to feel comfortable when you're clueless about what's going on."

"Oh?"

"I mean why exactly does he need an assistant? I still don't even know what I'll be doing out there."

Elliott nodded, sensitive to her bias about taking the assignment yet firmly resolved that it was a sound decision. A decision O'Hare himself had made.

"Well, as I told you the other day," he said, "Mr. O'Hare is scheduled for some minor surgery on his knee. Since he'll be confined to his home during the recovery period, he'd like to see that the flow of work continues uninterrupted. Hence, his need for an assistant that he can trust."

"But you said he already had some of his relatives staying there," Victoria reminded him. "Couldn't one of—"

The attorney's unmistakably dark expression halted her in midsentence. "The operative word is 'trust,' Victoria. That's why I'm sending *you*. Now, if you'll excuse me, I need to get ready for court."

Not exactly a chatterbox, Victoria categorized the uniformed chauffeur as she sat in the back seat of the limo and watched the rain-soaked Virginia countryside go by. Twenty minutes as a pampered passenger and all she had learned so far was that his name was Chan, he liked the Miami Dolphins, and he had a black belt in karate.

I must truly look dangerous, she thought to herself, wondering what had possessed him to so eagerly volunteer his knowledge of the martial arts. Either that or O'Hare's secret identity was the Green Hornet and she was being driven to her destination by Kato.

"So, have you worked for Mr. O'Hare very long?" she said, trying again to engage him in small talk.

"No," the young man curtly replied, his back ramrod-straight as he maneuvered the country roads.

"How would you rate him as a boss?" she casually asked.

Chan inclined his head, Victoria wasn't sure whether this meant that he hadn't heard her question or that he wasn't sure what kind of answer she was seeking.

"I don't mean to come off as nosy or anything," she said, "but since I'm going to be working for him through the holidays, I was wondering if maybe you could—"

"The storm has made driving very difficult," Chan answered.

Victoria folded her arms and settled back into the seat with a sigh.

What have you gotten yourself into? she asked herself. Correction: What had *Elliott* gotten her into?

Her independent sleuthing through the firm's files on Hunter O'Hare had yielded little more than the attorney's own disclosures. Five years previously, the man had inherited his great-grandfather's estate, a legacy predicated on his assuming residence of Patrick O'Hare's ancestral home. While Elliott clearly lauded the millionaire's shrewdness in circumventing the will's dictate, it made no sense whatsoever to Victoria why he should even have expended the effort—or wasted the law firm's time.

It wasn't as if he really needed any more money. Victoria had gasped when she came across the man's net worth and international holdings. Though his great-grandfather's castle and all its contents might be valuable for their historical significance, the cost of transporting them from Ireland over a three-year period well exceeded it.

Nor could his motive have been compassion for the servants left unemployed by Patrick's death. Provision for their continued care and housing until retirement had already been included in the voluminous text. Six of them, including Patrick's elderly personal valet, had relocated to America when the castle's completion rendered it safe for habitation. Elliott's own intervention and extensive correspondence with the Immigration and Naturalization Service had made the transition for all of them as smooth as possible.

What amazed Victoria the most, however, was that O'Hare had torn down a perfectly acceptable house—a spectacular house, by Thatch and John's assessment—and had the castle rebuilt on exactly the same site. Certainly someone with his resources could have purchased another parcel of acreage in the country and had his inheritance set up on it. That a wrecking ball had come down purely as an act of whim further attested to her opinion that he had never outgrown the childhood role of spoiled brat.

The limo had now turned off the main road and past a pair of open iron gates. Victoria leaned forward, conscious that her pulse had quickened with the realization that they were close to—if not actually on—O'Hare's property.

On either side of the road Chan was taking, huge trees mushroomed over a carpet of lush green grass, a pastoral scene where—were it not for the magnitude of the rainstorm—one would have expected to see deer or sheep peacefully grazing. No signs of life were visible today, though, contributing to Victoria's rising sense of uneasiness. Not for the first time that afternoon did she wish that Elliott were with her.

"Are we almost there?" she asked Chan.

Yet even as the last word passed her lips, the limo emerged from the trees and into the meadow's clearing.

Surprise drained all color from her face as she beheld the towering medieval structure that now loomed on the other side of the wide stone bridge they were about to cross.

"Yes, madam," Chan replied, oblivious to her state of shock. "We are here."

Though not one given to swearing, an expletive hovered on Victoria's mouth, her eyes wide with amazement as she stared at the battlements and cylindrical towers and arched windows on the upper levels. *Deja vu*, she thought with an inward shudder, stunned by the chilling awareness that she had seen the castle somewhere before.

As her gaze traveled downward to where jade green vines haphazardly serpentined the structure's darker first floor, she suddenly realized the source of familiarity. It was the castle in the picture hanging in Elliott's office, though its setting was now a verdant valley instead of a craggy cliff on the coast of Ireland.

"I want you to be surprised," the attorney said when she had asked him what the castle looked like. Had he been amused, she wondered, that the photograph of it in its original surroundings was hanging in plain sight the entire time and that she didn't even make the connection?

As the limousine soundlessly eased through an imposing archway into the puddled courtyard beyond, Victoria could not help but notice the thick, spiked gate of wood and iron that hung directly above them like a stage curtain poised to descend.

"That's some garage door you've got," she murmured. "Is it operated by remote?"

"It is not in use," Chan informed her.

As she started to pursue the subject, a burst of commotion off to her right distracted her. Two people—a woman and a man—had just come into the courtyard. Exploded into the courtyard, to be precise.

Though she couldn't hear what they were saying, it was clear that the exchange wasn't an amicable one. The young woman's long black hair whipped about her shoulders as she turned in midflight to wave her arms angrily at the man who had followed her outside. Both were clad in tight jeans and bulky sweaters; Victoria guessed them to be in their late twenties. Even at a distance, they were also, unmistakably, drop-dead good-looking.

With a final, guttural shout, the girl ran off in the opposite direction, indifferent to the water and mud that splashed across her knee-high boots and sides of her jeans. For a moment, Victoria expected the black-haired young man to run after her and drag her back.

"Who's that?" she started to ask Chan.

The object of her inquiry, however, suddenly noticed the limousine, too absorbed in his fight with the girl to have observed its presence before. With jaw clenched and eyes angrily flashing, he pushed up both sleeves of his sweater and defiantly strode toward the car, viciously yanking open the passenger door before either Victoria or Chan could react.

4

Victoria's *bewilderment* was mirrored in the young man's own face as their eyes met.

"Oh sorry, lass," he said, his voice thick with an Irish brogue. "I thought you were someone else."

"From the looks of it, I'm glad I'm not," a shaken Victoria responded, an answer that brought a chuckle to his throat.

"Pretty *and* witty," he complimented her with an engaging wink, extending his hand to help her alight from the limo. "Your servant, mum." The wet lock of hair that dipped across his forehead gave him a look that was simultaneously boyish and satanic.

Victoria hesitated a moment, casting a glance at Chan for guidance. When none was forthcoming, she determined that it was either because the volatile young Irishman was actually harmless or that the Chinese driver's responsibility for her safety ended once the ignition was turned off.

"I won't bite, darlin'," the black-haired man pleasantly assured her, "though I can't say it won't cross my mind. . . ."

Victoria smirked at his blatant overture. That Hunter O'Hare would condone such unenlightened attitudes among his staff was all the more reason to dislike him. "Mr. O'Hare is expecting me," she said, as she ignored the young man's offer of assistance and started out of the car on her own.

Instantly, one hand caught her elbow and the other slid around her waist. Victoria quickly rebuffed any further advance with a sharp glare and the command that he let go.

"Sorry," he said, taken aback by her unexpected directness.

"Please tell Mr. O'Hare that Victoria Cameron is here," she instructed him, wondering if she'd be made to wait in the rain or be taken inside.

"You're from the hospital, then?" he asked.

"I'm with the law firm," she replied. "Bowman, Johnson, and Williams."

"Oh," he murmured, nonplussed.

"He *was* expecting me, wasn't he?"

Annoyance flickered across the young man's face. "Who knows *what* the bloody bastard expects?" he snorted, pointing toward an arched doorway at the top of the steps. "Straight through," he said. "Hell if I care what to do with you." Whether perturbed by her rejection or disgruntled by his servitude, the young man clearly considered their association concluded, stomping off across the courtyard in the same direction where the girl had disappeared.

Fine, Victoria thought to herself, glad to be rid of him. "Will you be here when I get out?" she inquired of Chan, who had stayed clear of the entire interaction.

"No," he said. "Please close the door."

What has Elliott gotten me into? she thought to herself again as she watched Chan drive around the circular courtyard and back out the entryway. With a heavy sigh, she started up the steps, increasingly dubious of what she would find once she reached the top.

It looked like the set of a vintage Robin Hood movie, she decided, almost expecting Errol Flynn to step into her path with a full-antlered stag draped over both shoulders and deftly drop it at her ankles. The sound of her own footsteps on stone reverberated through the slate gray corridor, its depths lit only from one side by vertical slits about fifteen feet above her head. Even on a sunny day, she speculated, there would be little more illumination than now.

Thankful for a heavy winter coat and wool gloves as defense against the pervasive chill, she stopped midway, suddenly feeling very much a trespasser. They *were* expecting her, weren't they? The young man's reaction at least hinted they had been expecting *someone* that afternoon. She cast a wary glance back at the door she originally entered from the courtyard, half-wondering whether it had locked behind her, trapping her in some medieval nightmare with a rich loony.

The hallway was absolutely silent, save for the sounds of the storm outside. *Not exactly a warm reception from the castle's host,* Victoria thought, noting the absence of any obvious clues on which direction she should take next to find evidence of human habitation. A stout wooden door reinforced by iron cross-hatching lay to her immediate left. A little farther down was what looked like the entrance to another corridor. Farther still lay wide stone steps that curved up and disappeared behind the wall. "Straight through," the dark-haired man had said. Had he meant straight through and up the steps? Straight through and knock on a door? Straight through and wait for—

As she contemplated the alternatives, the door on her left suddenly opened.

"Oh my!" the woman who opened it gasped, obviously

startled to encounter someone. Her hand flew up to her ample bosom and executed a quick sign of the cross.

Victoria hastily introduced herself, lest she be thought a well-dressed prowler and shot on the spot. "Mr. O'Hare is expecting me," she said.

"Well, come in, darlin'!" the older woman invited her, displaying a broad grin reminiscent of Lewis Carroll's Cheshire Cat. "You'll be catchin' your death in the draft!"

It was Victoria's turn to express surprise as she was bustled into the castle's paraphrase of a modern foyer. Her expectation—honed from books and movies—of dank, cement-gray cells, musty animal odors, and an occasional tapestry of lions and unicorns fell by the wayside as she beheld what time and money had wrought to Patrick's ancestral home. Certainly, she thought, the original version had never looked this good, for if it had, the senior O'Hare might have hung on for another century to enjoy it.

"Take your coat, love?" the woman offered, her Irish accent as thick as that of the man she had met in the courtyard. Mesmerized by what she was looking at, Victoria almost didn't hear her.

"Yes, thank you," she murmured, grateful to be left alone for a moment that she might stare, unabashed, at the surroundings. It was definitely the farthest guess from the interior that Victoria had imagined as she stood in the cold, cavernous hallway just outside the door only a minute before. That corridor may as well have been in another world, another time.

Heat and light cast from a fireplace almost as tall as she was enveloped the room in a toasty glow, its warmth enhanced by earth-tone fabrics and an Aubusson rug of dark green and gold. As her eyes swept the contents of a visitor's first view of O'Hare's domain, she couldn't help but appreciate his blend of contemporary treasures and antique furnishings. Some lucky decorator, she decided, had made a mint off of this one.

The older woman's returning footfall and lyrical voice nudged Victoria back to the reality of her purpose in being there.

"So it's himself you're here to see, then?" the woman asked, encouraging her to take a seat by the fire.

"Himself?"

"Mr. O'Hare," she translated, planting her body in the opposite chair. "And a fine man he is, too."

"Yes, I'm sure," Victoria politely nodded. "I'm sorry, but I didn't catch *your* name . . . ?"

"Gwynna Maginn," she said, beaming, neatly folding her hands over her aproned waist in matronly satisfaction. "I see to things when himself isn't here."

"You mean like a housekeeper?" Victoria inquired.

By the woman's perceptible snort of indignation, Victoria wondered whether she had just committed a verbal faux pas. Maybe they're not *called* housekeepers these days, she thought. Perhaps she's a Domestic Administrator or an Internal Affairs Supervisor. Whatever the title, it was obvious from her ruffled reaction that Gwynna Maginn took her job at O'Hare's estate most seriously.

As she proceeded to explain the breadth of her duties—and they were numerous—it afforded Victoria the chance to take a better look at her under the pretense of hanging on every word.

Taller than Victoria by at least three inches, the first physical impression that Mrs. Maginn was likely to leave with someone was that of an ostrich, owing to a chinless profile, large brown eyes behind wire-framed glasses, and curly tufts of hair the color of marmalade. At least that was the first impression she left with Victoria, fixedly scrutinizing the latter as if she were an interesting—and edible—bug crossing the sand.

A delft blue dress—which may have been her regular uniform—sported an incongruously young Peter Pan collar and a hem length that was last popular in the 1940s. Her hose and black shoes were dated as well, reminding Victoria of a style the Pilgrims might have worn.

No jewelry, Victoria noted. No wedding ring. As for her age, it was probably in the neighborhood of fiftysomething, she guessed, though Mrs. Maginn struck her as the type who would never admit to anything unflattering.

"... now *there* was a devil to work for, rest his soul," Mrs. Maginn was saying, having already changed the subject during Victoria's study of her.

"I beg your pardon?"

The housekeeper pursed her thin lips as if she had just tasted something disagreeable. "Far be it from me to speak ill of the dead, darlin', but the saints rejoiced when *that* one passed on. And half the county, I'd wager, as well!"

"You mean Patrick?"

Mrs. Maginn ignored her question, either from poor hearing or impatience to ask a question of her own. "So you'll be workin' for himself then?" she inquired. "Isn't *that* a grand thing!"

"We still have some details to work out on it," Victoria replied, turning back her cuff to check her watch. "Do you know how much longer he'll be?"

Mrs. Maginn chuckled. "Harnessin' himself is like throwing a rope on the wind," she exclaimed.

"Could you be a little more specific? I usually go by eastern standard time myself."

"He'll be along when he comes," Mrs. Maginn noncommittally informed her. "So what is it again you're to be doin', love?"

I *wonder if she thinks she's subtle*, Victoria thought to herself, amused by the housekeeper's gregarious bid to extract information from her.

"A little of this and that," Victoria pleasantly played along.

"A jill-of-all-trades then?"

"Yes, I suppose you could say that."

"Keeps the hands busy," Mrs. Maginn observed, her mind clearly racing for some clever way to get down to details.

"Speaking of busy hands," Victoria spoke up, "it must take an awfully large staff to manage this place."

Once again, Mrs. Maginn's face registered the discomfort of insult. "Sure, I could do it all myself with enough hours in a day and still have plenty of breath to draw," she boasted. "Not like the *last* one."

"The last one?"

"'Miss High and Mighty,' they called her," she said, a definitive wrinkle creasing her long nose. "Not that *himself* didn't sing her praises like a chorus to St. Peter—"

Whatever Mrs. Maginn would have said next about her predecessor was cut short by the sound of the foyer door opening around the corner.

The housekeeper was on her feet at once, not unlike a terrier caught enjoying a forbidden nap on the furniture.

"Devil of a day out, isn't it, Mr. O'Hare!" she effusively greeted her employer as he entered the room. "Saints be praised you're home safe!"

O'Hare's focus, however, was already locked on Victoria.

And vice versa.

If the castle's interior had been one shock to her system, the millionaire himself was easily a double one. Try as she might to look elsewhere, Victoria's eyes were riveted on the handsome, chiseled features of the man Elliott had sent her to meet, the reflected light from the fire glimmering over his face and hair like an amber radiance.

It *can't be*, she told herself, embarrassed that the very man who had just come in from the rain was the same man—the same breathtaking hunk—whom she had met in the elevator on the Monday that she looked so terrible. Maybe he won't recognize me, she found herself hoping. Certainly her appearance today in a tailored wool suit was much improved over the bedraggled, wild-haired waif clutching a half-empty styrofoam cup on Floor 3.

One thing was certain, of course, and that was that he was even more handsome than her first look that day had estimated. The staggering challenge of his nearness, in fact, easily overruled all original intentions on Victoria's part to be aloof.

Broad shoulders filled the black, rain-splashed jacket that he wore, the jacket that Mrs. Maginn now eagerly offered to take. As the leather slipped off both arms, Victoria couldn't help but catch the sculpted outline of his chest or the thatch of dark gold hair in the vee of his open shirt. Unbidden came the lustful thought of sliding her fingers beneath the fabric and feeling the beat of his heart.

"Have we met before?" his voice intruded on her wicked daydream. Victoria's eyes snapped back to his face, having absently traveled downward to the jean-clad stance that emphasized the force of his thighs and narrowness of his hips.

"No," Victoria quickly replied. Too quickly perhaps. Not that it was a lie. "I'm Victoria Cameron," she introduced herself, stepping forward to offer her hand. His grip was firm and confident. For an instant, Victoria imagined that a full embrace from such a man would be just as solid, just as electrifying.

"Elliott's not with you," he remarked, arching a brow as if she had purposely hidden the attorney from his sight. "Does that mean I have you to myself?" A sensuous smile came to life on his lips.

The warmth of his handshake traveled up the length of her arm and back down her spine. "Mr. Bowman sends his regrets," she said, wondering whether Elliott's absence would declare the meeting impractical. "If you'd rather reschedule this for another time—" she started to offer.

"*You're* here, aren't you?" he said. "Since I'm here as well, it seems we're in the majority." His lips parted in a display of straight white teeth. "Shall we have tea?"

Victoria tentatively returned his smile, wondering whether he'd tug on one of the tasseled pulls above the fireplace to summon back Mrs. Maginn or if the tea service had already been set up for them in an adjoining room.

"Let's go see about making some," he suggested. Puzzled, Victoria followed him, steeling herself not to stare at his broad shoulders and tight buttocks.

Unlike the corridor she had first entered, the one they were taking was carpeted and well lit, broad enough to be a room itself. Maybe it *was* a room of some kind, she thought. A gallery perhaps, its walls adorned with portraits of dour matrons swathed in brocade and counterpart pictures of overweight, bearded men who looked like Henry the Eighth.

"The full tour comes later," her host promised as he led the way toward the back of the castle, oblivious to her discomposure over his looks.

Victoria was finding it impossible to take her mind off of his body. Thatch and John's teasing description of him as a beast now came back to nag her with a new twist. Even Elliott, she recalled, had been evasive in telling her much about him. Certainly, he had never divulged that Hunter was a hunk.

O'Hare was already pushing open a wide door similar to the others and announcing, "We've got company, Cook!"

The plump woman at the stove turned around to acknowledge him as Victoria entered the kitchen. "Hello," Victoria started to say, but the word was drowned out by the servant's sudden, earsplitting scream.

5

Victoria's initial reaction was to snap her head around to see if someone was standing behind her with a poised machete. Finding no one there, her second reaction was to wonder why on earth the very sight of her seemed to have such an adverse effect on every servant she had encountered at the castle thus far that afternoon.

It's even a good hair day, she told herself, so it couldn't be that she looked like Medusa, horrid enough to turn total strangers into stone.

"My God, it's her!" the plump woman hysterically shrieked, repeating it like a frenzied mantra in spite of her handsome employer's efforts to calm her with soothing words and gentle hands.

If I had both those hands on my shoulders, Victoria enviously thought to herself as she watched him from the doorway, I'd be absolutely placid in no time flat. The man should be arrested on the spot for being that handsome, she decided.

The woman's body—almost as wide as she was tall—was jiggling like Jell-o.

"What the devil's wrong?" O'Hare asked urgently when

no explanation was forthcoming from the flustered Irish-woman. He seemed to temporarily forget that Victoria was even present, much less the cause of his kitchen servant's immediate state of distress.

"It's *her*," the cook whimpered, not taking her startled eyes off of the redhead. "Sure, it's Alandra Monaco herself, sir!"

"Alandra what?" a puzzled O'Hare repeated. The name meant nothing to him.

Oh, great, Victoria muttered under her breath. Over two thousand miles away and the ghost of Marcine still blissfully haunted her. Obviously the cook was a devoted fan of mindless afternoon television.

"It's the Niagara woman!" the cook excitedly babbled away in her brogue, gripping O'Hare's strong forearm as if she were to lose her balance at any moment and plummet into a bottomless pit.

O'Hare arched a brow. "The what?"

"The one who's had herself five husbands," the cook eagerly explained, "but one of them twice and then, saints protect her, got arrested for his murder 'cept she was set up by her meaner, younger sister, don't you know, but sure an' the judge himself was the secret father of one of her sons, she was . . ."

O'Hare looked over at Victoria as the woman animatedly rambled on in great detail about the past season of Alandra's fictional exploits in Bayville, amusement underscoring his candid observation.

"Apparently there's a lot to your background that Elliott omitted about you," he remarked. "Sounds like you've led a colorful life for someone so young."

"Maybe I should clear this up," Victoria offered, conscious of the roguish wink that he had just cast but resolved not to read too much into it.

"Have at it," he encouraged her.

"I think you might be confusing me with someone else," Victoria diplomatically suggested to his servant, stepping further into the high-ceilinged kitchen that the woman might get a better look at her and thus realize her mistake.

The cook anxiously shook her head at the notion she was wrong, dislodging a few wisps of gray curl from the shapeless bun at the back of her stout neck.

"Sure, you're the spittin' image of—" she suddenly halted in midsentence and squinted at Victoria. "*You're* not Alandra Monaco!" she charged, her opinion now radically altered by the proximity of the subject and a different angle of light. "You're not her at all!"

O'Hare cleared his throat. "Am I the only one in the dark here?" he queried. "Who's Alandra Monaco?"

The Irishwoman indignantly puffed out her chest like a peacock. "Only the finest actress on the daytime television!" she proclaimed. "And even prettier than that Erica girl, bless her soul."

"Her real name is Marcine Cameron," Victoria said, finding it concurrently funny and sad that—to her fans— the popular actress was probably better known as the glamorous-but-martyred character who lived and loved in Bayville, New York, than as the real person who paid bills and resided in Sherman Oaks, California. Of course, maybe that's what came from playing the same silly part five times a week for the past sixteen years.

"A relative of yours?" O'Hare queried, nonplussed by all of it. "Or is 'Cameron' a coincidence?"

"She's my mother," Victoria replied, surprised that she should feel a tinge of irritation just then that a man as worldly as Hunter O'Hare not only knew absolutely zilch about the Hollywood scene but was oblivious to a physical resemblance that she had dealt with for most of her adult life.

Maybe she was more proud of Marcine's work than she liked to admit, Victoria thought, for certainly it was the first time she had ever experienced having to explain their connection. Most of the time, the nuisance of living in Marcine's omnipotent shadow created problems in developing relationships.

"So what kind of tea do you like to drink?" O'Hare asked, turning his back on Victoria to take a heavy teakettle from the far right burner of the stove.

The cook firmly pushed her way in to take it from him. "Now don't you be botherin' yourself with the water there, sir," she said as she reached for the wooden handle. "It's as good as boilin' its heart out if you leave it to me."

"Do you have Earl Grey?" Victoria asked, finding it unusual that a man accustomed to being waited on by a bevy of domestics had just insisted rather sternly to one of them that he was perfectly capable of boiling his own water.

Hunter affirmed that her choice was available. "Do you like yours strong?" he inquired.

"Strong is fine," Victoria replied, wondering if he intended all of his questions to hint at something else or if it was just her own way of interpreting them.

"Somehow I knew that," Hunter said. "I like mine strong, too." His eyes prolonged the moment between them.

The water, Victoria thought, wasn't the only thing that was edging toward a high temperature.

"We'll take it in *mugs*," he informed the cook, who—having reluctantly relinquished her efforts at the stove—had started to withdraw two delicate china cups from one of the oak and beveled glass cabinets.

"Very well, sir," the cook replied and proceeded to put them back. By the look Victoria briefly caught on her face, it was evident that she hadn't figured out all of O'Hare's quirky habits yet, either.

As the two of them discussed a concern on the evening menu, Victoria took the opportunity to scan her surroundings. Definitely the Middle Ages, she classed the circular interior, but endowed with enough modern conveniences to make Julia Child feel right at home. Obviously O'Hare had taken extensive liberties in the castle's reassembly to introduce twentieth century plumbing and electricity.

What still boggled the mind, of course, was why he had torn down his former home for this one.

"I haven't introduced the two of you," O'Hare suddenly remembered. "Ms. Cameron, meet Mrs. Pritchard."

"Oh, 'Pritchard' alone is fine enough, mum," the cook jovially countered, "seein' as how my Welshman's been dead and buried these twenty years past, rest his soul."

"Only if you call me Victoria," she replied, finding in the cook a more congenial personality than the zealously inquisitive housekeeper.

Pritchard shook her head. "Sure, it wouldn't be proper, mum," she said, "your bein' a guest of himself."

Victoria caught herself smiling at the second time she had heard O'Hare referred to on such a lofty plane.

"Actually," O'Hare corrected her, "Ms. Cameron is going to be working for us as an employee through the holidays."

The cook's pudgy hands came together in a joyous clasp. "Well, isn't *that* an answer to our prayers, sir!" she exclaimed. "And what is it that you're to be doin', mum?" There was no subtlety in Pritchard's head-to-toe assessment of the well-dressed young woman who stood in her kitchen. "Sure an' you're not another maid?"

"You and the others will all find out in good time, Mrs. Pritchard," O'Hare assured her. Just enough curtness laced his voice to preempt any further questions about Victoria's presence at the castle.

"Will you be havin' your tea in the parlor, sir?" Pritchard asked.

"No, the library," O'Hare replied, conceding to the woman's enthusiasm to be of service. "Please bring it in when it's ready."

Just before the door, he paused.

"You might bring some extra napkins, too," he recommended to Pritchard, "in case we spill any down the front of ourselves."

Victoria felt the color steal into her cheeks. *Damn*, she thought. He *had* recognized her.

"Mostly," O'Hare explained, "it will be errands and personal correspondence. I assume you know how to use a Mac PC and a modem?"

His reference to electronic technology struck Victoria as incongruous to the medieval setting in which they were discussing her duties.

"Was it the way I said it?" he asked.

"I beg your pardon?"

"You look like you want to laugh," he pointed out.

"Your place just takes some getting used to," Victoria replied, trying not to stare at the shadowed cleft in his chin or the muscles beneath his shirt. "I keep expecting a dragon to melt down the outer wall."

"He'd have to have pretty strong breath to do that, I think. In Duncan's time, they built their castles to last."

"Duncan?"

"Ancestor of mine," he replied with a shrug. "There'll be time enough later for you to catch up on seven hundred years."

As he continued to explain the scope of what he expected from her, it was all Victoria could do to keep her mind on the conversation and not let it stray to inappropriate speculations about his prowess as a lover. *You're here to work for the man*, she reminded herself, disturbed that she needed a reminder of it at all. *He's the same man who wastes money on moving castles*, her conscience chided her.

As she sat and listened to him, though, she could feel herself trying to justify the expense of what he had done. Unquestionably, it was a breathtaking structure, particularly the room in which they were seated.

A combination library and private office on the first floor, the room's parameters were dominated by twelve-foot-high bookcases, their upper shelves accessible only by ladder or tall stool. Not entirely practical, she thought to herself, but consistent with the vaulted museum effect appropriate to a structure that old.

Had O'Hare actually read every volume in his collection? she mused. He probably had, sating his need to know everything about everything. Elliott had praised his intelligence more than once.

A fireplace to her right boasted both a stone hearth and mantel nearly deep enough to dine on, were one given to such bohemian behavior. Its polished andirons were already cradling a fresh bed of logs when they entered, so O'Hare had merely to set one match to it to initiate a cozy flame. "A chimney sweep could make a good income on this place alone," O'Hare had told her, explaining that the castle had a total of nine fireplaces to help warm it in the winter. Not that paying a full electric bill instead would have dented his net worth, Victoria silently opined.

I wonder what this room used to be, she wondered as she

sipped her tea, *or what kind of view it looks out on*.

Only then did it occur to her that it didn't look out on anything, having no windows whatsoever.

"How's your shorthand?" O'Hare inquired.

Distracted by the oddity of a windowless room, Victoria nearly answered "Delicious," as if he had asked about her tea. "A hundred and twenty," she replied.

"Elliott tells me that you have good judgment and discretion," he remarked. "Can you keep secrets?"

"What kind of secrets would I be expected to keep?"

O'Hare's answer was cut short by the sound of the door bursting open behind Victoria.

Sudden anger lit O'Hare's gray eyes. "Does it ever occur to you to knock?" he sharply admonished the intruder.

Victoria turned in her chair to see the same young man she had encountered in the courtyard.

"Does it ever occur to *you* that you're not our bloody king?" the black-haired Irishman retorted.

A warning cloud settled on O'Hare's features in his pause of stony silence before replying. "I'm in the middle of something," he informed the man. "I trust whatever it is you want can wait?"

"Suit yourself," the intruder shrugged. "The silly mare can break her neck, for all it means to *you*."

"*What?*"

"Storm spooked her," the young man replied as he casually strolled toward them. "Broke down the fence again and got out."

O'Hare was already standing. "Where's Ian?" he demanded.

"Devil if I know. I*'m* not his bloody keeper."

In what seemed like only half a dozen strides, owing to his height, O'Hare had passed him and reached the door. "I'm sorry," he apologized to Victoria. "We'll continue this at dinner."

Before she could even open her mouth to tell him that she had plans for the evening, Hunter O'Hare was gone, leaving her in the company of a man she had already decided she disliked.

He was chuckling before her host was even out of earshot. "Worships the damn thing like a fool," he remarked. "Sure, that bloody horse'll be havin' her own room and puttin' me out of mine."

Victoria refrained from offering the opinion that a horse probably had the better disposition to live with.

"Seems I'm forgetting my manners, aren't I, lass?" he grinned. He was standing close enough that Victoria could smell his cologne and feel the scorch of his dark brown eyes as he covetously looked down on her. "Sean Michael Gleavy," he introduced himself. "His lordship's cousin."

6

At *least that explained why* he hadn't been fired for insubordination, Victoria thought, though it was hard to imagine O'Hare tolerating such a person—even a blood relative—under the same roof.

"Lordship?" she repeated, wishing that he weren't standing quite so close to her chair. "They don't recognize titles in America."

Sean Michael laughed and raked one hand through his hair. "Try tellin' that to *him*," he said, a glitter of lethal amusement dancing across his lean face. "Sure, I hear they still recognize a pretty *girl*, though," he added. "And a pretty name, I'd wager, to go with it."

Another short memory, Victoria thought to herself, having distinctly told him down in the courtyard who she was when she first arrived.

"Cat got your tongue, miss?" he teased, settling hip-shot with nonchalant grace on the edge of O'Hare's desk, his thumbs hooked in the front of his belt and index fingers casually pointed toward his crotch. "Or is it that you can't believe your good fortune?"

"And what good fortune is that?" Victoria inquired, irritated with O'Hare for leaving her in such a compromising position. Was it that he considered his cousin harmless enough company not to pose any threat? Or that his concern for a frightened horse took precedence over someone he had known for less than half an hour? Whichever the case, Victoria would have preferred being alone. Undeniably good looking but arrogantly abrasive, Sean Michael Gleavy reminded her of the stereotypical young actors who slept their way to the better roles in Hollywood but had only their sexuality—and not intelligence—to bank on down the road. Even his eyes held that same fierce gleam of competition to stay in the running.

Her question about good fortune made him laugh again, a broad laugh that seemed to reverberate off of the library walls. "Why, to be workin' for God's Gift to Democracy!" he sneered. "The man everyone loves!"

"Obviously not everyone," Victoria countered, seeing no reason to feign ignorance of the cousin's profound hatred.

His expression shifted to a critical squint. "Aye, but you're right on that count, darlin'. I'd as soon put a knife between his bloody ribs as kiss his American ass."

Obviously there's a story here that I'm missing, Victoria thought.

"There certainly doesn't seem to be any love lost between the two of you," she remarked.

"Never lost—and never existed," Sean Michael snorted. "But sure an' it doesn't say what *you're* to be doin' here."

"Just a secretary," she replied, wondering what sort of rumors were already circulating among his domestic staff.

O'Hare's cousin echoed her response with another laugh. "A secretary, is it?" he said. "Then I'll be wishin' you luck, lass."

"Why should you think that I'd need it?"

The voice of Gwynna Maginn interrupted whatever answer Sean Michael might have given.

"There you are!" she exclaimed from the door that O'Hare had left open in his flight from the room.

"Guilty and then some," he said.

"Miss Deborah is on the line."

Sean Michael's smile had a spark of raw eroticism. "Does she sound like she missed me?"

Mrs. Maginn pursed her lips in annoyance at his blatant conceit. "Will you be takin' the call up in your room, sir?" she inquired.

He had already slid his body into O'Hare's chair and was reaching for the receiver before Victoria turned back around. "This room's closer," he curtly informed the housekeeper. "And don't you be listenin' in on the extension."

With a miffed look on her face that he should even suggest such a thing, Mrs. Maginn took leave of them.

"Debbie, love!" he greeted his caller, his voice now underscored with a sensual huskiness that hadn't been there before. "And how's the light of my life?"

Victoria reached for her purse and stood up.

"Now don't be rushin' off on my account," Sean Michael insisted, cupping his hand over the mouthpiece.

Thankful for an excuse to leave him, Victoria merely smiled and left the room, not at all sure what she was supposed to do next.

Mrs. Maginn, she noted, had already vanished from the corridor, though there was no telling which direction she had gone—not that she necessarily wanted the housekeeper's company in substitution for Sean Michael's.

A return visit to the kitchen, Victoria decided, seemed a more prudent course than wandering around the castle by herself. Besides, she had found an ally of sorts in the amiable Mrs. P.

As she neared the open kitchen door, however, the sound of voices stopped her in her tracks.

"Tisn't a proper thing to do, to be chasin' a man like that," she heard Pritchard exclaim. "And her with the looks to have any lad in the county!" The cook clucked her tongue audibly enough for Victoria to hear it.

"Modern times, modern places," a male voice replied in a sermonic baritone, betraying no hint of the speaker's age. "The twig will grow as it's bent."

"Well then, she'll have *himself* to answer to for it!" Pritchard prophesied. "Mark my words, Nilly. A girl free as that never comes to no good!"

Paralyzed between the desire to hear more and the urge to mind her own business, Victoria would have remained rooted where she was were it not for the sound of a door opening and approaching footsteps from one of the corridors. Rather than be caught eavesdropping, her best recourse was to clear her throat to announce her approach to the kitchen.

"Oh, it's *her*, Nilly!" Pritchard brightly announced to the elderly man seated at the kitchen table. "It's her!"

Oh, no, Victoria thought for a moment, wondering if she'd have to relive the earlier scenario. Pritchard, however, had apparently already briefed her guest on the particulars of Victoria's celebrity background. With only a slur of hesitation, owing to his advanced years, the white-haired man noisily scraped back his chair and unfolded his skeletal body to its full Lincolnesque height.

"Miss Cameron," he said, gallantly offering a blue-veined hand, almost translucent in its frailty. "A pleasure to meet you." That such a decrepit—albeit well-groomed—man should have such a strong speaking voice was as much a surprise to Victoria as anything else she had encountered that afternoon.

"Nilly was Sir Patrick's valet," Pritchard proudly

explained, urging him to sit down again before the excitement of shaking hands taxed his system.

"Nilly?" Victoria repeated to make sure she had heard it correctly.

"It's a pet name, don't you know," Mrs. P said. "We're not ones to be standin' on the formality."

"So you're Mr. O'Hare's valet now?" Victoria inquired, recalling his mention in the docket of "possessions" that the millionaire had inherited.

Pritchard giggled. "Not to be laughin', Nilly, but sure an' *that's* a stretch of the thread!"

The older man laughed as well, though not with the exuberance of the plump cook.

At least they're easily entertained, Victoria thought, wondering what exactly had set them off. Wondering as well what had happened to the footsteps she had distinctly heard behind her out in the corridor. "Stretch of the thread?" she repeated.

"Himself's not one for the fancy caterin'," Pritchard offered at last. "And Nilly—well, by the looks of him, mum, would you get a fair day's work for the pay?"

"I'm not sure how to answer that," Victoria replied, not wanting to offend the gentleman by saying that he looked as if he should have been retired, if not buried, a few centuries ago.

"Himself, bless his soul," Pritchard continued, "knew Nilly was wantin' to see the States 'fore he met the Lord." The cook folded her hands in satisfaction over her stomach. "So that's why he's here and sure himself is to thank for it!"

In other words, Victoria silently interpreted, *Nilly is part of the furniture and just about as industrious*. Still, she couldn't fault him for being pleasant, his face crinkled with amusement as if enjoying a private joke.

"I wonder if I could bother you for some more tea," she

asked the cook, wishing that she had remembered to retrieve her mug off the desk. "I'm just waiting for Mr. O'Hare to come back."

"Where's he off to?" Nilly wanted to know.

"Something about a horse breaking down a fence," Victoria replied.

Pritchard's piggish eyes grew wide with alarm. "Not the mare?" she exclaimed.

"I don't really remember," Victoria answered. "It may have been."

"Ian will catch her soon enough." Nilly spoke up with the self-assured calm of a man who had weathered many a mishap. "The boy knows horses like the palm of his hand."

Pritchard snorted. "He should be so smart with the opposite sex!" With a flourish, she withdrew one of the delicate china cups and saucers from the cupboard that O'Hare had originally made her put away. "Shall I bring your tea to the library, mum?"

"That's okay," Victoria declined. "I'll just wait and take it with me, if that's all right with you?"

Pritchard beamed at Victoria's deference. "Long as you don't spill a drop and catch the devil," she said.

"You mean from Mr. O'Hare?"

Pritchard cast a sidelong glance at Nilly, then back at Victoria. "Have you met Mrs. Maginn?" she pointedly asked.

"Yes," Victoria answered, "when I arrived."

"A Bible in one hand and a knife in the other," the cook muttered under her breath.

Victoria tilted her head. "I beg your pardon?"

A pause hung heavy on the air between them. It was Nilly who broke the silence. "The walls have ears, Mrs. P," he said.

Pritchard's face tightened into one of stern restraint.

"Then that's all I'll be sayin', mum. Was it the Earl Grey you wanted?"

Darkness—and more rain—had fallen on the valley by the time O'Hare finally came back. Though he was drenched to the bone, his first inquiry upon returning was about Victoria's whereabouts.

"I've just been enjoying your library," she answered. At least it was partially true. After collecting a fresh cup of tea and some shortbread cookies to go with it, she had retraced her steps to the library and discovered, to her relief, that Sean Michael was already gone. Closing the door, she eventually settled into a chair by the fire with one of O'Hare's volumes on Irish history and proceeded to read. A nice, unassuming way to wait out the afternoon as a captive guest if she hadn't been bothered by a few other factors.

The first was her compelling desire to call Elliott and ask him to come and get her. Certainly an extended evening at the castle hadn't been part of her agenda, and while the curtailment of her talk with O'Hare about business was based on unforeseen circumstances, it nonetheless bothered her that he had automatically assumed her time was his own. "I'm not even working for him yet," she would have told Elliott.

In his usual sagacity, of course, Elliott would have told her that she *would* be on O'Hare's payroll and to respect his wishes accordingly. For as many times as she looked over at the phone, intuition about what the senior law partner would advise prevented her from using it. Besides, she reassured herself, it wasn't likely that Bowman or his two cohorts would let her be sold into white slavery or allow her to slip unnoticed from the face of the earth. If she didn't show up for work tomorrow morning, they'd be the first to storm the fortress with a battering ram.

Her second concern was that O'Hare's hot-tempered cousin would seek her out for a continued interrogation about what she was doing at the castle. It didn't take a rocket scientist to figure out why the millionaire would trust a stranger over his own family, she decided. If Sean Michael was any kind of barometer of kindred relationships in the O'Hare household, she was in for a rocky ride.

Last, but not least, among her distractions was the color photograph on the desk. She might not even have noticed it if she hadn't gotten up to stir the logs with a poker. Sandwiched between an onyx paperweight and the slender sculpture of an Egyptian maiden, it was the top of the frame that caught Victoria's eye as she returned to her chair. Intrigued by what it might contain, she came around the desk to look at it.

Haunting was the only adjective that really described what she saw. The image of the beautiful young woman in the picture kept reappearing in the fire and on the pages Victoria was trying to read. I guess I should've figured someone like Hunter O'Hare was taken, she told herself, concurrently disappointed and relieved. She wondered when he'd get around to making an introduction, or at least make mention to her that he had a significant other.

Hunter's unavailability shouldn't have surprised her, of course. The very nature of her job choices over the years had thrown many a gorgeous man into her path. Back in her youthful naïveté, she had even equated the lack of a wedding band with the absence of a commitment. Such assumptions, more often than not, had proven perilous to her heart and contributed to an attitude of cynicism.

By the time he returned, Victoria had willed herself completely immune to his rugged looks and blatant sex appeal. Or so she thought. "I forgot to ask whether you already had plans for dinner," he apologized.

Victoria felt herself hesitate. "If I could use your telephone a second?"

"Certainly," he replied. "But don't go changing something just for me. I can have Chan drive you back if you have a prior engagement."

The very fact that he had suggested it cancelled out any earlier opinions she had held that the man was domineering. "No problem," Victoria lied, for in truth the extent of her evening plans had revolved around a trip to the dry cleaners and a swing by the grocery store.

"I'll leave you to your call, then," he smiled. "Twenty minutes be okay?"

She decided to call Elliott at home and at least let him know what was going on.

"So how do you like our Irishman so far?" the familiar voice at the end of the line asked her.

"I think I've spent more time talking to his servants today than him," she replied.

"Something wrong?"

"Nothing I can put a finger on. What you said just before I left is beginning to make sense, though."

"And what was that?" Elliott inquired.

As Victoria opened her lips to reply, a definitive click prefaced the hollow reverb of someone picking up the line.

Elliott heard it as well. "Sounds great to me," he cheerfully improvised. "That Thatch sure knows a bargain when he sees one, doesn't he?"

"Couldn't have said it better myself," Victoria countered. "Tomorrow morning then?"

"We'll be there with bells on."

Victoria held the receiver to her ear for a second longer after her goodbye to Elliott, long enough to hear the eavesdropping party hang up.

7

"*So how was your dinner* last night?" Thatch inquired the following morning in his best imitation of Bela Lugosi.

"Straight out of the Addams Family?" John chimed in. "Did you get to pour hot oil down on revelers who came to the door?"

"Damn," Thatch muttered. "How come *we* never get to go to parties like that?"

"No hot oil, guys, but I wouldn't put it past a couple of the characters I met," Victoria replied, sharing highlights of her evening as the three of them walked together down the hall.

"Sounds like O'Hare's place just abounds with palace intrigue," John remarked.

"'Skulks' sounds more like it," Thatch corrected him. "I don't know, John—you really think we should let her do this?"

"What I think is that she's already made up her mind."

Victoria shook her head. "Not completely. Not until I talk to Elliott."

A few minutes later, she found herself hedging on the

very speech she had practiced all night. "I don't see a problem working for him," she said. "It's just that I really think—"

"He was impressed with you," Elliott complimented her. "I knew he would be."

"There are a couple of things that just don't gel."

"Such as?"

Victoria repeated the incidents with Sean Michael. "Being obnoxious and cocky is one thing," she said, "but this one's got a full-fledged vendetta going. If I were O'Hare, I'd be scared to turn my back on him."

"Oh, I wouldn't worry too much about that. I'm sure the man can handle the likes of his cousin—or anyone else—easily enough."

"But why so much hatred even to begin with?"

Elliott leaned back in his chair, reflecting on her question. "Well, you have to understand that Mr. Gleavy and his sister—did you meet *her*, by the way?"

"No," Victoria replied, "but I think I may have seen her in the courtyard when I first got there." It now made sense that the raven-haired beauty who shared Sean Michael's dark looks and explosive temper had to have been his younger sister, Peggy. Neither one of them had joined the table at dinner, leaving her alone with Hunter except for the occasional well-timed interruption by Mrs. Maginn.

"Patrick's estate would have been divided between the Gleavys," Elliott continued, "if O'Hare hadn't fulfilled the primary condition of the will."

"Living in the castle?" Victoria found her eyes gravitating toward the color photograph she had admired on Elliott's wall long before she knew whose castle it was.

"Everyone's assumption, of course, was that he'd forfeit. Certainly it wouldn't have been in his best interests to relocate to Ireland, not when his biggest investments are all here in the United States."

"Definitely a long commute," Victoria said, nodding.

"Although both Sean and his sister draw a monthly allowance of seven thousand, the two of them—"

Victoria's mouth dropped open. "Seven *thousand*? *Each*?"

"Not a bad wage for doing nothing but breathe, is it?"

"Go on. As you were saying?"

Elliott shrugged. "As high—and presumably comfortable—as that figure is, their contention is that it's not enough to live on."

"But they live with O'Hare. Unless he's charging them rent?"

Elliott shook his head. "Room and board was already guaranteed by Sir Patrick's will," he said, "but only until marriage and only if they lived in the castle." The attorney thoughtfully steepled his fingers. "Three months ago, they decided that life on their own in Ireland was too expensive. Much as the two of them detest Americans, they both came over and resumed residence."

"And there's nothing Hunter can do to contest that?"

"We're working on it," Elliott replied.

Like a slow-rising curtain, the truth about her impending assignment at the castle began to take form. "What about his surgery?" she inquired. "Isn't that a major interference if he's on any kind of time line to get rid of them?"

"Left up to him," Elliott answered, "he probably wouldn't have it at all. He's stalled it long enough as it is that the doctors are ready to bodily abduct him to the hospital before he does himself permanent damage. Even letting him convalesce at home is a concession they're not keen on."

During their talk at dinner, Hunter had told her very little about the operation, only that he'd been thrown by a horse and took the weight of the fall on his left knee.

Maybe it was even the same horse he had been so concerned about that afternoon, though he didn't elaborate. Hunter shrugged off the riding accident to Victoria. "I probably did worse damage playing college football."

Spartan, she thought to herself at the time. The man could have a nine-inch gaping gash across his chest and continue to conduct company business without so much as a whimper. In Victoria's imagination, it made him all the more virile, all the more desirable.

"Did you meet all of the servants while you were there?" Elliott asked.

"Only three," Victoria replied. "Four, if you count the chauffeur. Chan."

"I meant the Irish group."

"In that case, he's definitely not one of *them*. Which reminds me, what ever happened to Hunter's original staff? A man that rich must've had a whole house full of domestics before he inherited Patrick's batch."

"No, not really. He didn't need to, what with all of his globe-trotting."

"Well, are they still there?"

"From what I gather, only Chan and a couple of the groundskeepers stayed on after the castle got moved."

"How come?"

Elliott frowned. "Anybody's guess. My own is that none of them wanted to work in a building that was older than they were. That and the fact that the Irish staff was pretty territorial. All the elements in place for a full-scale war."

"With Mrs. Maginn at the forefront as commander general," Victoria smirked.

"I gather you didn't like her?"

"And I gather I'm not *alone* about that." Victoria repeated what had led her to the conclusion that Mrs. Maginn was not particularly well-loved.

"Well, she must be efficient at what she does or O'Hare wouldn't keep her on."

"What about Nilly then?" Victoria asked. "He doesn't seem to do much of *anything*."

"Funny name, Nilly," Elliott said. "His full name is Edward Niland. Sir Patrick's valet."

"Wouldn't it have made more sense to just let him retire in Ireland? He's got to be in his eighties, at least. A strong wind would knock him over."

"Sometimes people have a value we can't see, Victoria."

"Meaning?"

"Meaning that he's been around long enough to know just about everything about everyone. For a man in Mr. O'Hare's position, that could be a valuable asset." Elliott checked his watch. "Anything else I can tell you before I have to leave for court?"

Victoria hesitated. There *was* something she wanted to know, something she'd find out soon enough once she started working and yet, nonetheless, wanted to hear before she ever started. Certainly, she thought, Elliott had been dealing with the millionaire long enough to know the answer. "There is *one* thing I was a little curious about," she said.

"What's that?"

"Well, Hunter's around forty or so, isn't he?"

"Good guess," Elliott replied. "On the young side for so much wealth but smart enough to deal with it. Was that your question?"

Victoria shook her head, suddenly stymied at how to proceed. *Maybe it's not the question I'm stuck on*, she told herself. *Maybe it's the answer that I know I'm going to hear.* "Remember when I told you that Hunter had to take off for a while to catch a horse that had broken loose?"

Elliott nodded. "What about it?"

"Well, after I got my tea, I went back to Hunter's library to wait for him. I mean, I couldn't very well take myself on a tour or go sit out in the rain."

"You did the right thing," Elliott assured her.

"While I was in the library, I happened to notice that there was—"

Elliott's phone rang. "Sorry," he apologized to Victoria after he took the call. "We've got a pre-meeting in the judge's chambers in twenty minutes. Can you hold your thought until I get back?"

"Oh, it was nothing urgent," Victoria said dismissively. By this time next week, she'd be working for O'Hare at the castle. If there *was* a wife in the scenario, she'd be pretty hard to hide.

"Why *can't* you come home for the holidays, darling?" Marcine asked for the third time in one phone call. "You've been gone now for practically forever."

Even at long distance, Victoria could picture exactly what her mother was doing. Lounging in a rose satin bed among more fluffy pillows than was the legal California limit, Marcine Cameron had half of her brain engaged in conversation with her daughter while the other half was actively diverted to a zealous scrutiny of the latest Hollywood tabloid on who was sleeping with whom.

She was also—and Victoria would bet money on it—doing The Pout.

If there was one thing Marcine prided herself on having mastered as early as her midteens, it was the ability to win sympathy by thrusting her lower, luscious lip slightly forward and dropping her eyelids just enough to look wan and helpless. It was a technique that unfailingly worked for her both in private life and in front of studio cameras. It worked so well, in fact, that even those who had seen it a hundred thousand times could still be tricked by its sincerity.

Everyone, of course, except Victoria.

"Pouting's not going to persuade me, Mom. And don't deny you're doing it."

Marcine's voice registered astonishment. "Moi?"

"I *know* you, remember?"

"And I know how *you* used to love the holidays as a little girl."

"I still do."

"Yes, but it's just not the same back in—where is it again that you're living?"

"Washington, Mom," Victoria refreshed her memory. "Same address as last time."

Marcine emitted a sigh. "Oh yes, I try not to think about *that* place."

"What's wrong with Washington?" Victoria already knew what her mother was going to say before Marcine ever said it.

"Just a carryover from that—well, I really don't even like to bring it up after all this time. Water under the bridge."

"I'm glad you're over it," Victoria said. "Anyway, the assignment I'm going to be on is—"

"He didn't even send flowers," Marcine interrupted. "You'd think the president—especially *that* one—would be a big enough person to send flowers if something came up."

"I'm sure it's a guilt that he and Nancy will carry to the grave, Mom."

"So what is it that you're doing that's more important than coming home for the holidays?"

"Just doing my job."

"Well, can't the whales and the rainforests wait to be

saved until January?" Marcine asked. "Don't these politicians know that their employees have a life outside of work?"

"I'm working for someone else now, Mom. I'm with a law firm. Bowman, Johnson, and Williams."

At the other end of the line, Marcine gasped. "I don't believe it."

"What part don't you believe?"

"Remember that sweet-looking blond boy from Georgia who played Trevor Harley on 'My Silver Promise'? The one who turned out to be the illegitimate son of Crandall Westlake but they weren't reunited until he needed a bone marrow transplant?"

"Not really. Why?"

"Oh how could you forget him?" Marcine insisted. "He also does those cute Toyota commercials with the Scotch terrier in the fire hat?"

"Whatever you say."

"Well, he's just been cast to play Adam Hague in 'The Star-Crossed.'"

"Is that good or bad?"

Marcine sighed again, as if dealing with someone completely dense. "Adam's character has been dead for two years," she explained, "but now they're going to say he actually *ejected* from the plane before it crashed in the Himalayas and he's returned to Parma Heights to find Skye and Olivia."

"Will wonders never cease. . . ."

"They're just not going to buy it," Marcine murmured in dismay.

"Buy what?"

"Well, the first Adam Hague was played by Gregory Prescott, who's very dark, very Latin. Trés sexy. Honestly, darling, do you really think that viewers are going to accept that Adam changed that drastically after two years in a Tibetan monastery? This is just going to *kill* the ratings. . . ."

"Gotta go, Mom," Victoria signed off. "Someone's picking me up."

"At work? It's still early for lunch back there, isn't it? Not even eleven?"

"I'm at home," she replied. "The man I'll be working for the next couple of weeks is sending a car for me." Victoria eyed the two pieces of luggage that sat in the foyer of her apartment, hoping she hadn't forgotten anything important. Her original understanding of the arrangement was that she'd be reporting to the castle every morning the same as she did for her job, just a little longer drive. O'Hare, however, was quick to correct her. "The salary I'm paying isn't for a standard nine to five, Ms. Cameron," he said, explaining that international phone calls and faxes would require her presence on a more flexible schedule. Elliott had seen nothing odd or improper about the millionaire's hospitality. "How many people get a chance to live in a real castle?" Elliott reminded her. "Think of it as time travel without leaving your own zip code."

"Someone's sending a *car* for you?" Marcine repeated. "Don't they have cabs back there?"

"Of course they do. He just prefers to send a limo."

"Not to criticize him, dear, but don't you think politicians spend far too much on frills like that?"

"This one's not a politician, Mom."

"No?"

"He's a millionaire who inherited an Irish castle and had it moved across the Atlantic instead of going there to live in it. I'm going to be his secretary."

Marcine laughed. "Seriously," she said as Victoria's doorbell rang. "What are you *really* doing?"

8

"*I'll just be seein' you* to your room first," Mrs. Maginn announced. "Then we'll tell himself you're here."

Chan had followed Victoria to the foyer with her bags and, at a nod from the housekeeper, proceeded though the archway and up a flight of stairs beyond.

"How did the surgery go?" Victoria inquired, certain that Gwynna Maginn had availed herself of every detail possible, probably even down to a tablet count and expiration date on any prescriptions O'Hare had been given for pain.

"Well, sure as it's too early to tell, but himself's got the constitution of a horse. He'll be kickin' his heels up by week's end and, saints help us, there'll be no tyin' him down."

They had started to climb the stairs, Chan already well ahead of them. "Not bothered by stairs, are you?" Mrs. Maginn asked her. "It's a good climb and its brother to the next floor."

Victoria feigned astonishment. "No elevators?"

The humor, however, was lost on the older woman. "Kriskerry Castle is *authentic*," she informed her as if personally wounded by the remark. "They didn't *have* elevators."

So much for making a joke. "I can always use the exercise," Victoria replied. With the rainy weather curtailing her customary outdoor jog, the stairs presented a convenient alternative.

The housekeeper paused in midstep to look at her. "If *you* need the exercise with a waist like yours," she countered, "then my name's Ringo Starr." Compliment that it was, the slice of accompanying sarcasm didn't escape the redhead's attention.

"So how many floors are there?" Victoria asked. "From outside, it looks like almost three."

"That'd be three and a tower," Mrs. Maginn set her straight. "Third floor's for the servants."

"Then I guess you have a higher climb than I do," Victoria logically surmised. Once again, the housekeeper paused on the steps to address her.

"Sure as you're employed by himself same as the rest," she said, a twitch of smugness at the corner of her colorless lips. "You'll be takin' the room next to Pritchard."

Victoria wondered whose idea *that* was. For as little as she knew about him, it didn't strike her that a man like O'Hare would entertain such class-conscious opinions.

They passed the duration of the ascent in silence, meeting Chan at the top step on his return downstairs. Contrary to Victoria's expectation of a dimly lit corridor with bare floors scampered by occasional mice, the castle's third level was a continuation of the first two in its theme of medieval elegance. Carpeting and tapestries of burgundy and gold gave the hall a burnished warmth, as did the portraits and Irish artifacts that graced its walls. If the servants lived so well on the third floor, Victoria could only imagine the elegance of the level just below it.

"Aren't all of those stairs going to be hard for Mr. O'Hare to manage?" Victoria inquired. The lack of uniformity in their height, ranging from short steps to steep ones, made it cumbersome even for her. "How did you ever get him up to his room after he came home from surgery?"

"Sure, I've already seen to his comfort in one of the rooms at ground level," Mrs. Maginn matter-of-factly replied. "He'll not be leavin' it 'til he's good and healed."

"I'd think that would be next to impossible," Victoria remarked as they passed beneath an arch decorated with polished metal breastplates and antique sconces.

"*What* would be impossible?"

"Mr. O'Hare has a lot going on," Victoria said, shrugging. "I'd think he'd want to be out of bed as soon as possible and resuming a normal schedule. You'll have your hands full keeping him down."

They had stopped in front of one of the hallway's closed doors and Mrs. Maginn withdrew a set of keys from the depths of her apron.

"You'll be wantin' extra blankets, I'd think," she announced as she opened the door. "The room's not blessed with a fireplace. . . ."

No, Victoria thought, *but I bet it's well cursed with a certain housekeeper's resentment of an extra body in the castle*. "I sleep pretty warm," she assured her, stepping inside for her first view of the room to which Mrs. Maginn had assigned her.

Like the other rooms she had seen so far, this one, too, had a high ceiling. Though minimal in furnishings—a four-poster bed, a desk, a chair, and a wardrobe—it was the potpourri of shaggy throw rugs, dark, polished woods, and framed landscapes on the walls that gave it a personality unexpected in quarters relegated to the domestic help. It also, Victoria noted, had a narrow lancet window above the desk, its glass streaked with rivulets of rain.

As she crossed to where Chan had deposited her bags at the foot of the bed, Mrs. Maginn advised her that the bathroom for freshening up was at the end of the hall next to the dumbwaiter.

"Dumbwaiter?" Victoria repeated.

"Sir Patrick himself had it put in to take up the space," Mrs. Maginn replied. In response to Victoria's puzzled expression, the housekeeper proceeded to explain that the space in question was a cylindrical stone shaft whereby the castle's first occupants could escape by rope should their fortress come under siege. Mrs. Maginn sucked her mouth into a rosette as she divulged a seamier use of the secret passage. "They say it was Duncan's favorite place to—uh, take his lady, don't you know. . . ."

"You certainly seem to know a lot about the castle's history," Victoria complimented her.

"And why shouldn't I?" Mrs. Maginn puffed up. "Sure an' it's in our blood more than—" Though the sentence went unfinished, Victoria suspected that Hunter's name hovered in her throat.

"I can do my unpacking later," Victoria said. "I'm sure Mr. O'Hare will want me to get started right away." As they reached the door, she snapped her fingers in afterthought. "I almost forgot to ask you for the key."

"The key to what?" Mrs. Maginn queried.

"Well, the key to my room, for one thing. And I suppose an extra to the front door wouldn't hurt if I go out for a walk."

Mrs. Maginn answered the second request first. "The main door's locked up tight and proper every night at ten," she informed Victoria, implying that the access was free the rest of the time.

"Ten, you say? So if I get home late from too much carousing, I'm out of luck?"

"You could ring for Nilly or myself," the housekeeper said, not amused by so frivolous a lifestyle that mocked strict curfew. "We're both light sleepers."

"What about the key to *this* room?" Victoria reminded her.

Just above the top rim of her glasses, Mrs. Maginn's orange brows quirked in question.

"Sure, you're safe as a lamb without one," she replied with a smile. "There's no reason to be lockin' yourself away now, is there?"

Mrs. Pritchard was withdrawing with a silver tray of empty plates and glassware as Victoria and Mrs. Maginn approached the room made up for O'Hare's convalescence. Her broad smile of recognition for the young redhead all too quickly dissolved, however, on the heels of Mrs. Maginn's admonishment that she was too slow in clearing from lunch.

"It's himself who held up the progress, and not me," Mrs. Pritchard bluntly informed her. "The phone's never left his ear once."

"Has he seen to the mail, then?" Mrs. Maginn inquired.

The plump woman heaved her shoulders with no disguise of her total exasperation. "He's seen to the food, Mrs. Maginn," she replied. "I've not been concernin' myself with the state of the world beyond that."

With a definitive dip of her head as if to punctuate the remark, Mrs. Pritchard shuffled past them with her tray and down the corridor toward the kitchen.

As Victoria watched her go, Thatch and John's reference to palace intrigue never seemed more apropos, for certainly there was as little affection among the domestics as there was among the people who employed them. *I wonder what's up between these two,* she thought, half expecting Mrs. Pritchard to look back at any second and stick her tongue out at the castle's resident bully.

Mrs. Maginn swept up a stack of correspondence from the table just outside the door and turned to hand them to Victoria. "It's *your* job to be seein' to these, I guess." Without further explanation, she sailed into the room to announce the new secretary's arrival. Victoria followed.

Under normal circumstances—if such a thing even existed at Kriskerry Castle—the room might have been some sort of reception hall, more narrow than it was wide and dominated by a walk-in fireplace with a stone hood that traversed the entire height of the wall. Chairs and tables had been moved from a presumably cozy configuration to one of temporary storage against the perimeter of the room in order to accommodate a computer desk and a bed.

It was the man *in* the bed who immediately caught Victoria's attention.

Save for the madras robe that bared part of his chest, Hunter O'Hare could just as easily have been conducting business in an office, the phone receiver tucked between his jaw and shoulder as his left hand took notes on a laptop tray. "Seventy-eight percent growth over the next three," she heard him say, "plus they can convert the Michigan warehouses and subcontract with Wells and Rynearson for electrical." The Irishman paused, scowling at something said to him on the other end of the line. "No, Tom," he countered, "Evans is small potatoes. I say it's high time we give the other two a shot at the top. Between you and me, they've paid their dues."

Deals and deal-makers, Victoria thought to herself. Whatever investments and futures O'Hare was currently orchestrating from his bed were really no different from the backstage negotiations inherent in the Hollywood scene. One day a nobody, the next day a major star. No difference.

As he caught sight of Victoria and Mrs. Maginn in the

doorway, he waved them forward with his free hand. "Yeah, that's right," he said. "Listen, if I get it faxed to you by—let's say one o'clock your time?" O'Hare's smile widened in approval, a smile he shared with Victoria as if the success were hers as well. "Okay, give me those figures again and I'll get someone on it right away."

She hadn't seen him in glasses before but he wore them now, conservative wire-frames with a tint of amber that suited his coloring. Shades of an upscale Clark Kent, she thought to herself, wondering whether his knee injury was really from a horse or a miscalculated leap over a tall building.

"Best not to tire him with too much talk," Mrs. Maginn firmly advised Victoria as she prepared to take leave of them, seeing no purpose in remaining.

Like I'm the one doing all the talking, Victoria wanted to reply. Patiently, she waited for O'Hare to conclude his telephone call before stepping any closer.

"You'll forgive me if I don't stand up," he apologized as casually as if she had worked for him for years. "I see you've got the day's mail already."

"How did the operation go?" she asked, approaching the bed and making a conscious effort not to even glance at the crisp mat of dark gold hair that peeked through the vee of his robe.

"I think it'll go as far as Maui," O'Hare replied. "Maybe a full island tour."

It took Victoria a few seconds to realize he was talking about how his doctor might spend the surgery fee.

"At least you have a nice room to get well in," she remarked. "That should speed the recovery."

"The sooner, the better." He started leafing through the mail she'd handed him, methodically sorting the envelopes into separate stacks on top of the covers.

"Speaking of sooner, you may have overheard that last conversation. I need you to get a steno pad and take some dictation for a fax this afternoon to Seattle."

Victoria shrugged. "Just tell me where to find one and I can get started."

"Middle drawer of the desk," he instructed. "You may as well take an inventory and let Nilly know what you need. Did you meet Nilly already?"

"The older gentleman?" Victoria nodded as she crossed to the desk. "Yes, Mrs. Pritchard introduced him when I came out for the interview."

"Useful man," O'Hare remarked as he slid his glasses off of his nose. "How about Toby and Patty? Have you met them yet?"

The names weren't familiar to her.

"Toby's mostly outdoors," he explained. "Takes care of the grounds."

"Tall order to take care of," Victoria remarked.

"True, but he's got help from Buddy, one of my original staff. Between the two of them, they keep the place from getting overgrown. Patty," he continued, "is a maid and probably as hooked on American television as Mrs. Pritchard." O'Hare leaned over to see how she was managing. "Finding everything you need in there?"

"You must've been expecting me," she said as she held up a lined pad and pen. Now faced with the dilemma of where to sit for dictation in the absence of a convenient chair, she waited for a directive from O'Hare.

He was studying one of the envelopes as if trying to discern the contents without opening it. "Since you'll be handling all my correspondence," he said, "you'll probably be seeing a few of these."

Victoria took the sealed envelope from his hand, noting that it bore a local postmark but no return address.

"Go ahead and open it," he said, well aware of the typed "PERSONAL AND CONFIDENTIAL" in the lower left corner.

Victoria tentatively slit the flap open with her thumb nail and withdrew the folded paper from within. "They started coming about three weeks ago," O'Hare said as she read what was inside.

Victoria shuddered at the crude crayon drawing of a hangman's noose and stick figure identified as "H.O.H." In staggered formation to the figure's left were pasted black letters cut from magazines and newspapers. "'Burn in hell'?" she read out loud.

"It's only fair that you know up front what you might be getting into."

"And what's that?"

O'Hare indicated the piece of paper with a nod of his head. "I'm not exactly popular. At least not in *this* person's book."

"I gathered that."

"Actually, this is one of the tamer ones. Its predecessors lean toward the more graphic."

Victoria reread the note, even though its content was short enough for memorization. "Have you told the police?"

"Until something—if anything—actually happens," O'Hare replied, "telling them is the only thing I probably *can* do."

"Any idea who it's from?" Calmly as the words came out of her mouth, Victoria's mind was racing with scenarios, none of them pleasant.

One brow slanted in a frown. "No, but I think I've narrowed the field."

"Narrowed the field to what?"

O'Hare's gray eyes gazed off into some private space before coming back to settle on hers. "It's someone living here at the castle."

9

The bridled anger in Victoria's voice was only a glimmer of what lay beneath the surface, the escalating awareness that she was being drawn into something for which she was totally unprepared. That part of the trap was her growing attraction for Hunter himself was a breach of ethics that Elliott would never tolerate. "I don't mean to sound like the Countess of Pessimism," she said, "but you've just told me that you're getting death threats by mail, the police can't help, and, furthermore, that you also know who it is. That's not exactly a normal lifestyle. Even for someone who moves castles."

"Two out of three," O'Hare nonchalantly corrected her. "If I knew who it was, I would've taken action by now to have it stopped."

"Two out of three is enough, isn't it?" she replied.

"Depends on where you're sitting." The squared set of his chin was testimony of the inherited stubborn streak to which Elliott had alluded in an earlier conversation. "I was under the impression that you were a young woman who enjoyed a good challenge," he baited her.

Victoria shook her head as she set the notepad and pen back down on the desk. A challenge was one thing. A dilemma of the heart was quite another. "I'm afraid there's been a mistake, Mr. O'Hare. I'm not the person you really want for this job."

Her remark seemed to amuse him. "How do you know I don't want you?"

Victoria could feel the power of his gaze, a sizzling gaze that sought to strip her of all her defenses. She pointed at the letter she had returned to his hand. "It sounds like what you need isn't a secretary but a competent bodyguard." Certainly, she thought, the man had enough connections in Washington to land himself an ex–Secret Service agent with some free time.

"Don't you think I should be the judge of that?"

"Judging by the people you've surrounded yourself with so far—" Victoria let the statement drop, seeing no point to a continued argument. "I'm sure Mr. Bowman can recommend someone else to take my place."

O'Hare thoughtfully scratched his jaw as he contemplated the intentional sting of her truncated remark. "Elliott," he said, "recommended you. I have to consider that a gentleman's agreement."

Victoria responded sharply, abandoning all pretense of respect for the firm's most prestigious client. "He would never have agreed to sending me if he'd been told the full story about what's going on." None of them, in fact, would have compromised her safety or that of anyone else who worked for them, regardless of a client's importance or wallet. "I'm sorry," she said, "but I—"

"No apology necessary, Ms. Cameron, unless it's for your impatience to jump to conclusions."

Uncomfortable with the suggestion that her judgment might indeed be premature but loath to admit it, Victoria attempted to explain her perception. "We seem to be dealing with a serious omission on your part," she said, prepared to point out that endangering her own life for his wasn't included in "other duties as required."

"On my part?"

"Either that," she continued, "or something pretty major got lost in the translation between Mr. Bowman and myself."

"A diplomatic assessment," O'Hare commented. "So which is it?"

It was a rhetorical question, of course, O'Hare having clearly made up his mind already that he was in the right and fully justified to make whatever unreasonable demands he wanted. Why Elliott had ever assumed the two of them could be a compatible team—even for a few weeks—was beyond her. "If you'll just have your driver take me back to town," Victoria suggested, "I'm sure that other arrangements can be made to suit your purposes."

O'Hare smiled with the calm strength of one who held all the cards. In this case, he also held the power of transportation. "I don't think we've finished talking yet," he said.

Victoria, however, had certainly done enough listening in the past five minutes to know that Kriskerry Castle was the last place she wanted to be. Nor did she relish a daily battle of semantics with a man who enjoyed control as much as Hunter O'Hare. To even dream of wresting it from him was silly.

"Seeing as how I'm a captive audience, then," she observed, "what else did you want to say?"

O'Hare regarded her for a long moment before replying. "Well, in the first place," he said at last, "I think we need to establish that you're not a captive anything, Ms. Cameron. If it's your choice to end this meeting without the courtesy of hearing my side, then *I* have no choice but to give Chan instructions to return you to your office."

Even with O'Hare confined to his bed, Victoria felt the raw power that coiled within him, a power that both intrigued and intimidated her like no one else she had ever met. Certainly every man she had ever known—both romantically and professionally—paled in comparison to this one. Something that Elliott had said now flitted back and forth across her brain, too quickly for her to remember the exact words. All she could recall was an obscure reference to Achilles and the high price of keeping secrets. O'Hare has got plenty of those, she decided, as well as at least one person who wanted to see him dead.

Maybe she did owe him the courtesy of hearing what he had to say, her emotions temporarily colored by an empathy for his plight as an invalid. Dynamic and self-sufficient a personality as Hunter O'Hare possessed, his surgery had nonetheless rendered him dependent on the attention of others, a vulnerability in which his enemies might take delight. Elliott had told her that Hunter needed someone whom he could totally trust. Obviously the current candidates for such a role in O'Hare's life were limited.

"And if I *do* stay and listen?" Victoria countered, conscious that she was already involved whether she wanted to be or not, and conscious as well that she'd have to account to her mentor if she reneged on Elliott's personal commitment.

O'Hare arched a brow at her inquiry. "Such a sudden change of heart?"

"Just keeping an open mind," Victoria replied, refusing to be ruffled or perceived as waffling. "I'd like to hear what you have to say."

"So would someone else, I think. . . ." His voice had suddenly lowered and his eyes had left hers, their focus now locked on the doorway behind her.

Wordlessly, Victoria turned to see what he was looking at. Whoever it was had already disappeared.

O'Hare's tone was velvet but edged with steel. "As long as you're up," he advised, "I suggest you close the door before we continue."

"Well, aren't *you* the busy one!" Mrs. Pritchard proclaimed in admiration as she wiped her hands on the front of her pink bibbed apron.

From behind a coffee cup at the kitchen table, Nilly nodded his own assessment that the castle's pretty newcomer seemed to have her nose pressed to the proverbial grindstone. "A flower needs to see the daylight now and then or else it shrivels to dust," he said.

"Silly Nilly," Mrs. Pritchard teased him, waggling her fingers in his face as one would shoo a winged pest. "Now don't you be goin' on about dead petals 'n' such or you'll be scarin' the girl before she's been here a week!"

"All the same . . ." Nilly murmured, bringing the cup to his lips to drown the balance of his opinion.

"So you like the job, then?" the Irishwoman inquired, unabashedly eager for details.

Between O'Hare's confidential disclosures and almost two hours of dictation, Victoria had managed to stay sequestered ever since her arrival downstairs, emerging only at his behest to take a well-deserved break and get something to eat.

"Mr. O'Hare generates a lot of work," Victoria said. "I didn't even notice how much time had gone by until just now."

"But do you *like* the job?" Nilly repeated, not one to content himself with abstract replies or polite generalities.

"It's more than I expected," Victoria said, feeling no

guilt for speaking the truth. "But I'm willing to give it a try."

"And don't you know that himself's got the energy of ten and the temper of a hundred if it's not all done fine and proper!" the cook facilely volunteered.

Nilly clucked his tongue. "Now, Mrs. P.," he chided her, "we'll have none of your irreverence."

The cook dismissed his remark with a hearty laugh. "Himself's a saint and a good piece further," she said, presumably more for the redhead's benefit than that of her domestic peer. "Lord knows it's a praise and not a criticism to be workin' as hard as he does. Harder than *some*," she added, "though I'm not one to be namin' the names or throwin' stones at the boneless."

"No more than Saint Patrick would drive out a snake," Nilly sighed.

"I hate to interrupt," Victoria said, "but would you mind if I just fixed myself a quick snack? It'll only take me a minute and I'll be out of your way."

Mrs. Pritchard's mouth dropped open as if Victoria had just uttered a profanity. "Sure as I'm still standin' and drawin' a breath," she exclaimed, "it's not your place to be doin' the chores of a scullery maid! Now sit yourself down with Nilly," she insisted, "and I'll whip you up a ploughman's lunch faster than a leprechaun's blink!"

"You really don't have to go to—"

"No trouble at all," Mrs. Pritchard contended. "I could do it with my eyes closed. Why, I made one every day for my Welshman, rest his soul."

"May as well concede to the old girl," Nilly advised Victoria. "She learned her stubbornness from the master himself."

"So Mr. O'Hare has a stubborn streak?" Victoria played innocent, sliding out a chair and joining the valet at the table.

The question made Mrs. Pritchard laugh. "That'd be Sir Patrick that Nilly's referrin' to," she corrected her. "Now *there* was man who could give the devil a hearty run and not be budgin' an inch to do it."

Nilly cleared his throat, a signal that went blissfully ignored by the woman at the butcher block counter.

Intrigued to learn what she could, Victoria listened to Pritchard prattle on, her head still spinning from all that O'Hare had divulged behind closed doors.

"Elliott says that you've got a second sight when it comes to judging people," Hunter had complimented her. "I need to make use of that talent while you're staying here." Further, he added, the lack of prior association or time-tested loyalty on her part would not render her suspect as she quietly observed the goings-on of the household. "You can move freely," he said, "without arousing undue attention."

"Are you trying to tell me that Mr. Bowman knew all about this cloak-and-dagger portion of the assignment but didn't say anything to me?" she had challenged him, finding it out of character for the Virginia attorney not to at least drop a hint.

"He preferred that you hear it from me," O'Hare replied matter-of-factly, "and that you make the decision from there."

As punctuation to his remark, O'Hare had then picked up the phone receiver and encouraged her to dial the office. "Does that mean you believe me?" he asked with a charismatic but conspiratorial smile when she declined to take it from his hand.

"No," Victoria answered. "It means that I'd rather use a phone that won't have additional listeners."

"You *are* good," O'Hare nodded, apparently cognizant of the eavesdropping factor at Kriskerry Castle. "Not to worry about this one, though," he assured her. "I'm the only one who has this line."

Why didn't I take him up on that? Victoria now reflected as she watched Mrs. Pritchard pile a china plate with enough cold cuts, bread, and English cheddar to feed a third world country. Was it because she didn't want to look foolish to Elliott? Or because the very act of contesting her temporary employer's word would set an unpleasant tone for the rest of their working relationship? Victoria wasn't sure which.

"Now Nilly's the one who can be talkin' your ears off about Sir Patrick," Mrs. Pritchard was saying, bending her bulk across the table to refill his coffee cup.

"Were you with him for a long time?" Victoria asked, recognizing that their outward level of comfort with her presence could prove beneficial down the road.

"Longer than the devil," Mrs. Pritchard beamed in reply on his behalf.

"Sixty-five years," Nilly said. "Sixty-five years and seven months."

"You must have started very young," Victoria speculated, finding the number he had given a little unrealistic.

Mrs. Pritchard clucked her tongue. "Sure as he can remember *those* years better than his own age," she pointed out. "How old *are* you, Nilly dear?"

His refusal to answer suggested to Victoria that either he didn't know or that it was a game that they had been playing with each other for some time. "My living began with Sir Patrick," he gravely informed them both. "And it died the same day *he* did."

"Dead petals and dying lordships," Mrs. Pritchard sighed in dismay. "May someone take a shovel to my head if I ever get that dreary. ..."

Thankful that she could occupy her mouth with food

instead of words in the awkward silence that followed, Victoria wasn't sure whether she should feel sympathy for the valet's pronounced sorrow at losing his employer or annoyance that he hadn't cultivated enough outside interests to carry on after Sir Patrick's death.

"How's the food?" Mrs. Pritchard asked. "Is it enough to be keepin' you until supper?"

"More than enough," Victoria replied. "You've outdone yourself."

"Well, I'll not be havin' any guest of Mr. O'Hare go skinny as a zipper from a lack of soup on their ribs. Speakin' of soup, now—"

Whatever Mrs. P was about to offer next was interrupted by the tempestuous arrival of one of the most beautiful women Victoria had ever seen, the same black-haired beauty that she had first witnessed in the rainy courtyard with Sean Michael. Clearly, the anger she had held that day had not abated.

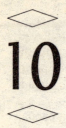

10

Mrs. Pritchard's *plump cheeks* tinted to crimson at the girl's profane salutation. "I'll not be hearin' such gutter language in my kitchen!" she admonished her.

"It may be *your* bloody kitchen in name," the brunette haughtily retorted, "but the house is Sean Michael's and mine!"

So that's the other cousin, Victoria thought to herself, recognizing in the young woman's arresting features and vicious tongue the very duplicate of her older brother. No prizes for congeniality with those two, that was certain. That she had initially mistaken them in the courtyard for quarreling young lovers now struck Victoria as ironic, for unlike a couple whose impassioned anger with each other could be settled by splitting, these two were bound by blood and, thus, forever linked.

Apparently, they were also bound by something else: a common hatred of their American cousin.

"Hell if it does!" the younger woman snapped at the cook's reminder that ownership of the castle rested with Hunter. "He's as much right to it as a frigging skunk on the road!"

Like a tape recorder, Victoria's mind quickly replayed what O'Hare had told her about Sean Michael's sibling. Twenty-eight, spoiled rotten, given to tantrums when she didn't get her way. "A clotheshorse, too," Hunter had added, alluding to the girl's unremitting arguments that her monthly allowance was far too small to live on comfortably.

There was something else as well that Victoria remembered from their conversation, something about a broken wedding engagement that had prompted her to accompany Sean Michael to the United States rather than remain behind in their native country.

Strange, she mused, finding her expectation of a sheltered and immature Irish ingenue in sharp contrast to the street-sassy spitfire currently confronting Mrs. Pritchard on the whereabouts of Ian, the stable hand. Jilted bride or not, Peggy Gleavy was hardly a candidate for anyone's sympathy, much less any long-standing friendship. The fiancé, whoever he was, could probably count his blessings that things had not worked out.

As yet unnoticed—or purposely ignored—by the girl, Victoria's eyes took in the swimsuit figure and defiant stance, the designer jeans and the red sweater that matched her lips and intensifed the black of her long hair. She may be undeniably gorgeous, Victoria decided, but her beauty just as assuredly ended at skin level.

"Where the hell is Ian?" Peggy demanded for the second time since she had burst in on them.

"One would assume that he's doing the job he's paid for," Nilly calmed informed her. "He's best to be left to it."

From the corner of her eye, Victoria saw Mrs. Pritchard's chin dip in smug approval of the valet's intervention. Either Nilly's authority in the household carried some weight she didn't yet know about, Victoria determined, or the chivalrous overture on the part of any male was enough to warm the cockles of the cook's generous heart.

As Peggy's lush lips parted to issue a sarcastic rejoinder, she finally noticed Victoria at the table. Not one to be taken aback or embarrassed by a stranger's presence, the younger Gleavy shamelessly took the offensive in extracting an explanation of why the redhead was there.

"I'm Mr. O'Hare's secretary," Victoria introduced herself with a composure she didn't feel. Just like Sean Michael, Peggy had an abrasiveness that would set anyone's teeth on edge. "And you're . . . ?"

Peggy's reply was delivered with the arrogance of a starlet who had just made the cover of *Entertainment Weekly* and expected everyone to have noticed. Los Angeles was replete with them, Victoria thought, none of them worth getting to know but all of them worth watching out for.

"Miss Cameron will be staying with us for a few weeks," Nilly informed Peggy, who declined Victoria's offer of a handshake.

"Her mother is Alandra Monaco," Mrs. Pritchard spontaneously added with the self-satisfaction of a privileged insider. "*The* Alandra Monaco, don't you know."

Victoria hoped such a novelty would wear off, nonetheless flattered that her connection to Marcine had earned her the cook's amiability and maternal protectiveness.

Nonplussed by the celebrity disclosure, Peggy tossed back her mane of hair and addressed Mrs. Pritchard again. "Sean Michael said to tell you there'll be an extra at dinner tonight," she said.

The cook's expression slid into one of suspicion. "And who's it to be, then?" Mrs. Pritchard inquired.

"I'*m* not a girl Friday," Peggy disdainfully shot back as a sidelong insult to Victoria.

"Perhaps not," Nilly said, setting down his cup, "but it seems a simple enough question."

Peggy glowered at him. "Another one of his sluts," she replied. "They all look alike to me." Message delivered, she started toward the door. "I'll find Ian myself," she snidely informed them, a postscript that made Mrs. Pritchard's hands clench into fists at her sides and her broad nostrils flare with fury.

"Now, now, Mrs. P," Nilly spoke up when Peggy had left. "It will pass soon and be done with."

"Sure, it's not soon *enough*," the cook muttered in undisguised disgust. "Not soon enough at all."

"What do I think so far?" Victoria echoed Hunter's question. "I feel like I've walked into the pages of Du Maurier's *Rebecca* and can't find my way back out."

O'Hare smiled. "I hope that doesn't mean you're giving up already?" He removed his glasses and slid them into the pocket of his robe. "Besides, as I recall, *Rebecca* had a happy ending."

Victoria smirked. "A dead body, a malevolent housekeeper, and Manderley burning like the Northern Lights—that's your idea of a happy ending?"

"I could remind you," Hunter said, "that it all worked out at the end for Maxim and Victoria."

"Her name wasn't Victoria."

"No?"

"She didn't *have* a name," Victoria pointed out, having encountered that literary oddity several times in Trivial Pursuit.

"Well, it *should've* been Victoria," he remarked as he scribbled his signature on the letters she had finished. "You share the same intrepidness and sense of observation."

"Elliott's words?"

"My own," he said of his compliment to her. "So what's the rest of your impression about Peggy?"

"Woman's intuition," Victoria said, "but she might have something going with the man who takes care of your horses."

"Ian?" The suggestion amused him. "Have you seen him?"

"Not yet. Why?"

Hunter shrugged. "Just curious how you jumped to the conclusion they were involved. Ian's not exactly in her league."

"Intuition, like I said. That much anger's either to throw people off or to confirm that she's a petty brat."

"The latter's a given. She and Sean Michael were *born* angry, I think."

"And you?"

"Me?" The easy smile that played at the corners of his mouth made him even more handsome. "*I* was born legitimate," he said.

The knock that came at the door just then preempted an explanation of his cryptic words.

"Beggin' your pardon, sir," Mrs. Pritchard apologized as she maneuvered through the doorway with a dinner tray. "I fixed your supper extra early so's you and Miss Victoria could finish your work."

"Actually," Hunter thanked her, "we were just about to wrap up. You can leave it over here on the desk, though, if you don't mind."

"No bother at all, sir." The cook grinned as she obediently followed his instructions.

"Smells delicious," he remarked.

"It's the lamb stew tonight," she proudly announced. "Your favorite, isn't it?"

"They're *all* my favorites," Hunter charmingly replied.

"You know you can't pin me down to a limit of one."

"Go on with you!" Mrs. Pritchard giggled.

Hunter shrugged with cavalier grace. "What can I say? It's true."

"So would you like me to be bringin' Miss Victoria a tray as well?" the plump woman asked, eager to be of further service to an employer she clearly adored.

O'Hare declined, reiterating that their business for the day was almost concluded. "Besides," he added, "I'm sure that Ms. Cameron would prefer to join the others in the dining room on her first night at the castle with us."

Victoria shot him a pronounced glance of disbelief, a look that O'Hare nonetheless missed. How *did he arrive at* that *conclusion*? she wondered, stunned by the outlandish suggestion that she share a table with his self-declared enemies, Peggy and Sean Michael. It was enough to thoroughly ruin one's appetite. Besides, she had secretly hoped to dine with Hunter.

Not one to acquiesce to a situation that made her uneasy, Victoria found the voice to speak up. "That late lunch you fixed me was really a lot," she told Mrs. Pritchard. "Great as that stew looks—"

The cook gasped as if mortally wounded. "Sure an' you're not to be skippin' a meal?" she said in alarm. "Why you're skin and bones as it is, girl, and the devil on my head for you to be gettin' any smaller!"

"Oh, I've got a long ways to go before *that* happens," Victoria assured her. "I'm just so full from all that you—"

Hunter interrupted before she could say any more. "There's a house rule," he said, "about turning down the cook's lamb stew on your first night. Isn't that so, Mrs. Pritchard?"

"Sure, I'd swear it on my Welshman's grave," the cook agreed, unable to hold back a broad grin.

"I'm sure Ms. Cameron can manage a couple of bites," Hunter said. "Besides, I know she's anxious to get to know my cousins."

House rules, Victoria determined, were synonymous with Hunter's rules and not subject to any latitude. "Maybe if I do a couple of laps on the stairs before dinner," she pleasantly said out loud, "I could rebuild my appetite."

"That's the spirit," Hunter remarked in approval.

No, Victoria thought, it was all politics and she was elected.

She should have asked what they wore to dinner in this place, she mused half an hour later in her bedroom as she pondered the contents of her wardrobe. The initial impression, of course, was that her dining companions weren't likely to stand on formality, if in fact they even showed up at all. Peggy's reference to an extra guest of Sean Michael's that night offered no clue, either. Maybe she should just stay in her skirt and sweater, Victoria decided. Certainly if there *was* a dress code and she unwittingly broke it by failing to pack diamonds and a feather boa, the fate of being brusquely sent back upstairs and out of their sight would actually be a blessing. "Sorry," she'd inform Hunter, "but my clothes were inappropriate for the occasion."

She was still fuming, of course, over the nerve of him to even ask her—no, *tell* her—to eat with his cousins. Spy-job or not that he expected her to perform, it grated on Victoria that he had handled it the way he did. First chance tomorrow, she resolved, Elliott would get a call apprising him of the circumstances. Tonight, she'd merely endure.

Victoria, of course, was no stranger to the laws of compulsory diplomacy. Groomed by Congressman Hoffart in the ways of Capitol Hill, she had sat through innumerable banquets, listened to interminable conversations, and suffered a multitude of fools—all while wearing a congenial smile and maintaining the highest level of professionalism. "The banquets and the gladhanders are a necessary evil," her mentor maintained. It was the grass roots work underneath all the glitz that really counted, he said. Where people got lost was when they reversed the importance of the two.

Maybe O'Hare did have a valid agenda underneath, she told herself. And maybe she *did* have to play along and be nice to his loser cousins.

She certainly didn't have to *like* any of it.

For that matter, she wasn't even sure she liked *him*. Charismatic, intelligent and well-read as the millionaire was, there was an edge to him that was unsettling, a veneer of dictatorship that made it difficult to know the layers of real person it covered. Now and again a brief glimpse of it surfaced, a hint of compassion. Hunter was not a man who let anyone get close to him. The disturbing desire to break down the walls herself, to become the one person he could trust with his heart, came to her unbidden. Silly goal, she chided herself. She was at Kriskerry Castle to do a job, not to get involved.

Resigned to the fact that no further answers would be forthcoming that night about her mysterious host, Victoria added a single strand of gold chain and matching earrings to her conservative ensemble and prepared to go downstairs.

Just to show that there were no hard feelings about their earlier exchange, her first stop before the dining room would be a visit to O'Hare. As she turned down the now familiar hallway, she also half-hoped he had changed his mind and would encourage her to stay instead with him.

The sound of a woman's laughter—and Hunter's—stopped her just outside the opened door.

"You could do a lot worse, from the looks of her," the voice proclaimed after the laughter had died.

"Leave it to you to know that," Hunter jocularly replied. "But great legs and a nice track record's not enough."

Too intrigued to walk away but too flustered to make an entrance, Victoria hesitated a moment. Hunter had put her on the spot at least once that day—why not reciprocate and at least find out who he was talking to . . . and who he was talking *about*?

Regaining her stride, Victoria entered the room and saw for the first time the young woman perched on the side of Hunter's bed, her curly blond hair flowing well past her shoulders.

11

It *was the cascade of fluffy hair* that triggered what Victoria had thus far managed to put out of her mind, the existence of a significant female in Hunter O'Hare's life. It's the girl in the desk photograph, she guessed, faltering in the new emotion that had suddenly engulfed her at seeing the two of them together, at hearing them laugh so easily at a joke.

And then the girl turned around.

"Sorry to interrupt," Victoria hastily apologized, startled that the summer-tan face she was now looking at was not the one she had expected at all. Where the girl in the photo sparkled with naïveté and sweet optimism, this one projected a cool sophistication and sagacity that came only with age and experience. The eyes and the mouth were different as well—the former ringed with thick, black lashes reminiscent of the 1960s vogue, the latter parting just enough to reveal an imperfect but engaging hint of gap between her front teeth. Not gorgeous, Victoria thought, but definitely cocksure and arresting. Even her clothes—trendy and expensive—made a statement.

"Yes?" Hunter said, waiting for Victoria to explain the intrusion for which she had just asked his pardon.

"I was on my way to dinner," she improvised, thankful to have inherited such acting talent—minimal as it was—from Marcine. "Is there anything you need before I go?"

"Is it that time already?" the blond murmured, pushing back the silky cuff of her blouse to confirm it by her own watch.

"No, I think we can call it a night," Hunter thanked her. "Oh, by the way, have you met Deborah yet?"

The blond simultaneously rose from her perch on the bed as O'Hare proceeded with the introductions. "Deborah Sheddmoore," he said. "You've probably heard of her father—Anthony Sheddmoore?"

Long before her foray into politics, Victoria had mastered from her parents the importance of learning a little bit about everything so as to converse intelligently. Where Marcine remembered celebrity names for the sole purpose of dropping them, however, Victoria mentally filed them as a point of interest.

"Anthony Sheddmoore? Who hasn't?" she now replied, returning the unexpected handshake that Deborah enthusiastically offered. For the past six Kentucky Derbys and twice as many other notable races, the thoroughbreds from Sheddmoore Fields had walked—or rather, run—away with an enviable collection of championship titles. Her complimentary mention of Anthony's latest winner brought an appreciative nod from Hunter's guest.

"Victoria used to be with Hoffart's office," Hunter continued, prompting the blond to express her condolences on the outcome of the last election.

"Daddy thought Larry was just about the finest man on the Hill," Deborah said.

"Must've been sincere about that," Hunter offered. "He wasn't even trying to sell him a horse." The remark, obviously an inside joke, set Deborah to laughing. "Take my word for it," he went on to Victoria, "his daughter's got even *more* knack for persuasion."

Victoria wondered what the comment meant. Out loud,

she asked if Deborah was involved with horses as well.

"A short-lived career, I'm afraid," Deborah sighed, inclining her head in Hunter's direction. The light from the nearest lamp caught the shimmer of diamonds at her ears. Large diamonds.

"I didn't say no," he responded. "I said I'd sleep on it and get back to you."

Deborah laughed. "Why don't I just check back after dinner?"

"What if my answer's still maybe?"

"Daddy doesn't deal in maybes," she glibly informed him. "Sullivan's Patty is a steal."

"Not with a name like *that*," he retorted in good humor. "That's almost as bad as Linda's Cookie or— what was that last one? Kaye's Life?"

"Men," Deborah muttered in annoyance at his teasing. "Victoria and I are going to dinner now. Try not to miss us too much." As if newly allied with Hunter's secretary, she issued a smile that prefaced their joint departure from his room.

"He'll come around," Deborah said as she and Victoria walked together toward the dining room. "Daddy's never known him to turn down a smart buy when he sees one."

Had Deborah spontaneously linked arms with her new acquaintance like a long-lost friend, it would not have come as a surprise. She seemed open and unpretentious enough to be likable, Victoria thought. And yet a sixth sense aroused her to be cautious in Ms. Sheddmoore's company.

"So Mr. O'Hare and your father know each other pretty well, then?" Victoria casually probed, still trying to fathom what Deborah's exact connection was to merit an invitation to dinner and so obviously comfortable a liaison with Hunter.

Deborah laughed.

"Did I say something funny?" Victoria asked, puzzled by the reaction.

As they entered the dining room, she suddenly found Sean Michael sweeping to their side. It wasn't Victoria, however, on whom his rakish gaze was now so dramatically locked.

"It's about bloody time, love," he said in a husky whisper, one arm sliding around Deborah's slender waist as his head bent to deliver a kiss.

Coyly, Deborah turned her head just as his lips were about to meet hers. "Later," she sweetly promised him, her eyes meeting Victoria's for only an instant, an instant that more than adequately explained her real motives for being at Kriskerry Castle.

Interesting, Victoria thought as she followed them to the table. And perhaps worth mentioning to Hunter.

The first opportunity to talk anything besides corporate business with him did not come until late the following afternoon. As it was, the outcome was not what she expected.

O'Hare regarded her for a long moment without saying anything. Perhaps, Victoria thought, he was letting the revelation sink in, digesting it before he voiced an opinion on the literal "state of affairs."

"You must think that I'm about as sharp as a bowling ball," he finally remarked.

"I beg your pardon?" Had it not been delivered with such a sarcastic sting, it was a line that Victoria would have found funny.

"Yesterday," he said, "you told me that you thought my cousin Peggy had something going with Ian. Today, you've decided that Deborah Sheddmoore's got the hots for Sean Michael. Am I with this so far?"

His derisive grin annoyed her.

"You told me to give you feedback," she reminded him. "I thought that's what I was doing."

"True," he nodded. "What I'm getting, though, sounds

more like a plot line from 'Splash Mountain' or whatever the hell that soap show is."

"'Niagara's Tears,'" Victoria corrected him, irritated that he was now throwing it in her face after his initial indifference that her mother acted at all.

"Whatever."

Victoria defiantly squared her shoulders, her hands on her hips. "Then maybe you should do a better job of defining *what* exactly it is you expect me to do."

"Well, for one thing, you could save yourself the trouble of telling me things that I already know."

Between his handsomely chiseled features and his expression of total calm, it was impossible for her to tell if he was bluffing. *Smart-ass*, she thought to herself, vexed at his capacity to keep her off balance.

"Oh, by the way," he said, freely changing the subject, "I'll need you to make some air reservations for Tapping for Thanksgiving week. Don't bother with a hotel—he'll be staying here."

With any luck, coupled with a call to Elliott, Victoria thought, she'd be gone by then. Out loud, she reminded him of her last question.

"Just observe," he matter of factly replied as if it were the most obvious thing in the world. "Comings and goings, deliveries, liaisons that seem peculiar to you—"

"You don't think it's a peculiar liaison," she pointed out, "that a girl with as much on the ball as Deborah Shedd-moore is involved with your cousin?" Even in spite of her discomfiture at dinner with their double entendres and open flirting, Victoria had paid enough attention to see in Deborah a bright, articulate young woman with the resources—and the family wealth and pedigree—to do whatever she wanted. Why she had attached herself to a ruthless and arrogant playboy with as bad an attitude as Sean Michael boggled the mind.

"What I find it," Hunter answered, "is probably on the hopelessly *stupid* side, but not that peculiar at all."

"Meaning?"

"You've met him yourself," he reminded her. "He may be brash and greedy, Victoria, but the exterior is an image that most women swoon over." There was just enough of an emphasis on the word "most" that she knew Hunter at least recognized she herself wasn't one of the giddy multitudes. "As a matter of fact," he continued, "if Sean Michael could sing, dance, or perform world-class illusions like flying around a stage or getting himself sawed in half, he'd probably be headlining at Caesar's Tahoe in Nevada instead of being such a royal pain in the rear to everyone like he is now."

"And yet you put up with him. Peggy, too, I gather."

"I put up with a *lot* of things. But only because the law and convention dictate it."

The unresolved statement about Hunter's being legitimate still hovered in her head, still alluded to things dark and improper about the cousins' past. "You started to tell me something about both of them yesterday," she reminded him. "You never finished."

"Just like you're not finishing today's conversation about Deborah?"

"I thought I had."

O'Hare questioningly quirked a brow. "You seem overly concerned about a relationship that I, for one, see as pretty superficial. Maybe you should give her more credit for only taking what she wants."

Victoria smirked. "So you're saying her attraction to him is purely physical?" From what she had witnessed at dinner the previous night, Sean Michael had done all but rape his blueblood date between the salad and the main course.

"Wouldn't *you* say it's physical?" he countered.

The telephone at his bedside preempted Victoria's reply.

"Oh, hello, Elliott," Hunter said. "Yes, as a matter of fact, she's right here." O'Hare handed her the receiver. "He's just calling to see how it's going."

* * *

I had my chance, Victoria chided herself. *I had my chance and I still held back*.

With the afternoon rain temporarily on hold and Hunter engaged in his paperwork, she had seized the moment to catch some fresh air, to go for a long walk on the grounds that had previously been off limits because of inclement weather. Not ten minutes from the castle, though, and she had caught herself regretting the brief exchange on the phone with Elliott Bowman.

"Is everything okay?" Elliott had asked. And as dutifully as if Hunter had been holding a loaded gun to her head, Victoria had replied that everything was fine.

The reason, of course, had made sense at the time, boiling down to the fact that the firm's high estimation of her as an employee had ingrained a level of loyalty that now ran counter to her personal desire to jump ship and start paddling fast. In five minutes of talking, she had asked Elliott only one pointed question, specifically, if he knew anything about the threatening letters that Hunter was receiving.

She had wanted to hear Elliott say no and, outraged by such a show of duplicity, to subsequently demand that she put Hunter back on the line to explain himself. Instead, he had said yes, adding only that he had wanted her to hear it from Hunter in person rather than muddying her perspective with a second-party interpretation. "He won't let anything happen to you, Victoria," Elliott had added to quell her unspoken anxiety. "I'd bet my reputation on it."

So why was she not convinced?

Her aimless walk had brought her less than a stone's throw from the stables. It brought her as well to a visual observation that jogged her memory about an earlier talk with Thatcher and John. Like the two gardener's cottages she had seen the first day near the entrance to Hunter's estate, the stables' rustic exterior was suggestive of the

Civil War and probably as long in need of a good coat of paint. Might even be an original building from that era, she mused, where many a southern belle might have lost her virtue in its hayloft and many a Union soldier had used its walls for cover from Confederate gunfire.

It was the stylistic dichotomy of a Civil War barn and a medieval castle existing on the same piece of land that bothered her, particularly since the millionaire's real estate holdings were nothing to sneeze at.

"You know he tore down the previous place he had," Thatch had remarked.

"Now *there* was a spread and a half," John added. "Should've been a feature piece in *Architectural Digest*."

"If it was so fabulous," Victoria had challenged them, "why did he take a wrecking ball to it?" Not only had it seemed a wasteful act but a juvenile one as well, signifying O'Hare's total indifference to nostalgia. Meeting him in person had clouded the issue even further, for if anyone in the household was a likely candidate to destroy something without a second thought, it would have been Sean Michael.

That Hunter had spared the stables and twin cottages in his zeal for renovation made as much sense as why he tolerated his relatives: Zero. Obviously she just didn't understand the rich.

As Victoria's eyes came back to study the main stable, she was surprised to see a young man watching her from the doorway. Staring at her, to be precise. The whippet thinness of his body was repeated in his long face and in mouse brown hair slicked back into a queue that was neither neat nor flattering to his angular features. Nor did his pencil-thin jeans and blue henley shirt with sleeves pushed up to the elbows give him any dimension of machismo.

Before she could give a thought to who he might be, however, both were startled by the sudden report of a single gunshot.

It had come from the direction of the castle.

12

She heard Sean Michael's voice well before she saw him in the castle's courtyard. " . . . like a bloody frigging circus!" he was sarcastically admonishing the spontaneous group that had spilled forth from the interior, alarmed by the shot.

"What's going on?" she inquired of Mrs. Pritchard, who stood closest, wringing her hands in what had become a trademark stamp of confusion.

As the cook started to reply, her piggy eyes caught something directly over Victoria's shoulder. "Back to the stables, now," she hastily instructed before answering Victoria's question. "It's nothing to do with you, lad."

As Victoria looked back, she saw that the pathetically skinny young man who had been watching her from the doorway had followed her back to the castle as well, no doubt as intrigued as she was by the source of gunfire and its intended target. Eyes locked on the cook as if in a silent communion, he hesitated a moment, his feet rooted to the ground.

"Go on with you now," the cook repeated, more gently than the first time, as if to coax a frightened animal.

"Who was that?" Victoria asked, but Mrs. Pritchard had already started to answer her original question.

"Sure, he'll be the death of someone, don't you know," Mrs. P bitterly remarked, nodding her head in the direction of Sean Michael. "Says it was a rat he saw, and a large one, too."

"Isn't a bullet a bit much?" Victoria commented.

Mrs. Maginn was speaking now, hands splayed on her broad hips like a parochial school teacher about to deliver thirty whacks on the knuckles with a ruler. "And where's *your* head?" she snapped at Sean Michael from the top step. "Are you meaning' to be scarin' us all to an early grave with your show-offs and bravado?"

A definitive sneer snaked its way across Sean Michael's face. "You're *not* my *mother*," he retorted as he strolled past her into the castle, twirling the revolver on his forefinger like an accomplished gunslinger.

"There'll be hell to pay for *that* one," Mrs. Pritchard muttered. The show now obviously over, she was wiping her hands on her apron and preparing to go back inside.

"Hell to pay for what?" Victoria queried, distracted by the uncharacteristically wounded look on the housekeeper's face. Was it that Sean Michael's remark had challenged her authority in front of an audience? she wondered. Or did his biting words go deeper than that?

"Sure as it's best to keep your own counsel," Mrs. Pritchard replied, squeezing Victoria's arm like a confidante. "No good's to be comin' from knowin' too much."

With the cook's departure, the courtyard was empty save for Chan, judiciously engaged in polishing the driver's-side mirror of the limo.

Victoria slid her hands into her pockets and strolled toward him. "Never a dull moment around here, is there?" she remarked.

"That would depend," he said without looking up, "on one's measurement of dullness."

"What would it be by *your* definition then?" Victoria inquired, intrigued by this somber young Asian who was simultaneously a valued member of the staff and yet purposely detached from any intimate association with it. While snippets of dialogue and visual clues were already building colorful composites of the rest of the castle's residents, this one remained—as he carefully chose to be—a complete enigma.

"Definitions," Chan philosophically replied, "have no meaning unless to justify one's existence."

"Confucius?"

"No," the chauffeur said. "Chan."

Victoria folded her arms as she watched him work. "So what does the Tao of Chan make of what just happened?" His almond eyes had missed nothing, she was certain. Whether he'd share any of it was questionable.

"You're referring to the gunshot?"

His open response escalated Victoria's hopes that she had magically scored a major breakthrough in communication. "Do you really think there *was* a rat?" she asked, eager to hear his version of the incident.

His meticulous polishing had now taken him to the mirror on the passenger side. "The fate of a rat does not affect me," he curtly informed her. "Nor should it."

Mr. Aloof, Victoria labeled him, imagining that the fate of his human peers probably wouldn't cause him to lose any sleep either. For one thing, of course, the cultural disparity between Chan and the others may as well have put them on opposite poles. Not gregarious by nature anyway, the chauffeur represented a corner of Hunter's prior life. B.C., she decided to call it. Before Castle. That Chan had opted to remain in O'Hare's employ after the influx of Irish nationals and the resignation of the prior staff certainly pointed to loyalty, independence, self-confidence.

Either that, she thought, or he just liked to wear a uniform with brass buttons and drive fancy cars.

"So how about those Dolphins?" she casually offered in postscript. "Think they've got a shot at the Super Bowl?"

Chan regarded her with a long look that might have passed for amusement had his face been capable of yielding to a smile. "Early prediction," he said, "is not often a wise choice."

"I'll keep that in mind," Victoria replied, perplexed by whether he was referring to more than a football team but too taxed by the prevalent mental games to pursue it at the moment.

As she crossed to the steps, the first faint droplets of new rain began to speckle the courtyard puddles that were already in abundance. *Works without fail*, she thought to herself. *Polish a car or wear a suede coat and the rain will always start up again. Probably one of Murphy's laws.*

Her foot was only on the third stone step when her absent glance off to the side caught what she had missed before, causing her to recoil in disgust.

There, not far from where she stood, lay the thick body of a dead rat, its neck stump ragged and bloody from where its head had been efficiently blown off by a bullet.

"A little late, aren't you?" Hunter remarked, his breakfast tray already laid to the side and his working papers well in progress.

After almost six days of conscientious work, his off-the-cuff comment was not a welcome one.

"Maybe if I left my room an hour earlier," Victoria replied, "I wouldn't be holding you up."

"You're only one floor up," he pointed out. "I'd think someone as enterprising as yourself would have taken to sliding down the banisters by now."

"Third floor," she corrected him.

By his reaction, Victoria could tell it was not something he already knew.

"What are you doing on the *third* floor?" he inquired. "I gave specific instructions for you to take the room next to Peggy."

"Well, it *would* make a shorter trip," Victoria acknowl-edged, "but there's no problem with the one I've got."

Indeed, she could not have been more mother-henned by anyone than Mrs. Pritchard, whose room was just next door. "As soon as I clear off a place to sit," Mrs. P had enthusiastically promised, "we'll have to be havin' some tea." If what Victoria had glimpsed through the cook's open door was indicative of the bedroom at large, spring thaw would reasonably be the earliest she could expect the invitation to come forth.

And by then, Victoria thought, she would be long gone from Kriskerry Castle and the engimatic man who owned it.

"Unacceptable," Hunter's voice cut into her reminiscence. "The room next to Peggy's is twice as large and has a fire-place. You could use it for the chill."

As if any fire could take the chill off of this *place*, she mused to herself.

"I'd like you to talk to Mrs. Maginn about it," Hunter said.

"Excuse me, but she's the one who originally *put* me there."

The housekeeper's subsequent entrance through the open door of Hunter's room could not have been better cued had it been scripted by one of Marcine's writers.

"Finished with your breakfast now, sir?" she cheerfully inquired.

"Yes, thank you, Mrs. Maginn."

"Another cup of coffee, then?" For all intents and pur-poses, the housekeeper was the epitome of efficiency, eager to spring into action at O'Hare's bidding.

Victoria wondered whether Hunter really knew what a sly fox the old girl was. A sly fox not above robbing the henhouse when she thought no one was looking. And if he did know, why on earth would he keep her around in a position with so much power?

"There is *one* thing I need you to take care of, Mrs. Maginn," Hunter remarked.

"And what would that be, sir?"

Hunter inclined his head toward Victoria. "Ms. Cameron was just telling me that there's a problem with her room."

The housekeeper's mouth gaped open in astonishment. "A problem, sir?" she echoed. "And what would the matter be?"

"It's not the room per se." Victoria joined the conversation. "I've just been told that it's the wrong one."

Mrs. Maginn stiffened, momentarily abashed to be addressed by so bold a remark from a newcomer.

"Is that true?" Hunter asked her when no ready explanation was forthcoming.

"And which room were you *meanin'* for her to have?" the housekeeper asked.

"I distinctly remember our discussing it the week before," he replied, neither raising his voice nor changing his tone. Even so, his annoyance with the error was obvious to Victoria. "I'd like her to have the bedroom next to Peggy."

Mrs. Maginn's colorless lips pursed at the suggestion. "I understood you to be wantin' *that* room to stay as it was," she said.

"Oh, I doubt Ms. Cameron's going to perform any serious alterations to it while she's with us," he replied. He cast a wink at Victoria.

"Sure an' the *Duchess* Room would be nicer," Mrs. Maginn recommended. "And the sheets already laid."

"No, I think I'll go with my first choice." Hunter held firm. "I'm sure someone as efficient as you, Mrs. Maginn, can have it ready for her?"

Concurrently flattered and flattened, Mrs. Maginn had no choice but to agree.

"Was there a meaning to that little exchange I just missed?" Victoria asked when Mrs. Maginn had left. Not only was the power play intriguing between two such strong-willed individuals, but the obscure reference to a bedroom being left as it was compelled her to wonder whose room it had been before.

Hunter's gray eyes had a sheen of purpose as he answered her question. "What it means," he replied, "is that maybe you'll be on time to work from now on."

"Are you coming or going?" Sean Michael queried as Victoria descended and met him, unexpectedly, at the second-floor landing, her arms full of clothes she had chosen to carry rather than pack.

"Just changing bedrooms," she informed him.

Sean Michael clucked his tongue. "Always the last to know. So is it mine or someone else's?"

"If you'll excuse me," Victoria said as he conveniently occupied her immediate path, "I'd like to get these put away."

Sean Michael extended both hands, palms upward. "Mind if I help you off with those?" The roguish wink accentuated his play on words.

"No, thanks," Victoria firmly informed him, stepping past toward the bedroom she had been told would be hers for the duration.

To her annoyance, Sean Michael followed her.

"I hear you've put ol' Spots in her place," he remarked with an underscore of admiration.

"Spots?"

"Our beloved housekeeper," he translated for her. "You hadn't noticed it?"

Victoria recalled the prominent dappling of liver spots on the housekeeper's hands and arms and, in spite of her dislike of the woman, found the nickname cruel.

"Oh, it's not *that*," Sean Michael said, chuckling. "Don't you know she's a beastie who'll change her spots to suit whoever's in charge?"

"Is that so?" Victoria murmured, wishing that he weren't standing in the doorway and watching her with a look that was pure lust.

"Sir Patrick was a dumb puss to keep her as many years as he did."

"You don't seem to think very much of him," Victoria commented. At the dinner with Deborah, he had maneuvered every story into a verbal castration of the elderly Irishman's character, showing no reverence for the fact he was dead.

"True." Sean Michael shrugged. "But the same could be said of a *lot* of sots I know."

What does Deborah possibly see in this man? Victoria had to ask herself. Aside from great looks, he had the congeniality of a piranha.

"I'd just think you'd have kinder things to say about him," Victoria opined. "After all, he was your great-grandfather."

Sean Michael's sensual mouth twitched with amusement at her remark. "Bloody wrong about *that*, love," he said. "Sir Patrick was only my *grand*father."

13

"*I must be missing a generation*," Victoria thought out loud. For Sean Michael to be a good ten years younger than Hunter and not a great-grandson as well didn't make sense to her.

"There's a lot more than *that* you're missing," he teasingly informed her. "But then Hunter's always been one for the secrets, hasn't he?"

"Everyone's entitled to their privacy."

Sean Michael tossed back his head and laughed. "Not in *this* place. Speaking of which," he said, "have you seen the ghost of Duncan yet?"

"I'd have to believe in them to see one," Victoria replied, annoyed that her uninvited guest had seated himself in the closest chair.

"Ah—but don't be letting little Peggy hear such blasphemy about the Other Side," he advised in a silky challenge. "She's *one* of them, you know."

"She looked alive enough to me."

Mischief twinkled in the depths of Sean Michael's dark eyes. "I meant a worshipper," he said.

"You mean of the devil?"

"That and the God of Money," he replied. "You don't

like her much, do you?" It was more of a statement than a question for which he expected an answer.

Victoria gave him one anyway. "From what I've seen, there's not much to like."

"At least you've something in common then," Sean Michael said, stretching to his full height as Victoria prepared to leave the room.

"And what would that be?"

Pleased to have hooked her curiosity, he wasted no time in delivering his message. "She hates *your* bloody guts as well."

Uneasy beneath his scrutiny, Victoria mustered a casual reply to his declaration. "I'll try to remember that."

"Oh, don't worry, love. My sister's not one to be letting you forget it."

It was the sound of a door opening that awakened Victoria late that night from an already restless sleep. Forgetting for an instant that she had safely barred her entrance from intrusion, her first expectation was that of Peggy with a butcher knife. Her second expectation was of Sean Michael in bikini briefs and an agenda of his own.

She was thankful that she didn't have to stay at the castle forever. If she did, the place would drive her as crazy as everyone else.

To have made two major enemies in just a week ran contrary to the usual popularity that Victoria enjoyed on every job she had ever had. While far from a Goody Two-shoes who conformed to everyone's wishes, her stint in the political arena had particularly enforced the practice of maintaining smooth relations. Only a week at Hunter's castle, however, and she already had a pair of strong-willed women who would sooner poison her than give her the time of day.

Mrs. Maginn—the more subtle of the duo—seemed to be the more dangerous.

O'Hare surely must be smart enough to see the housekeeper's cagey game, Victoria thought. Certainly their exchange earlier that day about the bedroom switch had demonstrated that it wasn't a case of misinterpretation but rather a case of Mrs. Maginn usurping her authority and doing exactly what she wanted.

"I don't think I'm scoring any points with your housekeeper," Victoria had mentioned to Hunter.

"I don't know that you'd want to," O'Hare had replied. "She's not the one paying your salary."

Pleasant as Mrs. Maginn had been when showing Victoria her new quarters, there was an iciness below the surface that telegraphed she would not easily let the incident go. "Perhaps *this* one will be suitin' your tastes better," she said to Victoria, the implication being that O'Hare's new secretary was a pampered snob who had whined her way into his sympathy.

Mrs. Maginn had also let drop—whether intentionally or not—the fact that the room had not been used for some time. "Sure, he forgot he *wanted* it that way," she cryptically remarked in reference to the man who employed her.

"Oh?" Victoria said. "Whose room was it?" Decidely feminine in color and fabric, it had obviously not been the bedchambers of one of the male residents. Mrs. Maginn ignored the question as blithely as if Victoria had said nothing at all.

"If you'll be needin' more blankets or pillows," she said, "there's an oak cupboard down the hall."

What I'm *needin'*, Victoria wanted to say, are answers, not blankets. The former, however, would clearly not be coming from Mrs. Maginn.

After several unsuccessful attempts to go back to sleep, Victoria switched on the bedside lamp. *May as well do something productive*, she decided. A half-finished letter to her mother beckoned from the cherrywood desk across the room.

Victoria tossed back the covers and reached for her robe, conscious of the chill that awaited outside the confines of a warm bed. *Easy enough to take care of that problem*, she resolved. With a stone fireplace nearly as big as the armoire, the corner where she'd be writing could be toasty again in a matter of minutes.

As she knelt down to pull a few pieces of wood and kindling from the copper log bin on the hearth, the faint ripple of a woman's laughter echoed down the flue, startling her. Victoria leaned forward to discern where the eerie sound might be coming from.

There be ghosts in these walls, she could imagine Sean Michael teasing her.

No merry ghost, though, was the instrument of the girlish giggles she was hearing now. If her guess was right, it was coming from Peggy's room next door, both fireplaces sharing a common chimney.

And from the new sound that now accompanied the laughter, it was equally obvious that Miss Peggy Gleavy was not spending the evening alone.

She had fancied herself immune to surprises in a setting such as this. Indeed, it struck Victoria that after her first week of adjusting to the tempo and oddity of so disparate a household, anything resembling the normal would have been starkly out of place.

An enemy's being congenial before breakfast definitely fit that category.

As flawlessly as if they had rehearsed it, Victoria found herself emerging from her room the following morning at exactly the same time as Peggy. For a split second, pinned by the brunette's galvanizing flash of disdain, she nearly considered going back inside as if she had forgotten something.

Why am I letting this girl get to me? Victoria chided herself. *So what if she hates my guts and practices witchcraft on the side?*

Such testimony, she reflected, had come from Sean Michael—hardly a credible source of anything significant. Maybe, for reasons of his own, he didn't *want* them to be on speaking terms.

Resolved to reserve judgment until the younger Gleavy could actually be accused of something tangible, Victoria took the offensive.

"Morning!" she greeted Peggy.

To her surprise, Sean Michael's sister responded in kind, even asking Victoria how she liked her room.

"It's a new experience," Victoria replied, wondering if a night of satisfying sex accounted for the otherwise sulky woman's definitive change in attitude. From the time she had started the fire to well after completing her mother's letter and reading four chapters of a novel, the erotic gymnastics next door in Peggy's room had been fairly audible. "I always sleep well in a good rainstorm," Victoria volunteered.

"Rains too bloody much for *my* taste," Peggy replied. They had fallen into step as they descended the staircase, both of them en route to the dining room.

"I'd think you'd be used to it from living in Ireland," Victoria continued, surprised to be carrying on a fairly civil conversation with a worshiper of the devil.

"You've been there?" Peggy inquired. There was an edge to her voice that hadn't been there before.

Victoria shook her head. "It's on my list, though," she said. Well traveled as she was in North America and the Hawaiian Islands, a trek across the Atlantic had yet to come to pass. "I hear that it's a very pretty country."

"It can blow off to hell for all I care," Peggy retorted, dismissively shrugging her shoulders. "Ireland was then. This is now."

Not exactly a profound observation but indicative of the Gleavy girl's sentiment for her homeland. *Obviously, Ireland is a red-flag word*, Victoria determined, trying to remember what had been said before about Peggy's decision to come to the United States.

As she opened her mouth to try a new subject of dialogue, the two of them nearly collided with Mrs. Pritchard, emerging from the dining room with an empty tray.

The broad smile on the cook's face at the sight of Victoria quickly changed to a scowl at the sight of her present companion.

"Have you seen Ian?" Mrs. Pritchard stiffly inquired of the latter. "Himself has been askin' for him."

"How the devil should I know?" Peggy insolently replied, sailing past them into the room where Sean Michael was already generously helping himself to muffins and fresh fruit from the sideboard.

"If I were himself," Mrs. P muttered beneath her breath, "I'd be takin' a leather strap to her bare backside."

And knowing Peggy, Victoria wryly thought, *she'd probably enjoy every minute of it*. Out loud, she asked Mrs. Pritchard which one Ian was that she might help to keep an eye out for him. "I haven't met all of the outdoor staff yet," she explained.

"Sure an' they keep to themselves, don't you know," Mrs. Pritchard replied, adding in postscript that it was a blessed condition she sometimes envied.

Her subsequent description of the Irish stableman matched that of the painfully thin man Victoria had noticed the same afternoon Sean Michael was doing his target practice in the courtyard.

"Ian's a good lad," Mrs. Pritchard sighed, "but sure an' his heart's too full of trust for the wrong kind."

"You mean Peggy?" They had moved out of earshot of the two Gleavys, though Victoria suspected they were both accomplished eavesdroppers, even at twenty paces.

"She's a witch, that one," Mrs. P declared in no uncertain terms. "That, and the word that *rhymes* with it!" The cook squeezed Victoria's forearm. "Don't be trustin' a word she says," she warned. "She's as evil an' black as her brother."

"I'll keep that in mind." Victoria thanked her, in spite of the fact she had already come to that conclusion on her own. "It's really nice of you to be so concerned about Ian," she said. "I hope he appreciates it."

That Mrs. Pritchard had so readily taken Victoria under her wing as well was a testament to the woman's generous and maternal nature. Obviously she considered the stableman a lost waif in need of some matronly guidance and advice, particularly as regarded the likes of Peggy. Unfortunately, to use the barn-door analogy, the horses had already gotten out at a full gallop and were off to a head start.

A smile returned to the cook's plump face. "Sure, I promised my Welshman at his grave twenty years past," she said, "it's a better life our boy will be knowin' here in the States than the one we left back in Ireland."

Well, I'll be damned, Victoria said to herself, the connection between them now clear.

"Ian is your son, then?" she queried.

Mrs. P beamed. "The joy of my life, lass."

Then I won't be the one to tell her, Victoria wisely decided, that the joy of Mrs. Pritchard's life had spent the better part of the previous night screwing his brains out with the castle's least-favored female.

Victoria strolled down the corridor toward Hunter's room, wondering if the morning's incidents were indicative of how the whole day would go. Notwithstanding Peggy's renewed coolness, Sean Michael's boyishly charming invitation to go horseback riding, and Mrs. Maginn's solicitous concerns about how she had slept and whether she wanted more jam for her toast, it had all the earmarks of a scene from *The Twilight Zone*. *My mother's writers would have a field day with these people*, she thought to herself.

As she passed by the hallway table with its silver tray for outgoing mail, she remembered the letter to Marcine in the pocket of her sweater and proceeded to withdraw it, certain she would forget to do so once her morning work with Hunter got started. Only three other envelopes were on the tray, the top one bearing the easily recognized logo of Alexandria's largest florist.

She wondered who had ordered flowers, not having seen any fresh ones since her arrival. Maybe it was a billing from the prior month. Maybe it was a bill of Sean Michael's, romancing his latest love with roses professing his devotion.

The door to Hunter's room was open, and from within she could now hear the voice of Nilly. "Sir Patrick himself carved it as a youth, sir," she heard him say as she stepped into the doorway.

"Beautiful workmanship," Hunter replied. "Oh, Victoria, you're just in time. Come and take a look at this."

As she approached, Victoria could see that it was a dark wood cane they were discussing, its handle magnificently carved in the shape of a horse head.

"It was his favorite, sir," Nilly respectfully informed him.

"That would be Clodagh's Crest, wouldn't it?" O'Hare asked, fingering the smooth sculpting.

On Nilly's nod, Hunter proceeded to explain what they were talking about. "My great-grandfather had a passion for thoroughbreds," he said. "Clodagh's Crest was one of the finest sires in the county, not to mention the meanest tempered."

"Ay, but Sir Patrick had a way with him," Nilly pointed out.

"That and women," Hunter remarked, turning his attention back to Victoria. "Want to help me give this a try?" He had started to toss back the covers.

Victoria hoped her face wouldn't go into a hot blush, for his words and companion action could be interpreted

on a sexual level. "Give *what* a try?" she casually asked,
pretending she hadn't made such a connection.

"You don't think I'm going to stay in bed all month, do
you?" Hunter motioned for her to come forward.

Staying in bed with *him for a month*, Victoria thought,
would be heaven. "Do you really think that's such a good
idea?" she challenged him, aware now of what he was
going to do. Aware as well of the delicious muscled
thighs she could see where his robe had edged up.

"I didn't get where I am," Hunter reminded her, "by
lying in bed all day long. Come on, I'm just going to need
some help standing."

Against her own better judgment that he was rushing
his recovery, Victoria found herself at the side of the bed,
Nilly having stepped back and out of the way.

"I'll just need you for balance," Hunter said, reaching
up to put his left arm around her neck.

God, give me strength, Victoria silently prayed, her senses momentarily dizzied by his scent and masculine nearness, in spite of her opinion that he was acting like a
bullheaded jerk. "Did your doctor tell you it was okay to
try this?" she asked, her arm automatically sliding
around his waist and tightening as he pushed himself off
the bed.

Whatever reply he might have given was superseded
by a wrenching groan as, off balance, the two of them
toppled to the floor.

14

Victoria's *spontaneous gasp* of alarm was muffled in the fabric of Hunter's madras robe as he fell on top of her, his chest hair grazing her nose and chin in their descent as she lost her balance and twisted beneath him. Crushed by his upper body weight and pinioned by his bad left leg wedged between both of her own, she realized that only a thick carpet and his quick thinking to break their final impact with his arms had prevented her from being completely squashed.

Hunter's voice, husky and unsteady, sought an assessment of her own damage in advance of his, a query at odds with her opinion that he was basically self-centered. "Are you all right?" Had he started to add an endearment at the end of the question? A word that sounded like "honey"? With ears still ringing from the jolt, Victoria couldn't be sure. Just as quickly, she dismissed it. They were veritable strangers, after all, who had shared little more than dinner and a Macintosh computer. Men like Hunter O'Hare didn't call *any*one "honey."

"I think so," she murmured, though the wind had been knocked out of her when they had landed. In a flash of horror, her thoughts turned to what the fall had probably just done to his knee, an accident for which she herself had to take partial blame in not being able to prevent it. "What about you? Is your leg—"

O'Hare groaned as he tried to shift his weight off of her midriff. "It's probably the damn best-padded part of me," he remarked, gritting his teeth in the frustration of attempting to extricate himself from between her splayed legs. "Nilly? Are you still there?" His breath was warm where it fanned Victoria's cheek, the expensive smell of his Obsession aftershave teasing her nose and reminding her of the fragrance's provocative magazine ads of naked couples engaged in highly compromising positions.

"Over here, sir," Nilly anxiously replied, not daring to venture any closer.

"We're going to need some help on this," Hunter instructed him, propping himself up on one elbow and trying to turn his head in the valet's direction. "Go get someone."

"Whom shall I get, sir?" Nilly respectfully inquired, reluctant to breach any order of protocol.

"Good lord," O'Hare muttered in annoyance just loud enough for Victoria to hear. Louder, he asked that Nilly bring whoever was available. "Hopefully," he said to Victoria after Nilly had shuffled off, "it won't be someone who will do worse damage."

Were they thinking of the same person? Victoria didn't volunteer a name, nor did Hunter.

"Maybe we can get out of this ourselves," she suggested, embarrassed to wonder what kind of spectacle they made. The fewer who witnessed it, the better. "I could try wriggling out . . ."

"Go for it," Hunter encouraged her. His grimace and guttural moan at her first movement, however, preempted the idea.

"Do you feel as ridiculous as I do?" he asked after a moment of silence.

"I don't think that's possible," Victoria replied, trying to put her mind beyond the sensation of his torso smothered against her or the intoxicating nearness of his lips when he spoke.

It took Hunter a beat to recognize what she had just implied with her remark, that his own vanity and impatience had precipitated the fall.

"You're dying to say 'I told you so,' aren't you?" he said.

"Not to the man who's signing my paychecks," Victoria diplomatically replied, much as she *wanted* to say it.

"But you are *thinking* it?"

At this distance, Victoria mused, he should be able to read her brain waves like a page of Braille. Out loud, she voiced the opinion that he could use a few more lessons on maneuvering a cane.

"Not the cane that's a problem," Hunter testily countered. "You're dealing with a southpaw."

"What does that have to do with anything? You're not left-*legged*."

"I was trying to use the cane for balance getting out of bed," he defended himself. "Problem was, I had it in my right hand." Hunter tried shifting his weight again, this time pinching her side. "Sorry," he apologized. "What the hell is taking that damn Nilly so long. ..."

"He only left us a minute ago," Victoria reminded him, just as anxious to be free of the situation as he was but cognizant of the fact that her own level of discomfiture fell far below that of this alleged paragon of perfection and master of all skills. He tried something and it didn't work, Victoria evaluated the situation, trying to understand it from his point of view.

Failure, of course, wasn't a word in Hunter O'Hare's operating vocabulary. He fairly well basked in that condition, she decided, building his empires and expanding his influence. And yet he had just experienced a dramatic measure of personal failure in front of not only a servant but a woman as well.

Be kind to his ego, her conscience advised, for in failing so miserably in a task he boasted was simple, he had just exposed a raw vulnerability Victoria might otherwise have never known existed.

"Want to try moving again?" Hunter asked her, his voice laced with impatience.

"Someone will be along pretty soon," she predicted.

"You sound pretty sure of that."

"I just don't think you should take a risk on any more injury than you have to," Victoria replied.

Hunter paused before answering. "Maybe I *was* rushing things," he reluctantly admitted. "I just hate being cooped up."

"Part of recuperation," she emphasized the second syllable.

"Maybe next time I'll listen to you."

His face hovered right over hers, their eyes meeting. Awkward with such intimacy, O'Hare was the first to look away.

"It's not your fault," he said. It wasn't until his next sentence that Victoria realized he was talking about the fall itself and not the graceless way he had just pretended she was invisible. "A week in bed and I'm too damned unsteady. That's all it was."

"Nilly *is* taking a long time, isn't he?" she commented, uncomfortable with the illicit thoughts that were sliding through her head at that very moment. Thoughts inappropriate for someone in her position to even be thinking about him.

O'Hare shifted again in another attempt to move his leg, the top of his robe pulling open a little farther as he did so. *Do that one more time*, Victoria's conscience screamed, *and I'm not going to be responsible for what happens*.

"He probably took a detour via Mrs. Pritchard's kitchen," Hunter speculated.

"He does seem to spend a lot of time in there, doesn't he?" For all of the caffeine that Nilly's system absorbed in the course of a day, it was a wonder to Victoria that the castle's valet wasn't in a permanent state of hyperdrive.

"True, but where else would he go?"

A humorous but nonetheless critical scenario unfolded in her imagination. "What if he forgets about us and no one comes all day?"

Hunter considered it for a moment. "Maybe it's what they'd call a case of 'extended floorplay.'"

Victoria caught herself laughing at his wit, a contagious laugh that made him chuckle as well.

It was in such a state of unrestrained mutual mirth that both of them were suddenly startled by the sound of someone addressing them from the doorway.

"Well, well, well," the jesting voice of Sean Michael rang out as he strolled into the room. "I guess I can see now why she never took a tumble for *me*, cousin."

Victoria felt Hunter's muscles tense beneath the fabric of his robe.

"Have you come to help or just be annoying?" O"Hare retorted.

Sean Michael was now squatting just behind Hunter's right shoulder blade, his face out of the latter's sight but in full view to Victoria. "Actually," he facetiously replied, "it might be amusing to pour honey down the length of your back and unscrew a jar of South American ants."

"I wouldn't put it past you," O'Hare countered, glancing down at Victoria just briefly enough to convey his fury that it was Sean Michael who had found them first.

"You seem to be in a position to bargain," Sean Michael casually pointed out. "Or rather, I do."

"Then you've misjudged the situation," Hunter firmly informed him, averse to letting an enemy see his pain.

Sean Michael laughed. "Have I? A moment ago you just asked for my help, didn't you?"

With the slow rage she could feel building inside of Hunter, Victoria expected him at any second to spring to his feet with superhuman strength and pound his sarcastic cousin to the size of a radish.

The fortuitous return of Nilly with Chan precluded Victoria's fantasy.

"I found Mr. Chan, sir," Nilly announced, nearly breathless from his quest to obtain aid.

"Well, then," Sean Michael sighed, "I can see that you don't need *me*."

He was gone before the sinewy and accomplished hands of the chauffeur had even come close to touching Hunter's sprawled body.

Victoria came in on enough of the conversation's end to hear the visiting doctor's admonition about Hunter's premature jump at mobility.

"Oh, there's no question that it's quality workmanship," Dr. Citi was saying as he ran his fingers down the smooth shaft of polished wood. "It's just not very practical for what you were trying to do."

"Excuse me a moment," O'Hare interrupted him when Victoria entered. "Is that the fax from Tapping?"

"Just came in," she said with a nod, stepping toward the bed with the latest transmittal in her hand. "He'll be sending the balance of it tonight."

"You've met my physician already?" Hunter asked, a device to get the two of them engaged in small talk while he scanned the awaited documents from the London attorney.

Victoria had earlier declined the doctor's offer to make sure that she herself had suffered no injury. Only a bruise to her ego, she had told him.

"Your secretary," Dr. Citi said, "shares my prognosis that you shouldn't rush things, especially after this kind of surgery."

"Does that mean I can pay *her* for the medical advice instead of you?" Hunter inquired without looking up from his reading.

Dr. Citi winked conspiratorially at Victoria. "As if he can't afford my fees . . ."

"How *was* Maui?" Hunter murmured, turning to the second page of the fax.

"Breathtaking. If you bang up the *other* knee, I can probably move my entire practice."

"Damn," Hunter snarled.

"Just kidding," Dr. Citi assured him.

"I meant the fax," O'Hare explained irritably. "Victoria, we're going to have to get Tapping here a week ahead. Has he already got his tickets?"

"Only a reservation."

"Seeing as how *you* have worlds to conquer and *I* have patients to attend," the doctor pleasantly interjected, "I think I'll let myself out."

Hunter looked up at him and arched a brow. "Lecture's over, then?"

"Don't try to use that thing again," he advised, pointing to the cane that now lay across the foot of Hunter's bed. "It's a gentleman's walking stick, Mr. O'Hare, not an assistive device."

"What's the difference?"

"About an eight thousand dollar corrective surgery bill if you try walking with it." The doctor picked up the cane to demonstrate his point. "Beautiful carving," he said, "but you've got too big a horse snout here to comfortably get a good grip on."

"It was carved from reality," Hunter said, briefly relating the story of his great-grandfather's fixation on a famous racehorse.

"Reality," Dr. Citi said at story's end, "isn't always practical, is it?"

"So I've heard. Anything else?"

"This tip's a problem, too." He tapped the end of it.

"Why's that?" Hunter asked.

"No rubber. The bigger, the better. Without it, you don't have any traction. And next time," he warned, glancing toward Victoria, "you might not have such a soft place to land on."

"So what's my alternative?" the millionaire wanted to know.

"First off," Dr. Citi told him, "no more walking for at least three days. Second, if you absolutely *have* to get up and moving after three days, you'll use the cane I'm having dropped off."

"Some ugly metal monstrosity straight out of a nursing home?"

"Ugly but practical. Now if you'll both excuse me, I really do need to get going."

Halfway to the door, the doctor paused and turned. "By the way, that young Asian man who got you back into bed? He certainly knew what he was doing."

It was the second time, to Victoria's knowledge, that Hunter's physician had commented on how Chan had handled the emergency and stablized the leg from further injury until the doctor's arrival.

"Chan knows a lot of things," Hunter replied. "That just happens to be one of them."

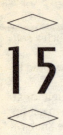

15

It *never ceased to amaze* Victoria how damning a perfectly innocent event could become on the tongues of a few well-seasoned gossips.

No sooner was the doctor's car out of sight and Victoria herself on the way into the kitchen than she heard from the lips of a flustered Mrs. P the currently circulating version of what had happened, a lusty tale that reeked of impropriety.

"'Now sure, himself is the proper gentleman,' I said back, 'and don't you be spreadin' the vile rumor he's not'—"

"Excuse me," Victoria interrupted, "but who told you such a ridiculous story to begin with?" It would have been funny, she thought, if Mrs. Pritchard weren't delivering it with such intense conviction.

"It's not the *source*, don't you know, but the scandal it puts on a lass's reputation." Mrs. P clucked her tongue in dismay at the very notion of it. "Sure an' a bad name's a stubborn stain to rub out."

What century is this woman from? Victoria mused, flattered by the cook's concern for her feminine virtue but disappointed in her obvious gullibility.

"Personally," Victoria said, "I'm more interested in the

source than any silly scandal. So who told you Mr. O'Hare was trying to seduce me?"

Mrs. Pritchard lowered her voice. "I'd not be wantin' you to repeat where I heard it," she said, "for sure an' I know *he* wasn't the one to be gettin' it started." The cook was clearly now more interested in preserving the integrity of the gossip chain's most recent link than in dismissing the gossip itself.

"Who?" Victoria firmly repeated. By the way Mrs. P was fidgeting, she already had a good idea of who the cook was trying to protect.

Mrs. Pritchard's voice was now a discreet whisper. "Ian said he heard it in the stables."

Victoria nearly laughed from the sordid scenario it conjured in her head, a scene equivalent to the back of a smoke-filled room or along the fog-shrouded, creaking wharves of a waterfront at midnight. "Well, unless one of the horses is named Mr. Ed," she countered, "I assume he heard it from another person? Maybe Peggy Gleavy?" Having only just learned who Ian even was, it seemed incongruous to Victoria that he'd fashion such a lie about a stranger on his own, relying instead on the gospel word of his manor-house lover.

Nilly entered the room and proceeded toward the cupboard for a coffee cup.

"Why don't you just ask Nilly?" Victoria suggested. "He was there in the room and saw the whole thing."

Mrs. P cast her an unexpected grin as if she had been teasing all along. "Oh, sure an' I'd swear it on my Welshman's grave, it's the truth *you're* tellin', love," she said. "But, saints protect you, it's a mean one you've chosen to cross. She'll not be at rest til you're gone."

"All the more motivation to stay," Victoria replied, perplexed by what she could have done to arouse such wrath in Hunter's female cousin.

*   *   *

Apparently Victoria aroused something equally potent and dangerous in Peggy's brother.

"I see you escaped from under my cousin," Sean Michael cattily remarked when he came upon her in the library later that afternoon.

"Yes," Victoria coolly replied. "Killer ants and all."

"I was joking about all that, you know." Sean Michael moved aside the books she had taken down so that he could settle hipshot in their place, his tight jeans displaying the firm contours beneath. "As a matter of fact, I came to apologize."

Yeah, right, Victoria thought. The word "sorry" didn't seem to fit his arrogance or street-savvy vocabulary.

"I think it's your cousin you owe an apology to," she pointed out.

"Hunter can go to hell," Sean Michael said. "But you— you're a different story." He was appraising her from head to toe and making no secret of it.

"I work for him," Victoria said. "That puts us on the same page."

"Your choice. You could at least hear my peace offering."

"Peace offering?"

"The rain's supposed to let up tomorrow."

"So?"

"We could go for a ride."

"In a car?"

Sean Michael laughed. "On horses. You do ride, don't you?"

"Only on carousels." Victoria gathered up the books that Hunter had requested, anxious to be out of the cousin's company.

"It's only the first mounting that's hard," Sean Michael said, his lower lip glistening from where he had just licked it. "Once you're on, the animal takes over." His double entendres weren't even subtle.

"I'm sure it does," Victoria said, "but no thanks."

"You're turning me down?" By his tone of astonishment, it was not an answer that Sean Michael Gleavy was accustomed to hearing from the opposite sex.

"In a word, yes."

Sean Michael caught her arm as she crossed past him, releasing it as she tensed in alarm and reeled to confront him. His next words were already out before she could say something herself. "That same page you're on with my cousin?" he said, reminding her of her own phrase. "You might want to read the small print before you do something you'll regret."

He was baiting her and enjoying every minute of it. "And what would I find?" she asked, disturbed that he was alluding to a romantic attraction to O'Hare that she had steeled her heart against ever acknowledging. Handsome, smart, and successful as the millionaire was, any kind of relationship beyond the professional would be a disaster. And yet here was Sean Michael, teasing that she was on the threshhold of involvement, hinting that O'Hare wasn't all that he seemed.

Sean Michael stood up and looked down at her a moment before turning and reaching for one of the objects on Hunter's desk.

The photograph.

Victoria felt her heart jump into her throat. Was he going to tell her who the young woman was? The mystery girl who occupied so special a place of display?

Sean Michael studied the angelic face in the frame a moment before looking back at her. "Don't be stupid, Victoria," was all he said.

"You seem preoccupied," Hunter remarked, studying her over the lowered rim of his wire-frames.

Two days had passed since his fall. Two days of him pretending as if nothing had happened, particularly his recollection of being only inches apart from her.

Two days, of course, had also been the life span of the

rumors, the household having moved on to loftier heights of intrigue about one another. To Victoria's relief, she had temporarily faded back into obscurity.

"Just getting squared away on all the details for Tapping's visit," she lied.

"I'm sure it's all under control," O'Hare complimented her. "Oh, by the way, I was just thinking that you might want to take a couple of days off while he's here."

"Yes." She nodded, "I'm sure that the work is stacking up on my desk back at the firm." She also missed the easy camaraderie of Thatcher and John.

"What I meant," Hunter said in clarification, "is that Tapping's never seen D.C."

"So 'tour guide' is being added to my ubiquitous duties?"

"Elliott never mentioned your propensity for second-guessing," he said. "Actually I was planning to show Tapping some of the sights myself and thought you'd like to come along."

"You're going to be up and about that soon?" The capital's reputation as a pedestrian's dream could be a knee-surgery patient's nightmare, particularly those sites accessible only by zillions of marble steps.

"I'm going to be up and about tomorrow," Hunter announced. "The doctor said three days, remember?"

"I remember," she affirmed, "but I also recall him saying only if it was necessary."

"It *is* necessary," Hunter insisted. "I have things to do."

"*What* things?"

O'Hare changed the subject.

Victoria changed it back.

"I don't know why you're blowing this out of proportion," he criticized her. "I promised him I'd use that institutional thing he brought, didn't I?" To emphasize the point, he indicated the metal and rubber cane that lay propped up in the corner.

"Just don't ask for my help," Victoria said. "The last time I broke my watch."

"What?"

"Actually it was just the crystal. I'll have it repaired next time I'm in Alexandria."

"Chan's going in this afternoon. I'll have him take it for you."

His zeal for control had surfaced again, in spite of the responsibility he seemed to be taking for the timepiece being damaged.

Victoria shook her head. "That's okay. I can do it myself."

"You can do a lot of things," O'Hare remarked. "You probably even pump your own gas."

"This is the nineties," she reminded him. "And speaking of Chan, as long as he's going to town, there are a couple of errands I need to run. Do you need me this afternoon?"

"Why don't you make a list? Wouldn't that be easier?"

"The list is in my head," Victoria replied. "I shouldn't be gone that long."

"Something bothering you, Victoria?"

"Why do you ask?"

"You just seem anxious to be away from here."

"You did say I had the freedom to come and go," she said. "Or have the rules changed since then?"

So maybe "rules" was a harsher word than she had meant to use. By the expression on O'Hare's face, she knew right away that he didn't like his authority contested. Braced for an argument, it surprised her when he slipped his glasses back on and picked up the papers he had been reviewing for signature.

"I'll need you back by two-thirty," he said, not meeting her eyes.

It was a concession she hadn't expected. It also left her in the awkward position of not knowing what to say in response.

"Can I get you anything while I'm out?" she asked.

"No, thanks," O'Hare replied. "I have everything I could possibly want."

His answer still lingered in her head a half hour later as she was opening the day's delivery of mail.

Another threatening letter had arrived, a letter that swore to deprive Hunter O'Hare of all he possessed.

"I thought you were going into town with Chan," Hunter said, glancing at his watch.

"Only if I finish up the filing you gave me," she replied, hoping her voice sounded convincing. "There was more to it than I thought."

"Just like *I* think there's more to your answer?"

His query set the alarm bells ringing in her head. Was she really that transparent that he had guessed why she had changed her mind? "What do you mean?"

"A little while ago," he reminded her, "you were hot to hit the road. A million errands, as I recall. How come you're still here?"

"Like I said, the filing—"

"The filing's a low priority," O'Hare said. "I also happen to know from Elliot that it's one of your least favorite office chores to do."

"Only when there's too much of it," Victoria explained, feeling the heat steal into her face. "If you keep on top of it—"

"It's the latest letter, isn't it?"

Victoria hesitated between the truth and a graceful lie.

Hunter took advantage of the pause to say something himself. "It's my problem to deal with, Victoria. If the author's that bent on carrying out the method in the picture, your being here or not isn't going to make a whit of difference to the outcome."

Victoria's eyes had gravitated toward the desk where the latest envelope lay in plain view.

"Besides," Hunter added, "I think I could put up a damned good fight if someone was trying to castrate me with a pair of hedge clippers, don't you?"

"What if they caught you off guard?" she said. "What if you were asleep?"

"I'm a very light sleeper."

"I'd feel safer about it if you called the police."

"You should feel safe anyway," O'Hare assured her. "Do you really think I'd let anything happen to you?"

There was a warmth in his words that brought back the feeling she had experienced a few days earlier, pinned beneath him as they waited for help. *Don't read anything into it*, her conscience advised. He probably just wanted to avoid the embarrassment of having to go to Elliott and tell him that the secretary he'd borrowed was dead and could he have a new one. "If you still want to go into town," Hunter continued, "I can take care of myself just fine."

"Maybe tomorrow," she said, still not convinced that leaving him right now would be the best thing to do. "Oh, by the way," she added, remembering something she had forgotten to ask earlier, "what did you do with the other cane? The one that was your great-grandfather's?"

She had first noticed it was missing when they had talked about showing Tapping around Washington, D.C., an observation dismissed when the conversation had turned to a debate about her freedom to leave the castle and go shopping.

"Nilly must have put it back in storage," O'Hare replied.

That he didn't sound definite about it bothered her. "Do you want me to ask him?"

"No big deal," Hunter said with a shrug. "The only thing it's good for would be to hit someone on the head."

16

"*Going out today?*" Sean Michael inquired the next morning at breakfast.

"You're either psychic or an eavesdropper," Victoria replied. Were she to place a bet, it would have been on the latter.

Sean Michael stabbed a generous piece of sweet Virginia ham off the serving platter with his fork. "Oh, I have my sources," he said with a sly wink. "I was also going to town myself." He was now standing closer than Victoria would have liked. "Ever had lunch at the First Lady's Rose?"

Victoria indicated the plate of food she was carrying. "I never think about lunch before I've finished breakfast." And, she felt like adding, she certainly would never consider a lunch date with *him*.

"Will you think about it after?" He had turned up all the decibels on charm, an approach that made Victoria all the more wary. "I hear they have a crab soufflé to die for."

"The month's got an R in it," Peggy sarcastically enlightened him, strolling in to join them with a Bloody Mary in her hand.

"So?" Sean Michael said.

"So don't say I didn't warn you."

The admonishment made him laugh out loud. "It's an old wives' tale, Peglet, that bit about the R."

Peggy turned up her nose at him.

"Silly superstition," Sean Michael leaned in to Victoria. "Like wicked ghosts that go bump in the night ..."

Mrs. Maginn's arrival with a fresh pot of coffee interrupted Peggy's sharp-tongued defense that her brother was doomed to hell for speaking badly of the spirit world.

"Speaking of spirits, sister dear," he retorted, "isn't it a little early for *that*?"

The reference prompted Mrs. Maginn to turn her head and see that he was pointing at Peggy's half-empty glass, a sight that distressed the housekeeper into an audible gasp of shock.

"Margaret Aileen Gleavy!" she snapped with the indignation of a parent at wit's end. "Is that liquor that I'm seein' in your hand?"

"She's really in trouble now," Sean Michael shared in whisper to Victoria as the housekeeper confronted his sister. "Spots never uses her whole name unless she's about to catch it."

"I'm past twenty-one," Peggy snapped, defending her right to a liquid breakfast.

"Sure, that's true enough," Mrs. Maginn said, "but the hour's not past a time that's proper to be drinkin' yourself free as a sailor." Her hand shot out to take it away but Peggy's reflexes were faster, a movement that sent the contents of the glass splashing out over her wrist and on to the dining room rug.

Whether more aghast by Peggy's childish disobedience or the ugly red stain that now saturated the carpet, Mrs. Maginn lost whatever personal control she still had left. "Clean it up!" she ordered Peggy. "Clean it up or himself will be hearin' about it from my own lips!"

"Do I look as if I care?" Peggy snidely replied before letting the crystal glass purposely slip from between her fingers and shatter at the housekeeper's feet. "I'm not his servant."

There's more to that whole picture than I'm seeing, Victoria told herself as she watched the countryside speed by from the back of the limo.

Pleased at having successfully eluded Sean Michael to enjoy the ride to Alexandria in peace, it nonetheless bothered her that the tantrum she witnessed in the dining room earlier that morning seemed to mask something deeper, darker.

Only in retrospect did it occur to her that it wasn't Peggy's immature attitude that garnered the lion's share of Victoria's curiosity at that moment, but rather the reaction of the Irish housekeeper to being put in her place by someone so much younger. Sean's indifference to the whole incident suggested, further, that the power play by his sister wasn't all that unusual, its venom defined by years of practice and manipulation.

Had tears indeed sprung to the woman's face or was it a trick of the light? Across the room, one couldn't be sure, nor was the definitive quiver of her lower lip the preface to a demand for apology or a plea to Peggy to not be so callous and cruel. Whatever clout Gwynna Maginn holds with the rest of the household, Victoria concluded from witnessing their brief interaction, it clearly stopped short of Hunter's obnoxious cousins, for almost on the very heels of Peggy's departure from the room, Mrs. Maginn had left as well, her face red with embarrassment.

O'Hare's bedroom, however, had apparently not been the housekeeper's destination. He was unaware the confrontation had even happened when Victoria brought up the subject after her own breakfast.

"I can't say that it surprises me," was all he said of Peggy's morning beverage. "It runs in the family."

Family. Victoria kept forgetting to ask him more about

that, still perplexed by the gap of a whole generation between Hunter and Sean Michael.

Chan was rolling down the glass divider that separated them. "How long will you be at your office?" he inquired, startling her back to the reality of her purpose in temporarily escaping from the castle.

"I really don't know yet," she replied. "Were you going to wait there for me?"

"Waiting is not a productive activity," Chan informed her.

"No, I suppose not." She wondered what a person like Chan did when he wasn't driving the limo, just as she had wondered what Nilly the valet did to pass the time when he wasn't drinking coffee with Mrs. Pritchard. "Why don't we say two hours, then?"

The first turnoff to Alexandria was just ahead.

"Two hours from now?" Chan asked. "Or two hours from when I drop you off?"

The man was such a perfectionist, she thought.

"I'll let you know," she replied, amused that the difference they were talking about was not much greater than ten minutes. Was his entire life that precise, that methodical, that geared to discipline? A funny thought crossed her mind and she suppressed a laugh.

"Yes?" Chan said, mistaking her squeak of amusement for a remark cast in his direction.

"Oh, nothing," Victoria answered, harkening back to Peggy's audible sex life as overheard through the fireplace damper. *What if it* wasn't *Ian in the room with her that night*? she thought, cognizant of the small number of eligible men on the premises.

Could it have been Chan? The idea struck her as ludicrous. Then again, Victoria had come to recognize an inescapable fact of life at Hunter's castle: Truly anything was possible.

* * *

It was disconcerting to see a stranger sitting at her desk.

"May I help you, ma'am?" the petite brunette inquired as she hung up the phone. Gone from the desk's surface was Victoria's wooden nameplate, in its place, a black and white plastic one that identified the perky usurper as Susan Stewart.

"Is Mr. Bowman available for a few minutes?"

"Mr. Bowman is in court all day. Did you have an appointment with him?"

"No, actually, I'm—"

"Victoria!" the familiar voice of Thatcher boomed out. "What a surprise!"

"On *all* counts," she replied, returning his hug of welcome and tilting her head just enough to acknowledge puzzlement about the unexpected newcomer seated behind her.

"Oh, this is Susan. Susan, Victoria." Thatch shifted his portfolio to beneath his other arm. "Susan's helping us out around the office while you're gone."

While it made sense for the firm to use temporary help, there remained the oddity that Elliott hadn't mentioned such a course of action to her. That and the first impression that Susan Stewart had settled in a tad too comfortably with her nameplate, mini-vase of silk flowers, and a few framed photographs of cherubic, dark-haired offspring.

"I'll be back before you know it," Victoria said, more for Susan's benefit than for Thatcher's.

"Not here to see Elliott, are you?" a puzzled Thatcher asked. "He's off at Superior on the Kiff case."

That the court date for one of Washington's more scandalous S&L episodes had already edged on to the firm's calendar without Victoria's even remembering it was a disturbing confirmation that she had been away from her real job for far too long. Under normal circumstances, of course, she would have had the courtroom number and even the presiding judge's name engraved on her brain for easy reference.

"I *was* hoping to catch him," she confessed. "A couple things have come up with his client."

"Nothing wrong, is there?"

"Just a few questions. Nothing that can't wait."

"Atta girl. Listen, I hate to run, but—"

"Don't let me hold you up," Victoria insisted, maintaining that her visit was just a whim of the moment and no cause for alarm. "How about John? Is he around?" To see one in the corridor or cafeteria without the other wasn't a normal occurrence.

"Took the day off," Thatch replied, "and you'll never believe how he's spending it." In response to Victoria's refusal to even guess, he supplied the answer. "Pricing out fifth wheels."

"What for?"

"Vagabond spirit," Thatcher shrugged. "He's got this bee in his bonnet that he wants to see the country and log a lot of miles before he cashes it in."

"Nothing wrong with that."

"Not if you don't mind traveling like a turtle with a house on your back." Thatcher smirked. "At least the models he's got an eye on are better than those aluminum ones that look like toasters with wheels."

"Excuse me, Mr. Williams." The temporary secretary waved to get his attention. "You were due in Mr. Cabrera's office ten minutes ago."

"We'll catch lunch next week," Thatch promised Victoria as he excused himself. "I want to hear all about how it's going out there."

"Would you like to leave a message for Mr. Bowman to call you tomorrow, ma'am?" Victoria's replacement asked.

Victoria thanked her but declined. "I'll get in touch with him at the end of the week," she said, reluctant to divulge to a total stranger that what she really wanted was to come home.

*   *   *

She had always liked the streets of Alexandria, meandering the cobblestone corridors that took her past pre–Revolutionary War mansions and upscale antique shops that catered to both novice and professional collectors. Spared by the ravages of the Union Army well over a century past, the tobacco seaport had been reborn into not only a trendy must-see for tourists but a comfortable homebase for the politically and culturally aware.

As she crossed the courtyards of city hall, the airy whimper of flutes and the rhythm of kettledrums drew her attention to a group of costumed Peruvian musicians who had set up a makeshift stage on the steps to entertain passersby. Just past the fountains, college students sporting T-shirts with a graphic depiction of government waste were distributing flyers, veritably thrusting them into the hands and against the chests of those who traversed their informal gauntlet. Across the street, a pink-haired little old lady was readjusting her purse, her aluminum walker, and the white and red plastic bag of Hallmark products she had just purchased.

So absorbed was Victoria in noticing the surroundings and the characters who currently peopled it that Deborah Sheddmoore was nearly at nose distance from her before she even realized she was there, much less that Deborah had been calling out her name for the last block.

"I *thought* that was you!" The blond greeted her with a boisterous, unrestrained enthusiasm usually associated with small dogs left home alone all day and eager for reunion with their masters. "How tremendous! How have you been?"

"You work in Alexandria?" Victoria queried in surprise. Even before the words were out of her mouth, she realized it was a stupid question to ask someone who was wearing a king's ransom in opals and gold. The Sheddmoore girl had probably never worked a day in her life.

Deborah tossed back her mane of hair and laughed.

"Just shopping til I drop," she replied. "What brings you here?"

"Chan and the limo," Victoria answered, a response that made Deborah laugh again. "Seriously," she said, "I had some errands and also wanted to check in with my office."

"Oh, that's right." Deborah nodded in remembrance. "You work for attorneys or something, don't you? That must be interesting."

"It has its moments, yes."

"Speaking of moments . . ." Deborah leaned in a little closer as if to confide a secret. "Stop me if I'm speaking out of turn."

"You haven't said anything yet."

An easy smile played on Deborah's full lips, rich with moist fuchsia to match the cowl of her sweater. "I understand that something happened with you and Hunter."

"Excuse me?"

"Sean likes to exaggerate a little," she continued, "but I'd heard the two of you had some kind of accident . . . ?"

Whatever excuse I give, Victoria thought to herself, *it's going to come out sounding worse than it is.* "Thanks for asking," she said instead. "Just a case of two left feet."

"Well, you couldn't ask for a better dancer," Deborah remarked. "That is, if you can ever get the man off a horse or out of a boardroom. Do you ride?" she asked.

Victoria shook her head.

"Too bad," Deborah sighed. "You're missing some great trails, especially up by the creek. And those horses of Hunter's? First-rate. Listen, I'm working up an appetite by standing here yakking. Want to get something?"

While the blond's dubious association with Sean Michael was reason enough to say no, Victoria nonetheless felt drawn to her, recognizing that Deborah's obvious familiarity with the family might yield answers to questions she couldn't comfortably ask of anyone else.

"Love to," Victoria replied. "Where do you want to go?"

17

"I *suppose there are stranger* ways a girl could meet people," Deborah blithely concluded after her story about the chance encounter that led her into a relationship with Sean Michael. "What matters is that it all works out in the end."

"And it didn't bother you," Victoria queried, "that he was buying jewelry for someone else?"

The tale Deborah shared with her over lunch fit the older Gleavy's personality like a glove—a rakish playboy lining up his next conquest before terminating the one he was already in. *Will she be so cavalier about it*, Victoria wondered, *when history repeats itself?*—for certainly with a man like Sean Michael the possibility was a strong one.

Deborah laughed as she slathered extra butter on her croissant. "Well, it wasn't like she was someone I actually *knew*. If there's one thing that's a no-no in my book, it's stealing a girlfriend's guy."

"I just meant about the part that he remembered you from the shop and tracked you down."

"Like a bloodhound." Deborah licked the ends of her fingers. "Flattering these days for a man to go to so much trouble."

Not if he's hot on the trail of a loaded bank account, Victoria thought, but kept it to herself. "Did you ever ask him about her?"

"Who?"

"The debutante."

"Old news, Vix."

Victoria inwardly cringed at the sound of one of her least favorite nicknames. Why did strangers always feel the compulsion to abbreviate long names to a more manageable form?

"Victoria," Victoria tactfully corrected her, lest the unwanted endearment take root in repetition.

"Sorry. Anyway, it's just one of those being-in-the-right-place love affairs. I guess it also didn't hurt much that she had one of those foreign last names with nine thousand syllables you can never pronounce right." Sean Michael, she clarified, liked things that were straightforward and simple. "So what about you?" she asked. "Single? Divorced? Heaven forbid, widowed?"

"Single," Victoria replied, her head still spinning at Sean Michael's ready trade of one girlfriend for another in the space of a week. Spinning as well that a girl who demonstrated at least some measure of depth had been so charmed by what Victoria saw as a well-polished macho routine.

"Single? That's getting as rare as virgins," Deborah remarked of Victoria's status, then apologized if she was coming across as vulgar. "Take me, for instance," she offered, "Daddy just dies if it ever comes up I was married before. Sort of like breaking a commandment or something." She took a deep sip of wine. "'Thou shalt not divorce' isn't even one of them, but you'd think so in *his* head."

Her candor amused Victoria. "How long were you married?" she asked, wondering what kind of husband Deborah Sheddmore had taken to the altar.

"Not as long as he's serving for white-collar crime," she replied.

Victoria thought for a moment that she was joking.

"Actually," Deborah continued, "Daddy had it anulled when the whole mess came up, so, technically, it probably doesn't even count."

"What does your father think of Sean Michael?"

"Oh, I'm sure he'd die if he knew. Probably want to lock me up in a convent or something until I came to my senses."

"He doesn't know that you're seeing him?"

Deborah laughed. "Well, I think he's got his little hopes up that it's Hunter I'm after. Why else would I be spending so much time out at the castle?"

Even though Deborah had spoken in jest, Victoria felt a short stab of unexplainable jealousy. "He *is* an attractive man," she observed.

"Too serious for my taste," Deborah shared. "I guess I just go for the bad guys, the wild-childs I can try to tame. It's a challenge, you know what I mean?" Deborah gazed off wistfully into space, lost for a moment in a private remembrance. "I guess it's like being told to stay off of motorcycles because they're dangerous but a part of you just craves having something that lethal between your legs."

Definitely fits Sean Michael, Victoria thought.

"The two of them sure don't get along, do they?" she casually tossed out as bait, hoping Deborah would volunteer an answer to the antagonism that existed between the cousins.

"Would *you*?" came the reply.

"Well, never having been in—"

Deborah was quick to interrupt. "Look, I'm not saying Sean walks on water or anything, but he *does* deserve a helluva better break than Hunter gave him for what happened."

"What do you mean?"

Deborah shook her head. "Sorry, kiddo. Don't even get me started on it. It's their problem to deal with, not ours."

"No, really," Victoria insisted, impatient to hear more, "I'm interested in what you think."

"What *I* think," Deborah said, "is that Hunter should've left well enough alone. I also think he should've left that castle in Ireland, great as it looks in the valley and all."

She was on the edge of learning something, Victoria could feel it. "Why do you think he moved it, then?" she asked. "I understand he tore down his other house?" Casual was the key to dealing with Deborah, Victoria had decided. If she appeared too anxious, she'd be left high and dry. Even worse, Deborah couldn't be trusted not to convey such curiosity to Sean Michael, touching off a chain reaction that would easily reverberate throughout the walls of Kriskerry Castle by dinnertime.

Deborah lazily soaked up the last of the Bernaise sauce with the end of her croissant. "Who knows?" the blond sighed. "When there's a woman behind it, men will do the damnedest things. . . ."

There was no clever way for her to pursue Deborah's cryptic remark, nor to segue back into it after the latter had changed the subject to her passion for horses and the world of racing. *She knows something*, Victoria's conscience taunted her. So, apparently, did Sean Michael, if his warning to her in the library carried any validity.

Deborah, of course, would be the easier of the two from whom to extract an explanation or a clue to the millionaire's past. It would just take time. The off-the-cuff hint that Hunter O'Hare's unorthodox actions involving Sir Patrick's estate had been influenced by a woman now thrust him into a new light in Victoria's opinion. A light that flashed yellow for extreme caution in dealing with him, particularly where her heart was concerned.

"Just listen to me!" Deborah laughed in mid-anecdote about Secretariat and Citation. "I could talk your ears off, couldn't I? And here you probably have nine thousand places you have to be."

Out of habit, Victoria looked at her watch, only then

realizing that the agreed-upon two hours had more than passed since Chan first let her off at the law firm. Was he still waiting for her? Or had he returned to Kriskerry Castle without her?

"We'll take a swing by and see," Deborah offered when Victoria voiced her dilemma. "If he's already gone, I can run you out there myself."

"I really don't want to be a bother." If worse came to worse, Victoria decided, she could take the Metro back to her apartment and pick up her own car. At least if she did that, she wouldn't be dependent on Hunter's chauffeur for her transportation needs.

"What's to bother?" Deborah countered. "Listen, I've got a hot date tonight and we can just start it a couple hours early. I'm sure that Sean Michael won't mind."

Deborah was already retrieving her purse off the floor and signaling for the waiter to bring them their check before Victoria could protest the woman's generosity.

A few moments later, the passenger view from the red Miata yielded no sign of the limo or its inscrutable driver. "A car that big," Deborah observed, "is hard to miss."

"Maybe I should call Hunter and just tell him what happened," Victoria proposed. She had, after all, promised to be gone only a few hours.

Deborah's laugh discounted any serious breach of conduct. "The way I drive," she promised, "we'll be pulling into the courtyard before he could even answer a second ring. Trust me."

Trust me. That was the problem, Victoria reminded herself as she acquiesced to Deborah's suggestion of driving on out sans phone call. As much as she had to offer in friendship—and as openly as she had warmed to Victoria from the very start—there still existed that nagging recognition of where Deborah's true loyalty resided. Anything Victoria might say would go straight from her lips to Sean Michael's ears.

"So what's it like working for attorneys?" Deborah

inquired, content to fill up their driving time with innocuous chatter. "Is it as much fun as it looks on television?"

My mother would love this woman, Victoria decided.

Mrs. Maginn stepped out to meet them with the smug satisfaction of someone who had just learned a damaging secret.

"So you've come back again," the housekeeper said as if their return to the castle hadn't been expected or particularly welcome.

Victoria couldn't help but exchange a glance with Deborah, unsure of whether the remark's caustic slant was intended for herself or Sean Michael's current girlfriend.

"Did we miss anything?" Victoria pleasantly asked.

"You're to be seein' himself at once and with no delay," Mrs. Maginn crisply informed her. "He said so."

Her remark put Victoria instantly on guard. "Nothing's wrong, is there?"

Mrs. Maginn's thin lips pursed, and behind her glasses there glittered a sparkle of undefined malevolence. "Sure an' it's all dependin' on what *side* a body's on."

"Excuse me?"

"It's not for *me* to be judgin' it," Mrs. Maginn proclaimed.

"Want me to go with you?" Deborah offered, as puzzled as Victoria about what was unfolding.

Appreciative of the offer and yet annoyed that Deborah assumed she sought safety in numbers against a bedridden invalid, Victoria declined. As she hurried down the corridor toward Hunter's room, she could feel Mrs. Maginn's eyes boring into her, relishing the fact that she knew something Victoria clearly didn't.

The sight of his empty bed caught Victoria off guard. Not nearly as much, though, as the sound of his voice from around the corner when she stepped into the room.

"And where the hell have *you* been?" he challenged

her, looking up from the book that had held his attention prior to her arrival.

Momentarily stunned by the sight of him standing in his bathrobe at the bookcase with the aid of the metal cane, Victoria nearly missed the anger that underscored his address. "I was in town," she replied. "You knew that."

Hunter snapped the book shut with his free hand and laid it on the table. "And *you* knew," he retorted, "that I needed you back here as soon as you finished your errands."

So that's why Mrs. Maginn was so pleased, Victoria thought. *Nothing like a good transgression to make her day.* "If this is about Chan—"

"No, Victoria," he sharply interrupted her, "it's about trust. When I gave you permission to take a couple of hours off—"

"*Permission*?" Victoria echoed, as confused as she was perturbed that he was displaying so much hostility toward her for coming back late. "Excuse me, Mr. O'Hare, but if you're familiar at all with labor laws in the state of Virginia—"

Sean Michael's distinctive laughter from the doorway made her stop in midsentence.

"What do *you* want?" Hunter snapped at him.

"Besides being entertained by a good fight? Actually, I was looking for Deborah," he said, inclining his head toward Victoria. "I saw her car outside."

"Deborah's here?" Hunter inquired, his tone softening just enough to be noticeable. "You didn't say so."

"We got delayed at lunch and she brought me back," Victoria replied, wondering how her presence could possibly make any difference.

"So what have you done with her?" Sean Michael asked playfully. "I'll find her, you know, wherever you've hidden her."

"She was talking to Mrs. Maginn," Victoria said.

In the awkward silence that followed Sean Michael's

departure, Victoria found herself looking everywhere except at the man who had so hotly contested her absence from the castle. Why, she wondered, *did her association with Deborah suddenly grant her a reprieve from his anger? Unless—*

"I guess I owe you an apology," he said at last. "When Chan came back without you and told me that you didn't show up when you said you would, the first thought that went through my head was that you had decided—"

He left the thought unfinished.

Victoria took a guess at what his thought might have been and responded to it. "When I make a commitment to something, Mr. O'Hare, I honor it to the end."

His cool gray eyes met hers. "So do I, Ms. Cameron. On that, at least, we're agreed."

18

"He'll *be catchin' the devil* from the doctor, don't you know," Mrs. Pritchard confidentially prophesied as she diced chicken for the casserole she was making.

Victoria caught herself nodding in agreement at the latest incident involving the millionaire's knee. Hunter's zealousness for mobility in the two days following his blowup at her had subsequently cost him a trip to the hospital for X rays. Chan had driven him, Victoria learned.

"Men are a funny lot," Mrs. P continued, her body bouncing in rhythm to her chopping. "Take my Welshman, rest his soul."

"Funny in what way?"

The cook's face split into its customary grin of satisfaction. "Strong as an ox and stubborn as a bull, but let the dear catch a whiff of the shivers and he was helpless as a babe. Sure, they're *all* like that, the silly lambs. Like a brick on the outside and a puddin' within."

The comparison, Victoria thought to herself, didn't match Hunter's constitution or attitude whatsoever, much as Mrs. Pritchard seemed to think that her observation was true of the entire male species. Certainly from what Victoria had seen firsthand of her employer, the man could be encased in a full body cast and still have the energy to raise hell with anyone who crossed him. If his sharp-tongued attack so early in the week had been roused by a little accidental tardiness, fortune had better protect those foolish enough to dare a *deliberate* slight of his omnipotence. Exactly *why* he had been so angry about her absence, of course, was still as much a mystery to her as why the mention of Deborah Sheddmoore had suddenly absolved her of wrongdoing.

Polite to a fault, Victoria temporarily shelved her annoyance with him to listen to the cook's reminiscences of her late husband. "Is Ian anything like his father?" she asked at one point to show she was paying attention.

Mrs. Pritchard picked up a broad knife to slide the contents of her cutting board into a bowl. "Don't I wish that he were!" she wistfully sighed. "He's like a wood sprite sometimes, don't you know." The allusion escaped Victoria, prompting Mrs. P to explain. "Sure, he's comin' and goin' as soft as a breeze and yourself not any the wiser. It's the horses, though," she said in a hush. "It's the horses that make Ian what he is."

"And what's that?" Victoria asked.

"Now don't you be laughin' to hear it, lass," Mrs. Pritchard prefaced her response, "but they talk to him as clear as I'm talkin' to you."

"I beg your pardon?"

The cook repeated exactly what Victoria had thought she heard the first time. "I swear it on my Welshman's grave."

"Oh, really?" Victoria said, wondering whether the whereabouts of Elvis or the existence of UFOs were among the many topics Hunter's thoroughbreds discussed with the cook's only son.

"Sure, it's why himself brought Ian over to stay in spite of the trouble."

It was a statement that begged the obvious query. "What trouble was that, Mrs. P?"

Mrs. Pritchard either missed the question en route to

the refrigerator or chose not to answer it. "It was the labor, I think," she said. "Thirty hours it was to the minute and my Welshman prayin' all the while for the priest to be gettin' there to give me last rites."

It took Victoria a moment to realize that Mrs. Pritchard was discussing Ian's difficult debut into the world as a baby and not his immigration to the United States as an adult.

"He's a good boy," Mrs. P finally finished her child-birth story, replete with more details than Victoria felt necessary or in good taste. "And if he's a wee bit slow," she went on, "then all the more's the blessin' he has to be knowin' the horses so well."

"I'm sure Mr. O'Hare appreciates that your son is so skilled at working with them."

"You can't *learn* a thing like that," Mrs. Pritchard declared of her offspring's talent for communicating with animals. "Not with a beastie like Paladdin."

"One of Mr. O'Hare's horses?" Victoria asked, helping herself to an apple from the centerpiece bowl.

"Sir Patrick's before that," the cook proudly replied. "Big as a house and a heart as black as his mane. Like saddlin' the wind, Sir Patrick used to say."

"A racehorse?" Victoria inquired.

Mrs. P vigorously shook her head. "Too hot a temper to ride 'round a track. Himself tried, don't you know."

"So what happened to him?"

"Well, himself said the next best thing was to breed him, bring him to America."

"So that's what he did?"

"Not without his Roxilaine," Mrs. Pritchard replied, building to the denouement of her story. "Ian told himself so, just as Paladdin told *him*."

"I'm afraid you've lost me," Victoria confessed, puzzled by the introduction of a new name to the narrative.

"The gray mare," Mrs. P proclaimed as if the answer were obvious. "They've a bond, those two, and there it is."

Roxilaine, it seemed, was an older horse with whom the high-spirited Paladdin had an attachment. Separated by an ocean from her—even briefly—Paladdin had fallen into the equine equivalent of severe depression. Ian, Mrs. Pritchard said, had proved the horse's godsend by simply telling Hunter that he needed to send to Ireland right away for the docile Roxilaine or risk losing his prize stud to a broken heart.

"And he's been fine ever since?" Victoria asked, quietly dubious that Ian had heard such a request straight from the horse's mouth.

"Fine as he *could* be away from home," Mrs. Pritchard sighed. The way she said it sounded as if she considered Palladin's residence in Hunter's stables a temporary one.

"Isn't *this* his home now?" Victoria suggested. Perhaps, of course, Hunter had plans to send him elsewhere. Maybe that's what Mrs. P had meant.

"Sure, we're *all* fish out of water, don't you know," Mrs. Pritchard retorted, shaking her head in dismay. "And Sir Patrick himself rollin' in his grave if—" The cook stopped short of finishing her remark. "Beggars can't be choosers," she said instead. "And there it is."

An odd conversation, Victoria thought to herself, *but a telling one in its own way*. Even the jovial Mrs. Pritchard, it seemed, had a reason to dislike her employer for taking away something irreplaceable.

Their roots.

With Jon Tapping's visit less than two weeks away, Victoria had more than enough to keep her busy—and to keep her mind off of Hunter and the dichotomy of emotions he could generate inside of her. *Concentrate on work*, she told herself. Mr. O'Hare was only a client to whom she owed a good job, nothing more.

Yet even when he was away from the castle, Victoria still felt his presence in the room where he had spent most of his time since her arrival. It had to be difficult, she thought, for a man so accustomed to power and control to have to depend—even for the short term—on other people.

That one of those other people also wanted to see him dead as a doornail and castrated with hedge clippers was disconcerting enough.

As she booted up the computer to update the correspondence he had requested, Victoria found herself making a mental list of suspects.

Sean Michael and his sister were too obvious as candidates, she determined. The death of their wealthy cousin, after all, would rob them of a comfortable living for which neither one had to work. While they might not like Hunter's control of the family purse strings, it wouldn't benefit them to end the arrangement with a murder.

Ian? So far, Victoria assessed him, his only quirk was a lack of oxygen to the brain during childbirth and an alleged aptitude for talking to horses. Oh yes, her conscience added, not to leave out his infatuation with Peggy Gleavy. What had Deborah said at lunch? That men did the damnedest things where women were involved? Just how much influence Peggy actually had on the smitten stableboy remained, of course, to be seen.

Victoria found her thoughts returning to the conversation with Mrs. Pritchard. Certainly, if the cook could voice an expression of homesickness, she could easily be speaking for the rest of the Irish staff. Nilly, in particular, would have felt the greatest discord at not only losing a beloved master but finding himself in a strange country. Would the unhappiness and sense of isolation, Victoria wondered, be enough to push him into a criminal act he felt was justified?

As Thatcher himself had once wryly remarked about an elderly serial killer, "There comes a time when a life sentence for murder isn't that intimidating a price for dispatching a thorn in one's side."

Much as Victoria hated to think it, the same could apply to Sir Patrick's unwaveringly loyal valet.

The bedside telephone rang, startling her out of her reverie about castle conspirators. Hunter's private line, she noticed. The one he had told her was for his exclusive use. Which meant, she realized, that no one else was going to pick it up and answer it.

On the bright side, maybe it was Elliott. It could also be Hunter, calling to remind her to do something.

"Hello?" she said.

No one spoke at the other end of the line and yet she could tell by the hint of breathing that someone was there.

"Hello?" she repeated.

"Is this Mr. O'Hare's number?" a woman's voice tentatively inquired.

"Yes, it is. May I help you?"

The woman paused before replying. "Is he there?" she asked.

"I'm sorry," Victoria apologized, "but I'm afraid Mr. O'Hare isn't available to take a call at the moment. Would you like to leave a message for him to get back to you?"

"Do you know if he's already on his way?" The tone had shifted to one of anxiety.

A business caller, Victoria thought, would have identified who she was. "Just a moment and I'll check his schedule for you," she said. "What office again did you say you were with?"

"Oh, no, that's okay," the woman hastily replied to the offer. "His car just pulled up."

She was gone before Victoria could even get her name.

It was irrational, of course, still to be dwelling on something that wasn't any of her business. It was Hunter's castle and he could get telephone calls from whomever he wanted. Even other women.

The fact that he didn't return until almost early evening and was in a more cheerful mood than when he had left only added fuel to the burning question in Victoria's head of what his private life was like.

"How was your visit to the doctor?" Victoria conversationally inquired, looking up from the book she was reading by the parlor fire.

"Enough to cover his next winter vacation," Hunter replied, shedding his raincoat with Chan's able assistance. "You'd think I was the man's only patient."

Victoria tactfully refrained from observing that he would *have* to have been the doctor's only patient to take up an entire day for his appointment. If, of course, that was really where he had been.

"So what's the verdict on your leg?" she inquired. As much as he grumbled about using the ugly metal cane, he seemed to be managing it well enough.

"Not ready to audition for the Rockettes," he said with a shrug, "but it shouldn't stop me from having dinner."

"With the family?" Even as the last word slipped out of her lips, Victoria knew it was the wrong one. The household at Kriskerry Castle was just about the farthest thing from fitting the traditional definition.

The laugh lines crinkled around Hunter's eyes.

"Actually," he said, "I was thinking of something else."

"And what's that?"

He hesitated a moment, as if it suddenly occurred to him that he hadn't completely thought through what he was about to propose. "Getting out today reminded me of how much I'm suffering from cabin fever."

"And you're not even in a cabin," Victoria pointed out.

"Castle fever then," he corrected himself. "And I think I've just thought of a cure."

Victoria tilted her head in question.

Hunter cleared his throat. "How would you like to have dinner with me?"

19

That *she was sitting* in the sepia-tint dining room of the Benedict Inn across from a man who could so casually tilt her equilibrium with a single glance was the kind of scenario Marcine Cameron would have loved. A pro like Marcine, though, would have handled it with greater aplomb than Victoria was currently managing. *What am I doing here?* she kept asking herself, knowing that she could have been eating Mrs. P's chicken casserole, deflecting Sean Michael's amorous advances, and suffering Peggy's barbed remarks instead if she had only exercised more willpower in the parlor.

Twice since sitting down she had nearly knocked over her wine glass, the second time barely preventing the domino effect of taking out a candlestick as well. Conscious of the occasional glance of other diners, it didn't occur to her until after the seafood and mushroom appetizers that her faux pas weren't as much the object of public curiosity as the other guests' recognition of the handsome companion sharing her table. *Who's the klutz with him?* she could imagine them saying.

It's only a dinner, her conscience reminded her. A dinner with someone who could influence Wall Street, receive death threats on a regular basis, dally with secret

women, and still have the energy to talk sports and foreign films. Absorbed in topics of his own choosing,
Hunter O'Hare was oblivious to the fact that almost
every couple in the restaurant was engaged in some level
of romantic tête-à-tête.

The romantic ambience, however, had not escaped
Victoria, leaving her to wonder why he had chosen this
restaurant for a business meal with his secretary—a
secretary with whom he argued more often than he
agreed.

"We'll just grab something at a little spot I know," he
had offered on the heels of his invitation.

The "little spot" he had in mind turned out to be a place
that consistently garnered its full share of Triple-A rating
stars and a premium slot on the respected Merriam list of
"Quality B&B's in America." Even Marinda Rugg, food crit-
ic for the *Washington Post*, had ranked the inn's cuisine as
well worth a trip to the East Coast.

Nestled on a Virginia knoll about five miles from the
nearest town, the Benedict Inn dated from the late 1700s.
George Washington, a brass plaque in the corner proclaimed, had once stopped there to take refreshment on
a summer day.

High-backed wooden chairs, pewter plates, and a
stout black cooking pot hanging in the stone fireplace
recalled an era when patriots met in secret to plot the
direction of a fledgling country. A thirteen-star flag, yel-
lowed from age but reverently displayed, reminded
restaurant patrons of the hard fight for liberty.

It was a theme cleverly repeated in the food servers'
Quaker costumes and the framed embroidery samplers
on the walls that depicted early colonial life. The burnished ale tankards, she noticed, even hung from the
walls on square nails.

Though she had never personally seen the two upper
floors of the Federal-style building, Victoria had read
once that they were modernized to B&B standards for

twentieth-century guests and yet retained the flavor of the inn's early times.

I should come back here and stay sometime with a significant other, Victoria made a mental note. That her first exposure to the inn at all was with a man like Hunter O'Hare was an irony she would not long forget. As Marcine would say if she were there, who'd have thought?

"In spite of her stealing my housekeeper," Hunter was facetiously remarking, "Maria's a hundred percent class act. She would have been foolish *not* to go to work for her."

"You didn't mind losing her, then?" Victoria inquired, more than a little surprised to hear that the same servant who used to manage Hunter's household had transferred to a post with a celebrity newswoman.

"Of *course* I minded," Hunter chuckled, "but do you really think I'd put up much fight with a lady married to the Terminator?"

He was opening up to her in a way that Victoria hadn't expected, discussing the times she herself had labeled "B.C."

"That must have been hard for you to start over with a whole new staff," she commented. "When the Irish came, I mean."

"Not any harder than selling out old stock and buying something new," he replied.

The waitress interrupted to serve their spinach salads.

Victoria waited until after the girl left to continue. "Do you think it might be one of *them* sending the notes?" she suggested. It was an idea she had been toying with for the past few days.

"Who are we talking about?"

"Your former staff," Victoria clarified. "From what I gather, no one was very happy with the new arrangement."

"Actually, it was a pretty amicable parting," Hunter corrected her. "You can always count on some degree of turnover in work like that. Domestic. For most of them, the time had probably come to move on to something else."

His gray eyes met hers over a fork full of salad. "What made you ask if I thought it was one of the servants?"

Victoria shrugged. "Just tapping all the possibilities," she said, knowing that "intuition" would never suffice as an answer in Hunter's estimation. "Chan seems to like what *he's* doing," she observed.

"Speaking of Tapping," Hunter artfully changed the subject, "are we all squared away for his visit?"

"Even down to a list of sights to see," she replied.

"By the time he gets here," Hunter remarked, indicating his leg, "the two of you may be hard pressed to keep up with me."

"So everything was okay with the doctor?"

"As fine as it was the *last* time you asked me," he said. "Thank you for the concern."

What Victoria had hoped would be a logical lead-in to how he had spent his day besides getting X rays wasn't turning out the way she wanted at all. "Oh, I almost forgot," she said, finally favoring the direct approach, "you got a phone call while you were out."

"From whom?"

"A woman," Victoria replied. "She didn't give a name."

"Well," Hunter shrugged, "if it was important, I'm sure she'll call back."

Try as she might over the course of their dinner to mention the phone call again, Victoria's efforts were unsuccessful.

The candles had melted down noticeably, but Hunter seemed in no hurry to call it an evening, calling instead for another refill of their coffee cups.

"There's something that really puzzles me," Victoria said.

"And what's that?"

"Sir Patrick was your great-grandfather, right?"

"Right."

"And yet he's only a grandfather to your cousins."

Hunter lazily stirred in his cream and sugar. "I was wondering when you were going to ask that," he said. "It's confusing to *most* people when they first hear it."

"I'm all ears."

"Well, to start out with, 'cousins' was about the nicest euphemism you can apply to a situation like theirs."

"A euphemism for what?"

Hunter winked. "Little bastards."

Victoria wasn't sure whether he was referring to their birth status or just their obnoxious personalities.

Hunter continued. "You'd have to have known Sir Patrick, I guess, to understand why things happened the way they did."

"And did you?"

"Did I what?"

"Know Sir Patrick. I mean, did you ever meet him?" For some reason, Victoria was under the impression that Hunter's inheritance wasn't the result of some deep-seated affection between the two.

"Twice," he replied. "The first time, I was just a kid, maybe ten or so. All I really remember of it was a grumpy guy who looked like Lon Chaney in a bathrobe and had a brandy glass permanently grafted to his right palm. Anyway, my father took me along on a business trip to Ireland to meet him. More so, though, to try and mend fences." Hunter thoughtfully sipped his coffee and decided it needed more doctoring.

Victoria leaned in on her elbows. "Mend fences?" she echoed.

Hunter smiled. "I'm getting ahead of myself," he apologized. "The real story starts back when my grandfather was born. That'd be 1905."

Saddened by the death of his young wife in childbirth but elated by the joy of an infant son, Patrick literally swore on the family Bible that his namesake would never know want or hardship.

"It was an easy enough pledge to make at the time,"

Hunter explained, "seeing as how Patrick and his ancestors had gotten rich off of having the poor work their lands for next to nothing in pay. By the time my grandfather was old enough to become a landlord himself, he was also smart—and compassionate—enough to see that he didn't want any part of it."

"So what did he do?"

"Why, what every red-blooded Irishman with a dream would do under the circumstances—take off for a land where he could be his own person instead of his father's son."

Not six months after arriving in Boston in 1925, Patrick junior had not only found himself a bride but a job in a shirtwaist factory. "Long hours, miserable pay," Hunter said, "but he kept consoling himself with the fact that fortunes could be made if a person just hung in there long enough."

"And did he make it?" Victoria asked, for certainly Hunter's own holdings had been built on earlier acquisitions.

"Unfortunately, no," Hunter replied, with a wistful catch in his voice. "There was such a rift between him and his father that he didn't even write to tell him when he and Annie had a baby boy, my father."

Annie, however, had a heart clearly more forgiving than her husband's and wrote to tell him of the birth.

"My grandfather hit the roof when Sir Patrick started writing to them, begging them to come home," Hunter went on. "He gave Annie strict instructions to burn any letters that arrived from Ireland."

Thoroughly hooked on the tale Hunter was weaving, Victoria inquired if the young Boston wife had followed the instructions.

"She must have been a lot like you," Hunter remarked. "She wasn't about to let someone dictate against what her heart thought was right." Confident that time would eventually heal the wounds, Annie took care to hide all of Sir Patrick's letters, never opening them but storing them away in a trunk until such time as her husband might be ready to read their contents.

"What she never realized, of course, was that Sir Patrick had been sending money in all of those envelopes so that their lives might be a little easier."

"Never realized?" Victoria echoed.

"Not until my grandfather died. My father must have been about fourteen when it happened. That's when Annie finally decided that the unopened letters should be brought out so that he'd at least know he had a grandfather back in Ireland who cared about him. To make a long story short," Hunter said, "there was enough over the course of fourteen years to not only put him through college but get him started in his first enterprise."

There was an obvious piece missing from the Horatio Alger narrative. "That still doesn't explain Sean Michael and Peggy," Victoria reminded him. "Where do *they* fit into all of this?"

Hunter studied his coffee cup a moment before answering. "Sir Patrick was devastated when he heard that his only son had died and not even on Irish soil. That's probably when he first started drinking, to kill some of the pain. Apparently, he also found solace in one of his own employees, an upstairs maid named Katie. Well, one thing led to another and Katie turned up pregnant with Sir Patrick's child."

Victoria was beginning to see where the story was going but waited patiently for O'Hare to continue it at his own pace.

"The decent thing, of course," he said, "would have been to marry her. If rumors are true, he even offered to do just that if she bore him a son."

"To take the place of the one he had lost?"

"Presumably. At any rate, she had a daughter instead, which nixed the whole deal."

Disappointed in the gender outcome but nonetheless adoring, Sir Patrick had continued to voluntarily provide for mother and child while disclaiming any legal responsibility.

"Things came to a head," Hunter explained, "when the girl—grown to womanhood—decided to run off with a married playboy from Monte Carlo and have his children. And that," he toasted with his coffee cup, "is where we get my cousins."

"At least Sir Patrick acknowledged them enough to put them in his will," Victoria pointed out.

"Only by default. With his daughter such a disappointment to him, it only stood to reason that her offspring would follow suit."

"But what about Katie?" Victoria inquired. "She must have meant something to him that he'd keep her around."

"Keep her around as a *servant*," Hunter corrected her. "Bearer of Sir Patrick's child or not, she was still an upstairs maid. That is, until she threw herself off the east parapet one day."

Victoria gasped. "Suicide?"

"I don't think she was *dusting* it. Anyway, after meeting him myself, I can't say that I blame her. He was pretty hard-ass and not very pleasant."

His remark jogged an earlier comment. "You said you had met him twice. When was the second time?"

Hunter paused a moment before answering. "I flew back a couple months before he died," he said.

"He had sent for you?" In light of the circumstances of O'Hare's inheriting Sir Patrick's wealth, it only made sense to Victoria that the old man must have summoned him to make his wishes known while he was still alive.

"No," Hunter replied. "I was actually back there because—" He shook his head without completing the explanation, adding only a passing comment that it wasn't that important. "Looks like they're trying to close this place," he remarked when he spoke again, calling Victoria's attention to the fact that they were the only couple left in the dining room. "What do you say we call it a night?"

20

"*You were easier to keep up* with when you were immobile," Victoria remarked, having tracked Hunter down out at the stables on the first November day without rain. With Tapping's flight due in at National Airport within the hour, she would have expected him to either have ridden with Chan or been back at the castle doing paperwork.

"I still can't take the stairs," he pointed out, leaning on the fence as he watched Ian work with the thoroughbreds. "Have I been missing anything?"

"You mean just now or upstairs?" Victoria queried, thankful that Hunter didn't possess the power to read her mind. If he could, he would have easily discovered that thoughts of him had assumed a prominent place ever since their dinner at the Benedict Inn. Ever the engima, he had nevertheless changed in his attitude toward her since that night, almost as if divulging his family's past had opened a door to the future, a future in which she might play a larger part than just his secretary.

No kiss on the cheek, no hand at the waist, no promise of another date. None of the customary things, in fact, that typified the beginning of a relationship. And yet in the days that followed, Victoria noticed he seemed more eager for her company, more insistent that they take meals together. Was he beginning to trust her with more than his business secrets? Maybe even his heart?

"I assume," Hunter commented, "that Peggy is still keeping you awake at night?"

"Do you think she'd be embarrassed if she knew I could hear her?"

"Peggy?" Hunter chuckled. "Probably not. She and Sean Michael are basic exhibitionists. Anything that will get them a little attention, they'll put their full store of energy into."

Victoria's eyes looked out toward the skinny stable hand, currently attentive to a delicate-looking gray horse that had to be Paladdin's companion, Roxilaine. "Do you really think that it's Ian she's involved with?" she asked Hunter. The more that she seemed to learn about Mrs. P's son, the less likely a liaison seemed with the Gleavy girl.

"What I think," he said, "is that Peggy would be involved with anything that shaved and had pants on."

"But what would an affair with Ian get for her?" Victoria went on, having determined some time ago that both Peggy and her brother never went into anything unless it would net them some kind of significant gain. As a servant, much less a slow one, Ian presented nothing tangible, not even sex appeal.

Hunter shrugged off the question. "Who knows why she does anything? Ian *is* good with the horses, though. I'll give him that much."

Victoria broached a question that had been on her mind for quite a while. "So what kind of trouble was he in back in Ireland?"

Hunter arched a brow. "Who told you he'd been in trouble?"

"A credible source," Victoria replied. "His mother."

"Call it a bout with bad company, then. Splitting the country certainly didn't help matters."

"What about now, though? Has it all been cleared up?"

A melancholy frown flitted across his features. "His employment here isn't exactly legal," was all Hunter offered. "I'm doing what I can to take care of it."

"So how many people know about it?" If Victoria were to guess, it was an easy assumption that Mrs. Pritchard had already confided the trouble to her kitchen cohort, Nilly.

"As of this moment," Hunter gravely replied, "one more than probably *should* know."

It was an offhand reference to her own integrity, a slight that Victoria found uncalled for.

"I'd never say anything," she said, but Hunter's attention was already diverted to something new beyond the fence. "Now *there's* a sight to behold," he remarked.

Victoria looked out just in time to see a beautiful copper-colored horse with black mane clear the far fence. It was the blond rider, though, who took Victoria's immediate notice.

Deborah Sheddmoore.

"You think I should add her to my stable?" Hunter remarked.

Victoria couldn't resist responding that she thought Deborah would be happier living in the castle. "Oh, you mean the *horse*," she pretended to correct herself. Hunter smirked at her.

Deborah cantered the horse up to the fence, waving an enthusiastic hello to Victoria. "Well," she said to Hunter, "made up your mind yet?"

"Hard to say. I'd hate to break the two of you up."

"We are quite the pair, aren't we?" she laughed as she effortlessly dismounted and offered the horse a treat from her jacket pocket.

"One of the better matches I've seen you with lately," Hunter replied, leaving no doubt in his tone that he was referring to her human companions.

Deborah, of course, picked up on it and tossed a casual aside to Victoria. "Makes you want to just bury a rusty ax in his little head, doesn't it?" she sighed. "So, Hunter darling, are you going to take her or do I have to tell Daddy you're waffling?"

"We'll settle it over drinks," Hunter informed her. "Besides, we already have a gentlemen's agreement."

"Speaking of gentlemen," Deborah said, "has Sean Michael come back?"

"I didn't know that he'd left."

"We're going to a matinee at the Kennedy Center this afternoon," she told Victoria.

"I assume you're springing for the tickets?" Hunter inquired.

"Why not? He's springing for the *dessert*."

Hunter rolled his eyes. "Spare me the details."

Ian had joined them by now to take the reins from Deborah and lead the horse away.

"Let's do lunch again soon," Deborah insisted to Victoria as Hunter let her out the gate.

"Sounds fine to me." At least, Victoria thought, it would be an opportunity to ask a few more questions.

"What do you think of her?" Hunter asked as they watched Deborah walk back to the castle, her blond hair bouncing on the breeze.

"Reminds me a little bit of Fergie," Victoria offered in comparison. "Definitely on the outrageous side."

What she didn't volunteer was that meeting Deborah and getting to know who she was had, ironically, tempered some of her own dark suspicions toward Sean Michael. Obviously not in the relationship with him for money or power, Deborah's open affection for someone so rakish and deceitful was in conflict with the otherwise level-headed attitude that Deborah Sheddmoore possessed toward life.

"'Outrageous' isn't the half of it," Hunter countered. "Her father's got his hands full just trying to manage her sometimes."

"How do you think he'll react if he ever finds out about Sean Michael?"

Hunter's reply wasn't what she expected. "Oh, he's known about it from the beginning," he remarked. "I told him."

Baffled, Victoria was slow to offer a comment on it. Slow enough for Hunter to make one of his own.

"He'd have done the same for me," he said with a cavalier shrug.

Why was it, she wondered, that whenever she felt she was getting close to understanding him, Hunter O'Hare would do a complete turnabout on her?

It was noble, she thought, that he was trying to square Ian's reputation and keep him from being deported. On the other hand, it was pretty despicable of him to meddle in Deborah's love life, even if her father *was* playing it cool and feigning ignorance. All of which, she realized, posed a tricky problem in her own future encounters with the Sheddmoore girl, pretending that Hunter had never said a word.

She had left him out by the stables and in the company of his beloved horses. Falling back on the excuse of files to attend to, Victoria found herself needing a respite from a man whose grand purpose in life seemed to lie in keeping other people guessing. *At least I'll be out of here in a few more weeks*, she reminded herself.

In a few more weeks, her life would get back to normal.

Victoria nearly laughed out loud even as she thought it, reminded of Marcine's frequently voiced conjecture that "normal" was a sad state for anyone to aspire to. "Hollywood's an oyster, darling," she'd say, "and most people don't even know what one *looks* like! Be thankful that you're on the inside."

Had it not been for the influence of her father, Victoria might well have grown to adulthood never knowing there were zip codes outside of LA.

It was a marriage that could have worked, Victoria liked to fantasize, if Marcine Cameron had never been discovered. Married right out of high school to the campus star athlete, their beginnings were the stuff of suburban America, complete with a picket fence and a wood-sided station wagon. A local talent contest, though, had suddenly thrust the senior high beauty queen into an acting contract, a contract that eventually led to more stardom than anyone might have predicted.

Where it left her husband was a spot on the sidelines, just out of sight.

With Marcine at rehearsals all day and dead tired at night, Victoria had consequently spent her early years by her father's side. Mindful that he loved her mother very much but equally sure he would've been happier pumping gas or slinging hash, Victoria often wondered what kept them together until his death the summer she turned thirteen. "A fairy tale's fine to live in now and then," he used to tell her in reference to Marcine's adoration of the camera, "but reality's where the real living is."

It was her father who posed questions like, "Were the seven dwarves covered by workers' comp insurance in the event of a mine collapse? Were criminal charges ever pressed against the evil queen for attempted murder with a spinning wheel? Did Cinderella ever seriously dance in slippers made of glass?" She could thank her father for the sense of humor he had instilled in her, as well as the encouragement to look beyond the Hollywood Hills for her own dream.

So here I am in a medieval castle with a bunch of loony servants, a psychotic note-writer and a brooding prince, she thought to herself. *If only Dad could see me now. ...*

The sound of Mrs. Maginn's voice at Hunter's door startled her back to reality, such as it was.

"Shall we be servin' dinner at the usual time?" she addressed Victoria.

"I don't see why not," Victoria replied. "I'm sure Mr.

Tapping will be hungry after his flight when he gets here."

"Sure an' he's got a big job ahead of him, don't you know," Mrs. Maginn observed.

She's baiting me again, Victoria recognized. "Yes, well, that's what lawyers get paid the megabucks for," she flippantly replied.

"You think he'll be successful, then?" the housekeeper inquired.

"I'm sure Hunter expects no less." Victoria picked up the day's delivery of mail, hoping that the act of indifference to her presence would send Mrs. Maginn on her way to annoy someone else.

"It'll be better to be sendin' him back," Mrs. Maginn matter-of-factly continued. "Sure an' that's what he's here for?"

"Hmmm?" Victoria continued what she was doing without looking up, knowing that it was driving Mrs. Maginn to total frustration.

Mrs. Maginn cleared her throat. "Sure an' it's the talk of the house," she impatiently informed Victoria.

Whatever talk it is, Victoria thought, *the housekeeper herself was sure to have started it*. "And what talk is that, Mrs. Maginn?"

"About Ian, don't you know?"

Victoria started to reply but was distracted at that moment by the sight of a familiar parchment envelope sandwiched among the rest in her hand. "I think if you have questions, Mrs. Maginn," she said, "you should take them up with Mr. O'Hare."

Had the housekeeper caught the change in her voice? Or was it the way she had hastily slid the envelope beneath the others to deal with when she was alone? Whatever the clue, Mrs. Maginn's thin lips melted into an evil smile. "They'll not be stoppin'," she said, tilting her head toward the mail that Victoria was holding. "Not until himself is dead as Sir Patrick."

Victoria maintained a cool she didn't feel, already dreading what the latest arrival might contain, the latest threat to Hunter's existence and body parts. "Oh?" she replied. "And what do *you* know about it?"

"Enough to be lockin' my door at night," Mrs. Maginn answered with the grim satisfaction of someone who had an advantage.

The arrival of Hunter at that moment coincided with the ring of the private line on the bedside telephone. Being the closest, Victoria picked it up, hoping that Hunter had heard enough of the end of their conversation that she wouldn't have to repeat it to him.

"Hello?" a woman's voice said. "Is Mr. O'Hare there?"

It was the same voice, Victoria was certain of it. The same voice that had asked if he was on his way the day he had supposedly gone to see his doctor.

"Yes, just a minute," Victoria replied. "May I tell him who's calling?"

Hunter, however, was already within steps of the phone himself. "Never mind," he said, "I'll take it."

Victoria maneuvered out of his way as he reached for the receiver. Mrs. Maginn, she noticed, had already vacated the room. I should do the same myself out of courtesy, she thought to herself, though natural curiosity compelled her to take particularly slow steps doing it.

"Oh, my God!" she heard a shocked Hunter gasp into the phone. "When did it happen?"

Victoria turned, frozen on the spot as she listened to him, conscious that he knew she was there and yet was making no sign of shooing her away. All color drained from his face, Hunter was firing off questions, questions that made no sense whatsoever to Victoria. "I'm on my way right now," he promised the caller, slamming down the receiver as an expletive exploded from his lips.

"What is it?" Victoria asked. "What's—"

"Get Chan!" he barked at her. "Tell him to bring the limo around."

Had the impact of bad news made him forget that his chauffeur was at National Airport? "He's picking up Tapping," she reminded him. "He won't be back for at least—"

"Then I'll drive *myself*!" Hunter snapped, nearly falling in his clumsy attempt at speed to reach the door.

Victoria blocked his path. "That's crazy!" she said. "There's no way you can do that if you can't bend your knee!"

Whether infuriated by his own incapacitation or the fact that a woman was pointing it out to him, Hunter cursed again. "Then get me a cab!" he demanded.

"No," Victoria held her ground. "Let me drive you."

His voice lashed at her. "Out of the question!"

"Why?"

"Because you don't know the situation!"

The volume of Victoria's own voice had gone up. "Then why the hell don't you *explain* it?"

Tall and angry he stood there, not knowing how to deal with the first woman—maybe even the first person—who had ever contested his authority.

"We're wasting time," he said. "Are you going to call me a cab or not?"

Victoria's breath burned in her throat, half of her wanting to tell him he was being a stupid idiot and the other half wanting to pull him close and squeeze out the obvious pain that was written all over his face.

"If you can't trust me to drive you where you have to go," she informed him, "then you can't trust me to be here when you get back."

The tension stretched ever tighter between them.

"What about Tapping?" he said.

"The man's found his way across the Atlantic," Victoria replied. "I think we can count on him to wait for us."

21

"*Are you planning to tell* me at some point where we're going?" Victoria asked over her shoulder of the passenger in the Mercedes' back seat.

They had been traveling northeast and, by Victoria's easy familiarity with the neighborhoods, would soon be crossing the state line and over into Maryland.

"I don't even like the *idea* of this," Hunter grumbled in response, alluding to his original request for her to get him a taxi.

"Maybe so," she countered, "but you can't very well put a blindfold on me and expect us to get there in one piece."

"Could you at least get us there a little faster?"

Victoria looked at him askance in the rearview mirror. "Not unless you want a speeding ticket. Which, by the way, I refuse to have taken out of my salary."

Hunter snorted something unintelligible, followed by the directive to take the Baltimore Parkway exit.

Where *were* they going anyway? Victoria wondered. More importantly, who held such power over the man that a single telephone call could turn him into one desperate character?

He had offered nothing, of course, in the way of explanation while she had helped him maneuver into the car. Nothing except the look of someone haunted, tormented by something valuable that had just fallen out of his hands.

Unexpectedly, a few droplets of rain started to hit the windshield. Victoria ignored them until they had built into a fairly steady rhythm, dappling the glass. "I thought it was supposed to stay clear today," she casually remarked.

Hunter, however, was lost to his own thoughts.

I may as well get lost in some of my own, then, she decided. Thoughts that, unavoidably, centered on her handsome passenger.

For one thing, she was driving his car. The same car with the HUNTER 1 plates that she had griped about to Thatcher and John not that long ago when she found it parked in her regular space in the garage. Her original assessment of the owner's image based on the macho license, though, could not have been farther from the truth if it had been on the moon. Hunter O'Hare was quite possibly the most attractive—and irritating— member of the opposite sex she had ever met in her life.

Victoria mentally clicked off in her head the number of weeks she had known him so far. It seemed that, ironically, the longer she knew him, the less she understood his actions. It was impossible to figure out what the man wanted, what the man needed from her. And yet he expected her to be a mind reader and respect his unspoken wishes.

That she was a competent assistant and secretary had already been established as well as praised. "Take care of this," Hunter would tell her, and she'd be back within the hour to report that it had been handled. As recently as that morning, in fact, he had generously complimented her on ensuring that Tapping's visit would be flawless.

"Elliott and his cohorts may have quite a fight on their hands trying to get you back," he had even remarked with the flash of a smile. "You're spoiling me."

It wasn't a hard thing to do, Victoria realized. And that was the crux of the problem.

Somewhere between being a professional employee and a vulnerable romantic had wedged that charismatic smile and twinkle of deep gray eyes and the scent of expensive aftershave that clung to her memory even when he wasn't around. Somewhere between efficiently doing what he expected and unabashedly doing what she really wanted had come the awful dilemma of recognizing that they were, after all, little more than strangers to each other. Even worse, that she was currently driving this particular stranger off to meet another woman. A significant woman.

Now, you don't know that for absolute certain, a voice in her head played devil's advocate. Maybe Hunter just has a female veterinarian and there's a problem with one of his prize-winning horses. That would certainly be a reasonable conclusion. Maybe it's about to give birth by cesarean and Hunter needs to be there to give a yea or nay on whether his vet should try to save the mare or the foal in the event of severe complications. Maybe his stalwart silence comes from not wanting to burden his secretary with any details or to show what she might perceive as weakness in his caring for animals.

It was a completely far-fetched excuse, and Victoria knew it. He was simply being an arrogant jerk and the less time she spent trying to figure him out, the less stressed her life would be. A lot less stressed than Hunter's apparently was, that was certain.

At least *she* wasn't the one getting death threats, she told herself, and in that instant, she remembered the parchment envelope she had been looking at earlier when the telephone rang. The same envelope that she had shoved into the pocket of her jacket in the confusion that immediately followed.

Obviously now wasn't a good time to show it to him, she determined. Maybe she should just open it and read it to herself while she was waiting in the car for him. Whatever life-threatening message it contained was probably no different than any of its predecessors.

"Take the next right," Hunter instructed from the back seat.

They had entered a residential neighborhood of Maryland that she wasn't familiar with. High stone walls and foreboding iron gates denied access, much less easy visibility, of the palatial homes that lay beyond.

It reminded Victoria of Embassy Row and the gracious mansions of an earlier era that had eventually been converted for the use of foreign consulates. While the mix of Italianate and Federal architectural styles she was passing along either side of the wide street could comfortably command a contingent of uniformed guards and Dobermans to patrol their perimeters, what struck her as odd at that moment was the total absence of any signs of life.

Even the rain, she noted, wasn't hard enough to have driven everyone indoors. Victoria refrained from whistling the theme from *The Twilight Zone*.

"Second place past the next corner," Hunter said.

"Which side?"

"Left."

In ways that alternately thrilled and frightened her, Victoria felt herself straining to catch the first glimpse of the address where he wanted her to stop.

"Right here is just fine," he said as she turned in and came face to face with the kind of imposing black double gate one would expect to find at Buckingham Palace. Ivy-covered walls at least twenty feet in height obscured any opportunity to see what kind of structure occupied so substantial a piece of land.

"Do we ring a bell to get someone's attention, or what?" Victoria inquired, for there was no gatekeeper to admit them, no video cameras in evidence.

Hunter was already opening his own back door of the car. "Do you think that you can find your way back to the castle?" he asked. "You might want to cut over and take ninety-five instead of the way we came. It might be a little easier."

Victoria jerked open the driver's side door that she might meet him on the other side in confrontation before he could press a magic button and escape from her.

"Now, hold it just a minute," she said with a bravado that was pure show. "You make me drive you all the way out to God knows where and then tell me to go home? Just like that?"

He was now standing to his full height, clutching the cane for support. "This doesn't concern you, Victoria."

"I happen to think that it does."

It *does*, she wanted to snap at him, *because it makes a difference in whether I lose my heart to you or write you off as a lost cause.* "I thought you said that you trusted me," she reminded him, annoyed that her reward for getting him to his destination was little more than a terse brush-off. "Is this the way you show it?"

"I trusted you to get me here," he said quietly. "And you did. And now I'm asking you to leave."

Victoria indicated the massive gates. "What is this place?"

Hunter took a breath, reluctant to answer but equally impatient to shed himself of her company. "It's a place where I have some business to attend to. Now, if you'll excuse me—"

"And how long are you going to be?" She had spotted a control box on a pedestal and what looked like a digital pad. No wonder there's no guard or anything, she rationalized. People who wanted to get in probably did it all by computer code or a plastic card like the kind banks used.

"I don't know," Hunter replied in answer to her question.

"Then I'll wait for you."

"That's not a good idea."

"What are you planning to do? Walk all the way back to Virginia?"

"I'm not going to stand here and argue with you, Victoria."

"Fine. Then I'll wait for you."

"No." It seemed to come out angrier than Hunter had intended and he immediately apologized. "I can get a cab back to Virginia when I'm through here," he said.

"Why pay for a cab when you have your own car?" she countered.

The brief hint of a smile started to come to Hunter's face, then vanished.

"I appreciate your desire to try and save me money," he said, "but I think I can manage the fare."

"Can you manage the walk?" she challenged him, not seeing anything that close to the gate but a wide expanse of green grass and a drive that sloped downward and out of sight. "Isn't there a front door or something where I can at least drop you off, save you some walking?"

"Victoria—"

"You're the one who said we had to trust each other if I was going to work for you," she pointed out. "Why is that so damned difficult for you to do?"

Hunter's free hand suddenly came up, startling her. As if embarrassed that she had interpreted the action as hostile, he stood with it hovered midway between them, unsure of how to continue.

"I'm sorry, Victoria," he said softly, his fingertips just inches from her jaw. "I have my reasons. Reasons that I just can't share with you—or with anyone—right now."

As his hand started to drop, Victoria's own reached up and grabbed it. Even beneath her gloves, she could feel the electricity of his touch. And in her face, she could feel a rush of heat start to spread. Now what do you do, she chided herself for acting so impetuously, wishing that she had something profound to say to accompany the physical contact.

To her surprise, Hunter's fingers tightened on hers instead of wrenching away for the spontaneous slip of indecorum. The impact of his gentle grip was almost more than she could bear, quickening her pulse at the speculation that the attraction she felt toward him might be mutual.

"Thank you for being so concerned," he murmured, his face coming close enough to hers that, for a moment, Victoria wondered if he wasn't going to kiss her. But, of course, he wouldn't, she mentally corrected herself. He was Hunter O'Hare, a man too locked inside his own painful secrets to let such vulnerability come out. "And now I really do need you to go," he said. "Please."

The worst he could do, of course, was fire her for being insubordinate.

At least that was what Victoria had been silently repeating to herself for the past twenty minutes. She had driven the car down the street, around the corner and back again just in case he had watched her go. In sight of the gates but hidden from easy view herself, Victoria sat and waited. The inclement weather was doing little to lift her spirits, nor did she feel especially optimistic listening to Dan Fogelberg's tearjerker melody on the radio about meeting an old lover in the grocery store on New Year's Eve. What I'm dealing with here, she reminded herself, is that Hunter was meeting an old lover—or maybe a current one—just over the slope of the hill and that there was absolutely nothing she could do about it.

Hadn't his look meant *something*, though? That, and the way his hand had closed over hers?

Victoria shook her head, baffled by the mixed messages he was telegraphing. Her gaze wandered back to the ominous black gates as her imagination began to conjure scenarios of what he and the mystery woman might be doing.

Forget about it and go home like he told you to, her conscience interceded. For although Hunter held the power to dismiss her if he felt like it, she recognized that she herself held a power to damage whatever thread of trust existed between them if she stayed a minute longer. Better not risk it, she resolved and turned the key in the ignition as Fogelberg's ballad slowly wound down to its final wistful refrain. Besides, she added to her decision, would she really be up to handling her emotions if Hunter returned to the car in a couple of hours with the scent of another woman's cologne and a look on his face that left no doubt as to how he had spent his afternoon?

As long as she had the car, Victoria opted to take a side trip back to her apartment before returning to the castle, just to remind herself that she did indeed have another life.

Being a woman who accrued few monthly bills, the short stack of mail she tossed on the dining room table held few envelopes that warranted immediate attention. Advertising flyers and solicitations went the way of the wastebasket. Letters from friends—and one from her mother—were sorted out to take back with her, for certainly she had enough free time in the evenings to answer them.

It wasn't until she went to slip a book of postage stamps into her jacket pocket that Victoria rediscovered the parchment envelope she had taken from the castle. Not having opened it in the car as she had intended, she debated whether she wanted to open it now, whether she wanted to expose her own safe haven to the evil so prevalent at Kriskerry Castle.

Logic finally won out over superstition, and Victoria slid her thumbnail under the sealed flap.

Just like the others, it was a patchwork string of words cut from magazines and newspapers. Only this one hinted at something more disturbing than those that had come before.

"I know where you're keeping Mary," it read, "and why."

22

Sean Michael and Deborah—laughing like giddy lovers and with fluted champagne glasses in their hands—were emerging from the castle as Victoria pulled into the courtyard.

"So now you're driving the old man's car around, hmm?" Sean Michael teased her as she stepped out. "Got your grip on anything else besides his throttle?"

Deborah playfully poked him in the ribs. "Oh, stop being such an ass, my love," she retorted before turning her attention to Victoria. "So where's Hunter?"

"You mean he's not back yet?" The trip to her apartment, plus getting lost twice in the Virginia countryside, had, she thought, virtually ensured that Victoria would find Hunter at the castle well before her own return.

"Back from where?" Sean Michael inquired.

Victoria sidestepped his question by directing one of her own. "How was the performance at the Kennedy Center?" she asked.

Deborah laughed. "At least someone like *you* would have stayed awake for it." She tilted her head toward her Irish playboy. "Guess who nodded off halfway through the overture?"

"I was nibbling on your shoulder," Sean Michael corrected her. "There's a difference."

Victoria could see the limo from where she stood. "Did Mr. Tapping get here all right from the airport?"

The question brought a chuckle to Sean Michael. "Don't worry," he assured her with a mischievous look. "My baby sister's already got him well in hand, so to speak."

Lord only knew what *that* meant, Victoria thought, excusing herself to go track down the English attorney and explain that Hunter was running a little late.

The sound of laughter was the first thing to betray their location in the parlor, Peggy kittenishly curled up on the floor at Tapping's feet and no doubt regaling him with examples of her intellect. "So you've actually *met* Princess Di?" she was asking. "Not just seen her from a distance?"

"Excuse me," Victoria interrupted, "but I'm Victoria Cameron, Mr. O'Hare's secretary."

Jon Tapping immediately rose to his feet from his chair by the fire. He was a slender dark-haired Englishman who was much younger than the way he came across in correspondence and on the telephone.

"A complete pleasure, Miss Cameron," he enthusiastically greeted her. "Miss Gleavy's been ever so helpful in getting me acquainted."

I'll bet, Victoria thought to herself, casting a glance at Peggy's ensemble—a turquoise spandex bodysuit straight from the pages of Frederick's of Hollywood. Not one's typical at-home attire by any means.

"I'm sorry I wasn't here when you first arrived," Victoria apologized, "but Mr. O'Hare had an unscheduled meeting."

Her eyes took in the conservative navy blue suit, the fair English complexion with rosy cheeks, and the slightly moussed crewcut that was either a throwback to the 1960s or a madcap stab at the avant-garde. His lips seemed perpetually parted and curved into an easy smile, a mole punctuating the upper right corner. Victoria's glance also took in the wide gold wedding band on his ring finger, an ornamentation that Peggy had either overlooked or, in her customarily perverted way, considered a personal challenge.

"No apology necessary," Tapping insisted of Hunter's tardiness. "I quite understand."

"We're having a séance tonight," Peggy matter-of-factly announced. "We were just talking about it."

Victoria arched a brow. "A what?"

"Summoning the dead," Peggy snidely interpreted for her over the rim of her brandy glass. "Interested?"

"Not really," Victoria replied, hoping that their guest wasn't basing his impression of the whole household on the twisted ideas of one of its members. "What brought *that* on?"

"Actually, it was my doing," Tapping blithely confessed. "I was asking Miss Gleavy to tell me all about the remarkable history of this place, and—"

"And we've decided to have a séance to learn more," Peggy finished his sentence.

"Count me out of the Ouija board crowd," Victoria informed her. "Besides, I'm sure Mr. O'Hare will have business he wants to discuss with our guest as soon as he returns."

"*If* he returns," Peggy said.

"Why shouldn't he?"

Peggy smiled like a Cheshire cat. "Spots just took a call from him," she replied, shrugging. "He's spending tonight away."

Much as she would have preferred to take a tray to her room, Victoria felt an obligation to stay close to Tapping, mindful of the fact that Peggy had already chosen him as her current prey. While the attorney was certainly old enough to look out for himself—not to mention committed to another relationship—it nonetheless bothered her that Peggy's chummy overtures masked a darker motive than just getting him into bed.

Across the table, Victoria purposely asked him about his wife back in London.

Tapping's mouth widened into a grin. "Doing splendidly," he replied. "We're due in early March."

The announcement surprised her, since she had discerned very little about the man from their transatlantic communications. "You're having a baby? I didn't know that!"

"Congratulations!" Deborah enthusiastically toasted him from her place next to Sean Michael. "Do you know yet what it's going to be?"

"Melissa does," Tapping admitted, "but she's a sly fox and not telling." It brought a collective laugh among those dining with him.

"So are you one of those modern fathers?" Sean Michael inquired, emphasizing "modern" as if it were something not quite acceptable.

"Come again?"

"The whole labor and childbirth thing," Sean Michael candidly explained. "Being there to deliver the bloody little bundle and all?"

"*Really*, love!" Deborah admonished him for his language at the dinner table.

Tapping, momentarily ruffled by the question, regained his composure to reply that Melissa's older sister from Lynmouth would help with the actual birth when the time came. "I'd be rather a wimp at it, I'm afraid," he told them, dabbing his mouth with his napkin. "I *have* been *singing* to it, though."

"Singing?" a puzzled Victoria echoed.

"They say that unborn babies are capable of learning quite extraordinary things," Tapping replied. "Melissa and I have both read a great deal about it in your American magazines."

Deborah joined in with her own knowledge on the subject. "They say you can buy tapes of Shakespeare or calculus or classical music and the fetus can hear it inside the womb."

"Wouldn't that be annoying?" Sean Michael interjected. "What if the little twit just wants to sleep?"

"So what have you been singing?" Victoria asked their guest.

A definitive blush came to Tapping's fair complexion. "I know all the songs from *Oliver*," he replied. "I don't sing them well, of course, but I *do* have a lot of spirit."

"I was afraid you were going to say Barry Manilow or Kenny Rogers," Sean Michael remarked.

"Well, *I* think it's very sensitive of you," Peggy spoke up, laying her hand on top of Tapping's wrist. "I really *like* that in a man."

Victoria avoided looking at Deborah, knowing that they'd both break out laughing if they made any eye contact.

"So what's the bloody point of this?" Sean Michael asked his sister as they adjourned after dinner to what had been the castle's chapel on the first floor. Minus the religious artifacts and altar where Sir Patrick's ancestors had come to worship, its modern use was that of a reading and game room for the family. That Peggy liked to use it for contacting the spirit world seemed, to Victoria, at odds with the room's original purpose and link with Christianity.

"The night's ripe for contact," Peggy curtly informed him. "It's a full moon."

"No moon at all with the storm," Sean Michael retorted. "Taken a look outside lately?"

"It's there," Peggy archly insisted, taking two candlesticks from the credenza.

Quietly minding his own business from an overstuffed

chair in the corner, Nilly looked up from his book at the current invaders of his privacy.

"Shall we give it a go?" Deborah nudged Victoria.

"I'm really not into this," Victoria replied, watching Peggy light the candles she had placed on the game table.

"Neither am I," Deborah said with a laugh, "but what's the harm?"

Tapping was pulling out Peggy's chair for her and taking the one she offered next to him.

"I'd think an old place like this would abound with spirits," he was saying.

"Yes," Sean Michael agreed, tilting his head toward Nilly. "It's certainly got its share of old relics."

Nilly ignored the remark and went back to the book he was reading.

Deborah had left Victoria's side and taken the chair across from Tapping. "So how does this work?" she asked.

"I see that you and I are of the same mind about this nonsense," Sean Michael remarked to Victoria.

As she started to reply, her eye caught Mrs. Pritchard's arrival in the doorway. With a steaming mug in each hand, the cook was clearly taken aback by the sight that greeted her. Only Victoria seemed to pick up on the fact that the elderly valet and Mrs. P had already staked a claim on the room for themselves.

"Going to join us?" Peggy's voice rang out. "Perhaps there'll be a message from your Welshman."

Mrs. Pritchard stiffened, meeting Peggy's invitation with an aplomb that Victoria couldn't help but admire in the older woman. "My Welshman's soul is in heaven," she informed the brunette, "so sure it's a waste of my time to be placin' a call to him through the devil."

"Guess she told *you*," Sean Michael proclaimed, with a chuckle at his sister.

"Go screw yourself," Peggy snapped as she briskly shuffled her deck of tarot cards. "Someone turn off the lights."

"I believe Nilly is trying to read," Victoria spoke up on

the servant's behalf, appalled that she was apparently the only one who had noticed or cared.

Nilly had closed his book and was now standing. "It's all right, Miss Cameron," he said quietly. "I'm sure the lights are much better in the kitchen."

"So are you two in or out?" Peggy sarcastically asked of her brother and Victoria. "The spirits won't come at all if there are disbelievers in the room."

"Oh, what the hell." Sean Michael shrugged and crossed toward the table. "Maybe they've got the inside track on the next race."

"Come on, Victoria," Deborah urged her. "Don't you want to know what the future holds?"

"It'll be here soon enough," she pleasantly replied. "I think I'll call it a night."

She was barely out the chapel door when she heard Peggy melodramatically gasp.

"Oh, God," the Gleavy girl announced with her first turn of a card. "It's the Death card," she said. "And it's meant for one of us. . . ."

"You wouldn't happen to have some hot chocolate, would you?" Victoria inquired of Mrs. Pritchard. Occupying their customary posts at the kitchen table, she and Nilly had been discussing Peggy's latest brazen flirtation when Victoria walked in.

"Good as done, lamb," Mrs. P replied, bouncing up from her chair to make some.

"Sorry you got bumped," Victoria apologized to Nilly. The heavy leather volume he had brought along from the chapel lay on the table. "What are you reading?" she asked, unable to make out the script title upside down.

"A history of Sir Patrick's people," he replied, his voice underscored with reverence.

"All about Duncan, mostly," Mrs. P added. "Now *there* was a randy chap!"

"Worse than Sean Michael?" Victoria said teasingly.

It brought a laugh to the cook's throat. "Duncan could outlast the boy and then some, don't you know!" she giggled.

"Now, Mrs. P," Nilly chided her. "None of us know that."

"Sure an' we do!" she insisted, revealing to Victoria that the castle's first owner had bedded over a hundred Irish virgins before his obsession with Marguerite.

"Who was Marguerite?" Victoria asked.

"You tell it better than I, Nilly," Mrs. Pritchard urged the valet.

"Marguerite was a witch," Nilly began his story.

"Not that anyone knew for sure," Mrs. P clarified.

"She washed up half-dead on the shore below the castle one day—"

"Drowned as a rat, she was," the cook emphasized.

"It was Duncan who found her," Nilly continued, "and brought her inside."

"Saints be praised, but the man loved her at first sight," Mrs. Pritchard sighed, clasping both hands to her chest. "Couldn't keep his hands off an inch of her, so they say."

"Is it your story or mine, Mrs. P?" Nilly inquired.

"Yours, of course!" Mrs. P proudly insisted. "Go on with you now, Nilly, and I'll just be gettin' to the cocoa as I should."

An hour later, amidst constant interruption, Nilly had finally finished the tale of Duncan and his bewitching bride.

"They still walk the halls together, don't you know," Mrs. Pritchard added in epilogue. "That and *other* things." Nilly's earlier reference to the couple's penchant for passion supplied ample clue of what those "other things" were.

"I don't know that I believe *that* part of it," Victoria replied, "but it was a beautiful story."

"And every word of it is true," Mrs. P reminded her.

Victoria scooted her chair back. "Well, I really should be calling it a night," she said, wondering if the séance group down the hall had been successful in conjuring a few castle ghosts. "Thank you again for the hot chocolate and the story."

As she started up the staircase to her bedroom, Victoria's thoughts turned once again to the envelope in her pocket. There was no way she could keep it from Hunter, of course, her intuition having already advised her that this particular note would mean more to him than all the others combined. Mary, whoever she was, probably mattered to the man more than his own life. That he was gone—and unreachable—for the night only made the situation worse.

I'll give it to him first thing in the morning, she decided. Even that, though, didn't feel quite right to her. In the first place, he would know that she had read the contents. In the second place, he'd know that she had questions about it, uncomfortable questions that he'd be put on the spot to answer.

He's going through enough right now, her compassionate side argued. *Leave it for him to find when he gets back*, the inner voice told her. If and when he wanted to discuss it with her, she had to give him the freedom to do it on his own terms.

Ignorant of the pair of eyes that watched her moment of indecision outside Hunter's door, Victoria slipped inside to leave the envelope on his bedside table.

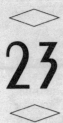

23

While it shouldn't have surprised Victoria that much to see Deborah Sheddmoore downstairs at breakfast the next morning, it nonetheless did. Swathed in a silky blue caftan from her neck to her ankles, the blond was already at the sideboard checking out the muffins Mrs. Pritchard had just brought in.

"So how did the séance go after I left?" Victoria asked following the brief exchange of pleasantries about how each of the other had slept.

Deborah shrugged. "So-so," she replied of the night's dabbling in mysticism. "Nothing to write home about."

"You sound disappointed."

"Well, it would've spiced it up a tad to see a genuine ghost or two. As it was, Peggy just dealt out the tarot cards and played interpreter."

"Any profound revelations?"

Deborah ticked them off on her fingers. "Let's see . . . fortunes are going to change hands, it's going to be an awful winter, and—oh yes, Duncan is going to kill someone before the next full moon."

Victoria helped herself to some orange juice. "Duncan's been dead for seven hundred years," she pointed out.

"And he's been pissed off for at least the last five of them," Sean Michael matter-of-factly proclaimed as he joined both women at the sideboard. "Haven't you heard him rattling his chains every night in the dungeon?"

His remark jogged Deborah's memory of something else the spirit world had menacingly imparted the previous evening. "It seems he didn't like his castle being moved clear across the ocean," she added. "Peggy says he's going to do something to put it back where it belongs."

"Short of an earthquake followed by an Atlantic tsunami," Victoria speculated, "that may be easier said than done." It had, after all, taken Hunter a matter of years, not magical minutes, to put the final stones back together. "He'd have to subcontract with David Copperfield if he wanted the job done any faster," she suggested.

Sean Michael laughed at the ludicrous vision her words had conjured. "She's got a point, doesn't she, love?"

Deborah replied that the occult warning wasn't necessarily a literal one. "It could mean anything," she said. "She only told us that his ghost was angry."

"I hate to be a naysayer," Victoria sighed, "but Duncan probably couldn't care less."

"You think it's a more localized opinion then?" Sean Michael good-naturedly challenged her.

"What I think," Victoria replied, "is that Peggy wasn't the most neutral party to be playing medium last night."

Sean Michael only laughed. "*Spots* seemed to take the whole thing to heart," he nonchalantly commented.

"Mrs. Maginn was there?"

"She came in a little bit after you left," Deborah answered.

Victoria scowled. "She doesn't strike me as the type to even be interested in that sort of thing." What little exposure she had to date to the housekeeper's philosophical leanings suggested a strong tie to her church, particularly the Sunday choir. While in truth the woman might not practice any brotherly—or sisterly—love toward her

peers, she'd be the first to claim religion as the corner-
stone of her existence.

"Dead wrong she's not into the occult," Sean Michael
corrected her. "You should see her grab the horoscope
page first thing every morning."

"Horoscopes," Deborah disdainfully scoffed as she
took a place at the table. "They're always so general. . . ."

"Have either of you seen Mr. Tapping yet?" Victoria
inquired as a change of subject, wondering if the attorney was sleeping in after his long flight from England.

"You'd have to have gotten up bloody early to catch
that one," Sean Michael replied. "He's long gone already."

"Gone? Gone where?"

"Peggy's taken him to see the sights," Deborah said.

"*Some* of them," Sean Michael said with a nasty chuckle,
"are even in Washington, D.C."

"Oh, great," Victoria muttered under her breath,
deflated by the realization that through no real fault of
her own, she had managed to let Hunter down.

Her initial hope that Tapping and Peggy might return to
the castle before O'Hare discovered their absence was
dashed less than a few hours later.

"Shall I be bringin' you a tray, sir?" she heard Mrs.
Pritchard ask.

"Thanks, no," the familiar voice of Hunter declined.
"Chan and I stopped for something on our way back."

Chan? That didn't make sense, Victoria thought to
herself from where she had paused at the top of the
stairs. O'Hare had made such a point of informing her
that he'd take a cab back when his business was finished.
That he had contacted the chauffeur without her even
knowing it added insult to injury.

As Victoria started down the stairs—allowing enough
time for Hunter to have returned to his room—she heard
Mrs. Maginn sharply address the cook.

"Sure, I heard you the *first* time," Mrs. P retorted after her name was called out twice.

"I'd not be so smart in the mouth if I were you," Mrs. Maginn icily warned her.

"Well, sure an' you're not, and the saints be glad of it."

Victoria, out of sight, couldn't help but smile at the cocky way Mrs. Pritchard held her own against the senior servant.

"You're not to be usin' the chapel for your dalliances," Mrs. Maginn sternly replied when Mrs. P asked her what she wanted.

"*Dalliances*, it is now?" Mrs. Pritchard exclaimed, outraged by the accusation that she and Nilly had done anything improper. "Who says I was?" she wanted to know.

Mrs. Maginn defended her charge. "You were seen and that's that."

"'Tis a bloody lie, and I'll swear to it!"

"I'll not be warnin' you again, Pritchard," the housekeeper said above the cook's protests that her actions the previous night were innocent. "Is that clear?"

"Clear as your ugly face," Mrs. Pritchard snapped back. "I've a mind to tell himself, don't you know?"

Mrs. Maginn laughed, a laugh that rippled with cruelty. "Would you now?" she called the cook's bluff. "And would you also be tellin' himself not to go sendin' Ian back to his kind like he's plannin' to do?"

What a snake she is, Victoria thought, knowing full well that Hunter had no intention whatsoever of turning Mrs. Pritchard's son over to the authorities.

"Sure an' you're lyin'!" Mrs. P blurted out.

"Am I?" The sound of footsteps walking away indicated that Mrs. Maginn had chosen to end their hallway confrontation.

"Damn you to hell and the devil!" Mrs. Pritchard cursed her, just loud enough for Victoria to hear. That and her guttural swear to see justice done if Ian came to harm.

* * *

Steeled for a lecture from Hunter about letting Jon Tapping so easily fall into the clutches of Peggy, it thus puzzled Victoria when he took the news with relative calm.

"Not your fault," he assured her. "Besides, I'm sure he can handle the situation."

Victoria wasn't as convinced, having witnessed how charmed Tapping had been the previous night by Peggy's eye-batting innocence. "He's up against a real pro," she reminded him.

Hunter smiled. "So is she," he replied, almost as if amused by the turn of events. "I wouldn't worry about it."

Victoria's glance traveled toward the bedside table and the awareness that the parchment envelope was gone. Was he going to say something? Was he going to explain?

He was systematically going through the rest of the mail, leaving Victoria to stand there without a clue of what to do next.

"Did everything . . . go all right yesterday?" she inquired after what seemed an interminable silence.

Hunter looked up, studying her face with that brooding, enigmatic gaze for an extra beat before replying. "Yes. Thank you for asking."

"You're welcome."

It was apparent that that's all he was going to say. With her heart and pride bruised by his complete indifference, Victoria saw no point in remaining in his company.

"I'll just be in the library if you need anything," she murmured.

When she was halfway to the door, Hunter's voice stopped her.

"There's something I need to talk to you about," he said. "Maybe now's as good a time as any."

Mixed feelings surged through her, but she imposed an iron will not to show it. Maybe he was finally going to open up and tell her what was on his mind. Concurrently, there lay the awful sense of apprehension that it wasn't going to be something she liked.

"Certainly," she said. "What is it?"

"Would you mind closing the door?" he asked.

Victoria complied without showing her inner reluctance, unable to dislodge the nagging reminiscence that people never asked that a door be closed unless they were about to deliver unpleasant news.

"Ever since you came to work for me," Hunter began, "you've exceeded my expectations. It's not hard to see why Elliott values you at the firm as much as he does."

Was he prefacing a reprimand by softening it with a compliment? she wondered. Victoria nodded and waited for him to continue.

"As you may know," he went on, "I had even spoken to Elliott about extending your time here through the end of December rather than the couple of weeks we had originally agreed to."

"He had mentioned it to me, yes." Was this a lead-in to a permanent offer with him? A raise for a job well done? An admission that it was total torture working side by side with her day after day and that if she didn't marry him tomorrow he'd die?

"Having had more time to think about it," Hunter continued, "coupled with the fact that I'm ambulatory again—" He paused before going on, a deep furrow creasing his brow. "I'm afraid there's been a change in plans."

"What kind of change?" Victoria cautiously inquired. Surely the stock market hadn't crashed when she wasn't looking, leaving O'Hare destitute and unable to afford her.

"Good news and bad news," he replied. "The good news is that it looks like I'll be sending you back to Elliott when Tapping leaves."

"That's the day after Thanksgiving," a puzzled Victoria reminded him.

"Yes," Hunter said. "I know."

"So what's the bad news?" she asked, hoping her voice wouldn't betray that what he had just said was bad enough.

A momentary look of discomfort crossed the millionaire's face, replaced by a half-smile of apology. "The bad news is that I'm going to miss you, Victoria. You're probably one of the brightest, most efficient, and . . ." he hesitated as if searching for the right word " . . . caring people I've ever had working for me."

"Then what you just said begs an obvious question."

"Yes?"

"If I'm so bright, efficient and caring a person—" Victoria cut herself off in midsentence. It's *not as if he's dumping a romantic relationship*, her conscience chided her. And yet for the feelings he had aroused in her the past few weeks—feelings that he wasn't even aware of—his announcement hurt just as much, just as deeply.

Victoria's eyes met his. He was waiting for her to continue.

"Was it anything I did?" she asked, already racking her brain.

Hunter shook his head. "It's nothing about you, Victoria," he gently assured her. "If things were different right now . . ."

This time it was Hunter who let a thought go unfinished.

"What's this?" Sean Michael remarked in surprise when he found her out by the pasture fence watching the horses. "Not inside talking shop with the boys?"

Victoria ignored him, just as she had ignored Tapping's return to the castle and his subsequent closed-door meeting with Hunter.

"You must be mellowing," he observed. "No verbal kicks to the groin for teasing you about his lordship?"

"I came out here to be by myself," she said.

"Then lucky for you I came out to ride. You can be my audience."

Victoria responded by turning away. Sean Michael, quick on his feet, maneuvered right into her path. "Oh come on, I was just—" His hand suddenly caught her chin before she could hide her eyes from him. "What's wrong?"

"Nothing that being by myself won't cure."

"You're either crying your eyes out or you did a bloody bad job of your makeup," he observed, planting both hands firmly on her shoulders.

"Get out of my way," Victoria snapped, "or I'm going to scream."

"Could you do it loud enough then for the next county?" he suggested. "It couldn't hurt my reputation. . . ."

In spite of her mood and current heartache, Victoria let a smirk escape, recognizing that—for all his talk—Sean Michael was basically harmless.

"I'm told I'm a good listener," he offered.

Victoria was dubious. "Who ever told you that?"

Sean Michael shrugged. "I'm sure that *someone* did once," he said. "I wasn't listening at the time."

"Well, thanks for the offer, but I'd really rather not talk about it."

"Would you rather go riding?"

"I don't ride, remember?"

Sean Michael indicated the gray mare standing closest to the fence and complacently eating grass. "You don't have to on Roxilaine," he said. "You just sit there and she does all the work."

"And where were *you* going to be?" Victoria inquired, having already determined he had an ulterior motive up his sleeve.

"On Paladdin, who else?"

"I thought no one was supposed to ride him except Hunter." At least that was what Mrs. Pritchard had implied.

"Piece of cake," Sean Michael insisted. "Deborah and I do it all the time when Hunter's not looking. Come on," he urged her. "Just out to the far fence and back again?" He was already climbing over the fence.

Against her better judgment, Victoria followed.

24

To her surprise, it wasn't as hard as she had imagined. Then again, she hadn't exactly done anything that could be classed as an act of daring equestrianism.

"I can't believe I'm really doing this," she said to Sean Michael as he led Roxilaine around the pasture to get her used to the feel of being on top of a horse.

"You look like you were born to it," he complimented her. "Sure you've never been on one before?"

"You're full of it," she retorted, nonetheless pleased that she'd been on Roxilaine's back for nearly ten minutes and not fallen off yet.

"Stay there a second," Sean Michael instructed, letting go of the reins. "I'll be right back."

"What?"

"I'm getting Paladdin."

Victoria momentarily panicked. "How do I get her to stay?" In her mind's eye, she could just picture the gray mare bolting for the woods, making a beeline for low branches, and dislodging her novice rider into the nearest mud marsh.

"Don't do anything," he shrugged as if the answer were an obvious one.

Victoria tentatively leaned forward to stroke the horse's head as she had seen Sean Michael do. Roxilaine shook her ears and snorted.

"I won't make any fast moves if you don't," Victoria murmured, anxiously looking back over her shoulder to see Sean Michael running toward the stables. "How did I ever let myself get talked into this?" she added under her breath, gripping the leather reins tightly as if they were a talisman.

At least the fear factor and concentration it required was taking her mind off of Hunter, she reminded herself.

Hunter. Damn him! Over and over, she had replayed what he told her, finding no solace in his praise of her work or in the impending return to familiar surroundings and friendly faces. All that she could hear, all that she could understand, was that he no longer wanted her around.

What she still didn't know was *why*.

Unbidden, the voice of Marcine intruded on her thoughts. "Of *course* he wants you around, sweetie," she could hear her mother say, "but right now, he wants to sit in the backyard, eat worms, and feel sorry for himself."

It was an excerpt from a real conversation they had had when Victoria was back in high school and smarting from the sting of her first broken romance with Steven Brehmer. Marcine—in one of her rare moments of actually making sense—had taken two hours off from the studio and had the commissary put together a box lunch for both of them to eat in the park across from Soundstage 40.

"How could a boy like that *not* like you?" she said as she dried Victoria's tears with the very same handkerchief that Ricardo Montalban had given her at the Emmy Awards. "You're smart, you're funny, you're pretty, and goodness knows, you have glorious hair just like me."

That the same woman had, three months earlier, told her she was too young to get serious about anything besides school was a contradiction to the loving empathy she was extending toward her heartsick daughter. Not even an I-told-you-so, for which Victoria was grateful.

She could close her eyes and picture everything about that afternoon, even the chiffon dress Marcine was wearing and how peculiar the sunlight made her TV makeup look. "We Cameron women," Marcine said with unmistakable pride, "have always been overwhelming to the opposite sex. It's a curse sometimes."

"All I want is to get him back, Mama," Victoria had whimpered. In retrospect, of course, the pathos of losing Steven in her freshman year now struck her as funny. Tall, skinny, and a contender for Super Geek, he had eventually grown up to sell cleaning products door to door, the profits of which all went to alimony and child support from three failed marriages. Sans crystal ball to see the boy's future that day, the young Victoria could only see her immediate sorrow at losing him. Worse, that she had lost him without any reasonable explanation. "It's not you, it's me," was all he had said.

"If you've lost him, honey," Marcine said, "it's because you were too good for him. He's probably feeling just as badly as you are."

Victoria brightened. "Does that mean he's coming back?"

"When he gets tired of eating worms, maybe he will."

It was an analogy that Marcine applied to a lot of things, not just romance. "If he decides to be an adult, sweetie," she said, "he'll come back indoors."

"And if he doesn't?"

Marcine shrugged. "Then he won't."

For a woman who spent a good two-thirds of her life in an atmosphere of cinematic fantasy and retakes, Marcine Cameron had demonstrated uncommon clarity of thinking that afternoon. Why else would her advice still come back to echo in her daughter's head so many years later?

I wonder what you'd make of Hunter O'Hare? Victoria

almost said out loud. Sean Michael's return at that moment made her thankful she had kept the speculation to herself.

"I see you haven't fallen off yet," he grinned, coming up alongside of her on the most beautiful animal she had ever seen.

"Was I supposed to?"

Sean Michael laughed. "So what do you think of Hunter's pride and joy?" he asked, indicating the prancing black behemoth on which he was mounted. Even beneath overcast skies, Paladdin's black skin glistened.

"Are you sure you should be riding him?"

Mrs. Pritchard's description of the horse came back to her. Black-hearted, the cook had said. Like Satan. Little as she knew about horses, Victoria could see that the animal had spirit. A wild streak. Not unlike the man in the saddle.

"No problem," Sean Michael shrugged. "As long as Roxy's in tow, he'll behave himself."

Victoria wasn't convinced.

"Come on, I'll show you," he insisted, clucking his tongue.

Victoria gripped the reins for dear life as both horses started to move.

"Just relax and enjoy it," Sean Michael said.

Easy for you to say, she silently cursed him, tightening her thighs to keep from being bounced out of the saddle and onto her behind as Roxilaine went from placidly standing still to loping in stride with the stallion.

"Want to race to the west fence?" her companion invited her.

"I don't even want to be out here, *period*," she replied above the clop of hoofbeats. "Slow down, will you?"

To her surprise, Sean Michael not only slowed down but stopped, drawing up beside her. "You're doing just fine," he said. "I'll make a horsewoman of you yet." Roxilaine whinnied as if in agreement with him.

Victoria brushed her hair out of her face. "It's not high on my list of aspirations," she informed him. "Staying alive, however, *is*."

"Damn!" Sean Michael muttered, his attention suddenly directed at something behind her.

Victoria looked back to see Ian walking down the path from the castle to the stables, no doubt having just finished lunch with his mother in the kitchen. That he'd arouse any kind of reaction in Sean Michael struck her as strange.

"What's wrong?" she asked.

"Dr. Doolittle and his big mouth," Sean Michael sarcastically replied. "Come on, let's get out of sight before he looks over here."

"What the—"

Even if she had wanted to stay where she was, he had already grabbed hold of the dangling end of the gray mare's rein and set both horses into motion again. Whether or not Ian or anyone else heard Victoria shriek as she clenched the horn of Roxilaine's saddle with both hands became a moot point as they galloped into the darkness of the green gully beyond, Paladdin breaking into the lead as befit the heritage of his Irish racehorse blood.

Not until they had reached a clearing did Sean Michael maneuver Paladdin to a stop, Roxilaine docilely following suit.

Fury almost choked the words that fell from Victoria's mouth.

"That," she angrily reproached him between gasps of breath, "had to be the most stupid, irresponsible, immature thing I've ever—"

Sean Michael chuckled at her reprimand, further incensing her. "You didn't fall off," he pointed out. "Why are you whining about it?"

He had effortlessly slid off his own saddle and onto the grass, raking both hands through his black hair as if invigorated by the entire experience. "Want to walk for a while?" he offered, chivalrously extending his hand to help her down.

The audacity of the man!

"I'm going back," she said.

Sean Michael shook his head, hands on his hips. "I wouldn't do that if I were you."

"And why not?"

"Ian," he matter of factly replied. "You sashay back there with Roxy and he'll be all over you about Paladdin."

"Why should he do that?" Victoria challenged him. "I'll tell him that *you* have him."

Sean Michael pasted on his most charming smile in an attempt to disarm her. "Why don't we go back together after a little while and sneak 'em in when he takes a break?"

Victoria cocked a suspicious brow. "You're *not* supposed to ride Paladdin, are you?" For all of his talk about doing as he wished, the look of discomfort that had crossed his face when he saw the stableboy was more than that of annoyance.

"Sir Patrick," Sean Michael countered with a sharp edge, "let me ride him whenever I wanted."

A part of Victoria delighted in raising a pertinent point. "He's not Sir Patrick's horse anymore," she said. Nor did she really believe that the dead patriarch of Kriskerry Castle had been so generous with *any* of his belongings.

The insolence in Sean Michael's voice was ill concealed. "He's really gotten to you, hasn't he?"

"Who?" Victoria asked.

"You think the rest of us haven't noticed?"

"I have no idea what you're talking about," she said, even though she was pretty sure that she did.

"Don't you?"

He was baiting her.

"If you want to stay here in the woods and talk to yourself," Victoria coolly informed him, "that's your business. I'm going back."

His hand shot out and grabbed Roxilaine's rein. "Not until I tell you something I don't think you want to hear."

His statement unleashed something within her. Whatever awful secret he was going to share was about Hunter, she told herself. It had to be. And much as she wanted to get as far away from Sean Michael as she could at that moment, she also knew that she wanted to hear what it was.

"Then tell me," she said.

Her reaction seemed to surprise him, as if they were each calling the other's bluff.

Sean Michael hesitated.

"What's wrong?" she pleasantly inquired. "Forget what it was already?"

Anger lit up his dark eyes. "Not when he's made me pay for it every day since it happened."

"Since *what* happened?"

He had dropped the reins and was walking toward Paladdin. Victoria repeated her question, louder than before.

As he started to mount the black stallion, he looked over his shoulder at her, his expression a mix of pain and hatred.

"Not even *you* can bring her back," he said. "It's best you not even try."

The one-word question that froze on Victoria's lips was drowned by Paladdin's hoofbeats as Sean Michael galloped away from her.

N*o*, she screamed inside her head. She'd just come close enough to the truth that she could practically touch it. He wasn't going to get away from her that easily. Victoria grabbed tight on the saddle horn and reins and prodded Roxilaine the way she had seen Sean Michael do to the black horse.

In spite of Sean Michael's head start and her own

incompetence as a rider, Victoria was determined to catch up, to demand that he explain what he had meant that cast such a pall over Hunter's life and, ultimately, the future.

How she managed to stay on Roxilaine's back through wet trees, over rotted logs and across two streams was something Victoria classed as nothing less than a miracle.

"Finally!" she muttered as she came upon Paladdin standing by a fence, a fence he could easily have cleared had Sean Michael urged him to.

Her sigh of relief at having caught up, however, quickly turned to a gasp of horror as her eyes caught sight of Paladdin's thrown rider, motionless on his back in a ditch.

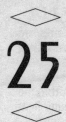

25

With *a clumsiness that would* have appalled her graceful mother, Victoria scrambled off of the hard saddle on Roxilaine's back and flew across the grass to where Sean Michael lay, not moving. It was sinking anguish that caused her to stumble almost on top of him, swallowing the ragged cry that rose in her throat as she laid her ear against his chest to see if he still had a heartbeat.

"Oh, God, please don't be dead." Her lips moved in anxious prayer, fearing that she had not only reached him too late but that, if he *were* still alive, her disorientation with the countryside would delay her in bringing back someone to help.

"If I didn't know better," he lifted his head and huskily whispered into her hair, "I'd almost think that you cared."

Outraged that she had been tricked, Victoria pulled away as Sean Michael's hands powerfully locked on her arms and tumbled her over on to her back, his whole body rocking with laughter at the success of his little charade. "God, but that was bloody fun," he roared. "You really fell for it, didn't you?"

Not even the adrenaline of her anger was a match against her well-muscled adversary.

"Is this what it felt like under my cousin?" he teased her, his weight pinning her down in the damp grass. "You don't really believe he was *that* helpless, do you?"

"Get off of me!" she demanded, refusing to let him see the panic that had suddenly welled inside of her from the fact she was probably miles from anyone who could hear her scream.

"And what if I don't?" he countered, enjoying her struggle.

Victoria repeated the command that he release her, furious with herself for walking into so foolish a trap, for believing that he meant her no harm by his supposed concern and flattery.

"Not until you listen to me," he said, his dark eyes flashing imperiously and just inches from hers. "Isn't that why you followed me? To learn the truth?"

"And whose version of it would I be hearing?" Precarious as her situation might be, Victoria recognized that her best—and only—defense was a verbal one.

"Are you that stupid not to see it, then?" he snarled.

Sean Michael didn't wait for her to answer, spatting out his opinion with a wild-eyed glare of contempt that knotted the fear inside of her.

"The bloody bastard's no good for you, Victoria."

"And I suppose *you* are?"

Sean Michael faltered at her snappy retort, a split second of indecision on his part in which Victoria managed to free a fist and slam it as hard as she could into his chin.

His grunt of total astonishment at the unexpected attack gave her a rush of satisfaction but not the necessary delay she had hoped for to make an escape. With bare knuckles stinging from the impact with his jaw, her immediate worry now was that she had just made their one-on-one situation all the more dangerous.

"Damn it, Victoria!" he cursed her, his brogue stronger than she had ever heard it as he pinned both of her wrists above her head. The accompanying rip at the shoulder of her blouse as he did so escalated her dread of how far his Irish temper might go to make a point. "I'm *trying* to do you a bloody *favor!*"

"And what favor is that?" the angry voice of Hunter O'Hare startled them both.

He and Ian were just on the other side of the fence. Only in her confusion of how fast they could have gotten there did Victoria get her bearings and realize that her ill-planned chase after Sean Michael had brought both of them almost full circle back to the stable beyond the trees.

Sean Michael rose to his feet and gallantly offered Victoria assistance, a gesture that infuriated her even more for its pretense of lighthearted innocence.

"Well?" Hunter demanded an explanation of his cousin's actions, his implacable expression enough to turn mortals to stone. "What the hell is going on here?"

"Just showing her how a *real* Irishman can kiss," Sean Michael jocularly replied before vaulting over the fence as easily as if he had been doing it all his life. Deaf to O'Hare's maddened call to account for riding Paladdin without permission, he was already on his way down the hill, leaving her to face the wrath of Hunter on her own.

"Take care of the horses," Hunter sharply instructed Ian.

Whether bewildered by the scene they had just come upon or fearful of reprisal for allowing the horses out of his trusted sight, the ashen-faced stable boy hastened to do Hunter's bidding, not once looking in the disheveled Victoria's direction.

The initial gratitude Victoria felt for O'Hare's fortuitous rescue was canceled out by the cold reality that he said nothing to her on the entire walk back to the castle, not even to inquire if she had been injured in the compromising scuffle with Sean Michael. Surely he had to know that none of it was her fault, she rationalized. Only an idiot would believe she had initiated—or enjoyed—what looked like a wanton entanglement.

"Don't you want to know what was going on?" she finally asked when they reached the courtyard, owing no loyalty to the cousin who so fiercely sought to discredit him in her estimation.

His stare was bold and assessed her frankly. "I think I have a clear picture of it," he said as he pulled off his gloves.

"And?" Victoria waited for what she expected would be his intention to speak to his cousin and extract an apology on her behalf.

No vestige of sympathy, however, was reflected in Hunter's face or his voice. "In your time remaining here," he remarked, "I hope that you'll exercise better judgment."

It was as impossible to sleep that night as it had been to pretend throughout dinner that nothing had happened. Deborah, at least, had not been present as a guest, relieving Victoria of any awkward moments with Sean Michael and his visibly bruised jaw.

Oddly enough, his relationship with her seemed to be exactly what it was prior to their altercation in the woods. Pride, she interpreted it. Far be it from a jock like Sean Michael to admit that a woman had repulsed his advances. By his own accounting, there was a long waiting list of females eager to do quite the opposite.

"Gave myself a real shiner on the fence today," he replied when Tapping inquired about it.

"Serves you right for ridiculing the spirits last night," Peggy snidely informed him as she helped herself from the platter of beef being circulated. "It was probably Duncan popping you one himself."

"I wouldn't doubt it one bit," Sean Michael said pleasantly, glancing at Victoria just briefly enough that she was the only one to see it.

At least he's got the discretion to keep this private, Victoria thought to herself. While it hardly qualified him for enshrinement on Mount Rushmore or nomination for sainthood, he was being man enough not to make it any worse than it was.

Hunter, though, was another matter altogether.

What on earth was going through the man's head, she wondered, as he sat at the table that night with the rest of them, making such a point of avoiding any eye contact with her that it almost became a game to try and catch some on her own.

Since he was the first to excuse himself when dinner was concluded, she barely caught his remark to Mrs. Maginn that he was going out and wouldn't return until late.

Was he going to Maryland again? Victoria speculated. Maryland and Mary? That she still hadn't gotten anything from Sean Michael that day besides a torn sleeve and a wounded ego made her all the more impatient to find out what Hunter was hiding. It was the unknown, she reminded herself, that always made it hard to function, to make rational decisions.

Her priority at the moment, though, was to straighten out what she deemed a grievous error on Hunter's part, the remembrance of his words in the courtyard slicing deep into her feelings. Unlikely as it was that their paths would ever cross again once her employment with him ended, it was an issue of principle to keep her reputation unsullied. The nerve of him to criticize her judgment!

It wasn't fair, the voice inside her head screamed. For whatever reason, Hunter O'Hare seemed bent on condemning her for something she hadn't done and for emotions of his own that he refused to come to terms with. It was bad enough, she thought, that he was terminating her early and for spurious motives. That he'd taken his attitude so far as to actually believe there was anything going on between her and Sean Michael—

"Excuse me," she said, a discreet moment after his departure from the dining room. Entertained by Tapping's perspective on whether the queen should impose a new tax on the commoners to restore the fire damage at Windsor, neither Peggy nor Sean Michael particularly cared about Victoria's early exit.

Though there was no one there to see her, Victoria tossed her hair over her shoulders in a gesture of defiance as she reached the hallway. You're going to hear me out on this, she silently declared to the castle's owner.

The next obstacle, of course, was getting an appointment to do it.

"Mr. O'Hare said to tell you he'll be along in a few minutes," Victoria cheerfully informed Chan as she opened the door of the limo and let herself into the back seat. Even Marcine would have applauded her initiative and panache.

Exactly as she might have predicted him to do, Chan came around and opened the door she had just closed.

"Excuse me?" he said, not having been apprised of an additional passenger.

"Is something wrong?" Victoria asked, stealing Peggy's tactic of bright-eyed innocence.

Chan considered her question but opted not to debate it, choosing instead to close the door again, leaving her in the darkness.

I have a right to do this, she kept repeating to herself as she waited for Hunter to come out. With no clue as to when he might return from his evening rendezvous, the prospect of leaving the matter until the next day was unacceptable to her. So, too, was her original plan to confront him in his room before he left, knowing that he'd brush her off with the excuse of having to be somewhere else.

No, the limo idea would force him to acknowledge her—and listen.

She didn't have long to wait.

Through the tinted glass, she could see him emerge from the castle and briefly confer with Chan.

A moment later, Hunter opened the door.

"If you need a car for the evening," he advised her, "you're welcome to use the Mercedes."

"That's not what I'm here for," she replied.

Hunter murmured something to Chan before getting into the back seat.

"Well?" he said when he was situated.

Victoria took a breath before proceeding. "I think I have an apology coming," she informed him, thankful that there wasn't a light on so he could see how nervous she was.

Hunter leaned forward and depressed a button to illuminate their compartment, bathing them both in an amber glow. "I agree with you," he said. "But I wouldn't expect one any time soon."

"I beg your pardon?"

"Sean Michael has never apologized to anyone in his life."

Stunned by the man's total lack of guilt, Victoria's response came out with a sharp underscore of irritation. "I wasn't referring to your cousin," she said.

Hunter seemed surprised. "No?"

"You said something to me this afternoon that was totally uncalled for," she reminded him.

"And what was that?"

"It's what you *didn't* say that I found insulting."

The corner of Hunter's mouth twitched a fraction as if he were about to smile. "If it's something I *didn't* say," he mused, "then how do you know what it was?"

Before she could regroup and start over, his hand reached out to close over hers. "I'm sorry," he apologized. "You were being serious, weren't you?"

"I *am* serious," she informed him, angrily pulling her hand out from under his and regretting it at the same time. "And what you had the nerve to say about my judgment—"

Hunter sharply interrupted. "—referred to your trying to ride a horse, Victoria. Nothing more."

Flustered but resolved not to back down, she stomached the lecture he delivered on what could have happened with her lack of experience in a saddle. "Not to mention," he added, "what could have happened to my horses."

Victoria carried her own argument—albeit diluted by now—into the shoddy way he had treated her throughout dinner, virtually ignoring her as if she didn't exist.

The scowl that had been on Hunter's face softened. "I know that you exist, Victoria," he said. "And all too well. That's never been the problem in having you here."

"So what *is*?" she demanded. That he had come out and acknowledged that there *was* a problem begged the obvious follow-up to reveal to her exactly what it was.

"This isn't the time or the place to be discussing it," he firmly replied. "And now, if you don't mind, I have an appointment this evening that I need to keep."

Victoria retied the sash of her robe and contemplated the fire that she had been absently prodding back to life for at least the last two hours.

Unable to sleep without reenacting the fiasco in the limo, it had become increasingly apparent that her mental health couldn't endure another single day. Obsessing about Hunter, dodging Sean Michael, and dealing with a passel of Gothic servants had contributed to a discomfiture that well exceeded the salary she was getting paid. *Elliott will understand*, she kept telling herself.

Besides, she added, Hunter was more than capable of looking after his own affairs.

What still puzzled her, of course, was why he hadn't mentioned the last note. Twice in the limo, she had nearly brought up the subject. "As long as I'll be leaving here anyway after Thanksgiving," she had been so tempted to say, "why don't you humor me and tell me who this Mary person is."

Instead, she had said nothing. And in the end, she had watched the limo pull out of the courtyard and drive away, leaving her more empty than ever.

Had he come back yet? she wondered. The bedside clock showed a little past one. Maybe he was staying away for the night again, she speculated. Maybe with any luck, he'd stay away through Thanksgiving and she'd never have to see him again.

As she replaced the poker back on its stand, a noise in the hallway drew her attention to the door. Probably Peggy, she guessed, wondering whether the Gleavy girl had managed to seduce her latest quarry yet, having pulled out all stops to attract his attention.

Poor Ian, Victoria thought, then nearly laughed. Poor Ian indeed, his life now significantly better for Peggy having dumped him.

There was a light tap on Victoria's door, startling her. A second one, a little more urgent, followed when she made no move to answer.

One o'clock in the morning? Certainly there was no one in the castle who'd have a legitimate reason to come calling at that hour. Had she remembered to turn the lock? Victoria wasn't sure. Maybe it's just Duncan's ghost, she shrugged off the noise, reluctant to investigate.

It was no ghost, though, who was now turning the handle and opening her bedroom door.

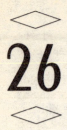

26

Even in silhouette, she immediately recognized who it was and gasped in astonishment. What paralyzed her senses more, though, was how he had managed to be there in her doorway at all.

"Victoria?" Hunter softly murmured. "Do you mind if I come in?"

The colliding sensations of desire and distrust chilled Victoria's eyes with reserve.

"What are you doing here?" she asked, suddenly conscious that he was still fully dressed while she was wearing only a silk robe and very little beneath it. The irony that their respective dress codes had been reversed only a few weeks ago might have made her laugh under other circumstances.

"I think maybe we need to talk, Victoria."

What had she done this time? "It's a little late, isn't it?" It was a dumb thing to say, of course. He wasn't likely to acknowledge the fact and, accordingly, go away.

He had closed the door gently behind him. "I had a feeling that you might still be awake." Hunter cleared his throat. "At least I *hoped* that you would."

"How did you get up here?" she inquired. Even the

mobility his cane afforded still denied him the knee-bending necessary to drive a car, climb steep stairs, or do anything else that required flexibility. Yes, her conscience mercilessly teased her. Even *that* called for limber limbs.

"Let's just say I had a little help from Duncan's trysting place," Hunter cryptically replied.

It took Victoria a moment to make the connection. "The dumbwaiter!" she exclaimed, pleased to have solved the mystery on only one clue.

The man in her bedroom, unfortunately, was not as easy to fathom.

"I'd just as soon keep the dumbwaiter secret between the two of us," Hunter recommended. "The pulleys weren't exactly designed for frequent flyer use."

It would certainly add a new dimension to Peggy's love life, Victoria thought to herself, though Hunter's smile betrayed he might have been thinking the same thing as well. Goodness knows how many more lovers the Gleavy girl could smuggle upstairs if they could bypass the main hall.

"You build a nice fire," he complimented her in a change of subject, taking a tentative step into its circle of light. "My Irish ancestors would have approved."

"Credit the Girl Scouts for it."

"You were a Girl Scout?"

Victoria held up the three middle fingers of her right hand. "On my honor."

"That's hard to picture."

"Being on my honor?"

Hunter smiled. "No. You being a Girl Scout."

"I was much younger."

"I assumed so."

His gaze was thoughtfully riveted on her face as if he were trying to imagine what she had looked like twenty years ago, then moved back to a study of the flames as a concession to their mutual embarrassment.

Victoria folded her arms to steady what would become a nervous shiver if he stepped any closer. "It's not cookie season and I don't belong to a troop," she pointed out. "So I'm not sure why you're here."

"I think that probably makes two of us."

Was it the heat of the fire or the nearness of Hunter himself that was making her uncomfortably warm all of a sudden? The answer was a rapid thud of her pulse as she awaited an explanation of what had brought him upstairs after the rest of the household was asleep.

Inexorably, her mind raced through a messy montage of what had transpired just in that day alone, a trio of painful scenes in which all verbal victory had clearly belonged in his court and not hers. That he had gone to the physical trouble to now seek her out after hours had to mean one of two things: he was either firing her or falling in love. The latter seemed unlikely.

Victoria felt a compulsion to fill up the awkward silence, even with a reference she had ascertained was off-limits.

"Did your . . . meeting go all right tonight?" she asked.

Hunter lowered his lids that she might not read the expression in his eyes. "It wasn't exactly a meeting," he said, drawing the fatigued sigh of one who was faced with an onerous task.

"Oh?" she replied, hoping it sounded detached, unconcerned.

Was he searching for the right word to define his liaison with another woman? Certainly he had to have figured out that she was already aware of it, that she wasn't dense to the fact he was an attractive man and had a pretty female's picture on his desk.

His voice was low, the kind reserved for dreaded subjects. "There are some personal obligations up in Maryland that I—well, just some things I need to take care of that I haven't mentioned to you."

Her hope that he would elaborate was short-lived.

Hunter pointed toward the chair at her writing desk. "Do you mind if I sit down?"

What choice did she have—to tell him no?

"Go right ahead," she invited him, moving her legs that she wouldn't risk tripping him. As the thought occurred to her, so too did Sean Michael's teasing about Hunter not being as helpless as he had projected the day he fell on top of her.

Maybe he could *have moved*, she speculated, for he had certainly been upset enough about the experience not to want to prolong it. Or had he?

Forcibly, she put the bittersweet remembrance of that moment—his scent, his nearness, his lips ever so close to her own—as far out of her mind as she could.

"So what did you want to talk about?" she queried after he had settled into the chair.

"Well, I thought a lot about what you said," he began. "Not just in the car this evening, but . . ." he hesitated " . . . a combination of several talks we've had since you came here." With elbows resting on the arms of the chair, Hunter steepled his fingers. "That was very enterprising of you, by the way. I can't say I've ever been ambushed before in my own vehicle." His praise sounded genuine. "Even Chan commented on it."

"First time for everything," she replied.

"Maybe in more ways than one," Hunter said. "You've opened my eyes to some important things I might have otherwise missed. I want to thank you for that, Victoria."

"I'm not sure what you're thanking me for. You seem to do just fine on your own."

An odd mingling of wariness and amusement flickered across his chiseled features as he turned his attention back to the dancing shadows on the stone hearth. God, but he was handsome, she thought. Handsome and thoroughly unattainable. The awareness of that had become a dull, throbbing ache that not even time could take away.

Hunter cleared his throat. "You remind me of someone, Victoria, and I'll be the first to tell you that it bothers the hell out of me."

Victoria waited for him to continue, expecting to be compared to an ex-girlfriend whom he had loved and lost.

"You remind me," he said, "a lot of myself."

"I'm not sure how I'm supposed to respond to that," Victoria remarked. It was not at all what she had expected him to say.

"I guess maybe that would depend on what your feelings are toward *me*."

"Right now or generally speaking?"

In truth, of course, the answer would have been one and the same.

Hunter ignored her question. "I think I've finally figured out why Elliott sent you," he said instead.

"Because you needed someone." Instantly, Victoria regretted her choice of words. "To work for you," she tried to add but the effect was far from seamless.

Whether he picked up on it or not, Hunter had the discretion to let it slide without remark. "We're both headstrong, opinionated, and risk-taking," he said. "I'm sure Elliott figured by now that our temperaments would either lead us to kill each other or—"

Victoria's attention hinged on the dangerous pause his unfinished sentence had just created.

"Or what?" she finally asked.

"Or that it might be crazy enough to actually work out between the two of us."

"Well, we haven't killed each other," she said. "If we can make it past Thanksgiving, I guess we're home free."

Hunter laughed at her remark. "I suppose so." He had settled back in the chair, obviously in no hurry to leave. "And what are your plans after that?"

"Plans?" Victoria echoed. "What do you mean 'plans'?"

"I meant besides going back to the law firm. It's hard to imagine that work would consume your whole existence."

"It doesn't."

Her bluntness seemed to amuse him. "So?" he asked, pressing to satisfy his curiosity.

"Whatever life has to offer," she replied, growing perplexed by his line of questions. "Why do you ask?"

"You're lucky to have that kind of freedom, Victoria. A lot of people don't. Myself included."

It was an odd comment for him to make and she chose to pursue it. "I wouldn't think a man who can move castles across an ocean is exactly hurting in the freedom department."

"Castles are easy," he replied, "compared to obstacles."

"Human or otherwise?"

"For the moment, a combination." He was gazing off into space, lost to some private recollection.

"I'm sure you'll work it out," she said.

The blackened center log of her fire had split from burning and toppled forward. Victoria reached for the poker to push it back, releasing a glittered spray of orange and red sparks up the chimney.

Hunter measured his next words carefully. "If I'm out of line to ask this, you're within rights to tell me."

"Ask what?"

"When all of this is over . . ." He had leaned forward while she tended the fire as if to make the shortened distance fill in the blanks for which words were not coming easily. "Would you mind if I were to call you?"

Stunned, Victoria straightened in response to his question, trying to assimilate its startling mix of awareness, invitation, acceptance. Trying to calm, as well, the rush of staggering reality that what she had been wishing for had just been miraculously granted.

"Call me?" Victoria cautiously echoed lest she had heard it incorrectly. "As in 'date'?"

Hunter tilted his head in a sheepish acknowledgment of what sounded so juvenile to them both when spoken aloud. "We should come up with another word for it," he said in an effort to lift what he perceived as a level of tension. "A date sounds like you have to ask your mother first."

"*My* mother," Victoria replied, "would insist on coming along."

Hunter laughed. "A chaperone," he said with a wink, "probably wouldn't be a bad idea." With no answer forthcoming to his original question, he inquired a second time.

"I'm . . . not sure what to say," she murmured. The urge to hurl herself into his arms was tempered by her uneasiness that a part of him already belonged to someone else. "Forgive me if I'm confused, but—"

"But what?"

"I guess I assumed that . . ." Victoria floundered for the right way to say it, never having rehearsed such an unexpected scene with him.

He was genuinely perplexed by her faltering. "What is it, Victoria?"

Victoria took a deep breath, knowing that she could no longer delay the inevitable. "There's a photograph on your desk," she said. "I noticed it the first day I was here."

The faint beginnings of a frown tugged at the corners of Hunter's mouth.

"Is she—" Victoria hesitated. "Is she the woman who's been calling you?"

"No." He seemed surprised by the question. "Is that what you thought?"

"I'm not sure *what* to think," she confessed, waiting for his reply and yet dreading it at the same time.

He was close enough to touch and yet he may as well have been a million miles away for his contemplative state, gazing into the fire. "Have you ever lost someone, Victoria?" he quietly asked. "Someone who meant the world to you and that none of your money could ever bring back?"

It was a rhetorical question, though she could have easily answered by telling him of her father.

"The girl in that picture," he said, "would probably turn cartwheels if she could see what I was doing right now."

"You mean asking me out?" Her voice had drifted into a hushed whisper, her senses struggling with the new uncertainties that had just been aroused.

"Asking you out and getting on with my life."

Had she just joined the ranks of competing with a dead love for Hunter's affection? If that were the case, she wished he had never come to her room, never looked at her the warm, galvanizing way he was looking at her at that moment.

"Who was she?" Victoria asked.

A woman's bloodcurdling scream—coming from somewhere outside—pierced the night's silence.

27

Hunter *grabbed his metal cane* and was out of the chair like a cannon shot.

"Stay here," he bluntly commanded as Victoria scrambled to her feet to follow him. "It's safer."

Her mind whirled at his chauvinistic response, for only moments before he had praised her independence and courage to take risks.

"I just thought you'd—" she started to protest, but Hunter's stance was adamant.

"Do as I say!" he cut her off as he pulled open the bedroom door. "*Please.*"

Victoria bit down hard on her lower lip as she watched the pained, erratic gait of his limp take him into the corridor. *Stay, indeed,* she wanted to shout at him. Already, she could hear doors starting to open and the castle's sleepy residents coming awake to investigate the disturbance.

She had as much right to know what was going on out there as anyone, she told herself, infuriated not only with the man's attempted domination of her but the fact that the scream—whatever its cause—could not have been more poorly timed. Just ten seconds more, Victoria wryly thought, and she might have had an answer to the mystery girl's identity.

That Hunter was moving in the opposite direction from the stairway momentarily puzzled her. Where was he going if the scream had come from downstairs? And then she remembered how he had gotten up to her room in the first place. Encumbered by the necessity of returning to the lower level in the same fashion—via the dumbwaiter—it wasn't likely that he'd reach his destination at any great speed.

She could be downstairs and back before he even got there, she concluded, curiosity feverishly superseding his orders that she obediently stay in her room and let him play hero.

Mindful of how she was dressed, Victoria slipped back inside her bedroom just long enough to grab her raincoat from the armoire and pull it on. Not exactly a fashion statement, but it would raise fewer eyebrows than her robe by itself in the presence of others.

The delay—short as it was—resulted in an unexpected encounter with Sean Michael, emerging from his own room wearing only the beltless jeans he was just now zipping up.

"You heard it, too?" he asked, raking both hands through his uncombed hair.

Hunter, she noticed, had already disappeared from the corridor, a fact for which she was grateful. All she needed right now were hurtful barbs from Sean Michael had he witnessed his cousin's departure at so late and compromising an hour.

"I was just on my way," she replied.

Barefoot and bare-chested, Sean Michael not only reached her side but was already past it in the time it took her to say it. Victoria followed in a race down the stairs.

Not to her surprise, they were the first to get there, the others having to travel a greater distance if they were all in their bedrooms.

"Came from outside," he muttered as they reached the main hall.

"Who do you think—"

He had already sprinted in the direction of the castle's front parlor before Victoria could even get the question out. His pause at the front door was only to turn and tell her to stay inside.

"It could be bloody dangerous out there," he informed her.

The adventurous glint that sprang to his own dark eyes as he said it affirmed that danger and risk were among the more satisfying things Sean Michael Gleavy lived for. Either that, or he was seizing another opportunity to impress her with his recklessness.

"I've come *this* far," she retorted, irritated that he was the second man in two minutes to tell her to stay put.

Rather than waste precious time arguing with her, Sean Michael yanked open the door and ran out into the courtyard.

Though the castle's drive was illuminated, the combination of jagged shadows cast by the castle's bulk and slippery puddles contributed by Mother Nature made Victoria less intrepid than her male counterpart. Sean Michael's guttural gasp of horror had, thus, already been made before Victoria was halfway across. All she could see from where she was when his outcry came was the odd sight of the pronged iron entrance gate being completely down, the first time she had ever seen it that way. Hadn't Chan told her that the gate was never used?

"For God's sake, *get* someone!" the strident but distinctive voice of Jon Tapping rang out from somewhere in the darkness.

She had nearly reached Sean Michael and could now hear a woman sobbing hysterically from the outer side of the gate. Who exactly it was, she couldn't tell.

"No, Victoria! Stay away!" Tapping shouted out in alarm, alerting Sean Michael to the fact that she was nearly upon him and the gruesome sight that had just assailed his eyes.

With lightning speed, Sean Michael whirled from where he had been standing to nearly tackle her, fervent in the goal to keep her from going any further, from seeing what looked to be something wedged up against—or possibly under—the castle gate.

"Call the police!" he demanded of her, his fingers digging so deep into her forearms that, even beneath the sleeves of her raincoat, it made her wince. "Now!"

"But what—" Her impatient determination to look around him was thwarted in a violent shaking of her shoulders by the hot-tempered Irishman.

"Get the bloody hell into the house, woman!" he yelled.

The unseen female's sobbing on the other side of the gate had turned into the sound of retching. Once more, Jon Tapping's voice urgently implored haste in going for help.

"Oh, God," Sean Michael murmured in the voice of one defeated. For now emerging from the castle in a collective din of confusion were its other occupants, his cousin Hunter among them.

"What's going on?" Victoria insisted on knowing. "And what's that thing over—"

Sean Michael's abrupt answer chilled her to the core. "It's Mrs. Maginn. She's dead."

The black police sergeant thoughtfully sipped from the mug of coffee Mrs. Pritchard had brought him as he added another reply to his notebook. Dividing up the household for separate statements, he and the lieutenant had already been at the castle for more than two hours before Victoria's turn had come. Now seated across from him at the kitchen table, she found herself grateful that Sean Michael had kept her from actually seeing the housekeeper's body, brutally impaled straight through the head and upper torso by the thick iron prongs of the portcullis.

"Like something straight out of a Stephen King thriller," she had overheard one of the officers remark about the means by which Mrs. Maginn had died. In and of itself, that comment alone conjured a graphic scene to turn anyone's stomach.

"Just a few more questions," Sergeant Daniels assured her. "I know you've had a long night."

Victoria nodded, still stunned by what she had pieced together of the night's tragedy.

"You say you didn't hear anything *before* the scream?" he inquired. "Nothing that sounded like the gate going down?"

"Nothing I can remember," she said, shaking her head.

Absorbed in her own thoughts prior to Hunter's arrival and centered on their conversation once he was there, Victoria had managed to tune out all else. Coupled with the fact that a castle of Kriskerry's vintage was replete with a number of sounds foreign to a city dweller, she might not have differentiated a gate descending from any other noise.

"You mentioned," the sergeant continued, "that Mr. O'Hare was in your room when Miss Gleavy screamed."

"Yes."

"Approximately how long was he there? Do you recall?"

"Twenty minutes. Maybe a little more." *I wish I knew what Hunter was saying*, she thought anxiously, praying that their stories corresponded. For although her alibi that they were together eliminated him as a suspect in what they were calling a murder, his use of the dumbwaiter that night also provided him access to the upper gatehouse where the portcullis had been released by a lever.

"And may I ask why he was there?" Daniels inquired.

Victoria hesitated. "I work very closely with Mr.

O'Hare," she replied. "There was some business we had to discuss for the following day."

A trace of a scowl flickered across the detective's face. "Was it customary for Mr. O'Hare to discuss business with you at so late an hour?"

I knew I shouldn't have said that, she chided herself. Yet the alternative—revealing that Hunter seemed to have an interest in her besides work—didn't sound right either. "As a special assistant," she explained it, "I'm expected to be available when he needs me."

He wasn't buying it, she could tell. And yet he continued to ask questions as if her explanation were perfectly plausible. "So he came to see you about doing work? To take some dictation?" He left his question open-ended for Victoria to supply an answer.

"Just talk," she replied.

Daniels nodded and made a few more notes. "Just one more thing, Ms. Cameron," he said. "Did Mr. O'Hare ever mention someone by the name of 'Mary' to you?"

"'Mary'?" she cautiously repeated.

"Yes."

"Why do you ask?" Stupid question to ask him, she told herself, saying it only to buy a little time to construct an answer.

The sergeant, as she might have expected, repeated his own question instead of answering hers.

"No," she replied, for in truth Hunter had never brought up the name 'Mary' himself, alluding only to someone special in his life who was no longer there to share it. "The name doesn't ring a bell," she said.

Daniels took another sip of coffee. "I think that's all I need for now, Ms. Cameron," he thanked her. "I appreciate your time."

His tag remark that she keep herself available if further testimony was needed prompted Victoria to tell him that her assignment at the castle would be up the end of the week.

"Excuse me?" he said, puzzled by what she had just volunteered. "I understood you were a permanent employee of Mr. O'Hare."

"Only temporary," she replied, briefly explaining how her assignment at the castle had come about.

"That name again was Elliott Bowman?" he repeated, making a note of it. "And the number where I can reach him?"

That's strange, Victoria thought, wondering what he'd possibly want with Elliott, save for a character reference about herself.

"He's been Mr. O'Hare's attorney for a number of years," she added.

Again, Daniels thanked her. "Oh, by the way," he said, "if you'll let Lieutenant Gibson know that we're just about to wrap up here . . . ?"

The shiver that Victoria had successfully managed to keep under control in the detective's presence resurfaced once she emerged from the kitchen. Like a horrible dream from which she couldn't awaken, she replayed what little she knew about what had happened that night, accounting for the household's whereabouts from what she had overheard or seen for herself prior to the arrival of the police.

Tapping and Peggy, she ascertained, had gone out for a midnight stroll, returning not only to find Mrs. Maginn's punctured body but to find themselves completely locked out of the castle, there being no outside mechanism to activate the gate once it was down.

That Peggy was in the company of the English attorney was not as much a surprise to Victoria's ears as the fact that they weren't pursuing their obvious flirtation with each other in the privacy of her bedroom. While no sounds of vigorous lovemaking had emanated that evening from the other side of the fireplace, Victoria was nevertheless certain she had heard *someone* moving around next door just before Hunter's knock. In the absence of a reasonable guess or proof of what she had heard, she omitted mention of it to Sergeant Daniels.

Sean Michael, of course, had been in his own bedroom when his sister's scream of discovery came, a fact that Victoria *had* chosen to mention. "He came out at the same time you did, then?" Sergeant Daniels had queried. *Of all the nights for Deborah not to be here*, Victoria found herself thinking, for in his blond girlfriend Sean Michael would have had an easy alibi of what he'd been doing all evening since dinner.

The murder, Victoria went on in her head, had to have occurred sometime after Tapping and Peggy left for their walk, as well as after Hunter and Chan's return from Maryland, for the limo could not have entered the courtyard with the gate down.

And yet when exactly *had* Hunter come back? Victoria racked her brain, trying to remember if he had told her when he first came into her bedroom. Intuition, at the time, had compelled her to think he had been downstairs for quite a while before his decision to see her, to speak his heart.

As for the servants, Victoria couldn't be sure, all of them having spilled out into the courtyard in their respective styles of nightwear at about the same moment. Even Chan, she noted, had presumably retired for the evening in a black kimono that ended at midthigh.

As she approached the open door of the game room, she could hear who Lieutenant Gibson was interrogating. Hunter.

"We found this note with your name on it in the deceased woman's pocket," she heard the officer say. "Are you familiar with it?"

"No," Hunter said after a grave moment. "I've never seen it before."

"So the reference to Mary—?"

Lieutenant Gibson stopped in midsentence, conscious that Hunter's eyes had just spotted Victoria uncomfortably hovering in the doorway.

"It's all right," Hunter said, unruffled by neither her presence nor the officer's question. "Ms. Cameron is my secretary."

"I'm sorry to interrupt, Lieutenant," she apologized, "but Sergeant Daniels asked me to tell you that he's ready to wrap up."

The blond lieutenant thanked her and waited for her to leave. For just the space of an instant, Victoria caught sight of the paper that lay on the game table and instantly recognized what it was, chilling her with the awareness that she had just caught Hunter in a lie.

As she exited the room, she heard the detective return to his last question.

"The name 'Mary,' Mr. O'Hare—?"

"Is my sister," came Hunter's somber reply.

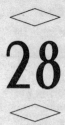

28

Victoria *absently drummed her fingers* on the desk top as if the rhythym would either hasten the impending sunrise or put the awful memory of the past few hours behind her. She doubted that anyone else was sleeping. Just like her, they were probably awake and wondering who among them was a cold-blooded murderer.

Most of all, Victoria's anxieties were centered on Hunter and what she had overheard him say to the police lieutenant.

Mary.

While it might have been a consolation to her ego and her heart that the one he had loved was a blood relation and not a girlfriend or wife, it did little for her spirits to remember that he had blatantly lied about ever seeing that last note bearing her name. Sooner or later the police would find out he was lying. And from that, she worried, they could draw conclusions to incriminate him in Mrs. Maginn's violent death.

What could have been going through his head when he gave that answer? she wondered, for surely he knew for a fact that at least one other person was aware it existed—Victoria herself. Or did he trust her that much not to reveal she had even left it, already opened and read, on the table for him to find?

What made no sense to her at all in retrospect, though, was what the note actually *said*, implying that Mary was sequestered away somewhere. Unless she was buried in some secret vault that no one knew about—

Victoria's spirits sank even lower, conjuring the scenario that Mary herself might have been the victim of foul play and hastily entombed to hide the truth, perhaps even beneath the castle.

Stop it, her conscience commanded. Hunter O'Hare was innocent until proven guilty. That she was attracted to the man and felt a kinship should be encouraging her desire to *prove* his innocence, not compelling her to find reasons to distrust him.

Besides, she rationalized, would a man who had just committed a heinous murder on his own property be able to so calmly come up to her bedroom and talk about Girl Scout cookies, mutual traits, and plans for future dating?

Perhaps, an inner voice cynically replied. Especially if he needed a credible alibi.

She had a hunch that they'd be there. For that matter, it would not have particularly surprised her to find the entire household, drowning their restlessness in chatter and caffeine as the darkness edged toward morning light.

As it was, only Nilly and Mrs. P were at the kitchen table when she walked in.

"Did you make any extra?" she asked the cook, indicating the mugs from which they were both drinking.

"We all need it, don't you know?" the red-faced Mrs. P sniffled, waddling to the cupboard in her shapeless robe and fuzzy scuffs to accommodate Victoria's request. Nilly, Victoria noticed, was already dressed, a man whose practice was to meet each day neatly groomed, even if he had absolutely nothing to do.

Victoria pulled out a chair and sat down, not sure what they expected her to say. Certainly there had been no love lost between them and Mrs. Maginn, and yet she felt the compulsion to at least acknowledge the woman's passing.

"It's been a terrible night," she murmured.

Nilly nodded without replying.

"'Tis a fact to be swearin' we had our differences, herself and me," Mrs. Pritchard started to remark but was promptly shushed by the valet.

"I'd not be saying too much, Mrs. P," he advised her.

"Go on with you now, Nilly!" she replied. "Why sure an' I'd be sayin' it to St. Peter himself that I wouldn't be wishin' it on my worst enemy." Mrs. P shook her head as she set down a fresh coffee in front of Victoria. "Bloody as sin, they said she was."

Nilly cleared his throat.

"It's strange," Victoria said, "that no one heard the gate come down. You'd think something that big—"

"Himself had it oiled smooth as a baby's behind," Mrs. Prichard volunteered.

"I beg your pardon?" Victoria said.

"Full of the creaks it was back home," Mrs. P went on, pleased to be sharing her knowledge. "Well now, himself didn't like it a bit so he had it oiled."

"But if he never intended to use it," Victoria pressed, "why go to the trouble?"

"Seems as *someone* did," the cook remarked.

Once again, the valet interjected his two cents that it was not their place to discuss such things.

Victoria recognized that she had found an eager talker in Mrs. Pritchard. "The gate must have come down awfully fast for her not even to be able to get out of the way."

"Like Satan hurlin' it himself," the cook proclaimed. "Not that I'm sayin' it was an act of the devil, but—"

Nilly had pushed back his chair and announced his intentions of leaving the room.

"It isn't respectful, Mrs. P," he admonished her before his departure. "There's no good to come from talking of it any further."

"The dear's right, I suppose," Mrs. Pritchard sighed, withdrawing a handkerchief from the pocket of her robe to blow her nose.

"Nilly seems awfully upset," Victoria observed.

"It's the whole thing of it, don't you know."

"Excuse me?"

"Out of the blue, he says he'll not be stayin' another week."

"Nilly?"

Mrs. P clucked her tongue. "He's homesick, the dear, and myself not to be blamin' him one bit." Without encouragement, she volunteered that Sir Patrick's oldest servant had not spent a single happy day since his arrival in America and yearned for a one-way trip home to the familiar sod of his ancestors.

"I hate to bear bad news," Victoria said, "but I don't think the police are likely to let anyone go anywhere with a murder investigation under way. Especially not out of the country."

The cook seemed startled by her suggestion. "Nilly wouldn't be hurtin' a fly!" she defended her elderly friend. "Even a pesky one, don't you know."

"A pesky what?" Sean Michael queried as he entered the kitchen, a plaid shirt thrown over his jeans and unbuttoned to the navel. "Am I missing anything interesting?"

Mrs. Pritchard bristled in indignation at his intrusion—either that, or at the sight of his naked chest in mixed company. "I'm sorry for your loss, Mr. Gleavy," she said, "but I'll not be lowerin' myself to the lie of sayin' we'll not be managin' without her."

Victoria's ears perked up at the words that had just slipped by her. Had she heard that right? Too late, the conversation had shifted before she could get a handle on it.

"I'm sure you'll manage just fine," Sean Michael replied with a smile. "Oh, by the way, how's Dr. Doolittle taking it?"

Had she not witnessed his snide reference to Ian the previous afternoon, Victoria might not have known who he was talking about.

The insult was not lost on Mrs. Pritchard. "Ian," she crisply informed him, "was out in the stables all night."

Though she said nothing, even Victoria saw the error of Mrs. P's statement, for Ian had numbered among those she saw herself in the courtyard. To be out in the stables as his mother so firmly attested, Ian would have to have been on the opposite side of the gate with Tapping and Peggy.

"The stables, was it?" Sean Michael said in amusement. "Was that before or after he pleasured my sister?"

"I'll not be listenin' to your lies about my son!" she snapped, furious with Sean Michael's remark.

"Was it something I said?" he asked of Victoria as Mrs. Pritchard bustled out of the room.

"Maybe it's just your personality," Victoria offered.

"Ever the charmer, aren't you?" he teased, pulling out a chair and turning it backwards so that he could straddle it. "So what's *your* excuse, pretty lass?"

Victoria retained her affability, but there was a distinct hardening in her green eyes as they met his. "My excuse for what?"

Sean Michael chuckled. "Ol' Spots was out to get you from the bloody start," he recalled. "Perhaps it was mutual."

"I was in my room," she icily replied, annoyed with the fact that she was even dignifying his accusation with an answer.

"Alone?"

"And what's it to you?"

Sean Michael studied her in obvious enjoyment. "I just thought perhaps you'd appreciate an alibi."

"Who says I need one?"

"Touché," he said. "I suppose I should know better by now than to argue with an actress's daughter."

"And what's *that* supposed to mean?" she challenged him.

"Should it mean anything?"

Victoria broke the verbal stalemate with a question of her own. "Was it true what you said to Mrs. Pritchard about her son being in Peggy's room?"

Sean Michael arched a dark brow, intrigued by her curiosity. "And if it was?"

"Well, it doesn't make sense, for one thing," she pointed out, cognizant that they both recognized Mrs P to be lying to protect her only child. "Peggy wasn't even in the castle."

Sean Michael laughed. "Seems as we *all* know that but Ian, don't we?"

Victoria felt a sudden pang of pity for the stableboy, though she couldn't have defined exactly why. Lovestruck and clearly enamored of the black-haired Irish beauty whose social class put her just out of his reach, it was not beyond reason that he was totally blind to her lascivious pursuit of other men. Had he shared her bed upon occasional invitation up until Tapping's arrival, it was possible that he had gone to her room and, not finding her there, patiently decided to wait for her return.

"Bloody misfortune he *wasn't* with the horses," Sean Michael remarked.

"What do you mean?"

"He's as easy a scapegoat as any."

"Scapegoat for whom?"

"Get bloody real, Victoria," Sean Michael sighed. "Who would have a better reason than Hunter to see the ol' girl dead? She knew his secrets. Every last one of them."

The pronouncement fell so effortlessly from his lips that Victoria wondered if he wouldn't perjure himself just to see it come true.

She saw no choice but to disprove his assumption of

Hunter's guilt. "I'm afraid he had a good witness to where he was last night," she informed him.

"Oh?"

It was worth it just to see the look of shock on Sean Michael's face. "He was with me," she said.

There was no more postponing the inevitable.

As many excuses as she had managed to muster all morning to avoid contact with Hunter, she knew there were things that they had to discuss, questions that couldn't remain unanswered if for no other reason than her own peace of mind.

He looked up from the papers he was signing as she entered the room, his tight expression relaxing into a smile when he saw who it was.

"Sorry I've been a recluse this morning," he apologized. "There were some calls I had to make to Ireland and—well, enough said. It's been a bad night for all of us."

"If I've come at a bad time—" she said, now paralyzed by the prospect of actually confronting him.

"You're a welcome sight, to be honest." The wave of his hand encouraged her to close the door. "I'm going to have to get something out to the newspapers this morning," he continued. "Are you up to taking some dictation?"

"I was . . . hoping that we could talk."

Hunter's voice was uncompromising and yet oddly gentle. "I really need to deal with this first and get it faxed," he said. "After that's done, we can talk about whatever you want."

He was studying her for a sign of objection. Either that, or a clue to her emotional state.

"That would be fine," she murmured. "I'll just go get a pad."

"There's an extra here," he said, tearing off the top sheet of the one he had been using and handing it to her along with a pen. Hunter cleared his throat as she sat down. "It's going to be an obituary for Mrs. Maginn." The long silence before he actually began only reinforced what had transpired in the early hours of that same morning.

It was peculiar, Victoria thought to herself as Hunter dictated, to learn more about a person dead than she had known about her alive. The housekeeper's full first name, where she'd been born in Ireland, the names of her parents. It surprised Victoria that the family name was also Maginn.

"Did she marry a cousin or something?" Victoria asked, amazed by the coincidence.

"The 'Mrs.,'" Hunter gently explained, "was a contrivance to cover her spinsterhood."

"Sorry to interrupt," Victoria said. "Go on."

"Preceded in death by her sister, Katie Maureen—"

Something was suddenly triggered in Victoria's head, but she didn't remember exactly what it was.

"—and survived," Hunter was saying, "by her great-niece and -nephew, Margaret Aileen and Sean Michael Gleavy."

29

   Victoria nearly dropped her pen, startled by this latest revelation of family history.

   "I had no idea," she murmured, though in a flash of
retrospect, it had always struck her that *something* was
curiously amiss about the housekeeper's strained relationship with Sir Patrick's grandchildren. Phrases and
looks that she had earlier discounted as the product of
bad tempers and cross purposes now took on a significant new slant, an affirmation of blood's thickness over
water.

   Impatiently, she waited for Hunter to finish dictating
and deliver on his promised explanation. Two letters and
four phone interruptions later, he was finally read to talk.

   "Gwynnelldylaine was only a baby when her older sister came to work for Sir Patrick," he said. Katie, in fact,
had been wont to bring the toddler along to play in the
castle while she worked as the upstairs maid, relieving
their parents of the exhausting task of looking out for
her.

   "Sir Patrick didn't mind?"

   "More likely, he didn't even *notice* for the first couple of
months. A place this size, she could probably have stashed

an entire preschool. At any rate, the two of them spent more waking hours here than at home, not to mention the bond they forged by always being together."

"No wonder Mrs. Maginn had such an attachment to this place," Victoria remarked, recalling several of the territorial comments the housekeeper had made about the proper way things should be done. Hunter agreed, citing some of the clashes Mrs. Maginn had experienced with the other servants, even while Kriskerry was still on Irish soil. "Blame it on her upbringing," he said.

Too young to understand the social division between Ireland's landed rich like Sir Patrick and the working-class poor like her parents, Gwynna—as she came to be called—had grown up regarding the castle as her very own, the place where she would live for the rest of her life. "She knew every inch of it," he said. "Every hiding place, every treasure, every picture. Probably the only one who knew more than she did was Nilly, and only because he had the advantage of age."

"Katie's subsequent pregnancy," Hunter went on, "didn't clarify their status in the household but, instead, confused it even more. All of that," he added, "thanks to my great-grandfather's decision to move both Maginn girls under his roof as soon as Katie started to show."

"Because he was hoping that she'd have a boy to carry on the line and justify him marrying her," Victoria filled in, remembering it from their conversation over dinner at the Benedict Inn. Matrimony, Victoria easily recognized, would not only have elevated Katie's social level but her little sister's as well. In the interim, keeping the mother-to-be happy, safe, and well fed was strictly an insurance measure from Sir Patrick's standpoint.

Hunter continued his story. "While Katie disappointed him by having a daughter instead, Gwynna couldn't have been more thrilled to have a new playmate." The very small age difference, he pointed out, made Gwynna and the baby more like siblings than, respectively, an aunt and her niece.

"But what about when they got older? Did they still stay close?"

"Oh I think at some point Gwynna was wise enough to the ways of the world to see that her niece had it a smidge better than she did, being at least the illegitimate *daughter* of someone titled rather than a coattail relative."

"So how come she never left?" Victoria queried, assuming that Mrs. Maginn had come up through the ranks of servitude and learned enough skills to take elsewhere.

Hunter shrugged. "Loyalty, I suppose. For all of the opportunities she had to move on, Mrs. Maginn had never worked anywhere else but Kriskerry Castle. She also had an unswerving amount of optimism."

Victoria scowled in puzzlement at his last remark.

"Katie," Hunter explained, "had pretty much resigned herself to being my great-grandfather's mistress and nothing more. Even if she had *wanted* to leave him, you have to consider that there weren't many places that would take her in." With public opinion toward unwed mothers what it had been half a century before, he reminded her, the Irish girl's options were starkly limited.

"Then you have Katie's daughter," Hunter said, "who was just looking for love in all the wrong places. Not unlike Peggy."

Finding her heart's desire in the arms of a playboy who wouldn't divorce his wife to marry her, Sir Patrick's love child essentially cut her own purse strings by refusing to end her affair and return to Ireland.

"As far as I know," Hunter said, "she only came back twice—to drop off newborn babies on her long-suffering Aunt Gwynna."

"And the name 'Gleavy'?"

"What the man refused to give her out of honor and respect, she went ahead and appropriated on both birth certificates. I don't know that she ever tried to collect support off of it, but maybe the surname was all she wanted."

"That doesn't explain what you meant about Mrs. Maginn and optimism," Victoria pointed out. "Her life sounded pretty bleak, to hear you explain it that way."

"Maybe it was one of the few things that kept her going."

The most vocal of the star-crossed trio, Gwynna Maginn had never given up the hope that Sir Patrick would one day do right by her older sister and make her an honest woman.

"She must've hated him for never doing that," Victoria said, wondering how exactly Sir Patrick had died. *Perhaps*, she thought, *the old man had received unbidden assistance at the hands of his lover's sibling.*

Hunter smiled. "Your face is an open book. I bet I can guess what you're wondering," he said.

"What's that?"

"Natural causes," he read her mind. "Although I'm sure my late housekeeper occasionally entertained thoughts of hastening it."

The will, Hunter wrapped up his story, had been Mrs. Maginn's last hope of justice. With both her sister and niece deceased, she must have reasoned, the kindness she had extended in Sean Michael and Peggy's upbringing would surely be reflected in a comfortable standard of living.

"I guess your intervention pretty much squelched *that* hope," Victoria observed.

Hunter cast her an unexpected, indulgent wink. "At least she still had a job with me," he said. "I doubt my ungrateful cousins would have kept her on payroll for five minutes after Sir Patrick's coffin was lowered."

The mention of burial turned Victoria's stomach with the remembrance of the funeral arrangements that Hunter was in the process of making. It was stupid to say it, but the words came out of her mouth anyway. "What an awful way to die," she murmured.

Hunter was silent for a long time. "I'm afraid that's not

the bigger thing that's bothering me right now," he revealed.

"You mean wondering who could've done it?" Victoria had spent most of the hours since it had happened wondering the very same thing herself.

"Did you know," Hunter said, "that you can't actually *see* the gate from up in the gatehouse?" In response to her expression of confusion, he went on to describe how the gatehouse—situated halfway between the second and third floors—was a medieval lookout station. "If you saw the enemy charging," he explained, "you lowered the gate so they couldn't get in."

"I'm with you on that part," Victoria nodded, "but—"

"If someone were standing directly *under* the portcullis," he said, "you couldn't see them from up there. You'd just have to hazard a guess of when they were right beneath you."

She could now see where he was leading, her thoughts dangerously racing for a plausible reason of why Mrs. Maginn had been in the wrong place at the wrong time. "What if she was meeting someone?" she offered. Mrs. Maginn, after all, had been fully dressed and not in her nightclothes like the rest of the staff.

"Meeting someone for what?"

Inadvertently, he had brought the conversation to the very doorstep of the subject she most dreaded discussing.

"Maybe," Victoria said cautiously, "it was about that note to you she was carrying in her pocket."

Hunter scowled, though Victoria couldn't be sure whether he was considering the possibility or was trying to think of a way to deny his knowledge of its existence.

There was no turning back what she had started. She had to know.

"Why did you lie about it?" she asked, daring herself not to show the emotion she was feeling deep inside.

"Lie about what, Victoria?"

She couldn't bring herself to look at the tense, drawn

face across from her as she said it, even though she knew that his eyes would mirror the guilt—or innocence—within. "The note about where you're keeping Mary," she replied.

His brusque answer surprised her. "How did *you* know about that note?"

Victoria's breath quickened, her senses conscious that she was playing a dangerous game of cat and mouse and that, somehow, she had just unwittingly become the mouse again. "So you *did* know about it," she said in a tone laced with resignation.

"Not until Sergeant Daniels showed it to me," Hunter informed her, leaning forward to cup her chin in his hand and tilt her head to eye level. "Which leads back to what I just asked *you*."

Victoria swallowed hard. "I could say I forgot to give it to you," she said, "but that wouldn't be true. Whatever was going on in Maryland—" she hesitated. "A person can only handle so much in one day, Hunter. Even you."

When they had finished talking, she wasn't sure whether she should feel better or worse. The censure by Hunter for keeping mail from him was almost worth the relief of determining that a third party had stolen it before he ever saw it.

"Do you think that whoever took it," she asked, "is the same one who killed Mrs. Maginn?"

Hunter shook his head. "About the only thing I'm sure of," he said, "is that you might want to pack your bags and go back with Elliott this afternoon." The senior attorney, he explained, was coming out on the police detective's advisement that Hunter speak with legal counsel in light of the investigation into Mrs. Maginn's death.

"Trying to get rid of me?" Victoria attempted to introduce levity.

"No," he replied. "Just trying to keep you alive."

* * *

The words still lingered as she sat in the game room a few hours later, trying to concentrate on a book to take her mind off of all that had happened.

"Penny for your thoughts?" Jon Tapping cheerfully interrupted, rapping on the open door.

"Is that the going rate?"

Tapping laughed at her remark, then immediately apologized for breaking the currently somber milieu of Kriskerry Castle with anything that resembled humor.

"Is your meeting over already?" Victoria asked. She had spoken with Elliott only briefly when he first arrived, assuming that Hunter would want as much time as possible with both attorneys.

"Oh, I'm out of this one," Tapping replied, expressing neither disappointment nor relief.

Victoria found his exclusion odd and mentioned it.

"It's really Bowman's show," he explained it as he parked himself in the chair opposite her. "My visit here's only a short one."

"The police didn't talk to you about extending it?"

"Apparently," Tapping shrugged, "I'm not one of their stronger suspects."

I *wonder who* is, *then*, Victoria thought.

"Throws quite a wrinkle in things, doesn't it?" he remarked. "The murder, I mean. Terrible."

"It's lucky your *wife* wasn't along on this trip," Victoria said, lest he had forgotten that he still had one back in London.

"Yes. Quite." In the next breath, he shifted the topic to Peggy. "She hasn't been down all day," he said in concern. "Perhaps someone should check in on her."

"Have you mentioned it to her brother?" Victoria asked. Given Peggy's rapidly shrinking popularity in the household, Sean Michael was probably the only one who'd care if she ever came out of her room again.

Tapping shook his head. "Angry fellow, isn't he?"

"Angry? I don't know that's the word I'*d* use."

"I pity Peggy to have grown up with him," the Englishman sympathetically continued. "We had quite a talk about it last night."

"On your walk?" It was a sniping comment to make but one that his demonstrated lack of ethics probably merited.

The sarcasm went over Tapping's head. "It's funny," he said, "but she told me last night that she had this awful feeling something was going to happen."

"Oh really? When?"

"Well, when she came to fetch me for a walk."

"No," Victoria clarified, "I meant when was something terrible supposed to happen?"

"Soon, she said. You know how vague these premonition things are."

"Yes. Very."

"Probably that séance nonsense. She kept saying Duncan was out for revenge." Tapping tilted his head. "Did I say something amusing?"

"Oh, I guess it's a little hard to swallow that a ghost who bedded a record number of virgins would object to his castle being moved to a place called Virginia."

Tapping laughed. "God, what a lucky chap Hunter is," he exclaimed.

"Lucky? In what regard?"

"Why to have *you*, of course. You're quite the stitch, Victoria."

30

Telepathy run amok, Victoria thought to herself, finding it peculiar that a newcomer like Tapping—amidst obvious distractions—had already tuned in to sensual vibrations that she and Hunter had yet to even act on. If ever, for that matter.

What on earth kind of message are the two of us projecting to everybody? she wondered, further perplexed by the fact that denial—rather than pursuit—had been their operating agenda up until last night.

From as early as her first day, she recalled, they had been the focus of all curious eyes in the household. While idle gossip about liaisons could be dismissed as a product of close quarters, its existence at Kriskerry Castle had recently taken on proportions that defied explanation. The reality of a murder only made it worse, casting unspoken aspersions on who might lie for whom if really pressed.

"Is everything going okay?" Elliott had asked her when his meeting with Hunter was over.

Dear, sweet Elliott, she thought. Just like Thatcher and John, he had a built-in radar for discerning when she wasn't quite herself. Either that, or Hunter had already told him that life at the castle was taking its emotional toll on her.

Victoria wasn't sure how to answer. Hunky-dory, the voice in her head retorted, considering the possibility that her handsome employer might be moonlighting as Vlad the Impaler. "Hanging in there," she said out loud.

"Hunter," Elliott continued, "said you might want to go back with me. Do you need some time to pack your things?"

Long before he asked, Victoria had already reached her decision. Reached it, actually, on the very heels of Hunter's proposing it himself.

"No thanks, Elliott," she declined. "I think I'll ride it out as planned til the end of the week."

As she now watched Elliott's car go out of the courtyard and back toward the tranquility of Alexandria, she couldn't help but wonder if the self-imposed stall of time she was creating would bring her any closer to Hunter or simply increase the number of days it would take to heal from ever having known him.

Sprawled across her bed with a tablet and pencil, Victoria studied the notes she had been making since Elliott's departure, scowling as she erased her last entry and moved it to a different column.

This isn't getting me anywhere, she muttered to herself in frustration as she surveyed the new result. And yet, she still felt the long-practiced compulsion to commit her confusions to paper, to confront the printed word in the hope that it would supply a needed answer.

In this case, the question at the top was who killed Gwynna Maginn.

So far, she realized after half an hour of scribbles, the only person with a claim to total innocence was Victoria herself.

Next—a little to her dismay—came Peggy and Tapping.

While they clearly provided a tight alibi for each other, there nonetheless existed factors that ruled out any question of conspiracy. Persuasive as Peggy could be with the opposite sex, Victoria decided, it wasn't likely that she could have talked a stranger like the London lawyer so quickly into a murder plot. Coupled with the logistics of their being outside the fallen gate with no exterior mechanism to operate it, it would have been impossible for them to be two places at once.

A similar argument, she maintained, also applied to Hunter. Acting alone, he could not have seen Mrs. Maginn from the confines of the gatehouse, even if he had been able to get there and then down to Victoria's bedroom without anyone seeing him, the dumbwaiter being at the opposite end of the hall. *Please don't have lied to me about that*, she found herself wishing, for it was his impaired mobility on which hinged the question of just how fast he could have moved.

Ian? Try as she might, Victoria couldn't picture the skinny stableboy commiting murder. And yet the fact that his own mother was already lying about his where-abouts to protect him couldn't help but conjure suspicion. Hunter's comment about trying to straighten out Ian's record with the immigration authorities threw yet another curve into the picture. Knowing as he must have that the millionaire was working on his behalf, it would have been foolhardy for the boy to risk as much as a parking ticket and draw undue attention to himself.

I wonder what his horses would say about it, she thought. *Probably "nay."*

Victoria's eyes dropped to the next entry. Mrs. Pritchard.

There was no denying that Ian's mother compensated for his weakness with a fierce sense of protection. Victoria flashed back to the bitter conversation she had over-heard between the cook and the housekeeper, punctuated by the former's muttered threat against the latter. Would she actually carry out such a threat? It was not beyond reason that Mrs. P would have believed every word of Mrs. Maginn's bluff about Hunter having Ian deported and, in an act of pure desperation, extracted brutal revenge on the bringer of bad news.

Victoria contemplated the cluster of erasures she had made around Sean Michael's name. Agile and conniving, the young Irishman would have had plenty of opportunity to slip up the stairs, do his deed, and be back down again before it was discovered. Even the fact that he had emerged from his bedroom in the process of zipping his fly wasn't proof that he had just awakened like the rest of the household.

What didn't fit for Sean Michael, however, was a lack of motive, particularly against his own relative. If he were going to ice anyone, Victoria decided, it would have been Hunter, not an older woman who posed no perceptible threat to his life.

Chan? The chauffeur lacked a murderer's motive as well. Certainly what little interaction he had with the housekeeper would not have been enough to prompt killing her.

Victoria's whimsical side had next made an entry of Duncan the ghost. Who was to say that supernatural elements *couldn't* be present in a castle that old, she thought, playing devil's advocate. Certainly a spiritual entity wouldn't be bound by the mortal conventions of time and space, and thus could dispatch the housekeeper with one flick of his transparent wrist and be back up to the rafters— or wherever he hung out—with no one being the wiser.

Yeah, right, her common sense chided her.

That leaves only Nilly, Victoria realized, for the other maid and the gardeners—staff she had seen only twice so far— lived off of the premises. *How much do I really know about the man?* she challenged herself. Seemingly harmless and diligently schooled in the practice of being seen and not heard, Nilly represented the most prominent link to the old ways of Ireland and Sir Patrick. Whatever sense of uselessness or displacement had brought about his sudden interest in returning home could equally be attributed to a guilty conscience. Advanced in years and essentially a loner, Nilly would have the ironic advantage over the others of serving a relatively short "life sentence" if he ended up being caught, tried, and sent to prison. A successful murder, Victoria mused, would definitely have been the most exciting thing ever to happen to him . . . if his conscience could actually *live* with his having committed one.

The mystery, of course, was how he had managed to lure an unsuspecting Mrs. Maginn to stand in just the right spot beneath the gatehouse for her own execution. There being no obvious affection or respect between the two, coupled with the alliance he shared with Mrs. Pritchard, it was an unlikely scenario that Nilly could have tricked her into much of anything.

A knock on her bedroom door interrupted Victoria's train of thought.

The caller didn't wait for her to answer, turning the knob instead and popping her blond head in.

"Oh good—you're here," Deborah exclaimed in relief as she let herself in without invitation. "Got a sec to talk?"

Victoria deftly flipped the cover of her notebook shut and rolled into a sitting position to address her unexpected guest. "I didn't know that you were coming," she said.

Deborah literally bounced onto the corner of the bed in her magenta jogging togs, tossing her jacket toward the pillows. "Just got here. God, what a creepy mess, huh? Are *you* doing okay?"

Victoria shrugged. "As well as anybody."

"I just *died* when my honey called to tell me what happened last night. I mean, can you *imagine*?" In the next breath, she quickly corrected herself, wrinkling her nose in disgust of the subject. "Oh that's right, you *saw* her, didn't you?"

"Fortunately not," Victoria replied, grateful that Sean Michael had prevented her from going any closer and actually seeing the damage that thick iron prongs could do to human flesh.

Deborah shook her head and dropped her voice to a

hush. "When I stop and think how close I came to nearly being here myself . . . "

The comment jogged Victoria's memory. "I missed you at dinner," she remarked on Deborah's absence. Indeed, if the Sheddmoore girl had been around to lighten the atmosphere with her humor, Victoria might have thought otherwise about leaving the table to go ambush Hunter in the limo.

"Well, he gave me a call to come over," Deborah said, knowing Victoria would recognize the pronoun as Sean Michael. "I almost did, too, except Daddy's getting so damn suspicious of all the time I've been spending out here."

Victoria guiltily refrained from telling her that her father was more likely disturbed about the company she was keeping, his suspicions already validated by Hunter.

"Anyway," Deborah went on, "I begged off 'cause it was too hard to get out of the house." The blond drew a deep breath. "Sometimes I think fate just has a way of maneuvering you out of trouble, don't you?"

"It wasn't doing a very good job of maneuvering Mrs. Maginn," Victoria observed.

Deborah wrinkled her nose again. "It was a pretty gross way to go, wasn't it?"

"I'd really rather not talk about it."

"Same here," Deborah nodded. "Anyway, when I think how close I came to getting my name in the papers and all . . ."

"I beg your pardon?"

Deborah was eager to explain. "Sean Michael said there was a reporter out here."

Victoria shook her head. "Not that I remember seeing. With so many police around, I'd be surprised if anyone got in." That, and Hunter's influence, would ensure a modicum of privacy.

"Well, it's not like it'll be a *major* story," Deborah continued. "If it happened in her own house, it'd probably end up on the back page in small print."

"I hadn't really thought of it," Victoria admitted, now seeing Deborah's point that Mrs. Maginn's employment by a prominent man whose life the press was committed to reporting about was a guarantee her death would merit greater mention.

"Anyway," Deborah said, "Daddy would just die if he read my name as being one of the suspects. Sort of like those couples who are the millionth guests at a downtown motel and there's all this fanfare and photographs and it turns out they're both married to other people?"

"I see what you mean."

"I guess it wouldn't matter, though, if it's an alibi we're talking about."

"Alibi?"

"I would've been with Sean Michael if I'd been here," Deborah volunteered. "Everybody knows that, right? There'd be hell to pay with Daddy, but you don't keep your mouth shut about a thing like that. Not when it's the man you love."

Why is she telling me this? Victoria wondered.

"I just hope Hunter doesn't go nasty on this one," Deborah said. "If he starts pointing a finger at my honey 'cause no one can vouch for where he was, it'll be all I can do to keep from coming out here and blowing his stupid head off."

"I'm sure it won't come to that," Victoria replied, remembering how Hunter's cousin had suggested they might be each other's alibi for the night. Maybe he had been more serious about the proposition than she thought.

"Sean Michael is so torn up about it," Deborah was saying. "I mean, being one of the first ones to reach her. Did you know she was his great-aunt?"

Victoria nodded, omitting that she had only learned earlier that day what everyone else seemed to have been aware of all along.

"She always wanted better for both of them," Deborah continued, in reference to the dead housekeeper. "I mean, the woman could be a real bitch when she put her mind to it, but those two were all the family she really had."

"So who do you think killed her?" Victoria decided to pick Deborah's brain, curious about what she might say.

"Well, if it weren't for how *you'd* feel about it," Deborah said, "I'd put all my money on Hunter. Not that he'll ever serve time for it . . ."

"How I'd feel about it?"

"Oh come on, hon. Just between us girls, I've seen how he looks at you and how you look back. I think there's something there. Chemistry, you know? It's absolutely nuclear."

Victoria dismissed it by staying with the original subject. "Why do you say it was Hunter?"

"It's obviously a man who did it, right? I mean women do things like poison or smothering."

"What about Lizzie Borden?"

"*You* know what I mean," Deborah defended her opinion. "Anyway, it had to have been Hunter, Chan, or the old guy. Take your pick."

Victoria noticed that she had conveniently left Sean Michael out of the lineup. "What about Ian?"

"Him? No way. The guy's gentle as a lamb."

"What about Tapping?"

"Wasn't he out with Peggy? God knows why, but that's what Sean Michael said."

"I just wondered what you thought."

"The only thing I think is that it's damn scary." Her next words verbalized the prevalent mood that had settled on all of the household ever since Mrs. Maginn's body was found.

"Whoever threw that lever," she said, "knew he'd be trapped in the castle like everyone else. I mean, doesn't it just freak you out that he's cocky enough to not even leave the scene of his own crime?" Deborah shuddered. "Makes you almost wonder if he's going to do it again. . . ."

31

"*Well, this is an unexpected surprise,*" Elliott exclaimed the next morning when Victoria put in an appearance at the office.

Just seeing the kindly face of her mentor was the salve Victoria's jangled nerves needed to remind her that the outside world was still fairly normal. "Not on your way to court or anything, are you?" she inquired, buoyed only slightly by the awareness that she'd soon be keeping his calendar again and know such things automatically.

"Desk work today," Elliott replied, closing his door that they might talk privately. "It must have been fate."

Fate. He was the second person in twenty four hours to say that, to allude to a cosmic design that maneuvered people where they were supposed to be for an appointment with death or conversation.

Elliott took an educated guess at why she was there. "Change your mind about staying on at the castle the rest of the week?"

Victoria shook her head. "No, it's not that. It's about—" She stopped herself, realizing just how unprepared she was to discuss what was most bothering her—particularly, discussing it with a man who filled the dual role of boss and father figure.

Elliott—practiced in the art of putting others at ease—took the initiative. "For what it's worth, Victoria, whatever you say won't go beyond these four walls."

She managed a smile. "I already knew that," she replied. "And it's worth more than you know."

"I guess I really threw you into the middle of a hornet's nest, didn't I?" Elliott shook his silver-haired head. "If I had it to do all over again—"

"You would have done exactly the same thing," Victoria finished the sentence for him. "Don't blame yourself," she insisted, conscious that her eyes kept gravitating to the same mesmerizing picture on his wall. The picture of Hunter's castle.

"How are things going out there?" he asked. "Any new developments from yesterday?"

"There's supposed to be a coroner's report. Probably more questions by the police." Sergeant Daniels himself had already been out once that morning to talk to Hunter.

"I'm a phone call away," Elliott reminded her. "That is, if you need anything."

Victoria noticed the folded newspaper on the corner of his desk. "I guess you already saw the write-up?"

"Sensationalism." Elliott shrugged it off. "I wouldn't pay it that much notice."

"Easier said than done." The reporter had spared few details of the alleged murder, including the properly spelled names of all who resided within the estate. Just whom the reporter had tapped for his information was unknown, leading Victoria to be suspicious of almost everyone.

"I've never known you to be without a theory," Elliott candidly remarked. "Is that what you wanted to run by me?"

"I'm afraid you couldn't be farther from the truth," Victoria answered, nonetheless flattered that Elliott was praising her talent for reading other people. "It's more of a . . . personal matter," she explained.

"Hunter?"

Obviously Victoria was not the only one adept at intuition and body language.

"How did you know?" she asked. Were her emotions that transparent?

"May I plead the Fifth?" he facetiously countered. Elliott folded his hands and leaned back in his leather chair with a sigh. "I'm afraid I have to admit to a combination of obliging a prestigious client and engaging in wishful thinking."

"Come again?"

"The first part you already knew," Elliott pointed out. "The second part I'll deny in a court of law if you ever tell my wife."

"Tell your wife what?" a puzzled Victoria asked.

"That I was trying to bring together what wouldn't have happened on its own."

It took Victoria a second to decipher his meaning. "You were playing matchmaker?"

Elliott smirked. "Sounds awful, doesn't it? But yes, I throw myself on the mercy of the judge and admit that that was exactly my intent."

"Objection," Victoria said, playing along.

"Overruled. I'm the senior partner."

"Elliott—"

"All right. All games aside. I suppose there were other candidates I could have sent out there who would have done an admirable job. You, though," he said, "you were the one person that a man like Hunter O'Hare would have taken a second look at, would have seen beyond the efficiency and the intelligence and the . . . " Elliott uncharacteristically floundered for the right word to complete his thought.

"Punctuality?" Victoria offered. "Good penmanship?"

"I thought you wanted a serious answer," he reminded her.

"I do," she affirmed, already having heard more than she bargained for or anticipated.

"It was a gamble," Elliott said. "If the two of you were meant to hit it off, all I did was bring about the meeting. If not, at least you got an interesting assignment out of it and a generous salary that's nothing to sneeze at."

"With a murder thrown in for good measure."

"*That*," Elliott said, "was the last thing I would have expected."

"I'm not sure what to say."

"You could say whatever it was that brought you here this morning. That is, if you can forgive me for meddling in your life."

"I'm not sure I'd call it meddling." She wasn't sure what she'd call it. As Elliott himself had said, he was responsible only for orchestrating the meeting; the rest had been left up to them.

"You're not having doubts about *him*, are you?" Elliott queried when a sufficient silence had settled between them. "Doubts about his innocence in this whole thing, I mean?"

"Of course not," Victoria said, loath to admit that the handsome millionaire had only her as an alibi, a tenuous link at best. "I was more concerned about his past than his present," she clarified, gauging Elliott's face for a reaction. "Mary, for instance."

Sobriety descended on Elliott's face.

"He told you about her?" he cautiously asked.

Much as she hated being deceitful with a man she respected as much as Elliott, his own admission of duplicity in playing matchmaker was enough to even the score. "You seem surprised that he would."

"He must trust you," Elliott remarked. "Hunter's not one to talk freely."

"I'd like to hear what he told *you* about his sister," she said, implying that there were discrepancies that only a third party such as Elliott could clear up.

"I'm really not sure what I can add that you don't already know. Hunter's always been a reasonable man, but—" He shook his head. "Six years is a long time to wait for something that may never happen."

Victoria anxiously waited for him to continue, thankful that he couldn't hear the increased beat of her heart.

"Sean Michael was driving the car outside of Dublin when it happened," Elliott went on. "Bad weather. Not a good road, plus his propensity for driving too fast anyway. The irony to everyone, of course, was that he walked away without a scratch, and Mary—well, it's so unfortunate to have happened to a girl that pretty, that young." Elliott gazed off into space, perhaps thinking of his own daughters. "I'm sure Hunter believes that she can hear him when he goes to visit, that someday she'll wake up like Sleeping Beauty and come home."

The place in Maryland behind the high gates, Victoria realized. It had to be some kind of hospital, some kind of private sanctuary where relatives of the wealthy—

"Under the same circumstances," Elliott went on, "I don't know that I'd be doing anything different."

"What do *you* think will happen to her?" Victoria asked after a moment.

"Do you mean if I think she'll eventually come out of her coma?"

Victoria nodded, another piece of the puzzle unwittingly supplied to her.

Elliott took a long time to answer. "Much as Hunter might wish it," he said at last, "I'm sure that even he knows that Mary's waking up could be a greater injustice to a girl who used to be so ..." Elliott faltered. "Well, you saw her picture. You know what I mean, I think."

She had debated with herself about bringing the subject up. Now in the light of new evidence, it was almost inevitable. Victoria proceeded to tell him about the last note, the one that Hunter claimed never to have seen.

"Obviously," Elliott replied, "the person who's been sending them knows that Mary is Hunter's Achilles' heel. If the notes have been going on all this time with little or no reaction on his part, it seems that he or she had to do something a little more drastic to get his attention."

"But for what purpose?" Victoria protested.

"If I could answer that," Elliott said, "I could also tell you who was behind it. As it is ..." He let the thought trail off, gravely meeting Victoria's eyes. "Perhaps it's your turn to tell *me* something," he said.

"What's that?"

Again, a hesitation settled on the senior attorney's delivery. "You really *didn't* know all of that about Mary, did you?"

There was no condescension in his attitude, no censure of her methods to secure the truth.

"No," she quietly admitted. "I only knew that she was his sister."

"I thought as much," Elliott nodded.

"And yet you went ahead and told me anyway."

"Only on a condition," he replied. "And one that I hope you'll honor, regardless of the personal outcome."

"What's that?"

Elliott's eyes probed to her very soul and held. "Let Hunter tell you about her himself. As far as we're concerned, this conversation never took place."

"Well!" Sean Michael announced. "The Prodigal Secretary returns!"

"You sound surprised," Victoria smoothly greeted him, doffing her jacket. "Have I missed anything important?"

Sean Michael shrugged as he followed her down the hall. "About the same, really. I suppose you knew about Thanksgiving?"

"It's this Thursday. What else should I know?"

"Just that we're having it," he replied.

"'Having it' meaning what?"

Sean Michael sighed in exasperation that anyone could be so hopelessly dense. "You don't think it's bad form? Pritchard's fit to be tied. Though it's hardly as if she has to make an extra trip to the store."

"I have to admit," Victoria said, "that no one's exactly in a holiday mood, but—"

"My point precisely. Want to boycott? Go find a cozy pub and drink ourselves senseless?"

"Is that what you're doing, then?" Victoria inquired. "Organizing a mass mutiny?"

"Wouldn't you?"

"Maybe we *should* have dinner," Victoria sweetly proposed, "just to give thanks that we all get along so well."

Sean Michael laughed at her joke. "She hasn't come down yet, by the way."

"Who?"

"Peggy. Although," he slyly added, "I did see Tap Dance take up a tray earlier. Lunch, I think."

Victoria had reached the foot of the stairs. "Well, if that's the extent of your news," she informed him, "I can see that I didn't miss very much."

"Oh, there's more," he added with a cavalier slouch against the bannister. "You got a telephone call while you were out."

"I'm not going to play Twenty Questions with you," Victoria informed him, distracted enough by the disturbing revelations about him imparted by Elliott that morning.

"I never asked you to," he replied. "It was the ex-con."

"Ex-con? I don't know any ex—"

"Congressman," Sean Michael said. "Although they're *all* a little bit crooked in this day and age, aren't they?"

There was only one person she knew who might have called and even that didn't make sense. "Hoffart?" she asked. "Was it Congressman Hoffart?"

Sean Michael shrugged. "I just heard it secondhand myself. Hunter's the one who talked to him."

"Did he say—"

Sean Michael was already giving an answer before her question was out.

"He sent Chan out to National to pick the ol' girl up, if that's what you're wondering."

"I don't have the foggiest what you're talking about."

There was no dulling the sparkle of amusement in Sean Michael's eyes. "Your mother," he matter of factly replied. "Quite a trick you pulled never to tell us she was coming. . . ."

32

Victoria's subsequent moment of indecision between looking up Hoffart's home phone number in her address book or seeking out Hunter to clarify the message received was abruptly taken out of her hands by the latter's appearance in the corridor.

"I need to speak with you, Victoria," he said, his tone leaving no ambiguity that, through no genuine fault of her own, she was once more in trouble.

"I got a strange phone call a little while ago from a former employer of yours," he prefaced their closed-door meeting.

"Congressman Hoffart, calling about my mother?"

Her directness caught him off guard, giving her the space to take the offensive before he could say anything he'd regret.

"It's as much a surprise to me as to you," she said with as much aplomb as she dared without sounding cocky. "I sometimes wonder what possesses her but—well, that's a mother for you."

It was clear from his reaction that Hunter hadn't anticipated her saying what she did, particularly in light of what he had yet to reveal about the conversation with

Hoffart. "You're saying that you *didn't* know about any of this?"

Victoria responded as if mortally wounded, though in truth she was paddling as fast as she could just to stay calm. "Of course not. Don't you think I would've mentioned it?"

"What about her letter?"

"Letter?"

"I understand that she wrote to you in the last week with the flight number."

The bravado that Victoria had just begun to feel proud of carrying off under the pressure of his company suddenly flagged, jarred by the memory of having brought mail from her apartment on her previous trip to the city but never having opened it. *Damn*, she thought to herself, remembering that there *had* been a letter from Marcine among the envelopes.

"Well?" Hunter said.

"I don't recall seeing anything to that effect," she replied. Well, it was *partially* true. "But don't give it a second thought," she assured him. "The District has plenty of nice hotels, and I know that—"

"Whoa," Hunter halted her with a raised hand. "Your mother is more than welcome to stay here, and I never said she couldn't. I just think it shows a lack of judgment under the circumstances we're all experiencing right now to have additional company."

Victoria bristled at the insult. "You know, that's the second time this week my judgment's been called into question."

"And the first time," he reminded her, "it was entirely justified. You could have been seriously injured riding a horse that you weren't used to. Riding a horse at *all*, for that matter."

"I can accept that one," she said, "but you can hardly hold me accountable for the actions of someone over two thousand miles away."

Hunter arched a brow. "You mean you haven't shared with her any of the things that have happened since you came here? You didn't *ask* her to come?"

"Of course not," Victoria retorted. "Didn't it strike you as a little strange that she tried to reach me through Larry and not Elliott?" Her explanation that Marcine Cameron wasn't on the cutting edge of current information brought a half-smile to Hunter's stern visage.

"I guess I owe you an apology, then."

"Apology accepted."

There was an awkward silence that settled between them.

"So you've never mentioned anything to her about me, then?" he finally asked.

"Not really," Victoria replied, puzzled at the trace of disappointment that registered in the corners of his mouth.

"Oh, there's just one other thing," Hunter added as a change of subject. "Because it's such short notice, and ordinarily Mrs. Maginn would have taken care of—well, I'm going to have to ask that the two of you share a room."

"You're sure you don't mind her being here?" Victoria queried again, hoping that it was only for a few days and that her mother was not arriving with her customary quorum of steamer trunks and staff.

"To the contrary," Hunter replied as he reached to answer the ringing phone. "I think it could be interesting to meet the woman who raised such an intriguing daughter."

By Mrs. P's reaction, rumor of a certain guest arriving soon from Hollywood was comparable to the highest ranking resident of the Vatican dropping in to borrow a rosary.

"Is it true that she's coming?" she eagerly asked of Victoria at first opportunity, clasping her hands together as if years of prayer had finally been answered. "I'm her biggest fan, don't you know! Sure, I never miss it!"

"I'm sure she'll be happy to hear that," Victoria replied, thankful that the one thing that the debauchery of Tinsel Town had not managed to change about her mother was the gracious—almost humble—manner in which she dealt with the strangers who adored her. Cognizant that it was the viewing public, and not necessarily talent, that kept her on the air season after season, Marcine had the capacity to make fans feel as comfortable as if they had known her all their lives. Mrs. Pritchard, Victoria was certain, would not be disappointed.

"Pity the lamb, she's still in a coma all this time," Mrs. P sighed in dismay.

Victoria nearly jumped at the bluntness of the remark, startled that the cook should volunteer it after so many weeks of silence. Startled even more that it should come within hours of hearing it from Elliott. "You mean about—"

Mrs. P's fortuitous rambling about Marcine's character on the soap opera preempted what would have been a grievous error on Victoria's part in assuming the reference was to Mary O'Hare. "Sure, it's that vile lass next door that's gone and done it," the cook animatedly continued, "and all to be havin' that fine Mr. Augustine to herself, don't you know, and Alandra not bein' able to speak up about it to save her soul. . . ."

"It will all work out at the end," Victoria assured her.

Mrs. P laughed. "Sure as it's the *lack* of an end that gives it the spirit!" she proclaimed.

Before Victoria could respond, Sean Michael came in to tell them that the limo had just returned to the castle.

She heard her mother's voice before she actually saw her, heard it lilting up from the confines of the limousine as Chan held the door.

"Well, no, I didn't know Bruce Lee *personally*," Marcine was saying to him. "We ran in different circles."

Victoria nearly laughed, recalling that her mother's favorite fallback line was usually that a particular person or event was well before her time.

"There *does* seem to be a return to that genre, though," Marcine continued. "Not that he and Carradine look a *thing* alike."

Her glance fell on Victoria in midsentence about the marketability of Chuck Norris and Van Damme. Enthusiastically, she rushed forward to embrace her. "Darling!" she exclaimed. "I was so concerned. Didn't you get my letter?"

"Let's talk about it after we get you settled," Victoria suggested, conscious that Mrs. P and Sean Michael had now come within earshot.

"I was just having the most interesting conversation," Marcine said. "Did you know that Kevin here once acted in a college play?"

Shows all that I know, Victoria thought wryly, never even having learned that his first name even *was* Kevin.

"It was only a small part," Chan said, handing Marcine her makeup bag.

"You're far too modest," Marcine complimented him. "He's also writing a book about golf." An uncharacteristic blush had just come to the chauffeur's cheeks. "Oh, and who's this?" Marcine inquired of the two standing near the doorway, already extending her hand in greeting as if they were the welcome guests and not vice versa. "Hello," she smiled. "I'm Marcine Cameron."

Victoria hurried through the introductions, more than a little anxious to move Marcine upstairs.

"What an interesting collection of characters you live with, dear," she remarked to Victoria when they were alone as she unpacked clothes from the two bags Chan had brought upstairs for her.

"Right. Tell me about it," Victoria agreed, nudging her

mother back to the question that she had asked just before.

"So, what am I doing here?" Marcine echoed it. "Well, as I said in my letter, if my little girl can't come to the Hollywood Hills, the Hollywood Hills can come to her. Besides, it's Thanksgiving and my character's in a coma anyway. Do you have extra hangers?"

Victoria got up to cross to the armoire. "I just wish I had more time to spend with you," she said. "It's not exactly convenient right now."

"Oh, we'll make the best of it," Marcine blithely assured her, turning the conversation back to the people she had met so far. "Doesn't it remind you of 'Dark Shadows'?" she said, likening the household and environs to the campy 60s series set in Collinsport, Maine. "Remember those vampires, werewolves, and witches?"

"None of those," Victoria replied, "but I do hear we've got a couple of ghosts."

"If they're as handsome as that Sean Michael," Marcine sighed, "I hope this room is haunted. What a rake, isn't he? Doesn't he remind you of that boy—oh, what was his name?—who played my second husband? The one who ran off in real life with the girl whose father was the ambassador to Chile? Or was it Nicaragua?"

"If you say so," Victoria said, too clueless to make a comparison. "Anyway, you haven't met Nilly yet. He was Sir Patrick's valet. Then there's Sean Michael's sister, Peggy. Maybe she'll be down at dinner. There's also an attorney who's visiting from England," she added.

Marcine withdrew a lipstick from the depths of her purse. "Enough about all of them," she said. "Tell me about that gorgeous man who owns this place."

"Hunter?" *What's going through her head now*? Victoria wondered.

"Such a strong name," Marcine rolled it off her tongue. "It suits him I think. I've always liked the chiseled, brooding type. Although *too* brooding can get tiresome."

Without going into much detail, Victoria told her mother that Hunter was a successful industrialist with enterprises all over the world.

"Well educated, well traveled, well dressed," Marcine mused. "Well?"

"Well, what?"

"I'd never be mistaken for any rocket scientist," Marcine candidly admitted, "but there are some things that you just know at first sight."

Oh, good grief, Victoria thought to herself. *Now my mother's in love with the man.*

"Do something for me, will you, dear?" Marcine said. "That is, if you don't mind."

"I'm almost afraid to ask."

Marcine laughed. "Don't be silly. Have I ever asked you to do something you didn't want to do?"

"How far back do you want me to take that question? Okay," Victoria gave in, "what did you want me to do?"

Marcine winked. "Don't let *that* one get away, sweetheart. I think he's perfect for you."

The snappy retort on the edge of Victoria's lips was interrupted by the sound of a siren, its volume increasing as it approached the castle.

33

Two *paramedics were ascending* the stairs with Sean Michael in the lead before Victoria and her mother had even reached the landing.

"What's going on?" Victoria attempted to ask, but the trio was too intent on their destination—the third floor—to give a reply. Downstairs, she could hear Mrs. Pritchard whimpering and Hunter's voice offering calm reassurance.

"They know what they're doing, Mrs. P," he was saying. "It's going to be all right."

Victoria's initial reaction that something had happened to Ian was dispelled before she had even posed the question to O'Hare.

"It's Nilly," he told her. "We're not sure just yet what the story is, but the situation's under control." Chan, he revealed, had remained upstairs while Sean Michael had gone to meet the paramedics and show them to the valet's room.

What was it in Kevin Chan's background, Victoria wondered, that qualified him for his other-duties-as-required?

"Sure an' I should've knocked sooner," Mrs. P berated

herself between sniffles and a floodgate of tears. "He was late comin' to tea, don't you know, and myself too busy to be takin' the stairs for a check. . . ." Overcome with grief for her elderly compatriot, the words that followed were too choked with emotion even to be intelligible.

To Victoria's surprise—or perhaps it shouldn't have been—Marcine gracefully moved past her to take Hunter's place and enfold the distraught woman in her arms.

"Now, I won't have you talking like that," she said in a soothing voice that was compassionate and yet firm. "Why don't we just go into the kitchen and I'll fix us both some strong coffee. . . ."

Marcine? Kitchen? It boggled Victoria's mind that someone like her mother even knew what a kitchen was, much less how to operate in one that belonged to a stranger. Back in LA, it was probably the least-used room in the whole house.

Mrs. P fervently clutched the actress' hand and shook her head as if just commanded to perform a mortal sin. "They'll be takin' him away, mum, and sure, I can't be *gone* from the spot when they do! Dear me, but I can't be desertin' him like that!"

Her tearful contentions that Nilly would be frightened if surrounded by people he didn't know might have weakened anyone else's stance. Not Marcine Cameron's.

"Well, you won't be doing your friend any good in an agitated state like this, dear," Marcine gently pointed out. "It would only upset him more, I think, that something is seriously wrong. Now why don't we just sit and talk a bit and then I'm sure Mr. O'Hare won't mind if we follow along after in the car to whatever hospital they're taking him to. How does *that* sound for a plan?" She looked to Hunter for any sign of objection, receiving instead—and graciously acknowledging—the show of his support.

"She's absolutely right," Hunter agreed. "I'll have Chan bring the limo out as soon as he comes down."

Like putty in her hands. Victoria marveled at O'Hare's unexpected acquiescence to her mother's subtle seizure of control under his own roof. That wasn't like him, she thought. Then again, he was not the first to have let America's favorite soap star have her way, clearly recognizing that the path of least resistance lay in letting her simply be Marcine.

"I'm surprised that you didn't go *with* them," Victoria remarked to Hunter a little later as they watched the limo depart, occupied by the still-whimpering Mrs. P and the ever-serene redhead who had just become her best friend in the world. "Shouldn't you be there as Nilly's surrogate next-of-kin or something?" Certainly his intention, she recalled, had been to accompany both women.

"I think I was outvoted from the start," he replied.

Had Victoria not been there herself to hear the exchange in the foyer, his comment might have puzzled her.

"Sure, I'm doin' better now, sir," Mrs. Pritchard had put on her bravest face for him, further assured by the paramedics that Nilly's condition was not as serious as first believed. "If you'd not be mindin', sir," the cook had broached the subject, "Miss Alandra—I mean Miss *Marcine*—here will be goin' with me to Mount Clarion."

"You're not a relative," Hunter had diplomatically pointed out to the cook's companion, refraining from mentioning the obvious fact that Marcine Cameron had never even *met* the fragile gentleman before his ambulance trip to the hospital. "They might not even let you in to *see* him."

"Celebrity," Marcine countered with no accent of boastfulness, "has its privileges, Mr. O'Hare. I'm sure that won't be a problem." Had her last line been spiced with just a hint of brogue? Even Victoria wasn't sure if she had heard one, recognizing only that her mother had never been a woman to let trivialities like rules and regulations stand in the way of what she wanted.

"Has she always been like that?" Hunter now asked, faltering for the right word to define his latest guest.

"Like what?" Proficient as she was at expressing herself, Victoria had yet to find any adjective that came close to describing Marcine's personality. Apparently, Hunter was having the same difficulty.

"I suppose I hold the same stereotypes as everyone else about people who make a living in front of cameras," he confessed. "She surprised me."

"She surprises *every*one," Victoria assured him, including herself in the statement.

"I can see now where you get it," he observed.

"Is that good or bad?"

"If you're asking whether I've changed my mind about what I brought up the other night, the answer is that I haven't. You're a remarkable woman, Victoria Cameron. And my intuition is telling me that I haven't even scratched the surface."

The shiver of wanting that ran through her when he said it was countermanded by the frustration of where they were, of what they were in the middle of.

"To coin one of your own phrases," she said, "this probably isn't the time or the place to talk about it."

Hunter smiled. "It *is* time, though, to get something to eat. Would you trust me to fix us a couple of sandwiches?"

"What about the others?" she inquired.

"They can fix their *own* sandwiches."

Two hours and two phone calls had elapsed before Mrs. Pritchard and Marcine finally returned from the hospital. Out of danger but still critical, all that anyone knew about Nilly was that he had taken more "medication" than the prescribed amount for a man of his constitution. Mount Clarion would be keeping him for the balance of the week.

"Sorry to be takin' so long, sir," Mrs. P apologized to Hunter as she waddled into the kitchen. "I couldn't be leavin' the place til I knew for sure."

"No apology necessary," Hunter assured her, using his free arm to give her a hug. "So what's the prognosis?"

Marcine entered the room with the elegance of Loretta Young, none the worse for wear after a cross-country flight and an evening of playing nursemaid to one of Hunter's servants.

"The doctors," she said, "prescribed plenty of bed rest, good chicken soup, and a couple of RNs in short skirts." In one swoop, she had piloted Mrs. Pritchard back toward the kitchen door. "Off to bed with you now, Mattie. It's been a long day for all of us, hasn't it?"

Mrs. Pritchard smiled for perhaps the first time since Nilly's rush to the hopital. "That it's been, mum," she agreed. "Now will you be havin' a full breakfast in the mornin' or shall I be fixin' you a tray for your room?"

Marcine smiled. "Only if that tray comes with more stories about your Welshman," she negotiated. "Would that be possible?" In a pleasant aside to Hunter and Victoria, Marcine asked them whether they knew that the cook's late husband could have been Tyrone Power's twin brother.

Victoria wisely kept to herself the opinion that all resemblance probably ended at the last name initial and shoe size. Hunter surprised her by feigning interest in this new divulgence of information.

"But wasn't Tyrone Power long before your time?" Hunter flattered Marcine.

I am truly going to gag, Victoria thought.

Marcine thanked him and deftly turned the conversation back to breakfast and her request for a tray.

"I'll be up quick as a whistle when the sun breaks through," Mrs. P promised. "And the best of dreams to you, mum." In obvious afterthought, she wished the same to Hunter and Victoria.

Marcine discreetly held her pose and pleasant expression until she was certain the cook was well out of earshot. "Goodness, what a night!" she exclaimed. "And these shoes are killing me. . . ."

"Tyrone Power?" Victoria said.

"It's her fantasy, dear. Why burst the woman's bubble?"

"You seem to have done my cook a world of good," Hunter observed. "I couldn't have begun to do the same myself."

Marcine shrugged off the praise, deeming it misplaced. "Just a woman's touch," she said, adding that Mrs. P was certainly one to prattle.

"So what really happened with Nilly?" Victoria impatiently inquired, recognizing enough of her mother's style to know when she was covering up something major.

Marcine sat down, folded her hands, and divided her scrutiny between them. "Either one of you care to tell me why a darling little old man like that would try to commit suicide with half a bottle of aspirin?"

"Suicide?" Hunter echoed.

"Aspirin?" Victoria followed suit. "Isn't the norm to take sleeping pills?"

"Someone *that* old," Marcine casually theorized, "could probably overdose on chocolate and cashews. Or even sex," she added. "And what's this about some horrible murder that Mattie kept talking about? I feel like I'm in the dark."

"Maybe I should let *you* fill her in," Hunter suggested to Victoria, realizing that mother and daughter had had very little time to talk since Marcine's arrival from California.

Disturbed that he might be leaving them, Marcine insisted that whatever it was could wait. "Besides," she said, "your cook and I didn't mean to barge in and interrupt whatever you two were doing."

"We were just talking," Victoria replied, a little too quickly.

The fact that it sounded as if she were defending her actions concurrently turned back the mental clock to reminiscences of when she *did* have to account to her mother. Neither Hunter nor Marcine, though, seemed to notice.

"If either one of you darling people could direct me to where I could find a good magazine," Marcine said, "I think I'll just go upstairs and read for a while." She gave Victoria a wink when Hunter wasn't looking.

"I think there are some current ones in the game room," Hunter said. "My cousin Peggy has a weakness for subscribing to every fashion magazine ever published."

"Oh, don't bother to get up," Marcine insisted as she saw him reach for his cane. "I'll just borrow my daughter a moment to show me where they are, and then I promise to send her right back to you."

Hunter smiled. "I certainly hope so."

"What was *that* all about?" Victoria asked in a hush after she and Marcine were in the hallway. The last thing she needed was her mother's intervention in her love life. Or lack of one.

"I'm your mother," Marcine shrugged. "You can talk to me whenever you want. With men, it's different. They're not always in a mood. Obviously this one is, and I think you should take advantage of it."

"A mood for what?"

"Talking, you nit. Now show me where those magazines are so you can get back to him before he loses his train of thought."

Victoria rolled her eyes and led the way to the game room.

Not having seen Peggy all day, it surprised her to discover the Gleavy girl and Jon Tapping engaged in a hand of blackjack as she and Marcine entered.

What surprised her more, however, was Marcine's

peculiar reaction to the introduction of the English attorney.

"What a small world," Marcine exclaimed as she shook his hand. "When did you switch from acting to law?"

34

"*Excuse me?*" *Tapping said*, blinking his eyes in confusion at this flamboyant stranger who seemed so certain that she knew him from show business.

Marcine was just as baffled by his response. "Oh, *you* remember," she said. "You did that marvelous summer stock show in Fullerton with Jazzy Daniels and Jordan Preston? I think it was 'The Importance of Being Earnest,' wasn't it? Yes, that's right. You played Algernon, as I recall, and to very good reviews."

"You must have me mistaken for someone else," Tapping insisted. "I live in London."

"Well, so did some of the others," Marcine enthusiastically went on, refusing to abandon the argument. "That's what I remembered about it, that none of you had to learn any accents to do the play."

"Sorry," Tapping said. "But you know what they say about everyone having a double."

Marcine pursed her perfectly painted lips. "I'm usually not wrong about those things," she said, collecting the magazines she had come for. "Your face is definitely familiar to me."

"I don't know what to tell you," Tapping shrugged. "But thanks anyway for the compliment."

As she and Victoria left the game room, Victoria heard Peggy snidely remark, "What a silly bitch."

"Yes," Tapping agreed, though his voice was significantly lower than Peggy's. "Quite."

True to her reputation as a woman of class, Marcine Cameron didn't dignify their comments with so much as an acknowledgment of even having heard them. Victoria, in contrast, felt her blood boil at the insult.

"Isn't that the strangest thing," Marcine finally murmured to Victoria as they reached the stairs. "I could have sworn that I recognized that young man."

"Well, it's like he said. Everyone has a double."

"Now *there's* a frightening thought, isn't it? Can you imagine two Marcine Camerons?"

Victoria kissed her mother on the cheek. "I have difficulty enough just dealing with the one."

"What a smart aleck I've raised," Marcine sighed. "I can only hope I'll do better by my grandchildren. Speaking of which—"

"I'll be up later, Mother," Victoria said, cutting her off.

"*Much* later, I hope."

Hunter had moved from the kitchen by the time Victoria returned. He was outside, in fact, lost in a pensive moment and staring out toward the raised iron gate. Whatever he was thinking about was shelved as she approached him.

"Did your mother find what she wanted?" he inquired.

"That, and something she *didn't* expect." Victoria told him what had just transpired in the game room.

"Has your mother ever been to London?" Hunter asked, alluding to the notion that her path might have crossed the attorney's overseas.

"No, but she's got a bee in her bonnet that Tapping's been to California and that she saw him in a play."

"Shouldn't you have a sweater on? There's a north breeze up tonight."

"You sound like my mother."

"I'm flattered," Hunter replied to her remark. "She's a very articulate woman."

"You're also changing the subject."

"Am I?"

"What *is* Tapping doing here?" Victoria asked insistently, reminding him that she had been pointedly excluded from their closed-door conversations since the Englishman's arrival. Even Elliott, she recalled, had had little or no contact with the man who supposedly shared the same career, the same quest for justice. "I gather it has to do with Peggy and Sean Michael's claim to the estate," she continued, "but you've never really—"

"Not all the business I conduct, Victoria, is for the world at large to know. When I think it's appropriate, I'll bring you in on it."

Victoria let his words settle a moment before responding. "If you want *my* two cents," she unabashedly offered, "there's a lot to dislike about the man."

"Meaning?"

"He seems to have totally forgotten that he has a pregnant wife back in England."

"Not by the length of his daily phone calls to her," Hunter countered. "Or didn't you know that?"

Victoria, of course, *didn't* know that but was not about to back down on her opinion. "He's probably calling her out of guilt," she speculated.

"And what exactly is he guilty of?"

Unless she was mistaken, he was taking almost a perverse pleasure in playing devil's advocate with everything she said. "You sound like you're condoning what he's doing," she remarked, irritated with the perceived lack of scruples.

"How do you know for a fact that he's doing *anything*?"

"Why would a married man go for a midnight stroll with someone whose only motive is to seduce him?"

"Maybe his ego likes the attention."

"The rest of him," Victoria pointed out, "seems to be tagging along without much encouragement."

"But you don't know that for certain?"

He had maneuvered her into a defensive position, a position Victoria hated, particularly when she knew she was right. To her chagrin, the sizzle of their interplay was also igniting her desire to experience fireworks of a more physical nature. "I think it's obvious to anyone who's been watching them," she argued, the thought only fleeting that others had drawn the same assumption about herself and Hunter.

"Have you asked *him* about it?"

"Of course not. Why should I do that?"

"Sometimes," Hunter said, "a direct answer is the best way to find out the truth."

There was no masking the annoyance in Victoria's reply or the target of its intent. "I've tried that. Believe me, it doesn't work."

As she turned to go back into the castle, Hunter's hand caught her arm, a touch of just enough possessive pressure to cause her to look over her shoulder at him.

"Maybe you've just been asking all the wrong questions, Victoria," he said, swiftly closing the space of distance between them and sliding his hand to her waist. His steady gaze—warm and sensuous in the amber glow of the courtyard lights—bored into her in silent expectation, as if his next move depended entirely on the answer to a request he had yet to make. As hard as Victoria's mind told her to resist, her body refused, yielding to the magnificent man who was now pulling her close, whose mouth was only inches from her own.

"Why don't you ask me what I'*m* doing?" he murmured.

As her lips started to part in response, Hunter's swiftly came down on them, claiming them with all of the sweet passion and ferocity that Victoria had only fantasized about until that moment. With all calm shattered by the unexpected hunger of his moist kiss, she felt her knees weaken as the curves of her body molded to his own contours in the crush of his embrace.

Oblivious to all that had happened before and all that was yet to come, Victoria's only thought was of letting this kiss, this magic, go on for as long as possible. With lips more persuasive than she had ever anticipated, their tender massage was interspersed with the insistent, probing thrust of his tongue and the smothered groan of pleasure which translated to only one thing. Hunter O'Hare wanted her as much as she wanted him. Languidly, his tongue pulsed and entwined with hers, setting vivid desires to course through her body, to imagine what it would be like to be loved by a man whose prelude to romance was so vibrant, so intoxicating.

The sound of his metal cane falling away and hitting the ground didn't even make her jump.

"Maybe we should slow down," he finally whispered, pausing that they might both come up for air.

Slowing down was the last thing Victoria wanted at that moment, not when it had taken so much of her willpower the past few weeks to push aside the kind of thoughts she had been entertaining. Hunter's next remark nearly made her laugh.

"I think we're victims of bad timing," he said. "All these weeks I could have kissed you, and what do I do but wait until the first night your mother is here."

My mother, Victoria wanted to say, *would also be the last to pass any judgment on what he had just been doing.*

His grip on her waist had started to loosen, compelling Victoria to tighten her own on his, to look up into the face that she had come to memorize from a discreet distance until tonight.

"I'm not sure where we go from here," Hunter said.

Would it be too forward to say "inside"? "Inside?" Victoria asked him.

Hunter drew a deep breath and reached up to gently caress the hair at the nape of her neck, to coil it around his fingers. "That would be the *easy* answer," he replied.

The way the light caught his eyes just then, Victoria thought she saw the glimmer of a tear. Just as quickly, he blinked and it was gone.

"What's wrong with an easy answer?" Victoria asked, seeing nothing complicated in the fact that they had just acknowledged they were both thinking exactly the same thing, desiring the same level of emotion, of love.

Hunter smiled at her with a tenderness that made her melt. "You deserve someone who can give a hundred percent of himself, Victoria. Right now, I just can't do that, much as I might want to."

"That kiss didn't feel like any fraction," she remarked, resorting to humor as her best defense against what was being couched on his part as rejection. "We seem to be using different units of measure."

Hunter met her defiance with the gentle tracing stroke of his knuckles along her jawline. "Oh, Victoria," he murmured. "What did I ever do to deserve meeting a woman like you?"

"Just lucky, I guess."

Hunter nodded, touching his lips in feather-softness to her forehead. "And it'll take all the luck of the Irish, I'm afraid, just to hold on to you."

Not nearly that much, Victoria thought to herself, knowing that just the two strong arms of Hunter O'Hare were more than enough to keep her by his side.

That, and the truth.

"Well," she said out loud, acquiescing to his request for her patience and understanding, "you know where I live."

It brought a chuckle to Hunter's throat. "Yes, I do," he agreed. "Centrally located right under my own roof. . . ."

"I thought you were asleep," Victoria said to her mother. Quietly as she had tried to undress in the darkness so as not to awaken her, the effort was for naught.

"What are *you* doing here?" Marcine drowsily murmured from the darkness.

"It's my room, remember?"

"I meant what on earth are you doing up here when that gorgeous Hunter person is—where *is* he, by the way?"

"Shouldn't you be taking a more conservative stance on this?" Victoria challenged her, knowing exactly what Marcine was referring to.

"Conservative stance on what, dear?"

"You're a parent. Specifically, *my* parent."

"I have no idea what you're talking about."

"Fine. I'm too tired to argue with you."

Marcine heaved a dramatic sigh.

"I know that sigh," Victoria reminded her. "Are you going to come out and say what's behind it, or do I have to play Twenty Questions with you?"

"Oh, I can wrap it up in just *one* question," Marcine replied. "Do you love him?"

"Love who?"

Marcine had reached over to snap on the bedside lamp. "Fidel Castro. What do you mean, 'who'?"

"Whether I do or not, Mother, is incidental."

Marcine shook her head. "Where do you get these radical ideas? Love isn't incidental to anything. It's *everything.*"

"If you say so."

"Of course I say so. I'm your mother and I'm always right."

"Always?"

"Always."

Victoria sat down on the edge of the bed. "What about Jon Tapping?" she reminded her. "Do you still think you're right about him?"

Marcine met her daughter's gaze with unflappable calm. "Oh, I *know* I am," she insisted. "I'll even prove it to you tomorrow."

35

There was no prying from Marcine the next morning her strategy to expose Tapping's duplicity, nor was Victoria particularly eager to see it happen. The Englishman's lie, she realized, would cast Hunter in a bad light as well, either in the context of withholding truth from her or in being ignorant of that truth himself.

The latter, of course, was totally inconsistent with O'Hare's reputation as a captain of industry, a man who prided himself on knowing the whereabouts of every nickel in an account and every skeleton in a closet. That he had dealt somewhat extensively with Tapping prior to the castle's transatlantic move would have indicated that he knew at least something about the man's past. Even more so, that he would recognize an impostor if that's what the attorney really was.

Even as she thought it, there flickered in Victoria's head the ironic awareness that she might have continued for an equal number of years knowing very little about Hunter O'Hare and the obsessions that compelled him to act as he did. Only the combination of accident and well-placed questions had enabled her to glean what she *did* know, relying on the selective gossip of others to fill in the blanks. Unfortunately, the blanks maintained a sizable lead over the facts.

Her conscience returned to the flip side of the puzzle. If Hunter *did* know that Tapping wasn't the genuine article, the suggestion ominously hovered that O'Hare himself had sanctioned it. And yet for what purpose? Vague to the point of annoyance about Tapping's presence at the castle, Hunter would have to have hired him to play a role that no one else could, gambling on the Englishman's credibility to get him exactly what he wanted.

The question, of course, was what. Or rather, who. There had to be some common denominator, some tangible quest that she had thus far overlooked and that would account for the shroud of secrecy at Kriskerry Castle.

Hunter himself had added only one postscript as punctuation to their reluctant goodnight the previous evening. "Your mother's had a long day," he observed in reference to the described episode in the game room. "It's pretty easy to make mistakes when you're that tired."

Victoria had tentatively nodded in agreement at the time he said it, still distracted in the tingling, hypnotic aftermath of being held in his arms and kissed until she was nearly senseless. Even in the sanctuary of her bedroom, she had managed to maintain the conciliatory posture that Marcine didn't know what she was talking about. Pacified by the passions Hunter had aroused and the sincerity she wanted so much to read behind his actions, it had been easier to discount her mother's phenomenal memory for faces than to further challenge a man who was clearly dealing with enough complications already.

By morning, though, Victoria's suspicions had renewed themselves and begun warring with her heart in a bid for dominance. Someone was definitely lying, and she was damned if she had a clue who it was.

While no words were spoken on that actual subject, Marcine was not insensitive to her daughter's uncharacteristic irritability as she readied herself for a new day. "So what's on our agenda, dear?" she asked pleasantly after dispatching the oversolicitous Mrs. P with enough compliments about the breakfast tray to easily last her for the balance of the year.

"I have work to do," Victoria replied, not meaning to snap and yet knowing that it had nonetheless come out that way.

Marcine tossed it off, unheard. "Well, don't worry about me," she said. "If I don't find something interesting to do, I can always go study my lines."

"What lines?" Victoria asked. "I thought you were in a coma."

Marcine laughed. "Well, it's not like the writers are going to leave me in one forever. *That* would certainly be boring, wouldn't it?"

"Sometimes that's the way they are."

"Writers?"

"Comas," Victoria bluntly replied. "Sometimes people *don't* come out of them."

She didn't even know for sure *why* she had said it, only that the conversation had triggered memories about the hopelessness of Mary's situation and the profound sadness in Elliott's eyes when he had told her about it. That Sean Michael could have walked away from the scene of a terrible accident like that, that he could seemingly function every day since without any show of remorse—

"Victoria?"

The softness of her mother's voice jerked her back to the present.

"Never mind," Victoria said to excuse her own remark. "I think I'll just go down and get some breakfast."

"There's plenty here," Marcine offered, gracefully indicating the contents of the teakwood tray with a sweep of her hand. "I may have to airlift the leftovers to Somalia."

Victoria shook her head. "I'm really not that hungry, Mother. Thanks anyway."

"Correct me if I'm interpreting this *in*correctly, dear, but why are you going *down* to breakfast if there's a perfectly good one up *here* that you're not hungry for?"

Why, Victoria wondered, *did her mother always pay attention at the wrong times?* "Maybe I'll work up an appetite on the way."

"Or maybe you're just in love."

Marcine was settled back in the pillows, looking every bit the glamorous star that she was. Looking like something else as well. Looking like a mother who knew her child better than the child would have wanted. "Your father made me feel exactly the same way." She was watching Victoria, waiting for an encouraging sign to share more.

"I'm really not up to talking right now," Victoria apologized. "Okay?"

To her surprise, Marcine didn't contest it or even feign hurt that her intimate disclosure was being dismissed.

"Well, I'm here if you need me, honey," she said.

"I know that. Thanks."

"Oh, you know that other thing we talked about last night?" Marcine added as Victoria's hand reached for the doorknob. "The thing about Mr. Tapping being an actor?"

"What about him?" Half of her wanted to advise Marcine to just drop it. The other half wanted too much to know.

"Just trust me, dear," Marcine assured her, implying with just a tilt of her head and a coy dip in her smile that everything would be all right. Movie magic. Marcine had lived it long enough that Victoria was convinced she had come to have faith that almost anything was possible.

"I do trust you," Victoria said, finding to her amazement that she actually believed what she was saying.

For in an entire household of people—her beloved Hunter included—Marcine Cameron was probably the only one who wasn't carrying a hidden agenda.

*   *   *

With Hunter sequestered behind closed doors already with an unscheduled visit by the police, Victoria found herself reacting like a caged animal, listlessly pacing in the absence of something constructive to do.

Twice, she had encountered Jon Tapping in the hallway and exchanged civilities so brief that only an idiot would fail to recognize that they bordered on rude. She had encountered Peggy one of those times as well.

"So that's her, is it?" Peggy had boorishly remarked. "The Big Star?"

Before Victoria could formulate a witty reply, Peggy proffered the opinion that she could now see where the Cameron girl got her red hair.

"Share the same bloody bottle of dye with your mum, do you?" Peggy sneered, tossing her own hair for emphasis before bursting into laughter.

"Haven't you some little old ladies to go kick?" Sean Michael spoke up, rounding the corner on the heels of his sister's nasty remark.

Peggy extended her middle finger at him before linking arms with Tapping and heading toward the foyer.

"At least she's back to normal again," Sean Michael remarked as he watched them go.

"That's not exactly an endorsement to be proud of," Victoria snapped, infuriated by Peggy's complete lack of respect for anyone or anything.

Sean Michael roguishly hooked his thumbs on his belt loops. "I meant about the ghosts," he said. "She was bloody convinced the murder was Duncan's doing, you know. Scared her witless to come out of her room."

"I'd have thought a ghost would be more creative than that," Victoria replied.

"And I'd have thought," he said, "that you'd be more grateful for my rescue just now."

"Rescue from what?"

"Why my evil little sister, of course."

"You flatter yourself," Victoria answered. "I don't recall

ever playing wispy damsel to your knight in shining armor."

Sean Michael pasted on a pout. "Perhaps if you did, you'd learn something you didn't know."

"Such as?"

"That I'm not as horrible as everyone paints me."

"Everyone? Or just Hunter?" Unbidden, the memory of what Elliott had told her came back, reinforcing that O'Hare lived with the daily reminder of Mary's condition, a human reminder who gleefully flaunted his own survival.

"Speaking of Hunter," Sean Michael said, "are they giving him the third degree?"

"Who?"

"The police. The black one and his sidekick are back again, I see."

"I'm sure they'll talk to all of us eventually," Victoria prophesied, more than a little concerned by the amount of time they had spent there already that morning.

"Pity they can't conjure up Duncan for a round of questions," Sean Michael shrugged. "He'd give them an earful, I bet."

"Do you think he's equally adept with a pair of scissors and a jar of paste?"

Sean Michael regarded her in puzzlement. "Meaning what?"

"Someone put that note in Mrs. Maginn's pocket," Victoria replied. "Perhaps it was one of Peggy's ghosts."

Believing until that moment that all of them had been provided the same details regarding the housekeeper's demise, it thus surprised Victoria to hear that Sean Michael seemed to know nothing about the note's existence. "Well, what did it say?" he inquired.

"I thought you knew *every*thing," Victoria pleasantly reminded him.

There was no reciprocal amusement, however, in Sean Michael's face. Anxiety, in fact, had replaced his usual facade of indifference.

He really doesn't *know*, Victoria realized, hesitating on whether she should be the one to now enlighten him on a matter of police evidence.

Fortuitously, Marcine broke the tension by sailing into their midst. "Oh, there you are, darling!" she exclaimed. "Would you mind if I borrowed her for just a moment?" she asked of Sean Michael, touching his forearm with the easy familiarity of friends who had known each other for years. "I need to make a call to my agent back in LA before it gets too—wait a minute now, let me see," she paused, consulting her watch. "Are we three hours or four ahead of the West Coast?"

"Three," Victoria and Sean Michael said almost in unison.

"Oh, good," Marcine divided a smile of appreciation between them. "Could you show me where a phone is, dear?" she inquired of her daughter. "And, of course, you'll have to say hello to Clyde while I have him on the line. He hasn't seen her," Marcine explained to Sean Michael, "since she graduated from high school. My, but time flies, doesn't it?"

"We can finish talking later," Sean Michael said. Though his tone was affable enough for Marcine's benefit, there was no mistaking the definitive ice in his eyes when they made contact with Victoria.

"I didn't interrupt anything important, did I?" Marcine asked her after they were alone and en route to the library.

"Not really," Victoria replied, hoping her mother wouldn't pester her for a more detailed answer. "So what do you have to call Clyde about?"

Marcine sighed. "Really, dear, I think you need to get out more. Didn't you know I was only making that up?"

Victoria lied. "I knew that," she said. "So who are you really calling?"

Marcine had already picked up the receiver. "You'll see," she promised. "Yes, hello," she said into the mouthpiece, "I'd like overseas directory assistance, please." A moment later, she was inquiring after the business telephone number of a certain London barrister named Jonathan Tapping.

Why didn't she just ask me for his number, Victoria wondered. Certainly she had called him enough times at his office in arranging his trip to Washington that—Victoria stopped herself in midthought, recalling a peculiarity that she hadn't considered at all until now. Not once, she remembered, had she ever been put through directly to Tapping; he had always telephoned her back a few minutes later, profusely apologizing for having been with a client or just returning from court. Until now, there had been no reason to ever question the delay in response time.

Marcine was already thanking the operator for the number she had just scribbled. "Which service does Hunter use for his long distance?" she asked Victoria next.

"Why?"

"Because I need to make a long-distance call, dear, and I'm not a mind reader."

"Do you really think you—"

"If I'm wrong," Marcine promised, "I'll reimburse him for it. Now what's the access code?"

She's like the Pied Piper, Victoria thought wryly as she obliged Marcine with the number. No one—not even Victoria—could resist dancing off to whatever tune Marcine Cameron chose to play. How else, she mused, could the woman have learned so much in less than twenty-four hours of getting there?

When next Marcine spoke, it was with a decidedly English accent. "Oh hello, love!" she cheerily said. "Is Jon about, or did we just miss again?"

Victoria had to give her mother credit for originality, for seizing the bull by the horns and feigning a convincing chumminess with her target of inquiry. *I probably would have asked for Mr. Tapping*, she thought in comparison.

Marcine's face suddenly changed from exuberant to dismayed. "Oh dear," she murmured. "You're quite sure?" Victoria was instantly alert, burning with curiosity about what was being said at the other end of the line.

"Shall he be gone long, do you think?" Marcine asked, projecting credible concern for whatever she had just been told. "Oh yes, well, of course, I suppose it can't be helped, can it, love?" Marcine sighed. "No, no, not at all," she insisted, and closed the conversation with what Victoria thought was a silly reference to the Queen Mum's health.

"Hmmm . . ." Marcine said as she thoughtfully replaced the receiver.

Victoria took a guess at what had transpired. "So did they tell you he was over here?"

Marcine looked up, her scowl subtly easing into her trademark smile of profound satisfaction.

"To the contrary," she replied. "Mr. Tapping is at Fortnum and Mason having afternoon tea with his wife."

36

Anyone else would have pushed the joy of being right to the fullest extension of gloating. Marcine, though, had read in her daughter's face at that moment the torment of a shattered illusion and could not bring herself to make it any worse.

"I was hoping that I *was* wrong about this one, honey," she said. "For your sake."

A dull throb of foreboding had settled at Victoria's temples and stubbornly refused to leave. Even while Marcine had been on the phone, her mental review of the things that had happened just since Tapping's arrival kept returning Victoria to the same conclusion, that he was somehow an instigator or at least a catalyst. His open liaison with the volatile Peggy Gleavy made him even more suspect.

She cast her mother a look of forlorn defeat. "So where do we go from here?"

"Option and outcome," Marcine shrugged. "Depends on what you want from it."

"What does *that* mean?"

"Exactly as it sounds, dear. Even as a newcomer to this," the actress explained, "I don't see that you have many choices. You can either come straight out and ask Hunter about it, or—well, you can just keep the whole thing to yourself and not let on that you're any the wiser."

"Oh, sure," Victoria smirked in response to the latter. "Like trying to hide a giant pink rhino in a room without furniture. Maybe if it keeps quiet, no one will notice it's there."

"Well," Marcine pointed out, "how many people so far have noticed Tapping?"

"You mean that he's not what he says he is?"

"Uh-huh."

"You were the only one, Mother."

"And why was that?"

"You mean why were you the only one who noticed?"

Marcine proceeded to supply the answer. "Maybe I was the only one *looking* for a pink rhino. The rest of you were sold on the empty room."

Victoria arched a brow. "It's the jet lag, isn't it?" she said.

"I'm going to pretend that you didn't say that," Marcine blithely replied, deeming her answers perfectly rational.

"Just like you want *me* to pretend that everything's copacetic?"

Marcine continued on her own train of thought. "Your father used to say I was always people-watching," she went on. "No matter where we went, I was always tuned in to what they were doing and what they were project-ing. Force of habit, I guess. Seeing what I could learn from them and how I could use it myself. It's sort of like a writer, I guess, who can't walk past a building without speculating what kind of people might live inside and whether they have a story."

"What does this have to do with Tapping and pink rhinos?"

"It's called motivation, dear. In front of a camera or on

stage, it's what you draw from inside of you to be convincing on the outside to your audience, to even render yourself invisible if you wanted to."

"Excuse me, Mother," Victoria reminded her, "but we were talking about real life."

"Same thing," Marcine said, defending her opinion. "If you're convincing and motivated enough, people will see what you *want* them to see and nothing more. Now take that sexy young man you were talking to in the hallway, for instance."

"Sean Michael?"

Marcine laughed. "Classic case of a bad boy in black leather who'd trade his Harley in an instant for a plate of warm cookies and a cold glass of milk. All he wants is a little attention, but he refuses to come out and ask anyone for it. Or take Mattie Pritchard," she went on, "and the way she still carries a torch for—"

"This has given me a major headache," Victoria interrupted, "and I still don't know what to do."

Marcine shook her head, unruffled at being cut off. "I can't tell you that, honey. *You* know what you want better than I do."

"I was afraid you'd say that," Victoria replied.

What she wanted more than anything, of course, was to retreat into the safety of Hunter's arms and to hear him say that everything was going to be all right. The problem, of course, was that it might never be right again.

It was the shimmer of a tear in his eye the previous evening that had shaken her more than anything else he had done or said, the painful vulnerability of a man who had the power to move castles but not the strength to lift the burdens off of his own heart.

Please trust me, she wanted to tell him. *Whatever it is, please just trust me to help you work through it.* A simple enough offer for him to accept, she thought. An offer made out of nothing but love.

For a man like Hunter O'Hare, though, any admission of weakness would be anathema to his system of values. Why else, she reasoned, had he kept from telling her about Mary or about his hatred toward Sean Michael or, for that matter, why hadn't he given in to the lustful, physical attraction that both of them yearned to consummate? *Stop being John Wayne*, she felt like yelling at him.

"I don't suppose *you* could go talk to him," she had suggested to Marcine, recognizing, even as she said it, the desperation inherent in recruiting her mother to unlock Hunter's secrets.

Marcine wisely declined. "I'm not the one he needs, dear," she said. "And I think both of you know that."

Much as she would have welcomed an excuse to delay confronting him with her discovery about Tapping, the departure of the police coincided with Victoria's presence in the same hallway.

"You remember my secretary, Ms. Cameron," Hunter reintroduced her, adding the side remark that he had some letters he'd be needing to dictate to her as soon as he returned from showing his guests out.

"Sorry to have taken your time, sir," the senior officer apologized, shaking Hunter's hand. Gibson extended a wish for a nice Thanksgiving, a rejoinder that seemed starkly out of place in the context of a murder investigation.

Victoria was waiting in Hunter's room when he returned. Would he take her in his arms again? she wondered. Would he pretend nothing had happened between them the night before? Or would his long session with the police have taxed all energy for concentrating on anything besides running the business portion of his life?

"You won't really be needing that," he said, indicating the steno pad and pen in her lap after closing the door.

"They might have talked forever if I hadn't let them think I had other things to do." His smile was tentative, as if testing whether it would be reciprocated.

Victoria merely nodded, waiting for a sign of what exactly he expected from her if not stenography.

"How are you holding up?" he gently inquired. "I meant to get together with you right after breakfast this morning but—well, I didn't know that they were even coming or that they were going to end up staying as long as they did."

"Doing okay," she replied, though in truth she was probably doing worse than ever. "So how did it go with them?" she asked.

"Before I get into that—" Hunter took a breath as if preparing for something arduous and unpleasant. "I've been doing a lot of thinking about what happened last night. About what *almost* happened ..."

Oh, God, Victoria thought with sinking dismay. He was going to apologize and tell her that it would never happen again, that the kiss had been a mistake he'd regret until the day he died and that the best she could do was go away and never come back. Let it be anything but that, she hoped. Anything but an apology for what they had both wanted.

"I sometimes think," Hunter said, "that I was born in the wrong century."

A *strange preface for an apology*, Victoria thought. Maybe he was going to say something else entirely.

"I believe that something worth having," he went on, "is worth investing time in. Maybe that's old-fashioned for this day and age, but I can't bring myself to imagine it any other way." Hunter cleared his throat. "Last night," he said, "I came close—literally inches—to jeopardizing a relationship that has more value to me than I realized, and all because it would have been an easy escape from the things I need to deal with."

Victoria's mind reeled with confusion. Where on earth was he going with this?

Hunter's hand tenderly closed over hers and yet he made no move to bring the rest of his body any closer.

"I'd like the time to properly court you, Victoria," he murmured. "I want to take you places and I want to buy you things and I want to one day show you that neither one of our lives were complete in the years before we knew each other." Though his bearing was stiff and proud, there was no mistaking that he had summoned every ounce of courage to say what he was saying now. To let her know that he loved her.

"It's not going to resolve itself overnight," he continued, alluding to the situation at Kriskerry Castle. "After what the police have now come up with . . ." He hesitated, unsure of how to proceed in a conversation that was already so fragile. "I guess what I'm asking you for is patience," he said. "I know it's not easy and that it probably frustrates the hell out of you, but I don't want to promise you things right now when I don't know myself how they're going to end up."

He was waiting for her to say something, to acknowledge that she had heard the same thing that his voice intended.

"I can be patient," she finally said, surprised at how calm she sounded in light of the heart-pounding realization that Hunter O'Hare wanted a future with her when all of this was over. "There's something I need from you in return, though."

Hunter's expression was grave, the man well aware of the trade-off she was so earnestly seeking. "You could be putting yourself in more danger because of it," he said.

"I can't imagine it could be any more danger than I'm in now," Victoria countered. Wasn't she already risking her heart to a man who held the power to break it?

While Hunter considered her proposition, she asked him what the police had found out about the housekeeper's death.

Almost welcoming the change in subject, O'Hare

revealed that they had at least determined how Mrs. Maginn came to be so brutally impaled beneath the castle gate.

"The coroner found some wood fibers on the left side of the back of her head," Hunter shared.

"What's so strange about that?" a puzzled Victoria queried. "The gate's iron and wood."

"The wood doesn't match," Hunter replied. "And neither does the time of death."

37

Victoria stared wordlessly across at him, her heart pounding as she tried to fathom the meaning behind his words.

"From what they've determined," Hunter went on, "the cause of death was a blow to the back of her head by a piece of wood, not the impact of anything sharp and heavy falling on her."

"But that would have to mean—"

"Yes," Hunter nodded, affirming the awful thought that had just crossed Victoria's mind. "She was *moved* into that position where she was found and the gate released."

All color drained from Victoria's face, a sensation of intense sickness sweeping over her. The earlier speculations they had pursued of how Mrs. Maginn had come to be standing in so fatal a spot were now supplanted by police evidence to the contrary. Neither returning to the castle nor leaving it at so late an hour for a rendezvous as previously assumed, the housekeeper had been attacked from behind, with no chance to cry out, to try and get away. Had she truly been the surprise victim of a mechanical accident, Victoria thought, she would have had a split second to at least do *some*thing, not just stand there and watch its descent.

So, too, did this new information negate the theory of coconspirators in her murder, one being up in the gatehouse and the second being at a ground-level distance to give a signal of precisely when to release the lever. A single individual, she realized with a shudder, could have done the entire ghastly deed alone and, thus, reduced the chance of betrayal by a guilt-ridden partner.

Hunter's compassionate inquiry of whether he could get her anything was dismissed with a quick shake of her head.

"I can't believe someone would do that," she murmured, stunned by the heinousness of a murderer so cruel as to further mutilate a body that was already dead. Was there some statement behind it? Some symbolic message that they had yet to discern? Unpopular and unloved as Mrs. Maginn was by the other servants and her own relatives, she had not deserved so gruesome a final act.

O'Hare read her thoughts, enhancing them with speculations of his own. "I guess whoever did it never counted on what police forensics can find out these days."

As little as three inches over, he delicately explained— more delicately than Daniels had explained it to him— and the thick iron that had passed straight through the housekeeper's skull might have obfuscated the evidence of the original blow.

"They also found minute traces of lemon varnish in her scalp at the same impact point," he added, discreetly omitting the more graphic details of the autopsy that the detectives had related to him.

"Varnish?" Victoria echoed in puzzlement.

"For as much wood as this place has got around the grounds," Hunter remarked, "the only kind that gets polished regularly is all indoors. Specifically, the furniture."

The image conjured of someone cracking Mrs. Maginn over the head with a Queen Anne dining room chair or a coat tree brought with it the conundrum of why no one had heard any commotion.

"And what about the time factor?" Victoria queried. "To hit someone on the head and move them outside that fast without anyone seeing—"

"That's the other piece of the puzzle," Hunter grimly replied.

As Daniels and Gibson had reconstructed it based on the coroner's findings, Mrs. Maginn had been dead for up to as much as two and a half hours before she was discovered under the castle gate by Peggy and Tapping.

"Since I didn't get back from Maryland myself until midnight," Hunter continued, "her body had to have been moved shortly after that time, or the gate would have been down when we returned."

"So whoever did it, then,"—and Victoria couldn't even begin to guess who—"had a pretty good knowledge of everyone's habits to know that no one would be up to see them moving her."

"Except for me," Hunter pointed out. "I didn't know myself when I left whether I was going to stay the night in town with my—with Mary, or just come back. Obviously it would have been awkward to be out moving a dead body and get caught in the headlights of a limo while you were doing it. A floating variable like I represented would be too much of a risk. Whoever it was had to wait until after everyone was accounted for and, hopefully, tucked off in bed."

"This isn't making sense," Victoria protested. "The killer didn't move her until after *you* came home. Are you saying that they just sat around waiting for that to happen?"

"Well, having me back *would* make me a suspect, if that was their intent. I really don't think they thought that far ahead, though," Hunter rationalized. "Like I said, no one knew I *was* coming back."

"But why do it at all?" Victoria argued. "The woman was already dead. Why not just leave her to be discovered wherever it happened?"

"Well, dropping a gate on her was obviously a ploy to

mask the real crime. Maybe even make it look like an accident, the gate being as old as it is."

For an instant, his words triggered something in Victoria's head. Just as quickly, the recollection triggered was gone. "I'm sorry," she apologized for the lapse of concentration. "It'll come back to me. What were you saying?"

"Only that moving her before daybreak was a necessity unless they had a really good place to hide her in the meantime and could account for her absence without any suspicion."

His answer clearly didn't satisfy her. "That still means they'd have to be *inside* the castle to throw the lever," she reminded him. "And that they'd be making themselves a suspect in the process instead of going out and getting an airtight alibi." Replete as the castle was with nooks, crannies, and a little-used dumbwaiter, even Victoria had been there long enough to know that there was no exit to the outside except through the courtyard gate.

"Although I suppose someone young and athletic," she speculated out loud, "could put crampons on his shoes and a climbing harness around his middle and scale his way down the back side like a mountaineer."

"You almost say it," Hunter observed, "as if you had someone definite in mind."

Was it the right time to even bring it up? Certainly the personal opinion that she had to share with him wouldn't alter the newly introduced facts about Mrs. Maginn's death—and yet Victoria couldn't help but feel it was all somehow related.

"I know who I *want* it to be," she replied. Were anyone else to be accused of the vicious crime, Victoria knew she would feel a degree of sadness about it, a sense that they had been driven to murder by a desperation that knew no other justice. Only two of them, she had thought for some time, possessed the cold-blooded wickedness for which capture and punishment would bring absolutely no pity to her soul.

"Care to enlighten me?" Hunter encouraged her.

"Things didn't start to happen," she cautiously volunteered, "until Jon Tapping arrived."

"What do you mean by 'start to happen'?"

"Well, there were the threatening notes already," she said. "And there was enough friction among everyone that you could practically cut it with a knife." Because those things had been in existence prior to his flight from London, Tapping couldn't be held accountable for them. "No one was murdered before he got here, though."

"And no one," Hunter countered, "tried to commit suicide before your *mother* got here."

Victoria bristled. "My mother has nothing to do with this."

"Was I claiming that she did?"

"The point I'm trying to make," Victoria went on, "is that you've got someone under this roof who doesn't belong here, and I think you know exactly who it is."

"Yes," Hunter nodded, "I can name at least two of them I'd rather see somewhere else. And no," he added, "it's not you and your mother."

His humor was an affront to the seriousness of what she was trying to convey. Victoria's voice hardened accordingly. "Jon Tapping is a fraud, and I can prove it with one phone call."

"You could also prove it with a look at his passport," an unperturbed Hunter replied, "but that's neither here nor there. The man was hired to do a job for me, Victoria, and I'll thank you to let him continue doing it. Uninterrupted."

The dry candor with which he acknowledged Tapping's charade startled her, for she had expected him to deny it with the same sangfroid that underscored the rest of his dark, brooding secrets. "What *kind* of a job for you?" she inquired.

"That's a longer answer than I'm afraid I have time to give you right now," he informed her, standing.

Victoria shot to her own feet as well. "So, in other words, just keep my mouth shut and let you play your game, right?" What was wrong with this man that he could profess love and chivalrous promises to her in one moment and then slam a door in her face in the very next? The words spilled from her lips, telling him as much.

"If you can't bring yourself to trust me, Hunter," she added in angry postscript, "then there's nothing we can build on. And nothing we can call a relationship."

Carried away by her own response, Victoria failed to notice the precise moment that he had stepped closer, that his hands had moved up and taken a possessive hold just below her shoulders, the warmth of his touch penetrating the whisper-soft wool of her sweater.

She felt his breathing quicken and felt her own fingers splay open against the broad chest that was edging forward, meeting her more than halfway. Achingly vulnerable to the need that was melting her insides but resolute to let this man know what she was made of, it was all Victoria could do to firmly reiterate the terms she so desperately wanted.

His gray-eyed gaze locked with hers and in that gaze was mirrored Hunter's own desperation, his need to trust someone outside of himself. His lips parted slowly, his tongue tentatively sliding across to moisten them. Victoria felt helpless as control began to spiral out of her grasp. She could hardly bear the wait to see whether he was going to say something or forestall her demand for the truth with a kiss they both knew she wouldn't turn away from.

Hunter's voice, when at last he found it, seemed to come from far away.

"You win, my love," he softly murmured, the emotion in his eyes drenching her, holding her captive. "I guess I have no reason to keep secrets from you any longer. But just promise me—"

Anything, the voice inside Victoria's head would have screamed if it could, knowing that there was nothing she could deny this man in her arms, no mortal weakness for which she could not—in retrospect—forgive him.

"It started," Hunter began a few moments later, "the summer that my sister Mary first went to Ireland. . . ."

38

The story was only *a few sentences* under way when a brisk knock came at Hunter's door. A knock that demanded an answer.

Victoria rolled her eyes. *I should have known that he wouldn't get that far*, she thought to herself, reflecting on all the previous times that something significant between the two of them had been interrupted by similar knocks, telephone calls, and bloodcurdling screams. Maybe it *is* best, she thought further, that Hunter wanted to abstain from a more intimate relationship with her until he either secured the services of a good locksmith or removed them both to neutral territory. Given the track record of the household on rudeness to date, its members had already demonstrated that they had no compunction whatsoever about bursting in to fink on each other and demand instant redress, regardless of what O'Hare was currently engaged in.

"Yes?" Hunter called out.

Victoria caught herself trying to guess which one of them it would be this time.

The one person she would not have guessed, however, turned out to be exactly who it was.

The apology was already in Marcine Cameron's eyes

before it made it out through her lips. She was, of course, the only one on Victoria's mental list of potential usurpers from whom any such expression of regret could be deemed heartfelt and genuine. "It's about Mattie," she said to Hunter. "I tried to calm the dear down but I thought you should come hear what she's saying."

Victoria and Hunter exchanged a quick glance, both cognizant of the fact that Mrs. P had gone to the hospital to visit with Nilly right after breakfast. Naturally, their first thoughts were that the elderly gentleman had taken a turn for the worse during the night and that Mattie Pritchard was beside herself with anxiety. Both of them spoke at once, giving voice to their own concerns that the venerable valet was not long for this world.

Marcine shook her head. "Oh, he's of hearty enough stock to have made it *this* far in life," she pointed out, "even if he *does* look like he should never have left Shangri-La."

In spite of the serious moment, her remark made Hunter chuckle. "So what exactly is wrong?" he inquired.

And please let it justify what you just interrupted, Victoria silently added, growing more and more dubious that she'd *ever* hear the private side of Hunter's sorrow.

"I think I better let *her* tell you," Marcine replied. "This whole thing's become too jumbled for a newcomer like me to accurately translate." Even Mrs. P's charming brogue, she said, bordered on a hindrance when drowned out by tears.

With Hunter and Victoria following in her graceful wake, Marcine led them back to the kitchen. A kitchen that was now empty.

Marcine scowled, her hands on her hips. "*That's* awfully strange, don't you think?"

"What's strange, Mother?" Victoria asked.

"Well, I told her to stay right here and that I'd be back in a minute," Marcine answered, looking about as if to spot the errant servant at any moment, cleverly blended in with the fixtures or fresh fruit.

Only Victoria, versed on an entire adolescence of observing her mother's velvet command over others, could appreciate Marcine's resultant confusion about why so simple and well-meaning an order had been ignored. What, indeed, could the cook have been thinking to willfully disobey a presence such as Alandra Monaco?

"Maybe she had somewhere else to go," Victoria offered.

Marcine raised a perfectly plucked brow. "Now, be realistic, dear," she gently chided her. "The woman has no life outside of this kitchen, especially the day before a major holiday. Where could she possibly be?"

"Maybe if you gave us some hint of what she said to you," Hunter recommended.

Marcine sighed. "Well, she prattled on a lot about that boy of hers and how hard it was to raise him by herself. Then, out of the blue, she broke down and said that Nilly had always loved him like a son and that that's why he had done it."

"Am I missing a page?" Victoria asked. "Done what?"

"This is where it gets confusing," Marcine said. "She seems to think that Nilly tried to kill himself as a way to protect Ian."

"Protect him from what?" Hunter cut in.

"Goodness knows," Marcine shrugged. "That's when I decided to call in some collective brainpower to figure it all out."

Victoria glanced toward Hunter. "Do you think that maybe she's gone out to the stables?" The fact that she had brought up Ian's name in the conversation with her mother rendered it a possibility.

"Worth a try."

Once more, the trio set out together, this time Hunter leading.

They heard Mrs. P well before they reached the open barn door, her brogue hitting strident levels as she furiously berated her flesh and blood.

"Maybe you better let *me* handle this," Hunter said to the two women with him.

The shrieking stopped right after Hunter entered the barn, changing into a guttural weeping. Marcine and Victoria stood rooted where Hunter had left them, neither one knowing what to say or do. A moment later, Mrs. P's scream at her son prefaced the young man's frightened emergence from the barn. Startled to see Marcine and Victoria on his intended path, Ian bolted in the opposite direction, scrambling over the fence and toward the grazing horses before either woman could react to what was going on.

"Do you think we should go in and try to help?" Victoria asked of her mother, alarmed by the heavy sobbing that now seemed to reverberate off the stillness of the November day. "It sounds terrible in there."

Marcine shook her head. "Let's wait a few minutes."

A breeze had nudged a few curls of Marcine's coiffure out of place, giving her an earthy elegance that Victoria couldn't help but marvel she had never really noticed before.

"Do I have something between my teeth?" Marcine said.

"What?"

"You're staring, sweetheart. And I know it's *not* because you've never seen a TV star in person."

Victoria shrugged. "Just noticing how you looked, that's all." There was no other way to put it. Nor any words to accurately define what she was seeing—the quiet, inner strength in a woman whom the rest of the world perceived as a pampered icon of daytime drama.

Marcine's smile faded a little as she looked on her daughter. "Would it have been better for your relationship," she unexpectedly asked, "if I had stayed in California instead of flying back here to see you?"

"I'm not sure that 'relationship' is the right term for it, Mother." It was also, Victoria thought, an odd time for her to even bring it up.

"Well, you're certainly having *something* meaningful with the man," Marcine countered. "It's not like you're total strangers who tripped over each other's camp stools at the Rose Parade and moved on."

"I'll concede to *that* part," Victoria said, frustrated that there was no label she could really put on what was happening between them, nor what would take it out of its current neutral gear.

"Is my being here a little bit awkward for you, honey? Because if it is, I'll catch the next plane back to LA." Unspoken but very much prevalent was Marcine's awareness that her knock had interrupted a tender moment between her daughter and the man who employed her. The looks on their faces had told her *that* much.

"Ask me that twenty-four hours ago," Victoria philosophically murmured, "and it would have been a different answer."

"Then why don't you just tell me what the answer is as of *now*."

It was hard to script a diplomatic response with the compounded distractions of Mrs. P's wailing and the inner-dialogue memory of Hunter's most recent words about courting and commitment. Still, Victoria tried. And in that telling, to her surprise, came the realization that she was actually *glad* to have her mother around.

"Just don't let me butt in," Marcine advised. "You and Hunter need all the time to nuzzle together right now that you can manage."

"Try telling that to Hunter," Victoria smirked. "Every time we seem to get close, he finds an excuse to push me away." Responding to her mother's look of puzzlement, Victoria related Hunter's earlier directives that she go away and out of his sight.

Marcine tenderly smiled at her. "Well, I haven't known the man for very long," she said, "but don't you think that if he really *wanted* you gone and never to darken his door again, he'd have stuck to his guns to see it happen?"

"Sometimes," Victoria replied, "I don't think *he* knows what he wants." The pulling together and pushing away had become more than she could fathom. And at the dilemma's center, Victoria was almost certain, Hunter's pain for his younger sister was inhibiting his ability to move forward, to give himself freely to another.

Marcine slipped a loving arm around her daughter's waist. "He wants *you*, honey. But first, he just wants to prove himself a worthy enough knight and clean up after his white horse before he pulls you into the saddle *with* him. It's as simple as that."

"You certainly make it sound that way."

"Only because it is. This all reminds me," Marcine said, "of the time I did that summer stock play where I was the mother of the young man who was blind."

"There must be a parallel here that I'm missing," Victoria observed. "What does 'Butterflies Are Free' have to do with my life?"

"Only that marvelous line in it about what people say they want and what they truly want." Marcine closed her eyes a moment as if trying to picture the stage and the cast and the precise shade of nail polish she had worn as the Scarsdale matron at odds with her son's bid for independence. "It's been a number of years, of course," she apologized for paraphrasing, "but the gist of it is that when you're head over heels in love and running out the door hell-bent to meet your destiny, you don't stop for a corned beef sandwich."

"I have no idea what you're talking about, Mother."

"Why don't I explain it over some lunch then?" Marcine suggested. "The sandwich line has made me hungry. And we're certainly not helping the situation out here by just standing around, are we?"

Victoria was not as convinced, glancing askance at the barn. "Do you think Hunter can manage this?"

"Trust me," Marcine knowingly replied. "Things are more in control here than I think we're giving the man credit for. And as for *you*," she added, "I think you need a reminder sometimes that you're Victoria Cameron and that you have the right-of-way."

"Right-of-way?"

"To take your heart wherever you want it to be."

It was some time before Hunter returned to the castle. But when he did, Victoria was the first one he came seeking.

"I'll leave you two to talk," Marcine immediately offered, collecting her magazines.

Hunter's invitation that it was all right for her to stay and listen was declined by Marcine as matter-of-factly as she would have plucked lint off a sweater. "I'll never get to learning my lines," she excused herself, "if I'm always with both of you."

"I thought that your character was in a coma," Hunter said, a remark that prompted a double-take by Victoria but which her mother accepted in cool stride.

"Have you become a fan now of 'Niagara's Tears'?" Victoria inquired of him after Marcine had left the room.

"No," Hunter replied to her question, "but its star *does* have a way of growing on a person."

Perplexed as to how to acknowledge that, Victoria turned the subject back to Mrs. P and what had transpired out in the barn.

"She's agreed to go talk to the police," Hunter prefaced his explanation. "As a matter of fact, I'm having Chan take her down there right now rather than them coming back out here. Considering all that came out of our conversation—well, I think it's more discreet to handle it this way. The less anyone else knows at this point, the better."

Victoria was on pins and needles. "So what's going on? And what about Ian?"

Hunter opted to answer the second query first. "Ian's the least of my worries," he said. "He'll come back when he's ready to. He always does."

"She sounded like she was really chewing him out," Victoria observed, thinking it odd that a woman who professed so much love for her only child could be capable of as much anger as she had displayed before Hunter's intervention.

"Well, his infatuation for my cousin hasn't exactly won his mother's support."

"So he *is* involved with Peggy?"

"Past tense. Unfortunately, he hasn't caught on yet that it's over."

"And that he's been replaced by Tapping?" The disdain in Victoria's voice was unmistakable.

"You're getting ahead of the story," Hunter said. "If what Mrs. P has said is true—and I have no reason to think otherwise—Ian was in Peggy's bedroom waiting for her to come upstairs. You mentioned you had heard someone but didn't know who it was."

"Which makes Ian a suspect, then," Victoria pointed out, recalling how Mrs. P had lied about her son being out in the barn with the horses that evening.

"Apparently we're not the only ones who jumped to the conclusion that Ian Pritchard had something to hide."

From his hospital bed, Hunter went on, Nilly had tearfully confided to Mrs. P his fears that Ian might have done something that was wrong, maybe not even realizing the consequences. "That in itself wasn't what disturbed her as much as what Nilly told her next," Hunter said.

"Which was?"

"Nilly explained to her that he took more aspirin than he should have as a way to treat the pain he was having in his back. When it wasn't getting any better, he decided to finish off the bottle as a suicide measure and go quietly."

"Back pain?" Victoria echoed. "Like the kind you'd get if you pulled something while doing work?"

"Or," Hunter said, "by moving a dead body."

39

Shock *caused the echo of* Hunter's *words to wedge in Victoria's throat.*

"Nilly? A murderer?" she exclaimed in disbelief. It didn't seem possible.

"No," Hunter countered, "I don't believe for one minute that he's the one who actually killed her."

"But you said—"

"He *moved* her. After someone else had already hit her on the back of the head."

An ugly truth began to dawn.

"Ian?" she ventured, barely above a whisper. Harmless as she had come to regard the young keeper of the horses, he nonetheless possessed the physical strength—if not sufficient motive—to wield a fatal blow against Mrs. Maginn.

Hunter shook his head. "Suffice it to say, I don't think Ian did it either, in spite of what may have been a noble attempt on Nilly's part to cover for him."

The valet's fondness for the cook and her son, Hunter went on, may have been the motivating force behind his desire to make Mrs. Maginn's death look like an accident. "All of us," Hunter said, "assumed exactly what Nilly hoped that we would—that she had been walking or standing under the gate when the mechanism failed that held it in place."

Victoria suddenly remembered the thought that had escaped her earlier.

"The gate," she said. "Nilly would have been around when it was oiled to know how easily—and soundlessly—it could come down."

Hunter completed the scenario. "And whether or not everyone rushed out after the lever in the gatehouse was released, he knew he'd have plenty of time to either come down the stairs or go down the hall toward his room. As it turned out, he had even more time than he anticipated."

Victoria brought the conversation back to Ian. "But why are you so sure it wasn't Ian who killed her when Nilly must have been pretty convinced that it was?" Convinced enough, she added, to take the blame for it if he got caught. Did the valet's remaining years hold so little joy and promise that he considered the sacrifice a reasonable trade for Ian's youth?

Unconsciously, Hunter's brow furrowed. "Too many factors that don't fit, that's why. A boy who loves living things as much as Ian Pritchard would never conceive of purposely taking a life."

"But what if his hitting her was an accident?" Victoria protested. "They do happen, you know."

Hunter was definite in his stance on the stableboy's innocence. "It wasn't Ian," he said.

"But what about the trouble he was in back in Ireland?" she reminded him, still clueless as to what that trouble was.

"That has nothing to do with what's going on over here. I promised both him and his mother that I'd deal with the authorities on his behalf if he did his job and kept his nose clean. So far, I've had no complaints on either score."

"But wouldn't you think that if someone went wrong once—"

"That they're doomed to repeat for all eternity?" Hunter interrupted, a little sharply. "That's pretty short-sighted and prejudiced, isn't it?"

Victoria bit her tongue to refrain from pointing out that that was exactly how he was regarding his cousin Sean Michael. Forever guilty because of one terrible mistake.

"How can you be so *sure* that it's not Ian?" she said instead.

"I just am, Victoria. I just am."

"Maybe," Marcine proposed as Victoria stoked the fire in their bedroom, "we're looking at this from entirely the wrong angle."

"Looking at what, Mother?"

"The murder motive, dear. Try to stay with this, will you?"

Victoria had filled her in on what Hunter had shared, leaving off in the same place where he had with the strong contention that Ian Pritchard might be slow but was hardly sinister. Stubborn to a fault, there had been no budging O'Hare from his belief in the boy's innocence. "All you can fault him for," Hunter concluded, "is his bad choice in women."

"Who had something to gain by the housekeeper's death?" Marcine now queried. "Tell me that."

"No one, as far as I can see."

"Oh, but there's always *some*thing," Marcine insisted.

Victoria shook her head. "Nope." Comfortable salary that Mrs. Maginn had made as Hunter's housekeeper, she had saved relatively little of it, donating the bulk to her church in the interests of eternal salvation. With no assets to speak of, any inheritance due Sean Michael and Peggy as her surviving relations would be minuscule.

"What about the blackmail-and-revenge theme?"

Marcine suggested. "Did she have the goods on anybody? You told me yourself she was a pretty snoopy goose."

"Oh, I'm sure she had something on practically everybody," Victoria shrugged. "But I can't imagine any of it being substantial enough to warrant her own murder."

"What about a setup?"

"Setup? You mean trying to pin it on someone else?"

Marcine reconstructed what might have happened. "Let's say that whoever clonked her on the back of the head intended to leave her there to be found, wherever *there* was. That means they were confident enough not to be tied to the crime. Then along comes Nilly who trips over the body, jumps to the wrong conclusion and thinks, 'Goodness, this is terrible! I can't let so-and-so get blamed for it.'"

"So he puts the body somewhere else," Victoria said, "and drops a gate on it. Honestly, Mother, this all sounds like a bad round of Clue."

Marcine smirked at her from her perch on the bed. "Well, if you were the original murderer in this," she blithely continued, "wouldn't it freak you out to discover that your dead body had suddenly moved from one spot to another? Obviously it didn't get up and walk there by itself. I'd think that would be rather unnerving."

"I suppose. What are you getting at?"

"Only that our murderer now knows that someone else found the body in order to move it and may start putting two and two together." Marcine shook her head. "I wonder what Jessica Fletcher would do in a case like this," she wistfully speculated.

"Probably get better writers," Victoria replied. "This whole thing is pretty sick, if you ask me."

Marcine slid back the cuff of her blouse to check the time. "I'll ask you when I come back," she said. "At the moment, I have a date downstairs to keep."

"A date?"

"Sean Michael wants to pick my brain over a glass of brandy." Marcine slipped her feet into the taupe heels she had kicked off earlier.

"I beg your pardon?"

"Such a cute little rake and great buns," Marcine sighed. "Anyway, I guess my flattery about his looks has gone to his head. He wants to know how to break into show business. I can see him doing something like that, can't you? Either that, or male modeling."

"Oh, sure. He'll be a real heartbreaker," Victoria sarcastically prophesied.

"Well, I *will* be getting a new husband when I come out of my coma," Marcine continued, "and they haven't cast anyone yet."

"What happened to the old one?" Victoria asked on cue, knowing that she was going to hear about it anyway.

Marcine eagerly filled her in on the story line. "Poor Cain just can't handle his guilt about Kacy's miscarriage and my accident and so he goes to The Spa instead of to Colorado and, after a couple of brief, unsatisfying flings with Heather the aerobics instructor and Tawny the towel girl, decides that the one he's really had feelings for all along is Curran."

"Curran's a woman's name?"

"No, no, dear. Curran is the handyman who's serving time for supposedly throwing a toaster in Sharon's swimming pool while she was seducing Martin in the buff at the shallow end." Marcine smiled in satisfaction. "So what do you think?" she asked.

"What I think," Victoria replied, "is that Sean Michael would fit in just fine."

He slipped into the room so quickly, so quietly, that Victoria didn't even know he was there until she felt a hand clasp over her mouth from behind and a stronger one grab her around the waist.

"Scream for bloody hell and I swear I'll break your neck," the intruder snarled in her ear, shaking her for emphasis.

Fear, stark and vivid, glittered in Victoria's eyes, though her attacker was not at a vantage point to see it. Just as well, she thought, more afraid of revealing her panic at that moment than she was of whatever harm he intended toward her. She could feel the muscles of his forearm tighten across her middle and feel his hot breath against her neck. "Not a single scream," he ominously warned her. Victoria nodded and felt his brutal grip release.

"Aren't you supposed to be meeting my mother?" she inquired with more composure than she felt, turning to squarely face Sean Michael.

She could tell that her reaction threw him off, that the resident villain had expected more than a cool glare and a confident reproach for the effort he had just put into his entrance. A fact he felt compelled to mention.

"Nothing scares you, does it?" he observed.

"Was it supposed to?" Victoria asked, glad that he couldn't feel her pulse or hear the stepped-up rhythm of her heart.

"We have unfinished business, you and I," Sean Michael curtly informed her.

"And what about the business you have with my mother?" she reminded him. "If you keep her waiting, you may as well know that she'll be back up here before you can throw on a sheet and say 'boo.'"

"What you have to tell me," Sean Michael said, "won't take that long."

His observation that she had avoided him all day now brought home to her a fleeting guess that the scheduled appointment with Marcine downstairs about show business may have been little more than a ruse to catch Victoria in the bedroom by herself. With Sean Michael's own room just across the hall, it would have been easy enough to know exactly when Marcine left.

Victoria feigned memory loss. "And what is it I was supposed to tell you?"

Sean Michael's dark eyes were compelling and magnetic, as if he could have easily hypnotized the answer out of her if he chose to. "The note, Victoria. Where is it?"

"Which note are we talking about?" Victoria stalled.

"You know bloody *well* which note I mean!" he snapped. "The one they found on Spots."

"Anything they found on the body," Victoria said, "would have been taken as police evidence. Why don't you ask *them* about it?"

There was no disguising the desperation that underscored his curiosity. "What did it say? Just tell me that much."

"Why don't you tell me why it's so important for you to know?"

"Don't play games with me, Victoria." The angry retort sharpened his features, his entire demeanor growing in severity.

"If I'm playing games," she said, "it's against a pro."

Sean Michael's mouth dipped into a deeper scowl. "It may be a matter of life and death," he warned.

"We seem to have already hit the latter," Victoria pointed out.

"Then for bloody sake, woman, tell me about the note before someone else pays for it."

Victoria's mind was racing. Racing between speculations that Sean Michael either knew the author of the notes or was perhaps the author himself. "I'll tell you on one condition," she bartered.

Sean Michael hesitated.

"Hunter is expecting me downstairs," Victoria lied, moving past him and toward the door.

Sean Michael caught her arm. "What's the condition?" he wanted to know.

"Just one question," Victoria replied.

"I didn't kill Spots."

"That wasn't the question I was going to ask," Victoria said. In truth, it really wasn't. Her intuition had already led her to dismiss him as a strong suspect.

Discomfitted that she clearly held the upper hand, Sean Michael bit his lip.

"The note they found on her," Victoria quietly volunteered, "said that they knew where Hunter was keeping Mary . . . and why."

Something disturbing replaced Sean Michael's smoldering look, something that looked as if he would be violently sick at any moment.

To her surprise, he found the words to ask Victoria what her question was.

"Did you know about that note before I told you?" she asked, bracing herself for whatever he might say.

Sean Michael gravely nodded, weighed down by a guilt that Victoria couldn't begin to understand. "I knew about it," he nodded, "because I took it from Hunter's room right after you left it for him."

40

"Oh, *there you are*," the unflappable Marcine addressed him upon entering the room. "Did we get our signals crossed, or what?"

Sean Michael faltered a split second before his mouth slid into its trademark cavalier grin.

"Have to cancel out, love," he said. "I'd stopped by to catch you but you'd already gone." He glanced toward Victoria as if seeking support for his lie. Stunned by both his audacity and the unexpected admission he had volunteered just before her mother's entrance, Victoria said nothing. Her eyes, however, spoke volumes.

"Well, no harm done," Marcine shrugged it off, affectionately reaching out to squeeze his forearm. "One nice thing about Hollywood—it will always be there tomorrow."

The door had barely closed behind him when the actress cocked her head, almost amused by what had just transpired.

"The little scamp was fibbing, wasn't he?" she observed as if discussing the antics of an incorrigible child.

"I'm beginning to think that lying is the norm around here, Mother." That such deceit spanned the full spectrum from family honor to guileless self-preservation could be demonstrated any day of the week.

"Bad news? You look upset."

"Confusing news. I asked him to come clean about something and—well, his answer muddied the waters even more, so to speak."

Marcine scowled when Victoria had elaborated. "What a strange thing for him to come out and admit to," she said. "Wouldn't that incriminate him in the murder?"

"You'd think so." Had she been asked earlier to guess who might have removed the note from the bedroom before Hunter's chance to read it, Victoria's first choice would have been Mrs. Maginn, not Sean Michael. Ever nosy, ever vigilant about all movement within the castle, it would have been only logical to assume that all entrances and exits—especially those involving Hunter's room—were dutifully marked by the housekeeper.

Ironic, Victoria now thought, that the missing note about Mary should end up in the dead woman's pocket when she had not been the one to steal it.

"So what does *that* mean?" Marcine queried, baffled by the household she had invited herself into.

"It means I've got to talk to Hunter right away."

Marcine's face registered instant dismay at being the bearer of a message that she knew her daughter wouldn't want to hear.

"He was just on his way out when I went downstairs, sweetheart. Something about going to Maryland for the evening."

He had to return *some*time, Victoria reminded herself, repeating it like a silent mantra as she sat on the hearth in his room, its interior lit only by the gold-orange glow of the fire she had set.

Dinner had been a makeshift affair, given Mrs. P's absence from the kitchen. Though she had returned well in time to cook for the castle's occupants, she had tearfully confided to Marcine that she was far too upset to attempt it.

"Don't even try, dear," Marcine had assured her. "We're all adults capable of wielding a can opener."

Satisfied to some degree that she was acting on the advisement of Alandra Monaco herself, Mattie Pritchard disappeared upstairs to her quarters. Ian, as far as Marcine could discern, had not only returned from the woods without a scolding but was spending the night in the stables conversing with his equine friends.

"He seems harmless enough to me," Marcine had remarked. "I'm sure Hunter knows what he's talking about when he says the boy isn't involved."

If that was completely true, of course, Victoria thought to herself, it narrowed the list of candidates who could have killed Mrs. Maginn. As she gazed into the fire, Victoria ran through the names once again, incorporating the latest clues but finding no resolution to the mystery.

Could it have been Mrs. P whom Nilly sought to protect by faking an accident? Certain that no secrets went unspoken between the two servants, a scenario was plausible that the cook had struck Mrs. Maginn in anger and, horrified to discover that the blow was fatal, pressed her best friend the valet into a plot to cover it up as efficiently as possible. That, Victoria decided, would account for Nilly's efforts to stop Mrs. P from divulging too much at the kitchen table.

Maybe Mrs. P, acting on the threat Victoria had heard on the staircase, had killed her nemesis but left the scene of the crime to go fabricate a credible alibi, never counting on her old pal Nilly to be the one to discover the body. Nilly, in turn, had drawn his own conclusions on who was the guilty party and simply performed out of loyalty.

Sean Michael? A part of Victoria didn't *want* to see him in so dangerous a role as a murderer. Falling back on

Marcine's assessment that the hotheaded Irishman was more bark than bite, Victoria found his confession about taking the note unsettling news. Somewhere between Sean Michael's hands and Mrs. Maginn's pocket, a third party had come into possession of it. And yet why had Sean Michael taken it at all, much less confided to Victoria about it?

Jon Tapping—or whoever he really was—constituted another piece of the puzzle that just didn't fit. While his working for Hunter would presumably lend some credence to his overall status as one of the good guys, Tapping nonetheless possessed the dubious distinction of being Peggy Gleavy's alibi on the night of the murder. Had he turned double agent against his employer, deeming the spandex-clad seductress a better investment of his time and energy? That he and Peggy might have joined forces for undercover work that was both literal and figurative was a frightening proposition to even consider.

The fire had become too warm to be comfortable, and Victoria slipped off her sweater, depositing it over the back of the chair in front of the computer desk.

When was *he coming back?* she wondered, frustrated that the past hour she had waited seemed almost like ten.

I could always leave a note for him and go back upstairs, she thought. In the next instant, she dismissed it. Notes, as evidenced by the recent past, had a disturbing way of disappearing and resurfacing in the wrong place. The last thing she needed right now was for one of hers—innocent as it might read—to end up under Chan's hat and the chauffeur run over by his own limo.

Victoria glanced toward the bed, conscious of just how drained she was both physically and mentally from all that had happened. *What harm would a short nap do?* she thought. In all likelihood, Hunter wouldn't be back for another couple of hours and, when he was, she'd be refreshed enough to talk to him about what she had learned.

*   *   *

The fire had died down long before Hunter's return. Acclimated to waking several times to half-darkness in strange surroundings, Victoria kept closing her eyes with the good intention of getting up at any moment and turning on a light.

The sound of a door opening—when it finally occurred—seemed to come from far away. So sluggish was the redhead at that point, she wasn't fully aware that someone had joined her in the room until she felt the concurrent weight of someone sitting down on the mattress and the warm touch of a hand on top of hers.

"It's okay," Hunter quickly soothed her when she awoke with a start. Backlit by light from the hallway, his rugged silhouette was at once a comforting sight.

"I must have dozed off," Victoria murmured, trying to collect her thoughts and remember what exactly had possessed her to kick off her shoes and stretch out on top of the covers. Her first awareness was that Hunter had not removed his hand but, instead, tightened his fingers, their loving warmth conveying the message that she had been missed. The second awareness was that he sounded tired, compelling her to wonder just how late it was.

"How did . . . things go?" she inquired, still hovering in the awkward limbo of whether it was appropriate to say his sister's name or ask after her.

Hunter shook his head. "It's hard to know from day to day," he replied. To her surprise, he continued. "Lately, she's been having a series of . . . well, I guess you'd call them seizures."

Victoria nodded in sympathy as Hunter explained, now realizing in retrospect that the first incidence of the seizures he described could well have been the day he received the phone call that threw him into such a panic to get to Maryland as fast as possible. The day he had relied on Victoria.

"Since they have no way of knowing just what kind of effect . . ." Hunter's voice dropped off, and a chill silence took its place.

"I'm sure that she'll be all right," Victoria comforted him, though in the absence of a crystal ball to affirm it, she knew as little as he did about the course Mary's life would take.

Hunter's voice had perceptibly tightened. Was he thankful for the darkness that hid his expression? Victoria wondered. Or did he now trust her enough with his emotions to let her see that pain? "I had started to tell you about her today," he recalled, though more to himself than to her.

Victoria waited, not daring to breathe lest the spell between them be broken.

"She called me her first night in Ireland," Hunter slowly related, "and told me that this was the most beautiful place she had ever seen. Just like the fairy castles in the books she used to read as a little girl."

Even in the darkness, Victoria could sense a half-smile crossing his face.

"She even informed me," he said, "that she was going to live in it forever." Hunter shook his head. "I reminded her rather firmly," he said, "that she was only overseas for the summer and that I expected her to come back in the fall and finish school."

Victoria's heart squeezed in sudden anguish at the realization of where Hunter's story was going. Mary *hadn't* come back to Virginia that autumn, not the way he had expected.

"Did Elliott ever tell you," Hunter queried, "about the house I used to have? The one that used to be on this same spot?"

"Not really," Victoria replied, though in truth its needless destruction had long been a source of puzzlement to her.

"Wasn't a bad place," Hunter shrugged. "It was always

the land that held the greater interest to me. A good place to keep horses and keep to myself when I just wanted to get away from the city. It was never the physical building that mattered."

Which is why, Victoria thought to herself, he had watched it fall beneath a wrecking ball without any remorse.

It was a long time before Hunter continued his story.

"Someday," he finally said after a labored sigh, "I know that Mary will wake up and, when she does, I want to bring her out here and the very first thing that she's going to see when the car comes into the valley . . ."

The words went unfinished, but enough of the thought had been conveyed for Victoria to finally understand the depth of commitment he harbored toward those he loved. Stone by stone on a long journey across the Atlantic, Hunter O'Hare had given no thought to expense or impracticality. Only the delight he hoped to one day see in his younger sister's eyes had motivated him to move heaven, earth, and an Irish castle. And if it were possible, Victoria realized, he would move a hundred more, all for the sake of making her happy, for seeing her live once more.

So many things she had not recognized before now fell into place, imbuing her with sorrow for the simple pleasures Mary might never know again. The loving voice of a brother, the smell of fresh flowers, the feel of morning rain on her face.

A deep sob began to wrack Hunter's insides and Victoria pulled him into her arms, wishing she could do more to ease the pain that his life had been dealt by Sean Michael. "It's all right," she whispered. "It's all right."

When at last he stopped, it was a hint of chuckle that prefaced his next remark. "I must be crazy," he remarked. "Here I've got the most beautiful woman in my arms and on my bed and what am I doing? Crying a flood."

It was too dark to see his features clearly, but Victoria

knew the tenderness and love and vulnerability that lay there.

"Speaking of being in my bed," Hunter murmured, "what *are* you doing here?"

Victoria hesitated. What had seemed such a good idea hours ago now struck her as a case of bad timing.

"Something wrong, honey?" Hunter gently inquired.

"I guess it's just this place," Victoria said, reluctant to proceed. And it was true. No secrets were safe within it, no moments truly private. "You never know who's listening. . . ."

Hunter glanced toward the open door. "Do you want me to close it?" he offered.

Victoria shook her head. "I don't know that it would do any good."

Hunter considered her comment for a moment before rising. "Then as I see it, there's only one solution." He extended his hand to her. "Do you mind driving?" he asked. "I've already had Chan put the limo away."

"Driving where?"

Hunter's voice was low and smooth, a mellow baritone edged with control.

"The Benedict Inn."

41

Thanksgiving morning dawned colder than the weather forecasters had predicted, cloaking Fairfax County in a pervasive chill that beat the past decade's record.

Victoria Cameron, however, had never felt warmer, glancing from time to time at the man on the passenger side of the Mercedes. No words had been exchanged in the last two miles. Indeed, no words were necessary.

How could I ever have been angry with him for keeping so much to himself? Victoria reflected. That he was a man whose financial success so easily put him head and shoulders above most mortals had, mistakenly, kept her from really seeing—until last night—that he was in as much need of gentleness as those who had far less. Devastated by his sister's tragedy, Hunter had sought refuge the only way he knew how—by burying it as deeply as he could within his heart and hoping it would remain there.

"Why do you try to do it all?" she had even brought herself to ask him in the solitude of the inn's darkness, alluding to his stronghold on control. Hunter's reply had saddened her in its emphasis on stalwart isolation. "Because everyone expects me to," he said.

"Maybe you should give those Y chromosomes of

yours a break and share some of the load," Victoria had softly recommended.

"Sure I'm not too old to learn new tricks?"

Victoria had countered with a favorite line of her mother's. "And how old would you be if you didn't?"

As they turned onto the road that led toward Hunter's castle, his hand reached over and came to rest lightly on her right thigh. Victoria responded by laying her hand on top of his, wishing that she could stop time and, thus, prevent their return to a household which, by now, had discovered their absence.

As if reading her thoughts, Hunter remarked that their night at the Benedict Inn had been relatively tame compared to the upsets of the preceding week.

"But I suppose I *will* have to answer to your mother when we go in," he predicted.

"My mother?"

The playful grin she caught on Hunter's face told her at once he was being facetious. "Of course," he insisted. "I'm sure she'll want me to make an honest woman of you as soon as possible."

"Get with the right century," Victoria teased back, knowing full well that Marcine would be more likely to ask why it had taken so long rather than what Hunter O'Hare intended to do about her daughter's honor.

"The century I'm in is just fine, thank you," Hunter replied as he squeezed her thigh. "Any other and I would never have met *you*."

As the car approached the castle's entrance, Victoria felt a brief shudder of trepidation, furtively glancing upward as they drove under the raised gate. Unconsciously, she accelerated as they passed through, then applied the brakes a little too quickly to compensate.

"Sorry," she apologized for the lurch.

"Understandable," Hunter said, offering the kind of smile that had been too long absent during the years before they met.

The sight of Sean Michael bounding down the steps and toward the car with a clenched expression on his face immediately escalated Victoria's anxieties. "Looks like a problem headed in our direction," she commented.

"Isn't it always?" Hunter said, opening the door just as Sean Michael was about to yank it open himself.

"Bloody nice of you to finally come back!" the younger man snapped at his cousin.

Hunter met the sarcasm with his usual aplomb.

"We need to talk, Hunter," Sean Michael curtly informed him. "Right *now*."

"I suppose it's as good a time as any," Hunter replied, pausing just long enough before his exit from the car to instruct Victoria on where she could park it.

Baffled by the source of Sean Michael's latest outburst, Victoria could only watch as both men entered the castle, recalling that her heart had been simultaneously enlightened and saddened just hours before by an odd twist on the adversarial roles in which they were cast. Certainly, what Hunter had revealed to her about Mary's tragic accident on a rainy night in Ireland put their ongoing conflict in a new light, leaving Victoria to quietly wonder which of the two men carried the greater burden of guilt for withholding a dark and dangerous truth, and further, how much longer either one could remain silent in their condemnation of the other.

As she eased the Mercedes around the curve of the courtyard, she caught sight of Chan, hatless on so cold a November morning but wearing his customary air of efficiency. She had always had a feeling there was something about him that went beyond the parameters of just a chauffeur. The previous night in Hunter's arms at the Benedict Inn, Victoria's suspicions had been confirmed.

"It was simple enough in the confusing transition of staff," Hunter had revealed, "to incorporate a bodyguard. Particularly someone who would never be suspected of *being* one."

Aloof to the point of ostracism by Hunter's Irish household, the young Asian had assumed the role so expertly as to pass among their ranks unnoticed, yet ever vigilant. The son of a San Francisco physician and a Hong Kong newscaster, Kevin Chan had chosen his own course in which to excel, coupling his knowledge of martial arts with his sixth sense about danger.

"He also likes driving expensive cars," Hunter added.

"But why did you need one?" Victoria inquired. "A bodyguard, that is."

"I'd think *any*one would want a measure of protection," he had casually proffered, "after willfully disrupting so many comfortable lifestyles." The arrival of the hot-headed cousins, Hunter added, had only affirmed the wisdom of his decision to employ a guardian angel.

Chan's eagle eye and alleged expertise, of course, begged an obvious question on Victoria's part.

"Isn't it sort of like hiring a security officer," she said, "and your bank getting robbed in broad daylight anyway?"

"If he had been *in* the castle on the night of Mrs. Maginn's murder instead of in Maryland with me," Hunter had answered, "I have no doubts but that he could name the person behind it." Chan, he added, had already observed enough of his peers to arrive at a few conclusions worthy of pursuit. Just what those conclusions were, however, Hunter refrained from telling her.

That reply came back to her now as Victoria watched Chan approach the car. What *did* he really think, she wondered, as she let herself out. And had he been watching *her* with the same inscrutable concentration as everyone else who dealt with his employer? If she lived to know him for a thousand Chinese New Years, Victoria was pretty certain she'd never know him any better than she did right now.

"Happy Thanksgiving," she addressed him, conscious of his cool censure that she had driven a vehicle under his purview and totally without his permission. He had probably even cringed at her lurch beneath the gate.

Chan nodded in acknowledgement of her greeting but didn't reciprocate the good wishes.

"Did you get a haircut?" she asked. Maybe it was just the lack of a hat. Or the conformity of his hair to wearing a hat too much.

Totally expressionless, Chan nodded and informed her that Marcine said his head resembled a cupcake.

Victoria had to bite the inside of her mouth to keep from laughing, so accurate had been her mother's assessment. "I'm sure she only meant it in the best way," Victoria said.

Chan regarded her with the cynical appraisal of a heavy-lidded crocodile.

"Happy Thanksgiving, Miss Cameron," he said, before sliding behind the wheel of the car she had returned to his safekeeping.

Victoria took the stairs two at a time, more than a little anxious to share the latest revelations with her mother. At the landing, she even caught herself smiling at the irony of the circumstances—rushing to see Marcine after spending all night out with a man and looking a tad disheveled for it in the previous day's clothes and make-up. Ten years ago, Victoria thought, and she'd have snuck in as unobtrusively as possible with a good lie about staying with a girlfriend.

Her anticipation of a heart-to-heart with Marcine was dashed as she opened the bedroom door and discovered her mother wasn't alone.

"Hello, dear," Marcine said. "How was your evening?"

The actress's guest did a double take at the remark, presumably surprised by the implication that mother and daughter hadn't seen each other in the interim.

"Hello, Deborah."

The blond was as effusive as ever. "You never *told* me your mother was so *funny*," Deborah exclaimed. "I haven't been able to stop breaking up."

Marcine's laugh rippled through the room. "Oh, we're all funny in our own ways, dear," she insisted. "It's what makes the world go round."

"I thought it was *money*," Deborah countered.

"Funny. Money. They both rhyme," Marcine pointed out, "so what's the difference?"

"I'll come back," Victoria said, suddenly feeling displaced in her own room.

"I really *do* have to be going," Deborah announced, almost as if sensing Victoria's discomfiture. "Daddy will have a cow if I'm not around to account for myself on Turkey Day."

"You're not here for Thanksgiving, then?" Marcine inquired. "I'd think your beau would want a pretty girl sitting next to him at dinner." To Victoria, Marcine asked if she had ever noticed Deborah's cheekbones. "Doesn't she have the loveliest bone structure? Sort of like that tall girl who married Stallone."

"Oh, go on," Deborah laughed. "You're too much." In the next breath, she asked if Marcine really thought so.

"Definitely," Marcine nodded. "Of course we move in different circles and she hasn't been with Sly for years, but I did meet them at a function once, and you remind me of her."

"Stallone is probably Daddy's favorite actor," Deborah said. "He'd die if I ever told him that I met someone who actually *knew* him."

"Why tell him *that*?" Marcine shrugged. "Why don't you tell him that *you* actually met Marcine Cameron and that she's staying a stone's throw away until Saturday morning?"

"You're too much," Deborah reiterated.

"And you, dear," Marcine said, "are too kind."

"What was *that* all about?" Victoria asked after Deborah had bounced out of the room and presumably off in search of Sean Michael.

"She came to see *you*," Marcine replied. "I was just the entr'acte."

"So if she wanted to see me, why didn't she see me?" Victoria queried, puzzled by Deborah's hasty departure.

"Probably the time factor. Is her father really the ogre that she likes to paint?" Marcine shook her head. "If a child of mine talked that horribly about *me*, I'd have to disown her."

"Sean Michael," Victoria explained the situation, "wouldn't be her father's first choice."

"Well, he's certainly *her* choice," Marcine said. "The sound of impending wedding bells was absolutely deafening."

Victoria scowled. "She said she was going to marry him?"

Marcine offered a coquettish smile. "Maybe she just said that because she thought I'd be competition."

"Are you serious?"

"About being competition, dear? Of course not. I *do* have my *standards*."

"No, I meant about her saying she was going to marry him."

"She seemed quite committed to it, yes. Something about Sean Michael finally coming into his own and her father not having anything to say about it."

"I don't see how *that* could happen," Victoria murmured.

Sean Michael and Peggy were both living off an inheritance which, without prudent investing, did not represent a limitless account. Only if something were to happen to Hunter and the estate were to revert—

"What's wrong, dear?" Marcine cut into her thoughts. "You look blanched."

"Let me think this out a second," Victoria begged off, new suspicions flying fast and furious within her head.

"Is it about your friend Deborah?" Marcine asked.

"I'm not sure yet," Victoria replied, reluctant to face

the possibility that the one person she had completely discounted as a suspect could cleverly harbor an agenda more dangerous than all of the rest.

Tapping was coming up the stairs as Victoria descended. "Have you seen Peggy?" he inquired. Something in his voice—an edge perhaps—compelled Victoria to ask if anything was wrong.

"Maybe she just forgot," he shrugged in reference to their morning plans. "After that ugly row last night with her brother—"

"I beg your pardon?"

"A wonder they didn't wake the dead," Tapping remarked. "You didn't hear them?"

"What was it about?" Victoria asked, sidestepping his question.

"Heaven knows. The sibling thing can get a bit nasty, can't it? And yet the next day they're inseparable." Peggy, he went on to explain, had stormed out and not been seen since.

"I'm sure she'll show up eventually," Victoria said. Whether or not she did, of course, wasn't nearly as important to Victoria at that moment as talking to Hunter.

The door was open and the room empty when she arrived. Either he and Sean Michael had concluded their business already or were meeting somewhere else. Maybe he had wanted to see Hunter about the fight with his sister, Victoria speculated, though she had long ago determined that conflict between them was more the norm than the exception. Even her first day at Kriskerry Castle, she recalled, the two of them had been royally battling in the courtyard.

Resolute to come back and see Hunter later, Victoria caught sight of her sweater, still draped over the back of the chair. May as well pick up after myself, she decided, and entered the room to reclaim it.

She might not even have noticed that the jade stone in her earring had worked free of its setting had it not tapped her shoulder blade in its bounce toward the floor and, then, made a noise upon landing. From the corner of her eye, she saw it roll under the bed; dropping to her knees, she peered beneath the dust ruffle to retrieve it.

With her fingers just inches from the stone, Victoria's body suddenly stiffened in shock, all senses stunned by the discovery of what lay hidden beneath the bed of Hunter O'Hare.

42

She had risen to her feet and yet not moved any further when the sound of Hunter's voice startled her from the doorway.

"I was just coming to find you," he said. What he initially thought was a flinch at being surprised was quickly replaced by concern for the look on her face when she turned, the horrified look of someone who had just seen a ghost. "My God, Victoria, what's wrong?" he exclaimed, reaching her side as fast as his stiff leg would permit. "You're shaking."

Victoria's composure was a fragile shell that threatened to shatter at any moment. "Under the bed," she managed to say, just above a whisper.

"What is it?" he asked.

"Just . . . look."

"A little easier said than done," Hunter replied, indicating his leg, "but if you really want me to—"

Victoria struggled with the new uncertainties that had been aroused, not the least of which involved the man she loved. "It's the cane," she said. "The horsehead cane."

Unbidden, Hunter's earlier remark at its disappearance from his room now came back to chill her, his comment that the only thing it was probably good for was to hit someone over the head.

An expletive escaped Hunter's lips as if he, too, had remembered the remark and, accordingly, saw the damning significance of the cane's being where it was.

Just as quickly, the man in control resurfaced, taking her gently by the shoulders. "You didn't touch it, did you?"

"Of course not. I—"

"You're absolutely sure?"

"Of course I'm sure."

Hunter's expression returned to one of stern restraint as he considered what needed to be done next.

"Shouldn't we call the police?" Victoria suggested, certain that she had unwittingly discovered the polished murder weapon used on Mrs. Maginn.

"I'd rather not do that just yet," Hunter cautiously replied. "Not until at least—well, let's just hold off awhile."

"Hold off until what?" Victoria angrily retorted. "If they had the cane, they could at least start looking for fingerprints or matching the wood or—"

"I need to handle this my own way," Hunter sharply interrupted her. "And I'm going to need you to let me do that without any interference. In fact," Hunter suggested, "I don't think it would be such a bad idea if you and your mother took the car into the city and—"

"I thought we were in this together," Victoria reminded him. "At least that's the impression I got last night, that you were finally willing to trust me."

"Please, Victoria," he implored her. "Don't bring last night into what I have to do here and now."

"But—"

"This is my problem to deal with, and I'm going to see it through."

Silenced but not conquered by his dark expression, Victoria found the voice to say one more thing. "You know who it is, don't you? You know who killed Mrs. Maginn."

Hunter started to open his mouth. But when he did, it was to address the third party who had just appeared, breathless, in the open doorway.

"No bloody sight of it anywhere," Sean Michael informed him. "I've looked all over the damned place and no sign of it."

"What's he talking about?" Victoria asked of Hunter, but the latter's attention was now all on his cousin.

"Does she know how to use it?"

Sean Michael's dark eyes flashed. "If she gets bloody close enough to either one of us," he said, "I wouldn't say that it matters."

They were talking about Deborah, she was certain of it. And yet the threat of danger they implied at the young woman's hands seemed extreme. Why in particular, Victoria wondered, would Deborah mean any physical harm toward Sean Michael, the man she loved? "She was just in our bedroom a few minutes ago with my mother," Victoria volunteered, her anxieties escalating.

"Who?" both men almost asked in unison.

"Deborah. Isn't that who you meant?"

Sean Michael and Hunter exchanged a look as if telepathically debating how much was safe to reveal.

"It's not Deborah we're looking for," Hunter said at last. "It's Peggy."

Her fingers ached to reach over and touch him. And yet she knew that he had to say what he must, without the distraction of her tenderness or love. Sean Michael, on Hunter's instructions, had gone off to find Marcine.

"He told me about taking the last note," Hunter gravely began, repeating the portion of the story that Victoria already knew. Sean Michael's past admonishments to Peggy to stop writing them had gone unheeded, widening the rift that already existed between brother and sister. "At least," Hunter observed, "he knew which side his bread was buttered on."

"You knew all along that she was the one doing it?" Victoria asked, recalling Hunter's earlier comment that the notes were being written by someone at the castle.

"I suspected it was one or the other," Hunter replied, "although for a while it seemed to point to Mrs. Maginn."

At least I'm not the only one who considered her, Victoria thought.

"Apparently," Hunter went on, "he confronted Peggy with the last note and warned her that if she didn't stop, he was going to come to *me* about it. From what he's told me, she grabbed the note out of his hand and, the next thing anyone knew, it ended up in my housekeeper's pocket."

"But how did *she* get it?"

"Probably," Hunter offered, "the same way the cane ended up being under my bed. Peggy put it there."

"But that would have to mean—"

"Yes," Hunter nodded. "Exactly."

"Well," Marcine announced, "this isn't exactly the way I intended to spend my Thanksgiving."

"You can still go to a hotel like Hunter recommended," Victoria reminded her.

Marcine, however, wouldn't hear of it. "You're not the only stubborn Cameron woman," she said. "If you insist on staying here by that wonderful man's side, I have no choice but to stay here *with* you." The actress proudly fanned her playing cards on the bed. "Gin."

"I wish I knew what was going on," Victoria murmured, casting a glance toward their locked bedroom door.

"I wish I knew *half* of what was going on," Marcine countered. "You never did finish it, you know."

Victoria shook her head. "It's hard to know where to start, Mother."

"I've always found the beginning a practical place myself. Do you want to start there or deal another hand so I can beat your socks off?"

Victoria leaned back in the pillows on the bed. "Things are never completely black and white, are they, Mother?"

"No, I suppose not. Unless, of course they're cows. Or maybe skunks. Or how about zebras?"

"How about real life?"

"Very gray, dear. In fact, I'd say almost always."

"Right. Tell me about it."

"No, dear," Marcine said as she took the deck of cards from Victoria's hand. "Why don't you tell *me* about it? Is it about Hunter?"

Victoria nodded. "It's about Hunter. And about Sean Michael. And about hating someone for a long time without knowing the truth."

Marcine tucked her legs underneath her, her most comfortable listening pose.

"I had mentioned the accident to you," Victoria refreshed her mother's memory. "The one in Ireland a few years back?"

"Oh yes," Marcine recalled. "That poor, tragic young girl. Mary, isn't it?"

"I guess a part of me just couldn't understand how Hunter could have the person responsible for that accident living under his roof day after day, a reminder of what had happened."

"Perhaps," Marcine suggested, "Hunter is a very forgiving man."

Victoria shook her head. "That's not it, Mother. Not it at all."

Marcine waited for her daughter to continue.

"You know that phone call you made to England?" Victoria said. "The one to Tapping's office?"

"Yes?"

"Apparently the walls had ears. Or, more accurately, the ears were on one of the other extensions."

Marcine pursed her lips. "Now that you mention it, it *did* sound like someone was there," she said. "I just thought it was my connection." A furrow suddenly lined Marcine's brow. "That wasn't a problem, was it?"

Victoria diplomatically skirted an honest reply. Without that phone call, things might not have been set in place as dangerously as they were now.

"You were right when you guessed about Tapping being an actor," Victoria replied instead, sharing what Hunter had told her the previous evening at the Benedict Inn. "Hunter," she said, "brought him over as a way to get close to Peggy."

"From the looks of it," Marcine candidly remarked, "the man is earning his money. Maybe even some overtime."

As Hunter had explained it, Victoria went on, a nice-looking young man with obvious resources would be exactly the kind to catch the Gleavy girl's eye. The addition of a sweet wife and a baby on the way simply enhanced the challenge for her.

"So he's *not* married, then?" Marcine sought clarification. "Well, that's good. A man who would cheat on a pregnant wife an ocean away would certainly have nothing to commend him." Satisfied that Jon Tapping was just another working actor, Marcine's next question related to why Hunter would want him to cozy up to Peggy.

Victoria took a deep breath before continuing, reliving the pain with which Hunter had told her his secret.

"About seven months ago," she said, "Hunter came into some new information about his sister's accident, the one that Sean Michael had walked away from."

Marcine shook her head in dismay. "How anyone could leave the scene of an accident like that—"

"He didn't, Mother."

Marcine looked at her in puzzlement. "But you just said that he did."

"That's what Hunter thought. For that matter, that's

what *every*one thought. And without Mary conscious to tell her *own* version of it, Hunter had only Sean Michael's word to go on."

"But if he came out himself and said it was his fault . . ." Marcine was clearly at a loss to understand what her daughter was trying to say.

"There was a witness that night," Victoria continued. "Two, in fact. Apparently they never came forward because of—well, compromising circumstances."

"A couple of marrieds making out in a marsh, were they?"

"Something like that," Victoria said. "Anyway, one of them has finally come forward with the story that Sean Michael never got a scratch because he was never *driving* the car that night. For that matter, he wasn't even *in* it."

"Then if Sean Michael wasn't driving, who was?"

"The one person whom he loves as much as Hunter loves Mary." The name hovered on Victoria's lips. "Peggy."

"But if that's the case—" Marcine started to say.

The report of a gunshot from outside stunned them both into silence.

43

With *her nerves at full stretch*, Victoria could think of only one thing: Hunter. The sound of that single, ominous shot had set all of her inner warning systems off at once, compelling her to fly toward the bedroom door. Marcine was just as quick, though her own motivations to spring into action contrasted sharply to Victoria's. "Are you crazy?" she snapped at her daughter, forcefully maneuvering herself between Victoria and the exit. "Didn't you just hear that?"

"Yes!" Victoria snapped back. "Please, Mother—"

"You'll only get in the way," Marcine firmly insisted. "Let Hunter handle this."

"But what if that was Hunter who just got—" Victoria refused to say it out loud, fearful that the utterance might make it so. "Just let me go, Mother!" Valuable time was being wasted.

"He *told* us both to stay here. And from the sounds of it, I don't think we have a choice."

"*You* have a choice," Victoria retorted. "Mine is to find out what's going on. Now are you going to move out of my way, or—"

"Or what?" Marcine challenged her. "Victoria, you're

not being rational about this at all. I don't want you to get hurt."

"I'll be careful."

"Nonsense. You'll rush right out there into the thick of things just like—" Marcine wavered, knowing full well that stubbornness was hereditary.

"Just like *you*?" Victoria shook her head. "You taught me too well how to not sit back and be a spectator, Mother."

"That was for lawn tennis, dear. Not gunfire."

With jaw clenched and green eyes narrowed in defiance, Victoria was a study in determination, a mirror of the woman who had taught her to follow her heart, no matter how treacherous the road. "I'm going."

"Then I'm going, too," Marcine bluntly informed her. "Someone has to keep you out of trouble."

They made it as far as the courtyard. Tapping—paled by the horrifying drama that was unfolding down by the stables—urged them to remain inside where it was safe.

"What's going on?" Marcine anxiously inquired. "We just heard the shot."

Tapping's words fell fast yet crisply. "It's Peggy," he replied. "She's got her brother's gun. Hunter and Sean Michael are trying to talk to her."

Hunter.

His proximity to danger slammed a hard fist of icy fear straight into Victoria's stomach. Without preamble, she broke away from Jon Tapping and her mother and started running at breakneck speed toward the gate, ignoring Marcine's command to stop. Whether or not either one of them tried to run after her, Victoria didn't really know; all her concentration was fixed at that moment on the need to see for herself that Hunter was still okay.

Just beyond the gate, a sudden blur in black streaked past the corner of her eye. Startled, she found herself overpowered by the uniformed chauffeur.

Simultaneously angered by her own immobilization and the fact that Kevin Chan was nowhere near the man he was hired to protect, Victoria let go a verbal curse. It had as little effect on her captor's conscience as her struggle to break free.

"It is under control, Miss Cameron," Chan replied with a coolness at odds with the explosive scene now being played out by the trio before Victoria's eyes.

Even at a distance, she could see the venomous hatred that flashed in Peggy's face as, across the pasture fence from Hunter and Sean Michael, she wielded a gun with the crazed unsteadiness of someone either drunk or drugged.

"Bastard!" the black-haired beauty yelled, alternating her unstable aim between the two men she perceived to be her worst enemies. "*You* did this!"

Sean Michael's voice rang loud and clear. "I love you, Peggy. You're my sister. I just want to help you."

"*Help*?" Peggy tossed back her shaggy mane of hair and laughed, an evil laugh that sent a chill down Victoria's spine. "Is *that* what you call helping? Breaking your bloody word?"

"Give us the gun," Hunter said, his voice firm and yet oddly gentle.

"Why don't you *take* it?" Peggy nastily dared him. "Take it like you took everything *else* from us!"

"We're not here to hurt you," Sean Michael promised. "We just don't want you to hurt yourself."

He may as well have been speaking to the wind.

"*You* did this!" Peggy accused her brother. "You *betrayed* me with your bloody lies!"

"I'd never betray you," Sean Michael insisted, but his sister would hear nothing of it.

"You went and told Spots!" she yelled. "You told her about the accident!"

Transfixed, Victoria watched the tension build between brother and sister, a violent volcano on the verge of erupting.

"No, Peggy," Sean Michael retorted. "She was *there*, remember? She took care of you when you were hurt that night. We both did. Remember?"

Peggy shook her head, her cruel red lips curved into a smile so sinister that it made Victoria's skin crawl.

"She loved you, Peggy," Sean Michael went on. "Just like *all* of us love you."

"You never loved anybody!" Peggy shot back.

"Listen to him," Hunter spoke up. "Listen to your brother, Peggy. He's telling the truth."

"Truth! What do *you* know about bloody truth?"

"We can get you help," Sean Michael promised. "Just trust us." He started to take a step toward the fence but Peggy clenched the gun even tighter.

"We know you didn't mean to kill her," Hunter said.

Peggy laughed. "How do you know I *didn't*? She hated me like the rest of you. She would have said something. I *know* she would!"

"We don't hate you," Hunter said, but Peggy was already readjusting her aim to now put Hunter in direct range.

Victoria felt her heart leap into her throat, paralyzed by the danger that Hunter was in at the hands of a crazy woman.

"I hate *you*!" Peggy yelled. "You took it all! And now I'm going to take it back!"

Sean Michael tried to calm her with words of love. "It's going to be okay, Peggy," he sought to reassure her. "We can go home . . . just like you've always wanted to."

"Home?" Peggy scoffed at the idea. "I *hated* it there!"

Chan was no longer holding Victoria's arms, yet when exactly he had released his grasp, she didn't know. Distracted by the sound of a horse's whinny, she noticed for the first time that Ian was also in this volatile picture, standing terror-stricken in the entrance of the stable and trying to calm the high-strung Paladin by grabbing tight on his leather halter.

"We can go home and start over," Sean Michael was saying. "We can do whatever you want, Peggy. Just give us the gun."

"I'm *glad* she's dead!" Peggy snapped back at him, then turned her vehemence on Hunter. "And I wish to hell that stupid bitch *Mary* was dead, too!"

"Don't say that!" Sean Michael admonished her. "I know you don't wish *any*one dead."

"I wish *you* dead!" Peggy proclaimed. "And you, too!" she yelled at Hunter. "And *that's* how it's going to be!"

Horrified, Victoria watched the scene as if in slow motion, nearly screaming out loud as she saw Peggy pull back the hammer of the gun and take calculated aim at her quarry, watched as Sean Michael literally threw himself on top of Hunter, knocking him to the safety of the ground as Peggy fired the bullet intended to kill him. Watched, too, as Paladdin—spooked by the sound of the gunfire—reared on his magnificent hind legs and broke free of Ian's control.

"Oh, my God," Victoria muttered under her breath as she witnessed what happened next.

Frustrated that her shot had missed, Peggy didn't see at once that the black horse had gone berserk from the noise and was running free in the pasture on the same side of the fence that she was. Certainly, Victoria thought, Ian would try to do something to catch him, fearful as he must have been that Peggy might take out her vengeance on an innocent animal. To Victoria's surprise, Ian did nothing, standing in the entrance of the stable, his eyes locked on the galloping beast that had now turned direction and was heading back. Headed toward Peggy.

Fixated on the two fallen men across the fence, Peggy started to take aim again, relishing her moment of victory over the enemies who had so hatefully betrayed her.

And then she saw the horse.

"No!" she yelled. As a startled Victoria looked on,

Peggy Gleavy turned back toward the stables and yelled at Ian, a bloodcurdling demand that chilled the senses. "Stop him!" she screamed at the top of her voice. "*Stop him!*"

With nostrils flaring and the temper of his breeding unleashed, Paladdin reared in fury and confusion once more on his powerful hind legs, a muscled devil in pure black satin.

And when his hooves came crashing down to earth, the desperate screams of Peggy Gleavy were stopped forever.

44

Sergeant Daniels closed his notebook and stood up. "I think that's all we'll be needing here, Mr. O'Hare," he said.

Hunter nodded and shook the detective's hand, offering to see him out.

From her wing chair by the fire, Victoria cast a glance at Sean Michael, his chin resting pensively on steepled fingers. As if sensing that he was being watched, the young Irishman looked over at her.

"Full circle, isn't it, lass?" he softly murmured.

Victoria shook her head, puzzled by his meaning. "I'm not sure I understand," she said.

Sean Michael gazed off into some private space. "We're not that different really, Hunter and I. The reasons we've done things, I mean."

You both loved your sisters, Victoria wanted to say, but didn't, all too aware of the pain so permanently etched across the hearts of both men for their loving too much.

Encouraged by Hunter to stay during the detective's questions, she had little by little pieced together more of the puzzle that made up Peggy Gleavy's life. Still, there were things she would never know, never fully understand.

"It would have gone worse for her," Sean Michael had tearfully shared the past with Hunter and the police, "if I hadn't taken the fall for Mary's accident." Cognizant of Peggy's past record of drunk and reckless driving, it had seemed only right to him that rainy night to accept the responsibility for it himself, to bear the awful brunt of Hunter's hatred from that day forward. Trusting the discretion of their great-aunt, Sean Michael had managed to keep his sister completely out of the picture, swearing that he had borrowed Peggy's car that evening to take their American cousin on a night tour of the Irish countryside.

"When she called to tell me that Mary had been injured," Sean Michael revealed to Hunter, "I had no idea how bad it was. By the time I got to the place where she told me it happened . . ." Sean Michael had broken down before the words were out, consumed by the guilt of protecting a sister who, in turn, had not been so deserving of his kindness.

"She was always on that fine line, that jagged edge," Sean Michael had described his sister. Certainly her discovery of Mrs. Maginn's body beneath the castle gate had been the final straw to push her over.

While there still remained investigations and evidence to be gathered, Victoria had gleaned some idea of what might have transpired that fateful evening when Hunter was away in Maryland. Whether Mrs. Maginn had actually overheard Sean Michael's confrontation with his sister about the notes, or whether Peggy had feared blackmail from the housekeeper for Mary's accident six years before, it stood to reason that she had reacted violently, seizing the most immediate weapon she could find and delivering the fatal blow.

That Hunter had left the castle right after dinner provided Peggy with the opportunity to stash the cane beneath his bed. Her subsequent invitation to Tapping to join her for a stroll around the grounds had been based on her assumption that Mrs. Maginn's body would be found during their absence. With Tapping as her obvious alibi, Peggy might have hoped to escape any attention as a suspect. What she had never counted on was her victim being moved.

Victoria recalled Marcine's casual remark of how upsetting it would be to discover a body in a second location after it had already been killed somewhere else. Only now did the true significance of Peggy's scream outside the lowered gate take on new meaning. Her long-standing belief in the occult, coupled with the very real awareness that someone had covered her tracks, was enough to unhinge her already delicate state of balance.

There would be more questions for the police to ask of Nilly, of course, when he was sufficiently strong to answer them. One could only assume from what they knew so far that the elderly valet had made a false assumption about the guilty party and attempted, in his own way, to do what was right.

Hunter reentered the room, a man wearied by all that had happened. And though Victoria longed for him to cross to her side and take her into the protective circle of his arms, a part of her was warmed by the fact that he crossed instead to his cousin, who was still stunned by the death of Peggy beneath Paladdin's hooves.

"Are you all right?" Hunter quietly inquired.

Sean Michael looked up to meet his eyes. "Time," he replied. "It's just going to take some time."

Hunter cleared his throat. "I owe you my life," he said. With only a moment of hesitation, Hunter extended his hand toward his cousin.

Victoria held her breath, hoping that Sean Michael would take it, that some resolution, some peace would come at last between the two men.

Sean Michael waited for what seemed an eternity before extending his own hand as well. The words that fell next from his lips were in a foreign tongue, one that neither Hunter nor Victoria understood.

"What does that mean?" Hunter asked.

Sean Michael glanced toward Victoria as he slowly rose to his feet, then back to his cousin. "It's an old Gaelic proverb," he said quietly. "From tragedy, there always springs a new beginning."

"I hope so," Hunter said. "I really hope so."

Epilogue

Four Months Later

"By *the power vested in me* by the state of Virginia," the judge solemnly proclaimed, "I hereby pronounce you husband and wife."

There was no need for him to cue Hunter O'Hare to kiss his bride. Beneath the dappled lacework of trees that were just beginning to show their spring colors, he pulled Victoria into his arms, sealing a future that neither mortals nor ghosts would ever put asunder.

Moments later, as their gathering of friends surged forward to offer congratulations, Deborah Sheddmoore made her way to the best man's side and affectionately slipped her arm around his. "Victoria's promised to throw me the bouquet," she teased Sean Michael.

He cast Deborah a roguish wink. "Sure it won't be a trial to be locked to a struggling actor?"

Marcine, standing just a few feet away with Lawrence and Joanne Hoffart, overheard the young man's remark and gracefully sailed over to join them. "I wouldn't worry about the struggling part," she assured Deborah. "I know real talent when I see it. Trust me, dear."

"It also doesn't hurt," Sean Michael candidly added, "to have the right connections."

No one had been more surprised than Victoria by Sean Michael's decision shortly after Christmas to take Marcine's advice and put his looks and voice to the test in Hollywood. Wistfully, a part of her had hoped that he would remain in Virginia, that they would somehow form a triumvirate, their past differences all set aside. In the short months following Peggy's death, Hunter and Sean Michael had grown closer, becoming almost the brothers that neither one had in their youth.

"I can't be a bloody leech," Sean Michael had explained his decision to them. "There comes a time a man's got to test himself."

"Just as long as you know," Hunter had assured him, "that the castle will always be home to you."

Just as it would always be home to Mary, Victoria thought to herself. A Sleeping Beauty who might never awaken, and yet whose life had touched them all in different ways.

Deborah's laughter now rippled across the gathering as she excitedly revealed their plans to Marcine. "And I'm going to get a job," she announced.

The remark amused Sean Michael. "Work?" he said. "You?"

Deborah playfully biffed him in the chin. "First time for everything," she replied, totally undaunted by the adventures that awaited them over two thousand miles away.

"Well," Elliott said as he kissed Victoria's cheek, "it all turned out, didn't it?"

"With a little help," Victoria smiled in return, reminded of how she had been introduced to Hunter's world to begin with.

"Are we good matchmakers or what?" Thatcher beamed.

Elliott raised a brow. "What?"

"It was all our idea, of course," John claimed, toasting

the new couple with a glass of champagne. "We just like to humor Elliott now and then and let him think he's smart."

Hunter slid his arm around Victoria's waist. "Why don't we settle this out of court, gentlemen, and just call it the luck of the Irish?"

Victoria's green eyes sparkled as she looked into the handsome face of her husband. "How about the luck of Hunter O'Hare?"

Hunter prefaced his kiss with a tender smile of approval. "No objection, Mrs. O'Hare. No objection whatsoever."